# FOURTH
# A LIE

# Fourth a Lie

## Goddess Isles
## Book Four

by

**Published:** Pepper Winters 2020:
**pepperwinters@gmail.com**
**Cover Design:** Ari @ Cover it! Designs
**Editing by**: Editing 4 Indies (Jenny Sims)

## Dedicated to:

*For those who fell in love with a monster, only to find your soul-mate hidden beneath fang and claw.*

# Prologue

SULLY SINCLAIR USED MASKS and murky morality to hide who he truly was. Our first meeting painted him as the villain, the procurer of women, and the ruthless mogul of his Goddess Isles.

However, day by day, spark by spark, his masks slipped, one by one, revealing that I wasn't a lunatic to fall head over heels for such a monster. I was justified because he was *worthy*.

Worthy of trust and love and a happily ever after.

I wanted to fight for that. To give him that. To give him *me*.

But…all things worth fighting for demanded pain.

Pain that sometimes cost far too much.

I wished we'd been immune to such a trial.

I wished Sully was an only child.

I wished he didn't have a brother called Drake Sinclair.

Where Sully wore devilishness to hide his decency, Drake wore decency to hide his devilishness. He was Satan walking amongst goddesses. Lucifer with no redemption. Pure evil in Sully's paradise.

And what was worse?

He ruined it all.

The spark, the bond, the happily ever after.

Sully made me come alive.

Drake made me want to die.

He stole everything.

He killed everything.
He murdered...*us.*

# Sullivan

# Chapter One

*"EVERYTHING YOU LOVE DIES, Sinclair. Everything you treasure is gone. That's your true curse. The one you can never run from."*

I pinched the bridge of my nose, doing my best to squeeze out the voice of my nightmare. The nightmare I'd had just before the bomb destroying *Serigala* ripped me awake.

I'd hoped the warning was some version of closure from my distrusting brain, throwing the masks of my past in my face, freeing me from lies and deceptions. A strange kind of acceptance that I was in love, that I'd felt joy, that I'd been happy mere hours before this shitstorm came knocking.

But I was wrong.

It'd been the opposite.

I couldn't shed those masks because they were a part of me. They were my armour against a world I could no longer survive in. They were my tools to reap death and decay on those who deserved it.

Those masks were the walls between Eleanor and our forever, condemning me with the truth that I was fucking delusional to think I could keep her, suicidal to give my heart to her, and utterly demented to think I could claim hers in return.

*I'd* done this.

I'd fallen for her and fallen from my power.

I'd adopted, rehabilitated, and nursed so many innocent creatures, and now they were chum in the sea, mangled paws and broken tails, missing ears and blown apart skulls.

I'd made a promise to keep them safe.

*Safe?*

Christ, my safety came with extermination.

Nothing was safe around me.

*Nothing.*

Especially not her.

*Three hours.*

*He gave me three hours to save her.*

My disgusting, gore-painted hands curled into fists as I leaned back and bashed my head against the plush helicopter upholstery.

Eleanor.

It didn't matter if I had three hours or three years, it was all the same—just a matter of time before I hurt her.

*If I keep her...she'll die.*

It was inevitable.

Inescapable.

My nightmare wasn't closure...it was a forewarning.

An omen filled with premonition and intuition that no matter how much time passed, no matter how hard I tried to find redemption, I hadn't been forgiven by fate.

I hadn't earned *her.*

I'd never earn her because I'd never fucking change.

I liked my life. I hoarded my privacy. I enjoyed playing with myths and falsities.

I was just as bad as the guests who visited.

I was owed no singular forgiveness for what I was. I wasn't any worse or better than my brethren. My one saving grace was I preferred the animal kingdom over my own and tried to buy better karma through their protection.

And I kept failing fucking spectacularly at it.

Humans were the disease. Animals were the pharmacon.

Eleanor was human.

*I* was human.

Drake was *human.*

And because Drake was a psychotic bastard, and I was a love-struck fool, and Eleanor was a girl trapped by me, we all had blood on our hands. We were all responsible for this animal carnage because Eleanor had distracted me from my calling, Drake had found my weakness, and I...

I'd been too busy being fucking happy to notice.

*Fuck!*

Groaning with fresh nausea, I glowered out the helicopter

window. Down below with black-shrouded oceans and star-dusted shores, life went on, things got eaten, new life was birthed, and a goddess existed who'd almost convinced me of the impossible.

The impossibility of *us*.

I bent forward again, digging hands through my hair, not caring that I spread viscera and biohazard, contaminating every part of me. Yesterday, I'd been making sarcastic quips to Jinx in Nirvana. I'd felt joy. I'd laughed. I'd indulged.

I'd forgotten about everyone and everything.

I'd allowed the very thing that I despised about the human race to intoxicate me.

I'd become *selfish*.

I'd become greedy and narcissistic—only thinking of *my* life, *my* lust, *my* love.

I'd given in to every dream and fantasy I had, thinking I could finally have peace.

And now…

I snarled in the din of helicopter blades. Fury tangled with loss, despair blended with violence, and every wall I'd dropped, every mask I'd shed, every denial I'd erased stabbed me with a thousand blades.

Eleanor.

*She'd* done this. She'd made me become *this*.

This…man. This blind, stupid man who'd forgotten his responsibilities and commitments. I was wrong to think her hex on me was purely about us.

It wasn't.

It was about my life. My future. My animals who'd died because I'd fallen in love.

And that…? Fuck, that was a price I wasn't prepared to pay.

Not again.

An avalanche of hate slithered over my shoulders, chilling me. My bones froze over, cracking with frost and filling with loathing for Drake. For me. Even for Eleanor.

She'd made me love her.

She made every drop of my frosted blood panic for her safety.

She came first.

Over everything.

She meant more.

Over anything.

*And look what fucking happened.*

*Those animals would still be alive if it wasn't for me.*

Drake needed to die.

Slowly.

Painfully.

Piece by piece.

That was a stone-chiselled certainty…but the rest?

The rest of my fuck-ups and failings? The fact that my heart belonged to a woman who had made me weak? The goddamn truth that I'd fallen for a goddess who'd shaken apart my dynasty and left my borders wide open for attack?

How did I fix that?

How did I go back to who I'd been?

*How do I stop the undeniable urge to sacrifice everything if it means I can keep her safe?*

Dropping my hands, I sat tall again. I was a fidgety, violent mess trapped in a tiny cabin, rapidly losing control, quickly fraying with the sickening desire to murder.

Cal sat quietly beside me, knowing not to interrupt.

He'd seen me on this knife-edge. He'd seen me this restless before. He'd felt what'd happened when I snapped and watched what I'd done when I broke.

I'd left a trail of corpses in my wake for payment for ten animal lives. A mix of mouse, monkey, and rabbit from a cosmetic group in Chicago. I'd made national news for the disgustingly gruesome and frankly morbidly-inspired retribution I'd delivered.

I'd been arrested.

I'd been trialled.

I'd been released because I had something that they didn't.

Money.

Lots and lots of fucking money and with money came untouchability.

But not this time.

Instead of coming after me, Drake had gone after my most vulnerable.

Bullshit.

*Motherfucking bullshit!*

I punched the fuselage in an explosive strike.

Cal flinched beside me, his voice piercing my ears via our headsets. "Just to distract you from your chaotic thoughts, I've called ahead. The guards have set the snares. They're armed. They know their position and protocol. She'll be fine, Sully."

I snarled in his direction. "What makes you think I'm worried about her?"

He snorted. "If you could sprout wings right now, you'd be down there with her already."

"I'd be looking for Drake."

"Well, whatever your first priority, she'll be fi—"

"She won't fucking be fine. Not while she's mine."

He shrugged as if this was a fucking shrugging matter. "Everyone has family they'd rather keep hidden." His lips twitched, delivering the twisted joke, hoping it'd shatter my rage but only adding to it.

I was not in the mood to let go of the shit I'd seen.

I was not going to be pacified just because I had men on my payroll who knew their jobs and were proven in merciless warfare.

The things inside me?

The fact that I would *die* for her? The knowledge that I would turn into anything, sacrifice anything, destroy everything for her…it made me a highly dangerous individual.

It made me volatile.

It made me unpredictable…even to myself.

*She can't be near me.*

"I want her gone." I glowered out the window as we began our descent. "Now."

His voice crackled, offering solutions to my fury. "We'll arrange for the goddesses to be sent to *Lebah*. They'll be close by and safe while we deal with Drake."

"There is no *we*." My knuckles cracked as I fisted my hands. "His pain belongs to me and every fucking creature he's just snuffed out."

"Fine." Cal nodded curtly, his reflection bouncing off the window. "I'll evacuate the guests too. They can go to *Angsa*. The fortified encampment there will keep them out of harm's way for a day or so. We'll ensure those who want to go home have transport available."

Two islands named after creatures with wings. One with feathers and one with membrane. A swan and a bee. Both far too delicate and defenceless.

My goddesses and guests could go there.

Frankly, I was done with humans for the time being. They could be casualties in this war; I didn't fucking care.

But Eleanor…she wasn't going with them.

She'd done this to me. She'd stripped me down to my final mask and shown me how lacking I was. I was a man who'd turned off his empathy toward his own race, only to cripple beneath the swarm of it for fragile animals.

I'd once told her that too much empathy could kill a person and not enough would kill someone else.

Well…my empathy had become a double-sided weapon, and I didn't want to be responsible when I wielded it.

Therefore, all my promises, ill-fated joy, and unbearable pleasure were over.

"Tell the pilots they have a flight to Java in one hour."

Cal stiffened beside me. "You're sending her to the mainland?"

I tensed, doing my best to stop my heart from leaping from my mouth. "She's going home. I'm done."

His silence was as damning as his sarcastic 'sir'.

My goddess island came into view, the helicopter sank, and I gathered up all the masks that Eleanor had stripped from me with bloody, gory hands, and put them back on…one lie at a time.

# Chapter Two

"STOP STRESSING, JINX. I'm sure he'll be back soon, and everything will be fine."

I ceased shredding the napkin from our untouched dinner, eyeing Jealousy. "He should have returned by now."

*Unless what he's dealing with is so, so much worse than I feared.*

I'd had no appetite all day, my stomach a riot of serrated knots whenever I thought of Sully and whatever carnage he'd faced.

*Are those animals okay?*

I couldn't shed the awful, awful feeling that we were over.

That Sully would be reminded of far too many things.

That he'd push me away before I could solidify just how important *this* was.

*We* were.

Yes, disaster had come.

And yes, things would need to be addressed.

But…unless he trusted me to have his back, trusted that I would be strong enough to put up with his stony silences born from grief and his explosive temper birthed from rage, then I had the tear-evoking sensation that my time here was borrowed.

I gnawed on the inside of my cheek. I had a cut there now. A cut that bled each time I nibbled because physical pain was the only distraction that worked against my emotional pain.

*God, Sully.*

*His creatures…*

My heart panged, filling me with fear all over again.

Was he okay?

What had he seen?

What nightmares now existed in that perfect, wonderful sanctuary?

I rubbed at the emptiness in my chest, agony swift and sharp cutting me right down the middle.

*How many lives have been lost?*

*What sort of state will he be in when he finally returns?*

Would he let me touch him? Soothe him? Hug him?

Would he share his exhaustion and emotional grief…or would he want nothing to do with me?

Once again, that sickening feeling that Sully would push me away rose with acidic bile. We'd admitted we were in love with each other, but that was just the tip of a very big iceberg to melt.

Right now, love was an idea, a promise, a word.

It could be snatched away as quickly as we'd conjured it.

Falling in love was the painful part.

It required the systematic stripping of who you were as an individual, a raw newness, and a terrifying look in the mirror that forced you to realise that the person you thought you were—the person you'd grown into on your own, without interference of another—wasn't who you were, after all.

The lies we'd fed ourselves. The tricks we'd used to deceive. The motives and methods to get through life were suddenly obsolete in the face of the one person who transcended all other people.

I supposed my young age permitted me to accept my evolution easily. I allowed the metamorphism to flow from girl to goddess to woman in love with a monster because I'd never truly grown to know myself. My youth kept me pliant for my truth.

But Sully…

He hadn't accepted me as easily. He had eleven years on me. That was eleven more years to build up his walls, smash down his bridges, and create an illusion that wasn't Euphoria-given but entirely of his own creation.

He saw himself as cruel and unyielding, severe and grim.

I saw him as gentle and forgiving, strict and generous.

Dark and light. Light and dark.

Two elements that cancelled each other out.

*Just as he'll cancel me out if that darkness has smothered him again.*

My shoulders rolled as I pushed away my untouched dinner.

Jealousy gave me a sad smile, her eyes glowing with sympathetic friendship. "It will be okay. It has to be. It's Sully."

I nodded and kept my fears quiet.

She reached across the table and squeezed my hand. Skittles chirped from my shoulder, eyeballing Jealousy's right to touch me. I got her possessiveness. I felt the same way about Skittles.

Jealousy patted my knuckles. "Don't just nod. Believe it."

I forced a smile. I'd never been one for casual touch between girls. I'd returned a hug if a school friend gave one, but I wasn't the instigator. However, Jealousy's touch was genuine and fierce; a bond that'd sprung swiftly but seemed solid.

I sighed, my belly once again squeezing with pain. My friendship with Jealousy was easier than my love with Sully.

I trusted that Jealousy would talk to me if I ever upset her. That we'd have an open dialogue if things got hard.

*Sully…I think he'll act first, then regret.*

*He won't trust in me.*

*Trust…*

Sully's hardest-earned gift.

I'd proven that I was trustworthy. That it was *him* I loved—the soul that resided in his handsome form—and not the pretty packaging he seemed to have contempt for.

But what it if wasn't enough?

If *Serigala* had been destroyed…would he still have a heart to give me?

If all those defenceless rescues who were alive because of him were dead…what would that do to him?

It tore out *my* heart, let alone his.

Would he return, still trusting we could be happy, or would death remind him that all connection was so fleeting? Death was the one thing he *could* trust in, and it might prove to be too much.

Because, regardless if we wanted it or not…we were linked now. If he hurt, I hurt. If I hurt, he hurt. We'd just doomed ourselves to a lifetime of pain instead of pleasure.

*Ugh.*

I dropped my face into my hands, shaking a little.

*Please, come back.*

*Please, still trust me.*

*Please, please don't push me away.*

Jealousy reached under the table and squeezed my knee. "Hey, stop it. Stop thinking about the bad and focus on the good.

It's going to be fine. He'll come back and things might be a little…aggressive…for a while, but then he'll be yours again."

I dug my fingers into my eyes, then swiped at my cheeks before I let my hands fall heavily into my lap. "I wish it were that easy."

"It will be." She patted my leg before withdrawing. "Just don't let him go all macho moron on you. If you feel him pulling away, just remind him that it's too late for that now."

"Too late to end things?"

"Too late not to be broken if he does."

I sighed heavily. "I truly hope *Serigala* and all its animals are okay. Maybe the treeline just caught fire. Maybe it only took them an hour to stop, and he's stayed there all day because he has a heart of gold and wanted to lavish his rescues with affection."

*That would be more believable if I couldn't smell the carnage from here.*

Jealousy's smile was unconvincing. "Yeah, maybe."

I glowered at the table, wishing I had some means to chase after him. I'd attempted to coax a guard into driving the speedboat there at lunchtime, but everything was on lockdown. The goddesses commanded to stay in their villas while the guests were requested to relax away from the main shore.

Skittles chirped softly, tucking her tiny feathery body in the crook of my neck and nuzzling my throat. Her sweet affection brought tears to my eyes. Pika sat on a lamp by the sliding doors leading to the deck, his wings slumped and grief evident in his black eyes as he waited for Sully.

He hadn't left his perch since Jealousy guided me from the beach and back to her villa, a few private beaches down from mine. She'd changed from her pyjamas into a lacy skirt and top, and allowed me to freshen up in her bathroom, then borrow a black sundress.

The remains of our unwanted dinner scattered between us. Seemed neither of us had the appetite to eat while the scent of charred flesh and fur coated the entire island.

*Sully.*

No matter what topic that popped into my mind, my heart immediately dragged it back to him. Almost as if my pining was a physical entity in the room, Pika squeaked pathetically from his lamp.

"Come here, little terror." I held up my finger.

He chirped once, then fluttered to me, ignoring my finger and landing next to his feathered sister, jostling her on my shoulder.

They squabbled for a second until Skittles accepted his presence and began to preen him. Almost as if she sensed Pika was suffering while Sully was gone.

Empathy from a tiny bird.

Compassion between two creatures.

Two emotions that could cause such pain to the affected and the ones who loved them.

Focusing on the claws of two tiny parrots digging into my skin, I asked softly, "Do you think he's okay?" Such a generic question. A question that couldn't be answered.

Jealousy scrubbed her face, then dragged her fingers through her blonde hair. Her attempt at consoling me stuttered a little as her hazel eyes caught mine with stark truth. "Are *any* of us truly okay?"

I slouched. "Do you have to be so frank?" I sighed with a weak smile. "I would've preferred the customary, '*He'll be fine. You're overthinking it. He'll be home soon and everything will be normal.*'"

"I tried that. It's not helping. You just mope harder."

"Sorry."

Silence fell, a third dinner guest who seemed to monopolise our conversation thanks to my obsession with what Sully was facing.

Skittles decided she'd had enough of her brother and flittered from my shoulder, picking her way through the unwanted meal, helping herself to a few grains of jasmine rice.

While Jealousy watched the tiny green, white, and apricot parrot, she murmured, "How many times have you had elixir now?"

I frowned, slightly afraid of the swift topic change. "Uh, three. Why?"

"Just wondering." She hugged herself, rubbing her palms up and down her arms.

"Wondering what?" I sat forward in my chair, grateful for Skittles as she provided somewhere to look rather than each other. Pika left my shoulder, flying back to his place on the lamp, staring out to sea.

Jealousy didn't glance up, almost as if she didn't feel comfortable admitting whatever she was about to. "Did it ever make you…sick?"

I sat taller. "Why…has it made *you* sick?"

She finally met my stare. "Can you answer my question first?"

I shrugged. "I fainted the morning after my first dose. I've never fainted before or since. But I think that was more due to the fact I hadn't eaten in over twenty-four hours rather than—"

"Have you felt weak?"

"Well, of course. Each time I wake up the next morning, I'm bruised and battered and it's a mammoth task to drag myself out of bed." I chewed my cheek, drawing more blood from my nervous, nibbled cut.

Should I admit it?

*Should I tell her how Sully reacted to elixir?*

If it was any other person, I wouldn't, but…Jealousy had earned my trust. "Even Sully passed out cold after his introduction to it. He almost drowned in Nirvana…far too focused on sex and forgot he needed air to breathe."

Her eyes narrowed. "Did he admit he felt totally out of it? Does he finally understand how dangerously strong it is?"

"He definitely endured the effects." I studied her, sensing something way more serious than she let on. "How come? Everything okay?"

Jealousy shook her head as Skittles continued her forage across the table, stealing a piece of wilted spinach. "I've lost count how many times I've taken it. For the longest time, I bounced back with no problem. Sure, I'd feel like shit the next morning, but my system always figured out how to reset itself." She sighed. "But recently…I can't fully shed its control. My resting heart rate is stupidly high. I regularly have palpitation attacks that can last over an hour. My limbs constantly buzz as if I have adrenaline running in my blood. I just think it's playing havoc with my inner chemicals."

I clasped my hands on the table. "Have you spoken to Sully about this?"

"Not directly to him no. I have had a check-up with Dr Campbell, though."

"And?"

"And…he's worried. He's never liked elixir. Always said it was too strong and that it will end up killing one of us these days." She smiled sadly as Skittles hopped onto her fork, pecking at a piece of discarded cantaloupe. "Ah well, I'm sure I'll be fine. It's just stress."

"Stress? Are you having second thoughts about staying? Do you want to leave, after all?"

She shook her head. "Oh, God, no. I never want to live anywhere else. My ultimate dream would be to run this place.

---

Maybe find someone who doesn't just want me for my body, and make Sully *hire* goddesses who have free will, instead of buying and trapping them. I'm glad he released Jupiter, Nep, and Calico. What they did to you is unforgivable, but also understandable when pushed to the brink of their tolerances. They're free now...but we aren't. Neither are the others who are still serving...and the ones he'll buy in the future."

I wanted to agree with her. To nod and forge ahead with sisterhood power—to revolutionise Sully's empire. However...my loyalties were also to Sully. Yes, he did bad things because he used the same rules against humans that we had for animals. And yes, he seemed to have no qualms about feeding us elixir and throwing us at the mercy of men for money. But...beneath those flaws, he cared enough that he deserved my fidelity. "I'm sure things will evolve for the better."

*Unless Serigala is blown up.*

If it had...then things might evolve for the worst.

"You're right." Jealousy looked up just as Skittles flew to my shoulder, squawking and hopping up and down. Pika let out a relieved trill, interspersed with excited squeaks, and shot like a green arrow down the night-shrouded beach.

Our eyes locked.

Hope exploded.

*He's back!*

# Sullivan

# Chapter Three

OF COURSE, SHE WAS there, waiting for me with imploring eyes, eager arms, and tangible fucking love.

Of course, she ran down the beach with my two parrots flying beside her, and leaped fearlessly into my arms.

Of course, she hugged a fucking monster who only had murder on his mind. A man covered in blood and brain, decorated with fur and charred flesh. A man who reeked of death and wore the cloak of the Grim Reaper himself, ready to repay the dismembered body parts to his brother.

But...

Her touch.

Her scent.

Her warmth.

It *broke* me.

Motherfucking broke me because I'd been so steadfast in my conviction. So black and white with my choice to send her away...for good.

She was too breakable in my current condition.

She was too much for me to survive.

But...

*How?*

How the fuck was I supposed to say goodbye?

*She'll die if she stays.*

*By your hand or his.*

I flinched at the agonising reminder. I jerked at my repeating nightmare.

*"Everything you love dies, Sinclair. Everything you treasure is gone. That's your true curse. The one you can never run from."*

Fuck, it made me angry.

Angrier than all my animals being blown to smithereens.

It made me rage worse than ever before because love was supposed to be the miracle of life. The one thing everyone chased relentlessly. The hardwired, unavoidable quest for a mate.

I'd found mine.

I knew the value of what I held.

I craved her kiss like a worthless addict.

*I want to keep her.*

But…

Her love made me weak.

My love made me powerless.

She was the catalyst of my ruin.

And that could never happen.

"Sully…please, hug me back." Her face pressed into my t-shirt that'd soaked up the lives of so many carnivores, herbivores, and innocence. She willingly shared the pyre my body had become, trying to offer me solace.

Her love threatened to create another form of weakness. The urge to buckle in the sand and allow her to soothe away the decay in my nose and the carnage in my mind.

I wanted to strip her, fill her, love her until I'd driven out the memories.

But that was selfish.

Once again proving me unworthy because when the time came for me to stand up for my creatures, I turned greedy just like any man.

"Let go of me, Jinx." My voice betrayed me. Curt and full of glass, my heartbreak crystal shards by my feet.

She shook her head, her gorgeous chocolate hair sticking to dried sinew and slaughter. "Don't do this, Sully. Please, don't."

How did she know?

How had she figured me out so quickly, accepted me so unconditionally, prepared to battle with me so fiercely?

I stiffened.

My mask threatened to slip. A mask that'd been firmly positioned to hide my trauma of *Serigala*, my hate of mankind, and my love for a goddess who'd broken me.

My arms twitched to claim her.

My tongue teased with the vow that whatever happened, I wouldn't end what we'd found.

I would keep her.

Forever.

Because I was desperate for the peace she could offer me.

But my peace would come at a price.

She wasn't safe with me.

And I'd just spent my day shovelling up the remains of those who believed my affection came without strings.

I clenched my teeth; my gruesome, filthy hands rose and latched around her shoulders.

I pushed her away from me.

I stared into her graceful grey gaze, and I prepared to destroy the final thing that kept me human.

"This is goodbye, Eleanor—"

# Chapter Four

I KISSED HIM.

I fought against his hold, tripped into his body, and smashed my lips to his.

If he couldn't say it…it wouldn't come true.

If I prevented him from saying goodbye…he couldn't end it.

My heart had punctured with a million tiny holes for every second I'd run to him, found him, and threw myself into his unreturned embrace. It was no longer whole but bleeding and weeping, filling the divots in the sand by our feet with bright scarlet grief.

Time was my enemy.

Fate was my prosecutor.

And Sully…he wielded the axe to kill all my dreams, desires, and dreadful premonitions.

I'd known he'd do this.

I'd sat on his island, alone with my knowledge, and wished, *begged* it wasn't true.

But the second I'd seen him…*God*.

His condemnation tainted him like a nasty aura. A fog thick with questions he didn't have answers for. *How could he be happy when so many lives had been taken? Who was he to take what I offered him when everything he cared for had been slain?*

The terrible thing was…I didn't have the answers either.

I just knew he couldn't stop what we felt for each other

because if he destroyed us now…we'd live a lifetime of aching regret.

Shoving back my fear at losing him, I crawled up his powerful, unyielding body and kissed him harder.

Pika and Skittles flew around us, their little wings buffeting us, neither of them attempting to land as if Sully's horror and my terror created a force field around us that no arrow or parrot could break.

I dove my tongue between his clamped together lips.

I ripped off the lid of his anger.

He snatched me.

Ensnared me.

His arms swooped around me, crushing me, sharing his filth and fury, plunging his tongue into my mouth, stealing my dominance and shoving me relentlessly back into submission.

He kissed me as if he'd forgotten how to be a man.

He kissed like an animal, taking all of me, attacking me, *hurting* me.

He tasted of smoke and blood and death, death, death.

He pawed me as if I was his enemy and not his ever after.

Violence replaced the blood I'd lost in my heart, blistering and bright as the stars above, giving me a dagger of nastiness to match his diabolical, uncontrollable rage.

I bit his bottom lip, making him snarl.

He kissed me so hard, I gagged on his tongue. He poured a rumbling roar down my throat, complete with teeth and spit and carnage.

And I lost it.

If he wanted to hurt me, so be it.

But I would hurt him back, bite for bite.

I let loose.

I kissed him with bottomless grief and endless stubbornness.

I kissed him…but he *devoured* me.

His fist curled in my hair, sharing the dirt on his hands, the blood under his nails, the strings of repugnant remains with me.

I bowed in his arms, imprisoned and manhandled, no longer a participant in the kiss but just surviving his violence. My lips burned from his facial hair. My jaw ached with how deep he kissed me. I let him pour his pain into me, gagging on the rancid ruin he'd dealt with, choking on the lives he'd lost.

And through it all, we argued.

*We're over.*

*Never.*

*I don't want you.*

*Liar!*

His kiss tried to beat me into accepting his compulsory closure.

My kiss ripped apart his determination and screamed a resounding *no*!

I couldn't breathe.

He couldn't breathe.

We attacked each other until we almost fucked right there in the sand.

Perhaps, that would work.

Give him my body in lieu of his nightmares.

Reaching between us, I fisted his rock-hard cock.

He snarled and threw me away, panting hard, his chest straining with madness.

I blinked at the wrathful god before me, and I saw past his lies before he ever uttered them.

He loved me.

But that wouldn't change a goddamn thing.

It wasn't agony that'd changed him but tightly bridled *rage*. Rage that I had no power against because it was too ingrained in him to master.

His entire body hummed with it. His nostrils flared with it. His skin crackled with it.

Pure, undiluted hate that had no outlet.

Once upon a time, I'd likened him to a volcano. His temper a steady flowing river of lava beneath the cracked veneer of decorum. He wore his civilised polish well, but he could never quite hide the diabolical vehemence inside.

That volcano was so, so close to erupting. A hissing cloud of warning was the only precursor to his impending detonation.

I understood his anger at losing *Serigala*.

I sympathised with his inability to shed such fury.

But I had no idea how to help him.

*How can I heal him when I don't know what happened?*

He kept a palm planted on my sternum, keeping me at a distance he could cope with.

Our eyes locked.

And a large piece of me threatened to die just from witnessing his pain. He looked as if he'd been to war and returned the only survivor. Harrowed and haunted, his blue eyes muted and no longer luminescent with male virility or power. They were washed out and filled with ghosts of the creatures he'd lost.

He reeked of sooty smoke and metallic blood, and his body tensed as I studied him, his muscles locking beneath his squalid clothing.

He flinched as my heart pounded beneath his palm, revealing the aching pity I held, my sadness, my woe.

"Don't pity me," he growled. "Pity them. The countless creatures who died...because of *me*." His fingers twitched and dug into my chest as the rest of him stood stoic.

"This wasn't your fault."

He laughed icily, murderously. "You don't know a goddamn thing about me."

His voice physically scarred me, but I kept my temper from unfurling. He was allowed to be angry. And I had to be the calm where he could find quiet.

"I know more than you want to admit," I murmured. "I know you love me. I know that I love you—"

"*Stop.*" He dropped his hand, curling his filth-blackened fingers into fists. "Just stop."

He looked satanic.

He'd left a man and returned a demon. A macabre mannequin who wore Sully's face and puppeteered Sully's body but had switched souls with him, leaving him with nothing but darkness.

My heart hiccupped with pain. If he'd closed every door to me...how the hell was I supposed to scratch my way back in? How could I teach a loveless titan that he could be both vicious and vulnerable with me?

He didn't have to push me away because of what he'd done and would do.

He didn't have to hide any part of his personality with me.

The urge to hug him crippled me.

I couldn't offer much, but a hug was a start. A hug was home and a haven and a place where he could unload and be exposed. No one should have to deal with what he'd seen and not have a place to vent or sift through his trauma.

But he shook his head to whatever invitation I gave, his jaw clenched in denial. His haunted eyes locked on the sand as if he couldn't bear to look up and see his untouched paradise and a goddess who loved him after surviving hell.

Without his condemning eyes hurting me, I was able to study him. His hair no longer had bronze-tipped strands—soot and dirt stained every strand black. His tanned skin was barely visible beneath streaks of gore, blood, and ash. His heavy five o'clock shadow held flakes of charred fragments, and his hands were unrecognisable with lashings of blackened blood.

His t-shirt was no longer white. The parts that weren't soaked in grim fluids of doomed animals were torn and smeared with charcoal. Every inch of him blared the fate of *Serigala,* and tears spilled over my eyelashes.

Just as I'd known he'd decided to stop our relationship the moment I'd watched him step from his helicopter, I knew precisely what'd happened on his island.

The playful otters.

The curious pig.

The rabbits and dogs and birds and mice.

*They're all gone.*

And their last mortal remains clung to Sully as if unwilling to say goodbye to the man who'd rescued them. The man who'd buried them, mourned for them, turned rogue for them.

Daring to touch him, I stepped closer and stroked his forearm. "You need to shower."

"You need to go."

I ignored my full-body quake of fear. "There's time to discuss—"

"That's where you're wrong, Eleanor goddamn Grace. There *is* no time."

"There's always time—"

"No." He bared his teeth. "I've made up my mind. You're leaving. Immediately."

It took everything I had not to buckle at his feet. I reinforced my spine with steel and narrowed my eyes. "You've made up your mind, have you? But what about my decision?"

"You don't get one."

"We're equals, Sully. I get a vote in whatever madness you've decided."

"That's where you're wrong. I brought you here. I can evict you just as quickly. You can scream and beg, but the fact remains, you will not change my mind."

I prickled with anger. "And you think by sending me away that I'll remain unhurt?"

He nodded savagely. "You'll be away from me. Therefore, you'll be safe."

"I'll be in more pain than I've ever felt if you send me away."

"Pain means you're still alive, so I'm okay with that." Arching his chin at the helicopter, he muttered, "That's your ride." Snatching me around the wrist, he tugged me down the beach. "Get as far away from me as you can."

My temper might've been locked up while I offered a haven for a broken man, but those gates smashed wide apart when faced with a stubborn jackass who ran on exhaustion and emotional bereavement. "Don't do this. If you send me away when you need me the most, you'll be the one who suffers."

"Threats now?"

"Just truth."

He stumbled as if I'd driven an ice pick into his heart. Swallowing hard, he growled, "And if I don't send you away, then *you'll* suffer." He kept his eyes far from mine, not denying that this would rip him into pieces, just ploughing ahead with his agonising choice. "I'll take the suffering, Jinx. I need you gone. I have too much blood on my hands to add yours."

"What makes you think you'll have my blood on your hands?"

He stopped and spun so fast, I smashed into him.

Our bodies collided.

Our chemistry ignited.

Lush, lusty connection that would never fade.

Our fight scrambled as our bodies primed for a different kind of battle. My nipples hardened to diamonds as his body shifted from raging to raw need.

His fingers spasmed around my wrist as if he had the uncontrollable need to break my bones, make me bleed, and fulfil his prophecy that my life force would one day stain his hands.

In his wild, washed-out stare, I saw just how stricken he was. How wretched and wounded.

And I didn't think.

I just acted.

We moved at the same time.

His head came down.

My mouth tilted up.

Our lips crashed and collided.

Our kiss was everything that love wasn't.

There was nothing gentle or kind, just nasty and noxious, sloppy and savage.

His gruesome hands cupped my head, twining his fingers deep within my hair, trapping me to kiss me deeper, rougher, with an unholy appetite that spoke of the hell that he'd stepped from.

I moaned as our kiss turned obscene with how much lust and loathing we shared.

Thanks to our bond, secrets couldn't hide, lies couldn't convince, and in the end, it was love that turned out to be our greatest suffering because it gave us nowhere to hide.

Nowhere to pretend.

We were both the poison and the antidote, killing and reviving each other with every plunder of our tongues.

His hands dropped from my hair, down my back, and grabbed handfuls of my ass. He hoisted me up until my tiptoes barely tickled the sand, and drove his hips into my belly, imprinting me with the pulsing hardness between his legs.

I choked on his tongue as he groaned so brokenly, so ferociously.

I pulled away and bit his ear, ensuring he listened with his body and not his mind when I hissed, "Don't say goodbye when you've barely said hello." I rocked my hips against him, making him shudder. "We have time, Sully. Take me home. Fuck me. Remember me. *Keep* me."

He grunted with tattered violence, tore me from the beach, and stormed with me in his arms away from the helicopter, away from our ending, away from the ghosts that haunted him.

# Sullivan

# Chapter Five

*"FUCK!"*

I dug my hands into my hair, dislodging a rain of ash and death as I bellowed at the ceiling and motherfucking destiny who'd given me a woman who shared a piece of my filthy soul.

A woman who knew exactly what I was going to do before I'd even decided.

Who sensed my decision before I'd even gotten up the strength to go through with it.

Who had an intuition about me.

Who defied me.

Who goddamn *ruled* me.

How the fuck was I here, inside her villa, primed to fuck her while covered in the massacred carcasses of rodent and canine and not waving goodbye as she flew away?

Pika and Skittles—who'd followed us from the beach on whispering wings—squawked at my violent, bitter curse, peltering around the rafters with green feathers.

In the clutch of my fury, I only saw them as more things to die because of my failures. I wanted to cage them up, ship them away, extract them from my calamity so they could be safe.

Just like Eleanor.

Yet she was still *here.*

On my shores.

In her villa.

Walking into my goddamn arms.

I stiffened as her embrace wrapped around my waist, her ear pressing against my heart, her body resting flush to mine. She dared kiss the absolute butchery of my t-shirt, making my stomach roil and pulse stutter with so many aggressive things.

"Sully...speak to me. What did you see? What happened? You can tell me." Her arms squeezed my waist, lying to me that she was strong enough to handle the spillage of such horror. Doing her best to convince me that the imagery of mangled paws blown from bleeding cadavers and snouts with broken teeth wouldn't turn her into what I'd become.

A sorry, pitiful, raging, rabid human who would give anything for his own claws and fangs—to be a powerful predator so he could rip out the jugular of his enemies and feel the gush of blood down his throat. To be able to kill in primal, chaotic ways instead of being so weak to require weapons to do his massacring for him.

A knife wouldn't be enough.

A gun wouldn't be enough.

Nothing would be good enough to exterminate the life of my brother. The brother who threatened my creatures and my goddesses.

Who threatened *her*.

Snatching her chin, I arched her face up and stole her gasp with my teeth.

I kissed her brutally, brokenly. I kissed her until blood tainted our taste and something inside me snapped.

She thought she could help me?

She thought she could convince me to keep her?

I'd prove otherwise.

I'd show her just how dangerous loving a monster like me truly was.

*It's still over, Jinx.*

*You've just delayed the inevitable.*

Seizing her from the floor, I carried her into the bathroom.

The same bathroom where she'd painted herself in magic, dressed in myth, and came to me gowned like a goddamn queen, all so she'd trick me into keeping her.

It'd worked then.

I'd fallen to my knees.

I'd fallen in love.

And look what happened as the result.

If I'd sold her to Roy Slater, my creatures would still be alive. They'd be barking and bleating, cooing and cawing. Instead of being silent for evermore.

Shoving her against the vanity, I snarled, "Stay right there. Do not move."

She licked her lips, tonguing the small cut where I'd bitten her, and nodded.

With my gaze locked on hers, I tore off my t-shirt, kicked off my boots, and ripped off my socks, jeans, and boxer-briefs, leaving the blood-soaked pile on the floor.

I shredded myself from material, revealing the putridity of my skin beneath. The bruises from kicking tumbled buildings in pure rage. The cuts from rubble and the blending of my blood with animal.

My body was as branded as my clothing.

I stood before her naked, a symbol of vulnerability, but I seethed with rage I couldn't shed so easily. Her grey eyes cast over me, lingering on the scars of my past, the lacerations and singes of my present, and the angry pulsing erection between my thighs.

I was desire and death all in one.

I scared myself with my ricocheting, ravenous needs, yet Eleanor just stared with an elegance I'd never been able to ruin, and a tranquillity that said I was safe to put aside my hate…just for a moment.

To find solace in her bravery and kindness.

A small part of me did want that. He wanted to drop to his knees and have her curl into his lap and rock. But the part of me that'd snapped no longer accepted her invisible crown or ethereal control over me.

I wanted her to *hurt*.

I wanted her to feel a tenth of the pain I carried.

Walking into her, I snatched her wrist again and yanked her into the shower.

I needed Nirvana.

I needed freshwater to surround me, drown me…but this would have to do.

Ripping on the cold water, I wrapped my arms around a struggling Jinx as she tried to outrun the icy liquid raining over us.

I added no heat, no comfort.

I needed the sleety needles.

I needed my temper to be extinguished before I did something I'd always regret.

*Stay, Eleanor.*

*Please, Eleanor.*

---

*Fuck, Eleanor.*

She gasped for air, the cold water stealing her breath. While she squirmed in my arms and her wet hair clung to her shoulders, I pawed at her black dress. I yanked it over her head and threw the heavy weight to slap drenched by the drain.

She was naked.

Her skin flushed despite the ice falling over us.

Her nipples puckered, her belly quivered, a slick of lubricant glinted on her inner thigh.

My cock hardened to the point of excruciation. "You dare be wet for a monster like me?" I shoved her against the wall and, once again, grabbed two handfuls of her gorgeous ass. I spread her cheeks, hauled her up, and slammed her against the iridescent tile. "Do I turn you on? Knowing I'm barely human? Knowing I'm hanging on by a thread?"

She shuddered as I pressed my body into hers.

"I'm wet for the man I'm in love with."

"A man who no longer exists."

Goosebumps scattered over her skin. "Don't say that."

"Don't be honest?"

Even in my fury, we were in sync.

Her legs wrapped around my hips as I thrust into her pussy.

Her lips rose as mine crashed down.

Our kiss connected as our bodies joined.

I stabbed into her.

A vicious, unrelenting possession.

Her cry echoed from her mouth to mine, but I didn't stop.

I didn't let her adjust.

I rode her all while dirt and decay sluiced down my body and onto hers.

We fucked in absolute filth and I was neither apologetic nor contrite.

Our kiss broke apart as I set a punishing rhythm. Our noses bruised, our foreheads bumped, our lips stayed wide and open, two silent screams as we clawed and attacked each other, sometimes kissing, mostly biting, both intent on destruction.

Her fire combated the icy shower. Her salvation tried to dilute my rage.

I pumped over and over, doing my best to punish her for ever showing me what happiness could be.

I took her until the first tightening tangles of an orgasm clenched my belly and balls. I used her until the first clench of her pussy announced she reached the same pinnacle as me.

And then, I stopped.

I withdrew.

I dropped her to the floor, wincing at my engorged cock and turning my back on her.

I sadistically took us to the edge where we might've found peace and denied us.

I denied us because we didn't fucking deserve it.

Her frustration puffed on my back as she panted. Her tiny mewl of need made pre-cum ooze out my tip. I trembled with the unbearable need to spin and finish what we'd started.

But...I wanted the torture.

I needed it.

I needed to live in that blistering, brutalising pain.

She could finish herself off. She could seek a cure for her agony.

But I wouldn't.

Not while I wore the death of so many innocent things.

*Get it off me.*

In a sudden panic, my desire to be clean overrode the crippling need to come.

Grabbing a bottle of coconut body wash, I dumped half the contents into my palm and scrubbed. I used nails to serrate my skin from entrails and innards. I attacked myself as if I was the enemy...because in reality, I was.

I lost myself in the mantra of cleanliness, clawing and scratching until trickles of crimson sluiced down the drain thanks to the sleet pounding from above.

Delicate hands touched my back. Sweet, formidable hands rubbing soap into my rotten flesh and down my spine.

My chin fell on my chest as the heaviest groan slipped from my lips. Eleanor sniffed back all the grief I'd caused and systematically rid my back, ass, thighs, and calves of any remains of *Serigala.*

I couldn't move.

My arms hung useless by my sides, swaying beneath the spray, corrupted and controlled entirely by a woman who would never permit me to send her away.

Once she'd cleansed my back, she squeezed herself between me and the wall, her nakedness slippery against mine.

Our eyes locked, shouting so many things.

I hated that a stare wasn't just a stare between us. A look

wasn't just a look but an entire paragraph of problems, turning into a battle of wills, forearming her with a rebuttal against anything I might decree.

*I love you.*

*I know.*

*You have to leave.*

*Never.*

She winced as she broke our stare, tracing the shallow scratches I'd covered myself with. I hissed as she soaped me, the coconut wash stinging my wounds. I closed my eyes with a haggard sigh, permitting a sliver of softness.

She washed me with reverence and worship, making my heart swell and suffocate.

She was a true goddess. The only one with sorcery over me.

Her hands slipped down my belly, making me twitch. She slowly, steadily lulled me into accepting a ceasefire, all while my heart chugged with memories, and charred whiskers filled my nose, and my mind was an amalgamated graveyard of extinction.

My rage blended with grief.

My fury fused with despair.

My muscles stopped seizing with nightmares and, just for a moment, I inhaled clean, untainted air.

But then, she touched me where she shouldn't have.

Her tight fingers fisted my cock, igniting pain and reminding me of my inadequacy. Reminding me that she shouldn't fucking be here. That I was running out of time. That she wasn't safe, no one was safe.

She had to *go.*

My temper barrelled through the thin veil of calm she'd granted. I grunted as her sinful lips encircled my erection.

My back snapped straight. My body jerked with unshed desire. My hands landed on her head, holding her while I thrust into her hot, wet mouth.

*Fuck!*

My orgasm that'd never vanished took my distraction as permission to explode.

The first splash coated her tongue as I drove to the back of her throat.

My anger followed swiftly.

My acrimony that she'd once again manipulated me raced through my veins and made me cruel.

Shoving her away, I pinched the tip, refusing another wave of pleasure. I locked down my muscles. I gritted my teeth against the natural pulse of my body to spurt. I groaned as the climax tormented me with talons then slunk back down my legs with irritation.

Eleanor remained on her knees, her grey eyes shadowed with annoyance. "Let me pleasure you, Sully. Focus on something else…it will help."

"Don't tell me what will help. I *know* what will help. The second you're off my island, I'll be happy."

"Happy?" She snorted. "You're so far from happy you're in denial."

"And whose fault is that, huh?" I bowed over her, flinching as cold needles continued to stab us. My cock ached with every droplet of unshed cum, making me snappish and savage. "I'll tell you whose fault it is. You and your goddamn curse. You've made me weak. You're the reason I didn't see this attack coming. You're as much to blame for the blood on my hands as I am."

She braced her shoulders. "I'll permit that one slander because I know how much you're hurting…but do it again and—"

"Get up." I fisted my cock, throttling it in warning to stop torturing me. "Your stay on my shores has come to an end."

Regally, seductively, she stood. "You can't send me away. We both know that."

This was the part I hated the most.

The utmost assurance in her tone of my feelings for her. The presumptuous boldness that said she wasn't afraid of me, that she could hear my lies even as I formed them, that she would always know the truth in my heart instead of the falsehoods in my mouth.

*Fine.*

She wanted the truth?

I'd give her the goddamn truth.

Wrenching off the shower, I grabbed her forearm and threw her into the bathroom. She tripped and skidded on the tile, quickly finding her balance to clash with me.

"I don't have the fucking strength to survive you."

She spread her hands in surrender. "I'm not asking you to survive me. I'm asking you to *trust* me—"

"Trust that you'll still be alive after I deal with Drake? Trust that you won't push me to my limit and make me hurt you? Trust that you're fucking immortal and won't end up like the creatures strewn all over my goddamn island?"

Her cheeks pinked with matching temper, water dripping

down her bare form. "Once again, I'm not asking you to drag me into whatever war you have to win. I'm just asking you to admit you want me—"

"*Want* you?" My nostrils flared, my hand still locked around my pounding cock. "Woman, I've never wanted anyone more."

"Then that's all that matters. I'm yours and—"

"I want you, Jinx…but I don't *want* to want you."

Her inhale pierced her lungs, air doing its best to cushion my intended dagger to her heart. Her hand rubbed her chest as I struck a successful blow. "You're walking a fine line, Sully. I know what you're doing. You're trying to convince me and yourself that what we have is cheap enough to throw away. That we aren't linked by something far more powerful than either of us."

"It's over, Eleanor."

"Like hell it is." She planted her hands on her hips, spreading her legs, her pussy still wet for me, her breasts still swollen for me, her entire body primed for my possession.

*Jesus*, I found her irresistible.

The most stunning, infuriating, maddening, *wonderful* creature I'd ever seen.

But if she died, the perfection of her would fade. It was her soul that made her perfect and her soul would escape the moment her body took its last inhale.

*I will not be fucking responsible for that.*

*I can't!*

I winced as an image of shovelling her broken body into a blood-soaked sack filled my mind. A rush of nausea swarmed me.

What I'd seen on *Serigala* would be nothing if I had to witness her death. If the bones I crunched and cracked over were hers.

I would spend my life in purgatory. I would sprout heinous blasphemy. I would hog-tie her and throw her on the helicopter gagged and trussed before I let that happen.

I balled my hands. "I gave you your freedom. It's time to take it."

"My freedom isn't worth a damn if I'm not with you. I wasn't free the moment I met you!"

"I rescind my ownership of you, Eleanor. Whatever bond you think we have—"

"God, you're a bastard. You think you can just snap your fingers and what I feel for you stops? You honestly think you can cut me from your life by sending me away?"

"Just accept that this is not open for discussion. My reasons

are my own and will not be swayed. You are no longer welcome—
"

"*Argh!*" She paced, her motions jerky, her breasts bouncing. "You know what, Sully, I called you a coward before and I'll use that word again. You. Are. A. *Coward.* You were a coward about admitting you were in love with me, and you're a coward now for trying to say that you don't. You're a coward for throwing me away the moment things get hard."

"Things get *hard?*" A sarcastic bark slipped my control, even as my cock swelled with deep-seated pain the longer I watched her.

I *needed* her.

Fuck, how I needed her.

She was walking fucking temptation.

A spitfire with temper crashing and igniting against my own. Every slur we threw at each other made the bathroom drip and shimmer with need.

"For fuck's sake, I've just wiped up the intestines of hundreds of animals. Do you think I want to wipe up yours, too?"

"My intestines are staying right where they are. You don't have to worry about that."

"I'm not worried."

"Then why are you—"

"I'm not worried about what *might* happen, Eleanor. I *know* what will happen. You. Will. Get. Hurt. It's a fucking guarantee. You are my weakness. He will use you against me, and because of the shit that I've done, fate will deem it fitting to allow him to hurt you. If you stay, he will hold you over me, and you. Will. *Die.*"

My body clenched with warning. I was near the ledge. A ledge that would only destroy both of us.

Breathing hard, I snarled, "I'm doing my best to stay calm here, Jinx, but I did warn you. I'm hanging on by a goddamn thread. I'm running out of time. If you continue to fight against me I—"

"You think he'll hurt me?" She crossed her arms, pushing her breasts up, making my cock weep cum. "That's the only reason you want me to leave?"

I laughed again, icy and cruel, so turned on I couldn't fucking see straight. "You mean, I need a better reason than *you will die?*"

"Do you still want me?"

My eyebrows tugged low, shielding my incredulous stare. "What a stupid fucking question. We just covered that."

"It's not a stupid fucking question. You're the one trying to convince me that you don't."

Anger had mutated to sexual frustration.

Despair had morphed to erotic stimulation.

I loved her for fuck's sake.

Yet I couldn't seem to protect her.

I gritted my teeth, answering her with clipped finality. "Whatever I feel is irrelevant. We're done, Eleanor. I no longer have any interest in keeping you because we have no future. We have no future because you will die by his hand or mine, and I fucking refuse to hurt you anymore."

"You're hurting me right now. You're acting as if you don't know me. You seem to think I'm some girl who won't stand up to you, won't fight you, won't fight *for* you." Marching into me, she planted her hands on my overheated chest. "You can lie to my face, Sully, but you can't change the truth."

My eyes snapped closed at her proximity.

My cock bounced with its own pulse, desperate to thrust inside her, hijacking my entire nervous system with hunger.

Her fingers were tiny electrodes, shooting current into my heart, down my belly, into my legs. Her closeness was a furnace, searing my flesh, making me sweat pure sin.

Her breath caught as my hands slammed over hers, digging her fingers deeper into my chest. My hips rocked, nudging my cock against her belly.

She moaned.

My eyes shot wide.

Our fight reached critical cataclysm.

Panting breathlessly, she dug her nails into my pecs. Her smoky eyes turned hazy, drunk and drugged on the potent, powerful thirst between us. "Are you forgetting Euphoria?"

Her voice did painful things to me, dangerous things.

"Did you not feel what I did?" She pressed her nails deeper, trying to claw out my angry, aggravated heart.

My skin, tight and tingly with passion, puckered beneath her touch, begging for more.

"You're trying to tell me you don't *feel* that?" She dared kiss one of my cuts, lick at my wounds, make me lose every shred of control I had left. "I touch your body, but you feel it in your heart, Sully. I see it in your eyes. I sense it in my soul. If you want to lie, by all means. But don't expect me to believe—"

I broke.

Seizing her from the floor, I stalked toward the vanity, spun her around, and folded her over the hard marble. "I suggest you hold on." Grabbing her hands, I planted them firmly on either side of the bowl. "I'm not going to be gentle."

# Chapter Six

MY HEART BOLTED LIKE a rabbit, darting and weaving, seeking a hole to hide in.

I looked at him in the mirror behind me.

Our eyes snagged and a cloak of dark depravity consumed him.

Instinct blared to run.

Basic survival said I would not like what was about to happen.

But I was trapped, turned on, and tangibly consumed by hate and love.

With a snarl, he jerked my hips back, kicked my legs apart, and ran his fingers from my clit, over my dripping entrance, to my crack and asshole.

I flinched as he pushed his finger against the tight ring of muscle.

I gasped as his cock found my pussy.

I screamed as he thrust both unforgivingly inside me.

His cock and his finger, claiming me two ways, ensuring he scrambled me, controlled me, *punished* me.

My knees buckled, digging my hipbones into the vanity as he mounted me without apology.

His hungry grunts and barbaric thrusts made me swell with my previously denied climax. My imprisonment and his nastiness only added gasoline to the fire he'd struck inside.

I billowed with it.

Orange and red and yellow.

I burned with it as he fucked me as if I was every nightmare he'd ever had.

He was nasty and revengeful.

He covered up his pain with blustering malice.

But I didn't care.

I surrendered to his spite because I found every facet of this man utterly irresistible. He was a weapon of lust even while my body screamed at me to *run*.

*To run and come.*

*To come and run.*

*To give in.*

My legs spread wider.

He snarled as his cock hit the top of my pussy, locking us together in carnal copulation. His finger in my ass only made his invasion tighter, deeper, dancing on the border of pleasure and pure pain.

My body switched from my ownership to his.

His touch filled me, defiled me, and sullied me in every way possible.

I rose on my tiptoes as he claimed me with every lash of his rage. His other hand grabbed my breast, kneading me, pinching my nipple, attacking me until I writhed in his hold.

"Please, Sully…God, *please*." My vision turned hazy as I looked at him in the mirror—watched the way he pawed me, flushed at the wildness he'd conjured in me.

All I wanted, all I *needed* was to be thoroughly fucked by this man.

A man who had no control over his actions. A man thoroughly hollowed out by an animal holocaust.

"Fuck…*fuck*!" He tore his finger from my ass and wrapped his hand around my nape, keeping my head facing the mirror, our eyes trapped on each other.

We watched each other fuck.

We learned how ugly we were, how hungry we were, how utterly desperate to convince ourselves that life would continue if we weren't together.

And we failed.

Because we no longer needed linguistics or lyrics to share our love, it was there.

The brightest flame, the loudest scream, the darkest disease imaginable.

My hands slipped on the vanity, sending me forward while his fingers around the back of my neck dragged me upright.

He sank every inch within me, clamping his fingers on my hip, holding me tight as he drove into me again.

And again.

He pulled me back until my spine bent and my breasts jutted forward. He kept my stare as he unsheathed his teeth and sank them piercingly into my throat.

I cried out as he nuzzled me, bit me, confused lust with loathing and handled me with peril instead of protection.

My legs buckled as he dragged me backward, sinking all he had to give inside me, rubbing his balls on my clit, keeping me pressed on the vanity and contorted in his hold.

His body pumped volcanic heat all while our skin still held icy droplets from our shower. His hair dripped onto my back. My hair dripped into the sink.

His tongue licked my neck, long possessive laps, running over the punctures from his teeth. His pupils blazed an otherworldly blue, glowing with dangerous curses and frostbitten rancour.

"Loving you is the hardest thing I've ever done. I hate it. I curse it." He bit me again. "I curse *you*."

I shivered at how dark his voice was—how dismal and destroyed.

The longer he fucked me, the more his eyes darkened until they no longer held blue, just shadows. Shadow-black curses and cusses, a dungeon trapping his kindness and making him mean.

"Sully, I—"

"Don't." He ran his nose over my wet hair, his eyes snapping closed. Misery etched his features, blending with frenzied ferocity. "You will let me fuck you. You owe me this. You owe me your soul, seeing as you fucking stole mine."

He rutted into me with single-minded determination.

My pain was his, and his was mine.

Fate's nasty trick where love was concerned.

Fall for someone, and you didn't just fall for their heart and happiness but also their flaws and fury.

I arched my back, giving in to the feralness between us.

I didn't need Euphoria to delete my decorum. I didn't wait for a drug to wipe away shame at being spread and at his mercy. I stared at us in the mirror, and I *liked* what I saw.

I shivered at the picture of two creatures fucking each other.

Not to procreate like nature intended. Not for love like romance dictated.

But for hate.

A hate born from the knowledge that we'd survived in a world on our own perfectly fine. We'd succeeded in chosen paths. We'd grown and evolved without missing the other.

But now...now that was impossible.

We would no longer be whole unless we were together. Our simplicity of being a perfunctory person was over now, now we knew what it felt like to belong.

Whatever Sully battled.

Whatever conversation would follow this could only hold one truth: two self-reliant people had gone and done the worst possible thing. We'd become dependent, obsessed, utterly and totally besotted with the one thing that would never let us be free again.

*I'm his.*

*He's mine.*

That irrefutable fact made my core clench around his invasion, possessive over him, my own temper snarling up my legs and into my heart.

I would always fight *for* him and *against* him.

I would never be so weak to let him destroy our bond.

That was my vow.

Just like his glowed in his eyes as his cock continued to pound into me. He loved me in every nasty, nice, wicked, and wonderful way.

And he hated it.

He hated that I knew how much he loved me.

He hated that I loved him as much in return.

Holding his stare, I licked my lips and let go. I gave myself entirely to him. I moaned and spread my legs farther, begging the way he wanted. "Fuck me, Sully." I tossed my head as much as I could in his grip, deliberately cascading my hair over my shoulder in wet coils.

His jaw clenched, fire burned in his eyes.

His pace turned from deep and penetrating to fierce and fast. "Stop it."

"Stop?" I shook my head. "I can't. I need you deeper. I want you to fuck me until you choose me. Choose me over revenge—"

"What the hell do you know of revenge?" His hand around my nape squeezed hard, his hips pulsing with vicious thrusts. "You know nothing about retribution—"

"Fuck me, Sully." I didn't want him chasing that path. I wanted him to be here. With me. Totally, entirely. *Mine.*

His creatures could have him once I was through. His loyalties and long lists of responsibilities could wait until we'd finished.

Shoving my hips back, making both of us groan with his depth, I begged, "Fuck me, fuck me, *fuck* me."

And that was it for his self-control.

He switched from man to monster and fucked me.

Hard and fast.

Painful and punishing.

Over and over.

Thrusting and rutting, bruising me just as I asked.

The wildness of him was what pushed me over the edge.

The beauty of watching sweat mingle with his shower, his pain bleed into pleasure, his loathing fire into lust.

He was undone.

I came as his head fell back, revealing the expanse of his powerful throat, the sweeps of his collarbones, the ridges of his muscles. I came as his balls pressed against my clit and his cock throbbed inside me. I came as he jerked and jettisoned, spurting his own release, dousing me in cum, over and over, coating me with every spasm and twitch of his powerful body.

I came harder than Euphoria.

Harder than elixir.

I came for him.

Because I knew what it felt like to be on the brink of losing him.

And I would never *ever* let that happen.

# Sullivan

# Chapter Seven

*ALL YOU HAVE TO* say is that you faked it.
*You don't love her.*
*You don't want her.*
*She means nothing.*
*Say that.*
*Only that.*
*And she'll go.*

I sighed heavily, my heart in fucking pieces on the floor.
We'd run out of time.

I'd already gambled her life by giving in to the desire between us. Our sex had been unhealthy. An act that had left us both scrambling in the dark for our stolen souls.

And now, I was supposed to find the strength to take away her choices all over again. I didn't have time for a proper negotiation. I didn't have time for a load of bullshit about tattered love and stubborn goodbyes.

Drake had given me three hours.

Those three hours were rapidly spilling through my fingers and I needed her gone before he appeared on the horizon.

I'd named this island *Batari*, thanks to the Indo word for goddess. *Serigala* hadn't been protected by deities or demons...but this island was. I would fight till my dying breath to ensure Drake never stole another goddamn thing from me.

And I'd start by sending Jinx home because I couldn't offer her what she deserved.

I eyed Eleanor as she dressed.

Leaning against the doorframe of her walk-in wardrobe, I remained naked from our war. I crossed my arms, cursing the well-spent cock between my legs.

I'd known if I'd touched her, I wouldn't have the strength to go through with this.

But now…now we were no longer joined, no longer fighting, and our energy had depleted to a tense surrender…perhaps I could finish it.

Maybe I stood a chance at saving her.

*Tell her.*

*Tell her you feel nothing. That it was all an illusion.*

*Tell her anything you fucking want apart from the goddamn miserable truth that you're a sad, pathetic bastard who can barely breathe at the thought of saying goodbye.*

Clearing my throat, I dug my fingers into my eyes, rubbing away the sudden sting, activating images of smoking pelts and the rancid stench of seared meat.

I doubted I would ever get such smells and memories out of my mind.

*Use them.*

*Wield them.*

If I continued drowning in death, perhaps then I would have the endurance to kick Eleanor from my shores before Drake arrived.

Dropping my hands, my gaze caught Eleanor's.

She stood in a simple teal sundress that skated around her knees. Her hair hung in seaweed coils over her shoulders. Her lips were swollen from mine. Her nipples still pebbled beneath the dress.

But it was her eyes that gutted me.

Those incredible silver eyes that'd once haunted my dreams and now doomed my future.

She knew.

She always knew.

She knew the moment she met me that I was hers just as I knew she was mine.

No matter what lies I fed her. No matter what fiction I tried to sell as fact, she would argue and defeat each one.

We could battle for hours, days, years.

We could battle until we found ourselves at a fucking altar, promising to live and die together.

The flash of her in a white dress with bare feet and an orchid in her hair, walking in the shallows of my shores, coming to marry me on my beach.

*Fuck,* I could barely stand.

My stomach fisted into an agonising ball.

My heart was no longer in pieces but devoured by monsters with the sharpest teeth.

She couldn't hate me for this.

After all, I had warned her.

I warned her so many fucking times that loving me was not a wise choice.

As she moved toward me, her dress swayed around her knees. My own knees threatened to send me crashing to the floor. The fact that she wore clothing and I wore nothing kept me extra exposed: a man with nothing else to play but still determined to somehow win.

"Sully…" Her eyes sprung with tears, knowing without words everything I thought. "Stop." She cupped my cheek, making me flinch. "Stop torturing yourself with lies you know are pointless."

I captured her wrist, pulling her touch away. "They're not pointless if they achieve what I need."

"What you need is me."

I huffed miserably. "What I need is for you to be free."

"I *am* free." She smiled sadly. "I'm free because I'm with you."

Skittles and Pika flew into the wardrobe, bravely venturing to see if the aggressive lust between us had dispersed. The aggression might've faded, but our lust would never dim. It existed between us in every stare, sigh, and stroke.

*Fuck…I can't do it.*

*You have no choice.*

Arming myself against the perfect image of Eleanor as Skittles descended trustingly onto her shoulder, I swallowed back my heartbreak.

Pika chirped, sensing my despair, and landed on my head despite my wet hair. He tugged at my strands, making my heart bleed harder.

I would still have one thing that loved me.

I'd survived my entire life with just a parrot's love.

I could survive again.

Balling my hands, I said as coldly and as carefully as I could, "Our time is over, Eleanor. I won't disrespect you by lying. I won't stand here and attempt to make you believe I never loved you. But I will demand loyalty and obedience. I'm not asking, I'm telling. You are leaving tonight. You may remember me, but you will never see me again."

I braced myself for her tirade.

I held an invisible crutch so I wouldn't fall into a worthless beggar at her feet.

But a fist hammered on the door, real life intruded, and the clock finished its final countdown.

Tearing my gaze from hers, I cupped my cock for decency and stormed to face my fate.

# Chapter Eight

PAIN.

There were different levels of it. Different methods of it. Different versions of different reasons full of different deliveries.

But this pain?

The pain Sully had just punctured me with?

I couldn't breathe around it. I couldn't see beyond it. I'd honestly never felt such catastrophic, claustrophobic...

*Pain.*

Not because I believed he didn't love me. Not because he'd dishonoured me by trying to make me swallow a lie. But because he was resolute, resigned...deadened to his decision and already suffering the accompanying agony.

*He can't do this.*

*He can't end us.*

It was unthinkable.

Stumbling forward, I clutched the doorframe as Sully marched naked with Pika on his head to answer the door. For anyone else, the image would be comical. For Sully, it made him all the more royal. All the more regal and untouchable.

Keeping his hand between his legs, he swung open the door, his back straight, his muscles locked.

A guard I'd seen lurking around the gardens during my weeks here bowed his head in respect. "Your clothes, courtesy of Mr. Moor."

Sully took the bundle. "Tell him thanks. His inability to keep his nose out of other people's business has proven to be convenient."

The guard nodded. "He also advised that the men are at their posts. We're ready." Pulling something from his waistband, he placed it on top of Sully's clothing. His eyes didn't stray from his boss's face; the fact that he was nude didn't seem to faze him. "Your weapon, sir."

*Weapon?*

My heart skipped, adding worry to my pain.

Why had the entire island suddenly turned black with foreboding?

I stumbled from the walk-in wardrobe as Sully closed the door and strode toward my bed. I followed him, dazed and soul sore, hating the dread covering my heart in sticky tar.

My eyes locked on the weapon.

A gun.

Black and lethal, despicable and menacing.

The sight of the morbid gun on my pristine white sheets petrified me.

The truth of the matter swarmed into comprehension.

His brother was coming here. His brother was going to try to kill him. His brother was the reason for all of this awful pain.

"Sully…" I moved toward him, my eyes drinking him in as he tugged on a black pair of boxer-briefs, black slacks, and a black shirt. A uniform intended to camouflage him in the dark. A solider ready for bloodshed.

I ignored his lies about us being over. I pretended what he'd said in the wardrobe never happened, and I tried a different tactic…in the hope that he'd stop being so stubborn. "If you want me to leave…come with me."

He sighed heavily as if my attempt at compromise was too hard for him to handle. "Enough, Jinx." He pinched the bridge of his nose, squeezed his eyes shut, and groaned low in his chest. "Enough."

"You don't get to shut me out just because you've made a decision. That's not how a relationship works."

"A relationship…?" His eyebrows tugged low over his tortured gaze. "We don't have a relationship. I told you…we're over."

"I'm doing my best to be respectful of what you've been through in the past few hours, but your decision to cut me from your life without talking to me is by far the cruellest thing you've ever done."

"Cruellest?" He chuckled darkly. "Has your love for me blinded you so completely?"

"It's *because* of my love for you that I'm willing to stand up and refuse your decision to send me—"

"I'm doing it so I won't do anything worse to you." His temper flared. "I'm doing it because I don't have a goddamn choice. *Enough*, Jinx."

Pika swooped from Sully's hair, dislodged by his shout. He landed on the sheets, glowering at the gun. He squawked in his stilted English. "Bye-bye! Pika!"

Skittles trilled loudly, landing beside her feathered brother, also glaring at the gun as if they both knew it caused mayhem and murder.

Sully huffed, nudging Pika away from attacking the trigger and grabbing the weapon from both parrots. Keeping his jaw locked against Pika's antics as he pecked at the sheets in frustration, he tucked the gun between his spine and waistband.

He sighed again, gathering final courage to finish this.

*I won't let him.*

*He can't.*

"Help me understand what you saw over there. Tell me, purge to me…maybe if you share—"

His lips thinned as he shook his head sharply. "I never want to discuss what happened there." He pinched the bridge of his nose, squeezing his eyes shut. "I can't get the images out of my head; I won't cement them any further with conversation."

"It might help."

His chin tilted up, his turbulent gaze meeting mine. "The only thing that will help is knowing you'll be far away from me. Far from my brother and his threats. Far from me with my tendencies. This was a mistake. *You* were a mistake. It's time I rectified that." With muscles braced, he stormed over to me, clamped his strong hands on my cheeks, and kissed me.

He kissed me as if he wanted to destroy me.

A crackle of chemistry.

A sizzle of sensuality.

A bone-deep longing that would never end.

*A mistake?*

This wasn't a mistake…we were the only thing that made sense.

I kissed him back, moaning as our tongues swept together.

Pika and Skittles took wing.

A gust of humid air whipped into the villa.

Energy prickled over our skin.

There *was* magic between us.

A rare, mystical connection. A bond that ought to be invincible and priceless…but Sully was determined to kill it.

He made a noise in his chest that dropped my stomach into my toes. A growl, a grunt, a groan of despair and damnation. His hands skated from my cheeks to my throat. His entire frame quaked with tightly reined rage, but his touch remained achingly soft. So, so soft as his thumb tickled my jawline.

My eyes snapped closed as he deepened our kiss.

Wet heat, endless belonging.

A goodbye neither of us wanted.

Ending the kiss, he wedged his forehead against mine.

His height meant he had to curl into me—a man who I could shelter beneath for the rest of my life if he'd have me. A man who could snatch that shelter away whenever he wanted.

Inhaling hard, he cupped my cheeks. "I only have the power to say this once. Don't interrupt. Don't argue. Nothing you say will sway my decision, so don't waste your breath."

I huffed with anger. "I'm not going to stay passive while you decide something I don't agree with, Sully."

His fingers bit harder into my cheeks. "What did I *just* say?"

"That you love me and you'll come with me if you're so determined to send me away."

His jaw twitched with temper. "This is my home. I will not leave it undefended."

"And *you* are my home. Therefore, I will not leave you alone."

"Christ, why did it have to be you, huh? Why couldn't I have fallen for a girl who obeys?"

I flinched, taking it personally because he *meant* it personally. He said he'd custom ordered me. He'd basically done this to himself by kidnapping me. "If you wanted a girl who obeys, you shouldn't have chased after a dream." I attempted to smile, despite the black cloud covering my heart.

"Yet the dream has turned into a nightmare."

"You're the one giving up on us."

He winced. "I'm protecting you."

"No, you're taking away my choice."

"Like I said, there *is* no fucking choice."

"There's *always* a choice." My snappish sentence hung in the air between us.

For a moment, I believed I might've broken his shields—that he'd tell me what was going on instead of commanding what would happen. But then his gaze slid over me, from my eyes, to breasts, belly, legs, and toes. He studied me as if he'd never see me again, and a heavy shadow fell over him, obscuring the man I'd fallen in love with, leaving behind a god with lightning in his blood, a vicious prince who wore anger as his crown, and a monster who no longer needed a mask.

He'd shut himself down.

He'd said goodbye.

I'd lost.

I sucked in a thin breath. "Sully...*don't.*"

He shrugged.

A simple, staggeringly painful move. "I love you, but it's not enough. It's not enough because I can no longer live in a world where my brother has the freedom to do whatever the fuck he wants. I cannot think of myself while the smell of my creature's fur still suffocates my lungs. I cannot put you in harm's way any more than I already have. It'll be the hardest thing I've ever done saying goodbye, but I will do it because I will *not* put myself first, do you understand?"

Without giving me time to reply, he winced and grunted with gravel and glass, "It's over, Eleanor. I won't repeat myself again. This fantasy of forever? This daydream of us? It's finished. I'm done."

# Sullivan

# Chapter Nine

I'D GOTTEN IT WRONG.

For all my science and theory, for all my successes in a sexual drug that reverted humans into animals and all the praise and profit I'd gathered...I'd somehow fucked up the recipe for happiness.

"Sully!" Eleanor clawed at my hand as I dragged her out of her villa and down the orchid-lined pathways. "Sully, *stop!*"

Orchids.

The main ingredient in my elixir and the trophy of my triumph. I'd spent years stripping every flora and flower down, seeking hallucinogenic, psychotropic, and experimental methods to tweak the human nervous system into accepting deeper pleasure, prolonged desire, and embrace the complete lack of inhibitions.

I'd achieved that quest.

Yet it'd been the wrong journey to chase.

Happiness was the fantasy, and sex was the consolation prize.

"*Let me go, damn you!*"

I ignored her.

I'd ignored her violent outburst when I'd told her we were finished. I'd ignored her rage as I'd carted her from her villa. And I would continue ignoring her attempts at fleeing because I had nothing else to give.

If we continued arguing, I would lose.

It was a certainty that stripped away my power as a man.

I could only repeat myself so much before my time ran out and Drake would hurt her.

"I'll just come back if you put me on the helicopter. You don't get to choose to keep me or send me away!"

My lips thinned as I swallowed back a retort. I could actually. I'd chosen to buy her. And now, I'd chosen to sacrifice her.

That was noble, right?

That showed some growth in my shadow-shaded heart?

If I didn't care, I would just leave her with the other goddesses. If I didn't love her with every fucking piece of me, I wouldn't spare a second thought of her survival.

I tripped in the sand, my heart circumnavigating my brain and trying to halt my stride.

The thought of her flying away?

The idea of never seeing her again?

It was a level of pain I'd never felt before—over any broken bone in my youth, over any massacred animal.

Eleanor had taught me a lesson I wished I could unlearn, but it was too late.

I knew better now.

I knew if she died…I'd die too.

I knew it wasn't elixir that granted joy.

It wasn't sex that gave unequalled ecstasy.

It was all the other shit that came from trading hearts with another.

The feeling of home. The sensation of staring into their eyes and knowing you were the most important person in the world to them. The most organic sensation of belonging.

Thanks to Eleanor, I'd tasted the first and only splash of sweet, sweet happiness I'd have. I'd finally learned, almost in my mid-thirties, that instead of bottling lust, I should've bottled love.

A stronger more potent drug that mimicked everything a human searched, coveted, and died for. An ingested endorphin that eradicated depression and loneliness. A priceless imposter for the real thing.

"SULLY!" Eleanor scratched my wrist, digging her nails into my flesh. "Stop for God's sake. We need to talk about this!"

I shook my head, gritting my teeth together.

*Don't answer her.*

*You couldn't get up the guts to tell her you lied about how you felt.*

*You told her point-fucking-blank that you're still in love with her.*

*You will lose if you speak.*

I couldn't be trusted to talk again.

My stride increased, dragging her kicking and screaming toward the beach and helipad.

Skittles darted like an aggravated hummingbird around my face, chirping and pecking, trying to get me to release her chosen mate.

I growled at her, swatting with my free hand. "Quit it."

Pika squawked and joined the fight, two annoying green mosquitos buzzing around my head.

Why the hell were caiques so fucking loyal? Skittles had known Eleanor only a few weeks, yet she acted as if I was about to rip out her tiny parrot heart. Even Pika had chosen her side…against me.

*You've only known her a few weeks, yet look at the sorry state you're in. You're as bad as they are.*

*Christ!*

I dragged Eleanor faster.

I was breaking.

My resolve splintering.

*Do it.*

*Get it over with.*

*Keep her safe.*

Eleanor sniffed as she watched me being attacked by two birds. "Not only are you evicting me from your island and heart but you're also denying me the right to see Skittles again."

I clenched hard. My teeth threatened to turn into dust.

*Stay silent.*

*Do not retaliate.*

We broke through the manicured jungle and onto the top of the beach. The sand remained white in the darkness while grey clouds danced over the tide that'd become an obsidian mirror.

It would still be my paradise if the air didn't reek of charred bone and pelt.

My chest ached.

My mind swarmed with so much death and decay.

My ears heard the whimpers of partially alive animals followed by the howls of those still fighting to survive even while missing vital parts. A woman's scream pierced my brain. Eleanor's scream. Her future.

My stomach roiled, and sickness blended with my rage.

My pain at losing Eleanor had overshadowed my fury, but now it nudged back into priority. My fingers curled tighter around her wrist, making her hiss with discomfort. My mouth watered to rip Drake's body limb from limb.

This peaceful, perfect world would soon be contaminated by my brother's blood, baptised in his death, and reborn from his tyranny.

"Sully...you've made your point. You win. Just let me go, and I'll find Jealousy and stay well out of your way. You won't see me until whatever is about to happen is over."

I raked a hand through my shower-damp hair. Pika and Skittles gave up their rampage, twittering and landing on Jinx's shoulders. I didn't think I'd ever find a more perfect woman.

Tall, willowy, graceful.

Stubborn, intelligent, kind.

Vegetarian, animal lover...*mine*.

*Fuck!*

I choked, clearing my throat as I stiffened and carted her down the beach toward the helipad. "If you stay, you'll still be at my mercy...even once this is all over."

"You would never hurt me, Sully." Her feet kicked up sand as she tried to tug against me.

"I would. I will. Eventually."

"That's not true—"

"Sinclair." Cal's voice whipped my head behind me, narrowing my eyes as he jogged to catch up. Like me, he wore all black. Unlike me, he carried a semi-automatic and the aura of squad commander. "You're going through with it then?" He nudged his chin at Eleanor who stood spitting mad beside me, still trying to unravel my imprisoning fingers.

Her neck arched with ire. "We're trying to settle on a compromise."

Cal smirked. "Sullivan doesn't compromise." He bowed. "It's been nice knowing you, Jinx."

"I'm not leaving!" She scratched at my arm, making me wince.

The helicopter was so close.

Only a few more strides before Eleanor would be gone.

My entire body revolted, but I pushed ahead, dragging her the rest of the way.

"Sully!" She squirmed and wriggled. "God, you're a stubborn bastard."

Cal followed us, his voice low and curt. "The men are ready, but the sensors are down."

I threw him a glower. "What do you mean the sensors are down?"

"The ones around the reef aren't working. Either the receiver is faulty or the perimeter line has had a break. We're sitting ducks with it being so fucking dark out there. I knew we should've gotten sonar."

"He flew over *Serigala*. What's to say he won't fly over this one?" I jerked Eleanor down the bamboo jetty and stopped outside the helicopter fuselage. She hadn't interrupted, her gaze darting back and forth between Cal and me, listening to warfare.

"He won't. This is personal."

"*Serigala* was personal."

"No, *Serigala* was a taunt. You're what he wants. He won't drop a bomb on you when he can have the pleasure of cutting you up with a fillet knife."

"Oh, my God. What the hell is going on? Why would he hurt Sully?" Eleanor stopped trying to get free and clamped her hand on my forearm in panic. "Come. Leave with me."

"I'm not fucking leaving," I growled.

The stricken look in her gaze made me add a soften snarl, "Drake won't touch me, Jinx. He's the one who will be dying tonight. Not me."

"All guests and goddesses have been evacuated, by the way. Arbi and a few guards will contain the girls." Cal narrowed his eyes.

"Good."

"I wish we had trained sharks," he muttered. "A few obedient crocodile or two. Maybe a rabid baboon."

I rolled my eyes. Not for the first time, Cal had tried to persuade me to come up with a pharmaceutical compound that could control any animal who drank it. To have access to powerful swimmers and jaws of death.

I'd half-heartedly given the request to Peter Beck—to see what he and his scientists could cook—but without the ability to test on animals, we'd reached a dead end. Besides, I wouldn't enslave a race just for my own gain.

Humans were my only hunting ground in that respect.

Shifting Eleanor so she stood right by the helicopter door, I grabbed her around the waist and hoisted her into the luxurious cabin.

"Wait. No—"

"You're going home, Eleanor."

"I'm staying." Tiki torches around the helipad flickered, bouncing golden flame off her glossy long hair as she leaned over me, refusing to go deeper into the cabin. She looked as if she'd embraced the fire itself, glowing from within with explosive temper.

"Sully—"

"Don't make me bind you," I snapped. "Because I will."

She attempted to push me away from blocking the door. "Let me off."

I nodded at the pilots, gritting my teeth as fresh torment ignited at the sound of engines firing on. Pika and Skittles took off with an agonising screech, fleeing from the noise.

Eleanor's gaze tracked them until they vanished into the undergrowth, rapidly filling with tears.

It broke my useless heart to tear her away from Skittles, but I'd do it all over again if I could keep her safe.

"Sit down." I pushed her back. "Buckle up."

Her tears spiked with frustration. Any sign of weakness or submission disappeared beneath dangerous tenacity. "I won't let you do this. Damn you, stop and just *listen* for a moment!"

"Listen?" I cupped her cheek, ignoring the splinters and daggers in my chest making it hard to breathe. "Don't you see? I *can't* listen. I can barely look at you without falling to my goddamn knees."

"Then don't do this!"

"It's already done." I gave her a grief-stricken smile. "At least you'll be safe. I'm doing the right thing by letting you go. You'll see. The second you're back in a city with people and freedom, you'll realise my enslavement of you warped your sense of—"

"My sense of love?" She bared her teeth. "Don't be ridiculous. I'm not like your other goddesses."

"Exactly. You're not. That's why you're fucking leaving."

The captain gave me a thumbs-up, hinting he had the envelope to give her, the flight path to fly her, the ending to sever us.

My knees threatened to buckle as I shoved Eleanor deeper into the cabin and attempted to step back. "I'll look after Skittles for you, you have my word."

"That's not good enough."

"It's all I can offer."

"Bullshit." She flung herself from the helicopter, her hair whipping in the wind generated by the rotor blades.

Tripping backward, I grunted and caught her weight, mindful that slicing blades whisked above our heads. "Stop making this harder than it already is, Jinx." I increased my volume over the din. "For fuck's sake, *please*."

Her body flush to mine made me achingly hard.

Her lips so close to mine made my mind swim with possession.

I'd reached the end of my control. I wanted the freedom to love her and the brutality to decapitate my brother. Two warring desires that should never live side by side.

"Cal!" I barked. "Get me some rope."

"No!" She shook her head, her arms twining around my shoulders. "Unless the rope is to tie us together so you can't do something moronic—"

"Cal." I glowered at him. "Go. Get something to restrain her. We don't have fucking time for this."

"*Sir.*" Storming away, he dashed up the jetty.

His sarcastic quip sent annoyance down my back. I didn't understand his attitude. He knew better out of anyone why I had no option.

Scooping Eleanor tighter into my arms, I marched up the helicopter steps and out of the downdraft from the blades.

The noise shredded any symbolism that this could be a romantic pledge. I was glad of the clamour. Thankful for the impatience of the pilots and the rising urgency of getting Jinx off my shores.

If I didn't have such hostile irritability, I'd probably carry her back to Nirvana and turn my back on Drake and on my creatures. I'd once again be so fucking selfish to put my pain first and keep her.

*I can't fucking keep her.*

Eleanor fought me as I wrangled her into the seat. "Why must everything be so black and white with you?"

Trapping her wrists, I struggled with the harness, looping it over her shoulders and draping it down her belly. "Because you either survive or you die. It can't get any more black and white than that."

Hot puffs of anger hit my throat as she breathed hard, glowering at me as I leaned closer and tried to do up the buckle one-handed.

Her rage was a physical thing, squeezing out every remaining pain in my chest. She ripped her wrists from my hold, her hands landing on my chest as if to push me away.

But then…she stopped.

Our eyes locked.

She annihilated me as she licked her lips and stood up to me, just as she had so often in our short connection. "Temporary."

I froze, raising an eyebrow. "What?"

She shook her head, as if trying to form thoughts after such a blurted comment. "I'll go…if you agree that it's temporary."

My chest tingled where her fingertips pressed into me. "I can't agree to that. My brother isn't the only problem."

Her eyes flashed silver. "You're doubting yourself because of what happened today, but I need you to listen to me. You. Will. Not. Hurt. Me."

I let out a black laugh. "You don't know enough about me to be sure."

"I know enough to fight for permanent when my whole life has been temporary until I met you. You are permanent, Sully— regardless of your pig-headedness and uncouth ways—and I'm not going to run away with my tail between my legs just because you say so. But…if you agree that this separation is *temporary*, I promise I'll go without a fuss. I'll sit here and fly away even though every instinct is telling me to stay…if you promise me that I can come back."

Cal jogged down the jetty, carrying a coil of rope in his hand.

*Temporary.*

Could that work?

Could I possibly have the freedom to be the monster I needed to be, the murderer without a shred of compassion, and somehow keep her once he was dead?

Cal skidded to a stop, holding out the rope.

Eleanor's hand landed on my cheek, guiding my eyes back to hers.

She smiled softly. "Do you trust me?"

*No.*

*Yes.*

"Fucking hell, you're killing me." I ran a hand over my face, catching her palm pressed against my cheek. I couldn't look away from her perfect smoky eyes. "I thought I knew who you were. I thought I had an answer to my question…but…who the fuck are you, Eleanor Grace?"

Her hand twitched beneath mine. "I'm your future…regardless how much you're trying to deny it."

My eyes closed. My heart raced. Her offer galloped through my blood, tangling fury with fear and fear with ferocity.

I wanted what she offered so fucking much.

But…men like me didn't get the girl.

Men like me didn't change and suddenly become redeemable. The moment she returned to a place where she'd have access to internet and information…everything she felt about me would go up in dirty smoke.

All it would take was one search on my name.

One article of who I truly was and her commitment to me would be over.

With that knowledge came a strange kind of peace, a solidifying dread.

I flinched against the slam of inevitability.

*Fuck, I'm an idiot.*

What did I think? That I'd keep her away from her family, friends, and facts for the remainder of her life? That I'd continue trading in goddesses and elixir, and she would stand by my side and plug guests into Euphoria?

That she'd still love me when she knew what I was?

It'd been a pipe dream.

A goddamn stupid fantasy.

And Drake had just woken me before it was too late.

I didn't get to keep her.

There was no happily ever after for me.

I clutched her fingers, making her wince.

"What happened? What did you just decide?" Her gaze searched mine, prying and diving, yanking out my secrets and sins one by one.

The only problem was they'd all been buried by the truth. I didn't even have to put a mask on to lie anymore.

"Okay, Eleanor…temporary."

I expected her to smile, to hug me, to kiss me with gratefulness. Instead, she peered at me suspiciously. "You're saying I can come back?"

"I am."

"When?"

"In a few days. A week? Give me a week…and then, come back." I shrugged. "This is my home. You'll know where I am. I'll be here…if you want me."

"What's that supposed to mean?"

I smiled away my sadness. "It means I'll still be here, trading in women, selling their pleasure, being the man who bought you from traffickers."

Her forehead furrowed. "Reminding me of your downfalls won't prevent me from returning, Sully. I know what you are."

I nodded, reaching forward to do up her harness. "I'm aware."

She shivered as my knuckles brushed the bottom of her breasts, clipping the buckle together. The pilots added more power to the rotors, making the cabin shudder in eagerness to leave gravity behind.

Giving myself one final good memory—a memory I would hold onto for the rest of my life—I linked my fingers behind her nape and tugged her forward until our foreheads touched. "Only you could turn an ending into a temporary pause. Only you could strike a deal with the devil about returning to his side instead of running away from him as fast as possible. Because of you, I know what it feels like to be happy. And thanks to you, I'm now condemned to a half-life without you."

"No." She shook her head. "Only a few days. I'll come back...you'll see."

I wanted to trust her.

I wanted to trust that I would survive Drake's invasion, that I'd be a better man afterward, that I could move on from *Serigala*, and somehow find the strength to trust in *us*.

But...trust had always been my downfall, and I knew deep in my gut that this wasn't temporary.

This was permanent...Eleanor just didn't know it yet.

I pulled away.

Our time was up.

Her hair slipped over my hands as I released her with awful reluctance.

Cal's presence lurked outside. The pilots were seconds away from soaring into the sky. I tried to order my tongue into saying something poignant, something that she'd always remember.

*I love you.*

*I need you.*

*You're mine...even if I'm letting you go.*

But in the end, I just kissed her.

I sank my hands into her hair one last time and crushed my mouth to hers.

I braced for harsh finality.

To kiss her with savagery and sin.

Instead, I kissed her softly, slowly, longingly. A final farewell even while she said temporary. My tongue slipped past her lips, tasting her, groaning with regret.

She moaned, opening wider, inviting me to take her deeper, to blend us together, to twine her lust with mine.

Her hands swooped up and clutched my shirt, yanking me into her.

I stumbled, resting on my haunches while we kissed and the helicopter gave us its last jerky warning before it winged into the sky.

I needed to leave.

To plan for war.

But still, I kissed her.

I lost myself in her.

I gave myself one exquisite moment where I trusted in a future I could not have.

And then, I let her go.

I leaped from the helicopter.

I punched the fuselage with all the pent-up fury inside me.

I slammed the door, keeping my gaze far from my greatest jinx.

And I locked my knees against the downdraft as Eleanor soared toward the stars.

Fuck.

Fuck.

*Fuck, it hurt.*

Cal stood with me, silent against the slicing screech of the rotor blades until the pilots banked and headed out to sea.

I rubbed at the bleeding within my chest.

Jesus, it *hurt.*

I'd been torn in two. Ripped apart. Turned into half of everything that I'd been.

As the palm trees calmed, and Pika and Skittles darted from the jungle, too late to say goodbye, Cal's hand landed on my shoulder, squeezing hard. "You're a fool, Sinclair. A goddamn fool."

I growled in warning. I felt *exactly* like a fool, but I didn't need the goddamn staff rubbing my face in it. "I'd stay silent if I were you."

"Someone has to knock some sense into your thick skull. I don't envy you, but…I get it."

"Get what precisely? That I went against my every rule, and

now I'm paying the price?"

"Get that you didn't have a choice."

"I did have a choice." I flashed him a cold smile, doing my best to ignore the lacerating holes in my heart. "I just chose wrong. I fell, and now she's gone."

He scowled. "I've never seen you lie that well before."

I sighed, rubbing again at my heartache. "It wasn't a lie."

"You told her she can come back?"

"I did."

"And you meant it?"

I shrugged, doing my best to stand still without stumbling with regret. "It doesn't matter what I meant. It's over."

"She was good for you, man. I think you've made a mistake."

I glowered. "Back off, you don't know a goddamn thing—"

"She'll come back, you know. You can't be that stupid to think she won't."

Keeping my eyes on the night-beacon flashing in the sky, I balled my hands. "Once she learns who I truly am, she won't. She'll make the decision for me. I won't have to break her heart...she'll break mine."

"She's not like the others, Sullivan. She's fallen for you, but she's smart, too. She'll figure out a way."

I turned to face him, dislodging his hold on me. "We both know I don't do well in love. Either they get killed because of my good intentions, or they die directly at my hand. This way, she stays alive."

"She might break the pattern."

"Or she might be exactly the same."

"She'll still attempt to come back."

I sighed, exhaustion creeping over my rage. "She can try...but she won't succeed."

Cal's green gaze sparked with understanding, shaking his head. "Oh, you sneaky son of a bitch."

Striding up the gangway, I held out my finger for Pika. He descended gently, chirping with worry, sensing my scrambled emotions. Skittles continued to zip in the darkness, her mournful squeaking breaking my fucking heart all over again.

Cal sniffed. "She won't be able to come back because no one without an invitation can find us."

I gritted my teeth, swallowing more pain. "Exactly."

Without the dark web coordinates, my islands were only accessible by fluke or fortune. I'd sent her away knowing that. I'd agreed to her promise of temporary, all while knowing she could never return.

*Permanent, Jinx.*

*It's over.*

*Christ, will the pain ever stop?*

"Fuck, she's gonna be pissed when she realises," Cal muttered.

"She'll be grateful because she'll hate me."

Cal followed me toward the beach, tossing the unneeded rope on the sand. "I don't envy you, Sully. Not one fucking bit."

I huffed, placing Pika on my shoulder and yanking the gun from my waistband to check the safety was off and the chamber was full.

I didn't have time to be tired or sad.

Those two words were no longer permitted in my vocabulary.

*She's gone.*

*Drake's coming.*

I would ensure my shores were fortified with every weapon I had in my arsenal.

I ignored Calvin; I'd done enough talking without dissecting my doomed relationship.

"You know…if she does find a way back, I think you should keep her."

"She's not a goddamn pet, Cal."

"She could be."

I bared my teeth. "I preferred it when you cockblocked me. Stop with the psychological bullshit. She's gone. It's over."

"I only cockblocked you because you asked me to. You ordered me never to let you get close to another human. You asked me—"

"To stop me from falling because I honestly don't have the strength. Animal or human, I'm done with loss, alright? She's gone. *Serigala* is gone. It's done. I suggest you shut your mouth before I shut it for you. My last warning."

He pulled out his own handgun, checking he had a full clip. "Fine. Noted." He huffed before shoving it back into his trousers. "Just for the record, though…I like her. I think—"

A shot boomed over the ocean, shutting Cal up.

We spun around, our eyes shooting skyward, skating over stars just as gunfire blazed through the night, aiming straight toward the helicopter.

# Chapter Ten

SULLY GOT HIS WISH.

I was no longer on his shores.

I gasped at the suddenness, the aching grief, the plummet of my tummy as we climbed higher and higher.

Sully stood below; his hair tussled by the wind as his black shirt snapped around his powerful torso. The harsh brackets of horror around his mouth, the stress etched into his forehead, the grim stamina and exhausted despair in his gaze vanished as intimate details were hidden by distance.

*Why did I tell him I'd go?*

Why had I obeyed when every part of me screamed that I should never have left?

This was a complete reversal to my unwanted arrival here.

This eviction hurt a *thousand* times worse.

The higher I climbed, the more my chest ached. My heart fisted with thorns as two parrots dashed from the forest, no longer buffeted by the downdraft—two tiny birds who'd wrapped their talons around my soul.

*God, Skittles.*

It didn't matter he'd agreed to temporary. It didn't matter that he loved me.

Nothing mattered against the bone-deep foreshadowing I'd felt when he'd agreed to let me return. He'd agreed, but there'd been *something*—something wrong lurking behind his voice. A harsh resignation. A decision that agreed with my suggestion yet reeked with a lie.

Had I adopted too many of his traits?

Had my trust turned so fragile that I couldn't believe he shared the same need for me? That he could survive sending me away forever?

*No, he loves me.*

*This doesn't need to be permanent.*

*You'll be back in a few hours...you'll see.*

I balled my hands in my lap as we climbed higher and higher, blurring both parrots as they circled Sully, refusing to land while he remained drenched with goodbyes and grief.

I couldn't shake the feeling that this was the last time I'd ever see him.

I couldn't stop the god-awful premonition that this was permanent...for him.

His island shrunk from a place I'd found such torment and pleasure to something so small I could pluck it from the ocean and place into my pocket for safekeeping.

The helicopter banked.

The pilots added speed.

And a streak of light blazed up the sky beside my window.

I baulked. My pulse thudded with adrenaline.

Was that a shooting star?

Another came, followed by the unmistakable screech of metal punching into metal.

"Shit!" The captain's curse filled the cabin, despite the din of rotors.

Grabbing the headset beside me, I shoved it on. "What's happening?"

More streaks of light. A *rat-tat-tat-tat* of illumination. A few pings against the fuselage.

"Tighten your harness!" the co-pilot snarled. "We're under fire!"

"*What?*" I bounced in my binds as the helicopter swerved up and to the side just as another spray of light originated far below us, spearing through the stars directly for us.

"Dammit!" The captain angled us steeply to the left, putting distance between us and danger.

Danger.

*Shit, Sully!*

"Take me back! Right now." I grabbed the microphone, holding it close to my lips. "*Please!*"

"Quiet! Stop yelling through the damn headset." The pilots angled us forward, encouraging rotor blades to slice almost vertically through the sky, soaring with speed.

My stomach flipped with weightlessness.

"No!" I struggled with my harness, my terror bouncing through me like a rogue frog. "Please, *please* go back!"

"Our orders are to take you to Java. We need to get to a safe altitude." The captain reached across to his controls and flicked a switch, muting me.

"Hey!" I screamed. "Go back. If they're shooting at us, they'll be shooting at Sully. We have to go back!"

Nothing.

The pilots ignored me, their chatter of flying maneuvers and technical speak filling my ears but forbidding me the right to talk.

*Sully!*

"Please…" I ran my fingers over the headset, trying to find a button that would allow a two-way conversation. "*Please* turn around."

No reply.

Nothing but their clipped curses and crackling feedback.

Daring to squish tight against the window, I looked down, down, down toward a black, black ocean and the flickering lights of Sully's shores.

And my heart died as the spray of bullets that'd attacked us aimed for land instead.

A morbid firework, seeking victims, streaking with comet fire toward the man I loved.

Death in the darkness.

An enemy he couldn't see.

*Sully!*

# Sullivan

# Chapter Eleven

"GET ME A GODDAMN radio!"

I ran up the jetty toward the guards lined up on my shores. Each had a machete, shotgun, and semi-automatic. Each was well-versed in hand-to-hand combat as well as being accurate shooters.

"Aim at the boat!" Cal ran beside me, yelling orders, preparing for war. "Sink those motherfuckers!"

The men moved toward the tide, a march of weapons and wrath.

A man ran toward me and slapped a walkie-talkie in my palm. "Here."

Spinning to stare at the sky again, flinching as more bullet-fire shot toward the flashing light blatantly giving away the helicopter's location, I pressed the radio button, and snarled, "Captain Jondal, turn off your fucking anti-collision light!"

A crackle of feedback hissed while everything I was as a man scrambled.

The pain at saying goodbye.

The rage at Serigala.

The suffocating *fury* at Drake's tricks.

*Fuck!*

More gunfire, all aimed at shooting Eleanor from the sky. My heart ceased beating as I dropped my stare, following where the bullets had come from.

Squinting into the distance, I saw a boat ghosting on the

horizon. No lights. No announcement. Just sly unfairness and my bastard brother who'd not even honoured his time for battle.

*He's an hour fucking early.*

The gentlemen's code broken because he was a cunt and I was once again a motherfucking fool.

Another spritz of bullets aimed straight for Eleanor.

The helicopter's spotlight made them the perfect target.

"Captain! Turn off your goddamn lights!"

I thought I'd saved her.

Instead, I'd put her directly into harm's way.

My rage ignited. A rush of wildfire through my veins, and this time...this time I didn't try to leash it.

I let go.

I allowed heat and hate to lick through me.

I *thirsted* for Drake's death.

I wanted his heart limp and lifeless in my hand.

I wanted to cut up his corpse and decorate every island in my atoll with pieces of him.

The helicopter suddenly vanished, and the radio came alive in my palm. "Done. We're out of range, sir. We've gone stealth."

My stomach clenched, fear blending with my fury. "Is she okay? Did you get hit?"

"A few pockmarks. Nothing serious. Cargo is intact."

Cargo?

Fucking hell, it was my world up there.

A woman who'd turned me into a useless, stupid idiot.

"Get out of here. Fly directly to Java."

"Copy."

The radio went dead just as a crack of violence aimed not at the sky but my shores.

A few of my men grunted, tumbling forward as blood spurted from wounds.

For fucking shit.

My temper broke through the veneer I wielded. I bulldozed through my decorum and failed attempts at being civilised.

My eyes locked on the boat ahead. A boat that should never have been able to come so close to my shores, manned by a cocksucker who I should've killed decades ago.

Cal yelled at the guards, giving instruction to return fire.

I wasn't needed.

He had his job...*and I have mine.*

Stepping into the fugue of fury, I ripped off my shirt and

welcomed the insidious pull of demonic instincts. I embraced the part of me that I'd always run from—the part of me that tainted me as a man and kept me firmly ruled as a beast.

Unbuckling my belt, I strode toward the sea.

Drake would not be allowed onto my shores.

No *fucking* way.

As warm ocean lapped around my ankles and seeped into my shoes, I shed the final part of myself. My teeth felt sharper. My senses acute. My mouth watered for gore. I was wrong when I thought I'd harness the wolf I'd named *Serigala* for.

Tonight, I'd become a shark.

The monster I'd swam with so many times before.

A crack of bullets returned fire on Drake, shooting out to sea. I kicked off my shoes and buried my feet into wet sand. I ripped off my trousers and trembled with the primordial urge to shed off my human skin and *hunt*.

To dive into the ocean.

To swim to him.

To drag him into the deep.

My gun fell, splashing into the salt, useless for where I was going. The sea lapped around my calves, welcoming me back into my domain.

My hand curled around the radio, still tight in my grip. I went to throw it away…but…

I pressed the call button, wading deeper into warm water dressed in just black boxer-briefs. Once I dived into the sea, any remaining humanity inside me would vanish. I wanted it. I hungered for the freedom of no longer obeying rules and civility.

But I honestly didn't know if I'd find myself on the other side.

I might cross an irrevocable line I could never return from.

I'd said goodbye to Eleanor.

I'd given her no way to find me again and no promises to go after her.

After tonight, there would be nothing left of the Sully she knew.

Bringing the radio to my mouth, I murmured, "Jinx…"

If Eleanor wore the headset in the cabin, she'd hear me. She'd know, even with her above me and out of reach, I was still hers, for the next few heartbeats at least. "Eleanor…I'm sorry."

*Sorry for betraying you.*

*Sorry for loving you.*

*Sorry for saying goodbye.*

My thumb stayed on the call button, not wanting to hear a reply. I braced to dive into the ocean, only for a spray of hot fire to ricochet over the horizon, thudding into my men, wounding more, knocking them to the sand.

"Shit!" I turned, violence crashing through me.

I stormed forward, inhaling a final breath to vanish into the brine, but a creature rose from the ocean before me.

No, not a creature…a man in full scuba gear with a harpoon aimed at my chest.

I saw red. I threw the radio at his masked face.

Calm water around me danced with a volley of bullets as Drake shot toward his own men, seeking me. "Fuck!" Ducking to the side, I dove into the wet darkness, only for a harpoon to hiss with release.

A spear sliced into my thigh.

A rope jerked me back.

And a foot planted squarely on my back, shoving me underwater.

# Chapter Twelve

"HERE."

I looked up, my eyes unable to focus on what the pilot held.

*"Jinx…"*

*"Eleanor…I'm sorry."*

For the past sixty minutes, Sully's voice echoed like a terrible melody in my head.

His apology set fire to all my fears that he'd agreed to a temporary separation, but really…it'd been a terrible lie.

He'd sent me away knowing he'd never see me again.

His voice gave the truth.

His violent curse following his despair hinted that the gunfire that'd been aimed at me had been aimed at him instead.

*Dammit, Sully!*

While I'd been flown against my will, he'd been shot at, attacked, and possibly died on the very beach where I'd been delivered to him.

*Oh, God.*

I curled up, hugging my hollow stomach, my heart long ago reduced to ash.

"Take it." The captain who'd ripped me from war and left Sully to battle alone entered the cabin and grabbed my lifeless hand. "You'll need this. Read it carefully. Obey completely. And your life will continue without further harassment from Mr. Sinclair."

I blinked, forcing numb fingers around the envelope. "What…what do you mean?"

"I mean your time as his goddess has ended. You're free."

"I don't want to be free. I need to go back. He's in trouble—"

"Stop." He rolled his eyes as if he'd heard it all before. "He is not in trouble. And regardless of what you want, it doesn't matter. Come on." Leaping from the cabin, he brushed down his pilot's uniform and held out his hand. "I'll pass you over to the ground staff."

I sat straighter, refusing to move. "Take me back to Sully."

His body stiffened, illuminated by the lights from the private hangar outside. "I only take orders from Mr. Sinclair."

We'd landed on the outskirts of a busy airport. Jets and commercial planes all went about their business in the distance, unaware that the man I'd fallen for might not breathe air anymore.

"He might be hurt."

"He has guards. They'll defend—"

"The last radio call…it sounded as if he'd been ambushed."

"The sooner you remove yourself from my aircraft, the sooner I can return and offer assistance."

"Take me with you."

He crossed his arms, his nostrils flaring. "You will not be returning to Mr. Sinclair by my services, Miss."

I flinched, lost and alone, doing my best to figure out how to stop this runaway train separating me from Sully. "I'll pay."

"You have been evicted. You can bribe me all you want, but you will not find Goddess Isles again. By me or other means of transportation."

A flush of panic tried to resurrect my heart. "Just because you won't take me doesn't mean I won't—"

"You can't find his islands, ma'am." He clenched his jaw and launched into the cabin again. His fingers unlocked my harness; his hand wrapped around my arm and jerked me unceremoniously from the helicopter. "No one can find Mr. Sinclair if they don't have an invitation. And you, Miss, no longer have an invitation."

I fought him. "His brother found him. I doubt *he* was given an invitation."

The pilot sniffed. "Forget about Mr. Sinclair. Don't waste your time trying to find him. No one will help you. No one will take you."

"Stop it!" I struggled against his strength as he dragged me closer to the hanger. My bare feet grazed on the tarmac, flaring with pain. My simple dress fluttered with the night breeze. I'd been sold to Sully without a single personal belonging. I'd been removed from Sully in the exact same condition.

I hadn't even taken the diamond he'd given me.

I had nothing of his.

No photo to prove it was real. No promise that he'd come after me.

Just a false admittance that I could return.

And a pilot who told me that was impossible.

Panic added new power to my body and I fought harder. "I'll find a way. I won't let him do this."

"It's already done." The blast of air-conditioning as he jerked me into the large hangar was a slap of reality after living on a tropical island. An island that might be under a siege with no one alive to protect it. An island that'd become unreachable.

A small waiting area welcomed, complete with travertine floors and flocked seating.

A young man in a black uniform with SSG on his lapel came forward. He bowed at the pilot, uncaring that he held me while I struggled. "I will ensure she is properly taken care of."

His words could mean kill me or help me.

"Take me back to Sully. He's in trouble. Stop wasting time and—"

"Hold her while we take off. Remind her that Goddess Isles is no longer available to her and destroy the letter once she's memorised it." The captain shoved my arm at the new man.

"Wait, don't—" I tried to backpedal, only for the slim Indonesian man to wrap his bony, strong fingers around my wrist.

"I'll hold." He nodded curtly, digging his fingernails into my skin as the captain gave me one last look, then stormed from the luxury office in the hangar and strode swiftly back to his helicopter.

I tried to run.

I did my best to pry my new jailer's claws off me, but I was too late.

Rotor blades swirled faster and faster, engines screamed, and my only method of returning to Sully shot into the sky.

The second the helicopter no longer touched earth, the man let me go, shaking out his hand as if touching me had been an affront to his job description.

"Do you have a preference in airlines, ma'am?" he asked

politely, moving toward his desk where a computer waited. "If you advise your hometown, I can book you on the next available flight."

"Flight?"

He nodded. "We might have to transfer you through the Philippines or Hong Kong. A lot of the main routes fly from there, but that won't be a problem." Pointing at the envelope in my hand, he added, "Inside, you'll find a new passport, cash, and any other identification you might need according to your place of birth."

Ripping open the paper, I peered inside.

Sure enough, a freshly minted American passport rested inside.

*Forged or real?*

"Huh, that's strange." The man clipped toward me again, his shoes echoing on the tile. His eyebrows rose as he peered into the envelope, perplexed that the passport seemed to be the only thing given. "Normally, there is a letter from Mr. Sinclair. I ensure you've read it carefully, before destroying it and confirming that you understand that the four hundred thousand dollars is yours to use as you wish…as long as you keep your employment secret."

I choked. "*Four hundred thousand?*"

"Yes." He nodded with self-importance. "All goddesses upon their release earn a salary for their service."

"I'm not just a goddess. I'm his…partner. His friend. I need to go back…before it's too late."

"Not possible." He crossed his arms. "No one goes back."

My fingers dipped into the envelope, pulling the passport free with shaky fingers.

"Mr. Sinclair is very grateful for your time in his employ, but you are no longer needed."

*I am needed. More than ever.*

*He was shot at.*

*I know he was.*

*He might be bleeding and wounded and—*

*Don't break down.*

*Nothing good comes from breaking.*

The best thing I could do—the *only* thing I could do—was keep my fear in check and focus on arranging swift travel back to Sully.

Regardless of what these men said, I *would* find Sully's islands again.

*I have to.*

It was unthinkable to accept that Sully had sent me away with a bald-faced lie about me returning, knowing full well I could never attempt such a thing.

*He sent you away for your safety…*

*If he's dead, then—*

*Stop it!*

Sniffing back terror, I flipped to the photograph page. I flinched as my image gleamed back. Somehow, I'd been captured simple and travel approved—sitting primly with my hair loose and sun dusting my features, the image must've been photo-shopped onto a white background.

It looked legit with the requisite glowing seals and hard-to-replicate watermarks.

I flipped to another page.

Something slipped free, slapping against the floor.

The man ducked to pick it up, standing slowly and passing it almost reluctantly to me. "It seems you do not get cash, ma'am."

I took it from him, my mind whirling with fear over Sully's safety and the roadblocks that'd been so smoothly slammed in my way.

A credit card.

A black Amex with no spending limit in the name of Sullivan Sinclair. "But this isn't mine. It's a mistake." I flipped it upside down, my stomach clenching at the sexy scrawl of Sully's signature. Elegant swooping Ss and aggressive slashes for the V.

The man touched my wrist, making me flip the card back to the front. He frowned. "No mistake. See? Your name is authorised beneath Mr. Sinclair's." He looked me up and down, as if judging what I'd done to deserve such a gift.

I didn't want a damn credit card.

I wanted a ride home.

A way to return to Sully's side, despite the danger.

My trembles increased as I looked closer. Goosebumps sprang over me as, sure enough, my name was scribed beneath Sully's.

*What the hell does this mean?*

That he'd given me the power to clean out his bank accounts? His version of showing me his trust? His way of tracking me with every swipe of his card?

*He doesn't want me to find him, but he wants to be able to find me?*

The man strode away in his dress shoes, returning to his desk.

Swiping the screen to activate his computer, he asked again, "So…which airline would you like to fly home on? I can book first class anywhere you need."

I shivered, unable to fight the chill from the air-conditioning snowing over my shoulders and the fear of what happened to Sully.

He'd premeditated this.

He'd had time to request a card be issued with my name on it. *Why?*

Had he known Drake would attack or had he planned on getting rid of me all along? And if he did want to get rid of me—if he wanted us over—then why give me access to his damn bank accounts?

"Ma'am? Your flight. Most large airlines leave around dawn, so it's advisable to book—"

"Send me back to his Goddess Isles."

He blanched, genuinely afraid for my mental capacity. "You cannot return, ma'am."

"Why not?"

"I told you. Because you are not welcome. No one is permitted to return."

"And like I told you, all I want is a private charter back to Mr. Sinclair." I strode toward him, clutching Sully's credit card. "That's the only destination I need."

"Not possible."

"*Make* it possible." My anger appeared. "I don't care who you are or what your guidelines require. Mr. Sinclair is in danger. He only sent me away because he believed it would keep me safe, but I need to go back. I need to make sure he's—"

"Mr. Sinclair does not permit anyone to know his location. Only those who have been carefully screened and approved—"

"I'm not a guest seeking to indulge. I was a goddess who *lived* there. We're going around in circles."

"What country are you from? I'll book that—"

"You're not listening to me!"

The man glowered. "And you are not listening to me. Your return is not possible." He hovered his fingers over his keyboard, his teeth clenched as he snipped, "Preferred airline?"

"I'm not leaving until I get a lift back to Sully Sinclair."

"No one will take you, ma'am." His black eyes narrowed as his patience reached its limit. "Please advise me the airline you'd—"

"No flight!"

He sounded like a damn robot with pre-approved sentences. He was the gatekeeper.

And Sully...*God, Sully.*

*Please be okay.*

I crossed my arms, Sully's credit card dug into one hand and my fake/real passport dug into the other. "If you won't help me, I'll find someone who will."

"No one will help you, ma'am."

"Sully is well-known. Someone will spill."

He bared his teeth. "You are not permitted to stay in Indonesia. What airline—"

Swooping toward him, I let go of my temper. I shouted like I should've shouted at Sully. "I am staying in this damn country because I deserve answers. I deserve to know what the hell he meant sending me away with no way of going back to him. I deserve to look him in the eyes and see which was the lie...loving me or getting rid of me. You and his pilots and all the guards in the world cannot stop me. Put me on a plane, and I'll fly back. Ship me off to somewhere, and I'll swim back. I will leave when I'm good and ready. And I will find a way back to him with or without your help."

His eyebrows soared into his black hairline, his own temper fading under mine. "But...it's just not *done.*"

"I don't care. I'm not just any goddess." Pointing a finger in his face, I snapped, "So, what's it going to be? Will you help me, or do I have to find someone else?"

He licked his lips. "I will not help you, ma'am."

"Fine." My heart fell.

More delays.

More worry.

More time when Sully could die before I ever found my way back.

Bracing my shoulders, I commanded, "Take me to the closest hotel then. I'll find my own way from there."

# Sullivan

## Chapter Thirteen

THE SEA DIDN'T HAVE favourites.

The predators she kept safe one day could become chum for a bigger beast the next. I'd spent long enough in the salty embrace to know how traitorous the depths could be. But I couldn't hate the ocean for choosing me as its next casualty.

I couldn't be pissed that my blood now blended with brine, ringing the dinner bell for sharp-toothed creatures to swim swift and hungry.

But I could be worse than any of them combined.

Ignoring the harpoon stabbed clean through my thigh, I pushed off against the sand beneath me. My lungs burned from lack of air while the surface above me taunted. So close yet so unreachable unless I could get the bastard's foot off my spine.

A slither of oily black appeared in the darkness.

A quicksilver whip of a fin.

The reef sharks were always present here. Most no bigger than a small dog. Most passive and content to swim side by side without challenging for dominion.

But their teeth were sharp and their nose for blood incomparable.

And I was wounded in their waters.

One brushed past my leg where the harpoon delivered blazing pain.

A scream sounded above the surface, warbled and followed by splashing of another diver as someone got bitten.

Digging my hands deeper into the sand, I searched for a weapon. Any weapon. Oxygen was needed. Breath was paramount.

Finding a piece of dead coral, I fisted it and struck with every last bit of power I had. I reached behind me, striking at the leg of the bastard drowning me.

I connected.

His foot vanished.

I shoved to the surface and stood with a huge gust of fury and air.

A shark oozed between my legs. The sharp nip of teeth against my already shredded flesh shot me from the sea and toward the beach.

The twine imprisoning me to the harpoon gun, shot by some hired mercenary, jerked me to a stop. Twisting, I reached down and fisted the rope, searching for a way to rid myself of the harpoon as three divers launched themselves from the shallows thanks to the cruising hungry sharks.

The diver holding the gun attached to me had a hole in his wetsuit and a trickle of blood down the back of his calf.

Yanking the rope, I jerked the harpoon out of his hands, making him slam to a stop, pinning his gaze on me.

Tearing out a hunting knife from a sheath around his thigh, he advanced on me.

Pain flared in his gaze. Panic a debilitating emotion.

I was above all that.

I felt nothing.

Heard nothing.

Saw nothing but rage.

Throwing myself at him, I whacked the coral against his temple, cracking his mask and most likely his skull, sending him plummeting to the sand.

Two other divers rushed toward me, their harpoons thrown away in the shark attacks, their hands fumbling for blades.

It only took a single heartbeat before I crushed the windpipe of one with a well struck punch and plunged the blade of the other into his heart.

Three bodies in the shallows, more blood dripping into the sea.

White water appeared in the darkness as the small sharks turned into a frenzy.

Breathing hard, I glanced at the horizon, seeking Drake's

boat.

*Shit.*

He was so much closer than he'd been before.

No longer barely noticeable, his black craft sped toward my shore and beached itself in a heavy wake. My guards immediately added more firepower, shooting and surrounding the boat. Some aimed at the hull and the men hiding within while others aimed at the engines to create an explosion.

Only…it was pointless.

Drake proved once again he had no respect for life.

A machine gun spritzed my shores, mowing down my men, a blanket of bullets all firing faster than their fingers could squeeze the triggers on their semi-automatics.

Forty guards.

Reduced down to nothing.

*Fuck!*

I stumbled as the throb in my leg amplified. My gaze drank in the carnage, my golden sand turning black in the moonlight with blood.

Cal.

*Where the fuck is Cal?*

A rush of bile burned my throat as I found him. Flat on his back, his black shirt torn apart, blood all over his chest.

His eyes closed.

FUCK!

Grabbing the harpoon gun so I didn't drag it behind me, I ran.

I ran with a goddamn spear in my leg the second the machine gun stopped reaping death and bellowed, "Still a fucking coward, Drake. Too much of a pussy to do the dirty work yourself!"

I dropped to Cal's side, my hands shaking as I searched for a pulse.

*Thud-thud.*

*Thud…thud.*

Weak and fading, but there.

*Hold on, my friend.*

Drake appeared in the boat, laughing under his breath. Smoke from his gun curled into the sky, hazing him as if he'd stepped from a crack in the underworld. "Well, that was easy." He pouted. "I'm rather disappointed."

Standing, smearing Cal's blood with my own, I grabbed a discarded gun from a dead guard and fired.

I fired again.

And again.

I emptied the entire fucking clip, wishing each bullet lodged firmly into my brother's brain.

When I had no more ammo and the sky rang with noise and reeked with gunpowder, he stood up in the boat again.

With a sneer, he plucked at the small graze I'd given him. A simple cut on his side.

My aim fucking sucked.

"Always were a loser when it came to guns, baby brother. Should've come to the shooting range with me and dear ole Dad instead of hanging out with your mangy rescues."

I threw the useless weapon to the side and yanked a knife from a guard's leg scabbard. I advanced on him as he pressed a hand against his side and leaped awkwardly from his boat.

His feet were in *my* ocean, walking up *my* sand, infecting *my* paradise with his motherfucking filth.

*No.*

I didn't care that his mercenaries leaped off the boat to surround us. I didn't care that I would die. All I cared about was killing him.

Over and fucking over again.

"Hey, Drake." I ran full tilt, harpoon in one hand and knife in the other. I ignored all weakness and the stickiness of blood and roundhouse-kicked him in the chest. "Surprise, motherfucker."

I shoved him straight off his feet.

He sprawled in a jarring jumble in the sand.

That was all I needed.

I fell on him with a rain of fists. I stabbed him, lodging the blade into his shoulder, making him scream.

I struck his face, his body.

I used both hands at once.

"Fuck!" He rolled beneath my onslaught, trying to get far enough away to collect his breath and retaliate.

I wouldn't let that happen.

"Time to die, Drake." I kept hitting. My knuckles crunched. My wrists threatened to snap. My blows ranged from feral to ferocious, growing sloppy and savage.

I forgot about the knife sticking in his flesh. I needed to feel him die. Needed brunt force to break him rather than a knife to slaughter.

He gave up trying to run.

Twisting to face me, he struck my jaw, making my teeth rattle and blood geyser in my mouth from biting my tongue.

"Fuck you!" he snarled and struck me again, thinking he could win. "Someone get him off me!"

Hands reached for me. Punches rained on my back.

But I had the upper hand.

I had the power of hate. The corrosive fury of being weak. I hated that he'd gotten this far in one piece. I despised that my life refused to change tracks, preferring instead to hit the rewind and repeat button, forever making me the loser and him the gloating asshole.

Not today.

Today, I would take his life and—

"*Stop.*" Metal bit the back of my head, digging past my hair and into my scalp. "Get off him unless you want your brain splattered all over your fucking beach."

I glanced behind me while I continued strangling Drake.

I'd won.

I had his life in my palm.

My teeth clenched as I weighed up the likelihood of killing him before I had the same fate.

My leg pumped fresh blood, making my mind skip with light-headedness.

*No.*

I shook my head, refusing to allow my body to ruin this for me.

I squeezed tighter.

I ripped the knife from Drake's shoulder and held it against his throat. "Shoot me and I kill him."

The mercenary paused, assessing the situation.

"Get him the fuck off me!" Drake tried to push me off, making me see nothing but red.

I dug the knife against his neck and slammed my fist into his nose, making blood gush and a garbled grunt spill from his lips.

"I said *stop.*" The gun dug deeper into my skull.

Four other men pressed their weapons against my head.

Drake choked and squirmed beneath me.

I balanced on the edge of committing worthwhile suicide just so I could continue murdering my brother.

But...even with a knife, I couldn't be guaranteed he'd die.

I wouldn't have the satisfaction of seeing his lifeless eyes.

It would be my lifeless eyes.

My end.

My loss.

With bared teeth, I pushed to my feet, blinked back the heavy throb in my leg and spun. My arm lashed out, knocking into one of the guy's wrists and sending a gun smashing to the sand. A second later, I punched him in the throat, making him gag for air. "I don't take orders very well."

My vision went black for a second.

I shook my head and stepped away from Drake, throwing a punch at the remaining men surrounding me.

I stumbled.

My heart galloped with adrenaline, mixing with the sedative of losing too much blood.

*Shit.*

I struck again, making contact with a man I couldn't see.

I tripped as a wash of heaviness made gravity twenty times stronger.

*No!*

*Stay awake, goddammit.*

Shaking my head again, I bent and scooped up the gun I'd removed from the first mercenary. Nausea clawed my stomach, sickness made the world swim.

I pinched the bridge of my nose, doing my best to stay conscious.

How much blood had I lost?

"Drop the gun."

Gritting my teeth against the creeping greyness, I gave him the finger and aimed at my brother.

A *rat-tat-tat* volley of bullets made me jolt as a guy on the boat sprayed the sand by my feet. "He said drop the fucking gun!"

I fired instead.

I swayed and tripped and pressed the trigger in the general direction of my cunt of a brother.

The kickback sent me falling to my ass.

The sand embraced me.

My teeth rattled.

Darkness hovered on the edge of my vision.

Six men surrounded me, all with guns aimed at my every body part, their tension feeding into mine and helping me stay awake.

My leg looked like fucking mincemeat.

A strange kind of spaghetti of muscle and blood.

More nausea clawed up my throat, making me sweat and

shiver all at once.

The men surrounding me swam in a blur. I licked my lips, tasting sand and salt. "Whatever he's paying you, I'll quadruple it." I struggled to breathe as my leg continued to drain me of everything. "Kill Drake and leave, and I'll give you whatever you goddamn want."

Drake climbed gingerly to his feet, rubbing at his bleeding nose, favouring his stabbed shoulder. "They can't be swayed, Sullivan." He sniffed loudly and spat a large glob of blood right by my bare feet. "They don't want money. They want this." He waved his hand at my island. "They want what you've created here. They want a goddess for themselves. They want their dicks sucked. They want ultimate fucking power."

He stumbled toward me, hissing, "I'm going to take it all, and unlike you…I'm going to share."

Hissing hate ran through me. "My islands are not for sale."

"I don't remember offering you a price."

"You think you can take my business by force?" I smirked and tapped my temple with a wobbly hand. "It's all up here, cunt. The programming. The cypher. The way Euphoria works. The recipe for elixir." I shrugged. "You can't have a damn thing because I fucking refuse to give it to you."

"Oh, you will. I'll trade you. Eleanor Grace for everything."

I grinned. "She's gone. You couldn't shoot her down. You're too late."

"I'll find her. I know her name. The world is an open book these days." He smiled and rubbed his mouth with the back of his hand, spreading more blood. "I already have her parents' names and addresses. I'll just make myself at home here, we'll have a family reunion while she flies to her folks, then I'll arrange for her transportation back here. When she arrives, we'll have ourselves a little chat and see how firm you are on the idea of business over pleasure."

I flinched as another wash of sickness made me sway. *Fuck!*

"And you call yourself a man." He clucked his tongue. "Can't shoot. Don't eat meat. Have to buy whores to sleep with you. And think just by sending your girl away that I can't hurt her. You're an embarrassment, Sullivan."

My heart galloped, oozing more blood from me to the beach. Terror I'd never felt before crippled me at the thought of Eleanor being tortured and raped by my sibling.

I wanted to launch at him.

I wanted to tear him into shreds.

But my own body imprisoned me.

My own blood forsook me and soaked into the sand instead. Balling my hands, I snarled, "Yet for all my downfalls, you still wish you were me. The older brother envious of the younger."

I screamed as he kicked me in the leg, his boot catching on the spear, sheer fucking agony bellowing through me. "Not jealous. Just owed what's rightfully mine."

I gasped and groaned, writhing with uncontrollable pain.

Fuck, I'd been blind all over again.

I'd given Eleanor access to my credit card so I could track her whereabouts.

If I could do that…of course others could. She would never be safe until Drake was dead.

I hadn't learned a fucking thing.

It was *my* fault she was in danger.

My fault all my rescues had died.

My fault that Cal was barely breathing.

My fault that my beach was decorated with the bodies of my guards.

My fucking fault for *everything.*

Drake clucked his tongue again. His forehead shined fake-perfect, his eyes unable to fully squint with intimidation.

It'd been a few years since we'd seen each other, and instead of letting nature weather him, he'd turned to pharmaceuticals to reverse the hints of aging.

"You know…" I coughed as my pain levels crept to all-consuming. "Injecting your face with botulinum toxin might do my job for me." I attempted to stand. To grab him, kill him. "You'll die wrinkle free, Drake, but you'll still fucking die."

I wobbled and fell sideways, cursing my failing body, eyeing up the pool of blood beneath me.

"What's the matter, little brother? Feeling woozy?" He grinned and kicked my leg again, crunching the harpoon against my thigh bone.

"Mother*fucker*!" I jack-knifed up and shoved him away.

He snickered, his own injuries making him trip. "I can take that out of you. I could be nice like that. However, the hooked end will mean I'll rip off most of your leg…but you don't need to walk anymore, do you, Sully? All I need is that genius brain of yours."

He ducked to his haunches beside me, his hands locking

around the spear. "By the way, this look is good on you."

I went to punch him in the jaw. His mercenaries pre-empted my strike by pressing the muzzles of their guns against my head.

I would pass out if he touched that spear again.

I would vomit and choke and die.

Forcing myself to speak through clenched teeth, I snarled, "What look? A gutted pig?"

"The 'bleeding out like a slaughtered cow' look." He jerked the spear, making me pass out for a second.

Nothingness.

Then back on the beach.

He chuckled. "Thought you'd gone then, brother." He let the spear go, dragging his finger through the congealing blood beneath me. "Wonder how many litres you've lost. How many can a human lose before they die?"

I shivered, suffering a stabbing pain in my belly and thickening greyness over my vision. "Piss off, Drake."

"Nah, not yet. Not until I've fucked that sweet girl of yours, you've watched me slice her into pieces, and then given over every worldly possession you own."

My heart kicked me into blackness again.

Gone.

Then back, blinking into colour, narrowing my eyes on my greatest enemy. "Who told you?"

Drake grinned. "What little spy told me about Euphoria and elixir?" He touched his swollen nose, wincing. "That's a secret."

"No secrets between brothers…" It was a struggle to work my tongue. The urge to slur and slip through words became harder and harder to ignore.

*I'm dying.*

The thought popped into my head with terrifying conviction.

My body felt wrong.

Cold.

Distant.

A shell I could no longer operate.

I clawed my way back into comprehension. I couldn't die. Not until Drake was shark food.

Eleanor.

Fuck, Eleanor.

*I'm so, so sorry.*

My eyelids turned heavy.

I forced them wider.

I looked at the sky, and a flutter of emerald caught my attention.

*Ah, shit.*

My heart rate increased, keeping me alive but ensuring I died faster.

Two green parrots zipped from above, dive-bombing Drake.

*No!*

Pika squeaked and attacked Drake's head, his little talons outstretched, sharp enough to scratch above his eye.

Drake ducked, throwing his hands up. "What the——?"

Pika fluttered around me, cawing instructions for me to sit up and give him somewhere to land.

"Leave, you damn bird!" I swatted my hand as he tried to perch on me, fighting the final wash of light-headedness. He puffed up like a menacing cotton ball; his black eyes filled with fury. "Go!"

Skittles circled both Drake and me, shredding the air with an ear-piercing squawk.

Mercenaries tried to catch her with outstretched fingers.

Drake eyed my caiques with the same malicious glee that he'd worn when he'd hurt Pongo.

I turned ice fucking cold.

"Well, well." He sneered. "You have more pets other than Eleanor."

"Hibiscus, Pika. *Now.*"

The flowers he favoured were by Nirvana. Far enough away to keep him protected, hidden by tall, thick trees and safe from whatever would happen to me. "Skittles, fuck off!"

Pika squeaked, darting around my head, so stupidly unaware that Drake prepared to pounce on him.

"Pika!" I waved my arms, creating air eddies, giving up the last of my energy to scare away my feathered friend. "Go!"

"Sully!" he chirped. "Lazy. *Lazy!*"

I glowered at Drake as he crouched, coiled and cruel. I knew his intentions. He watched Pika as if he could snatch the parrot from the sky and wring his tiny neck.

My heart hammered, I flickered between darkness and awake.

"*Go*, Pika! For fuck's sake, *go!*"

He chirped again, his little face full of concern. I'd dealt with so many animals in my time and all had a high level of intelligence, but birds…they were different.

They *knew* things.

They understood what wasn't said and could read a situation that might seem friendly but was filled with violence.

Pika had called me lazy because he saw me lying down and knew just how close I was to death.

He put his own life on the line to encourage me to stay alive.

Tears sprang to my hazy eyes. "GO!"

Drake held out his hand, cooing, "Come here, little birdie."

Pika let out a huge screech, swooping toward him.

I whistled loud and piercingly, stopping him mid-attack. If he got anywhere near Drake, I'd be forced to witness fourteen years of man and parrot brotherhood being decapitated before me. *"Pika!"*

He snapped his wings and hovered just out of Drake's reach. He squawked again, throwing me a rebellious glower.

"Hibiscus, Pika. *NOW!*"

He erupted in a chorus of angry chirps before finally darting into the jungle.

My energy levels plummeted.

My heart skipped with an odd rhythm, running out of blood to pump.

Skittles still hovered above.

Drake continued staring into the jungle after Pika, like the cat wanting to chase the juicy canary.

I'd saved one bird.

But Skittles was too brave, too bold, too loyal.

She pinned in her wings and attacked Drake on my behalf. *"No!"*

She dive-bombed, pecking at his eyes, scratching at his nose.

Drake bellowed as she darted off, only to swoop in again, drawing blood on his cheek.

"Skittles, stop!" I cried, my voice fading and weak.

She didn't.

She continued attacking him, taking more and more risks, getting closer and closer to his flailing hands as he tried to protect his face from her beak missiles, so, so close to snatching her from the sky.

*Shit!*

Gritting my teeth, I gathered every remaining shred of power.

I shoved off from the sand.

I shut down every pain receptor.

I ignored the blackness whispering over my mind.

I hopped and threw myself on Drake, pinning him to the

beach.

His guards were on me a second later.

Punches in my kidneys, kicks on my spine.

My hands found his throat, squeezing tight, all while our legs tangled and the spear dug deeper.

My vision blacked out, stuttering with warning.

Skittles squeaked and plummeted from the dark sky, aiming straight for Drake's eye.

It happened in slow motion.

Drake's attention slipped from me to Skittles.

His lips spread to reveal sharp teeth, his hand curled into a fist, and he struck at the perfect point of her trajectory.

He punched her.

Clear out of the motherfucking sky.

*"No!"* I scrambled to the side, hauled back with the harpoon rope now wrapped around both Drake and my legs—a morbid, agonising mousetrap.

My heart stopped as Skittles went from a fierce little fiend to a lifeless pile of feathers, tumbling from speed to silence. She splattered against the sand, somersaulting with a spray of golden granules.

She came to a stop.

Lifeless.

Not moving.

Dead.

Skittles represented all the love I had for Jinx and all the things I'd failed at.

I lost it.

I howled and crawled back to Drake.

I hit him, over and over.

I got his jaw, his eye, his collarbone, his temple.

I didn't care where I hit, only that I did.

I hit and struck and pummelled him with undying ferocity.

My gaze caught the carnage of green feathers, unmoving and sand-covered.

I hit harder, faster, crazier.

I hit and hit and hit.

But my body had reached its limit.

I had nothing left.

No life force.

No blood.

My fingers went from berserk to broken.

My heart gave up beating.
My eyes rolled back.
I tumbled forward…
…and the world went deathly dark.

# Chapter Fourteen

*SULLIVAN SINCLAIR, OWNER AND CEO of Sinclair and Sinclair Group, faced trial for the fourth time today. Rival companies, Craden and Co, and Smart Int, hope for a conviction of life imprisonment. However, just like his previous arrests and subsequent court appearances, Sullivan Sinclair will most likely walk free this afternoon thanks to having the best lawyers that money can buy and no useable evidence against him. It seems this pharmaceutical mogul cannot be touched and continues to walk amongst us, murderer, whistle-blower, and all.*

I frowned.

For the past hour, I'd been online, googling Sully's atoll, clicking on Wikipedia links and doing my best to locate his forty-four islands that'd seemingly vanished without a trace. If I hadn't spent time there, if I still didn't taste salt in my hair from his oceans and feel his touch upon my tanned skin, I'd fear it'd all been a dream.

The World Wide Web ought to have *some* mention of his location. After all, everything was on the internet these days.

But…nothing.

No link to his address. No mention of where he lived. No social media or tags from other people's albums. The only thing I'd found was a corporate website for his company and a stern photo of him in a navy suit glowering at the camera with a simple bio stating he was the boss.

I gave up trying to find his home and instead tried finding out about the man. Perhaps a hobby would lead me to him, or an old bill that'd somehow found its way into public knowledge would give me a starting point.

However, googling Sully made my heart pound and palms perspire. I didn't find a man known for deviant virtual reality or libido-enhancing drugs. I found no information on his proclivities about buying trafficked women. Instead, I read about a monster who, on paper, sounded utterly heinous and disgustingly powerful.

Clicking on another article from a few years ago, I bit my lip and read.

*Upon taking ownership of his parents' science research and highly lucrative drug business, Sullivan Sinclair, promptly fired most of the board, forbid animal testing, and enforced strict guidelines on the future of Sinclair and Sinclair Group. Stock market shares plummeted to a historic low when members of his board turned up dead a few weeks later. No evidence was found to the cause of their deaths, even though Sinclair's own scientists made noises that they'd been working on a highly volatile compound that stopped the heart of any animal they'd tested it on.*

Ignoring the five-star hotel room that I'd rented—the first accommodation the man from Sully's hangar had driven me to—I clicked on more links, skimming faster and faster.

*Sullivan Sinclair was once again arrested today for his involvement in the illegal recording and video sharing of a slaughterhouse in West Virginia. The footage has gone viral with over three million views in just twelve hours. At two a.m. on Thursday 15th February,*

*Sinclair and two other men (who he refuses to name) were seen breaking into the slaughterhouse and recording footage of pigs crushed in pens, chickens walking over skeletal remains, cows sick with bovine spongiform encephalopathy, and recently slaughtered carcasses inhumanely dispatched and prepared for human consumption.*

*Charges have been brought against TMT Feeds with more videos being leaked of employees physically mutilating the animals while in the chute waiting to be dispatched and one even performing sexual acts. Regardless of the seriousness of evidence, TMT Feeds will most likely be unaffected by allocations due to the law stating it is illegal to enter and film without consent. Therefore, all evidence is inadmissible. Sullivan Sinclair faces fifteen years imprisonment for entering private property and recording restricted activities. To this date, he has not released the names of his accomplices.*

*Breaking News: Sullivan Sinclair walks free from murder.*

*In a shocking tragedy today, Sullivan Sinclair—owner and CEO of Big Pharma Sinclair and Sinclair Group—has been interviewed by local enforcement for the murder of Sally Scoon. Ms. Scoon headed the campaign to bring back the right of fur use from fox, rabbit, and other animals. Her social media was thrown into controversy when she filmed the killing and skinning of a rabbit to reveal the process of how pure her fur products are. Mr. Sinclair has declined an interview but eyewitnesses put him at the scene of the crime, the day before the gruesome discovery of Sally Scoon, who'd had her throat slit and skin removed in the same methods as those revealed on her Facebook page.*

I slapped a hand over my mouth, reeling away from the computer.

Could the newspapers be right?

Could Sully have been cold-blooded enough to murder a woman in the exact same way as she'd done to countless of creatures?

*Yes.*

A little voice shouted in my head.

*A thousand times yes.*

Sully could be cruel, cold, and completely unreachable if he chose. But he was also warm and caring and suffered far too much empathy for creatures he couldn't save.

He was the flip side of a coin. The yang to yin. The ocean crashing on a beach.

He could be calm and gentle, but he could also be ruthlessly merciless.

My heart thundered as nausea swam up my throat. If he could buy women and farm them out to guests for sex...of course he could kill. Of course he could turn off any guilt or wrongness because in his mind, he wasn't doing something barbaric; he was doing something protective.

Running shaking fingers through my hair, I glanced away from the countless articles painting Sully in black and white gory detail.

The luxurious hotel room—complete with living room, huge bedroom with a four-poster bed, and giant ensuite—paled under the knowledge of what Sully had done. I'd booked this room with his money. I'd paid for this from wealth he'd made while killing fellow humans.

It made me sick.

All while a part of me understood.

Sully had never pretended to be a good guy. His patience was non-existent when it came to men and women, yet endless when it came to creatures.

He'd removed himself from society and cloistered himself in a paradise no one could find.

For their protection or his?

I skimmed the screen again, wincing at the pages and pages of hits on his name. All either blood-soaked or crime-etched—a manifesto of every dark and disgusting depravity he'd done.

*The notorious owner of Sinclair and Sinclair Group, Sullivan Sinclair, was questioned earlier this week on the death of his parents. His own brother, Drake Sinclair, has pointed fingers, suggesting the yachting accident and subsequent drowning wasn't as innocent as first believed. Sinclair's lawyers refused to comment.*

*For Feathered Sake—an online group that has successfully exposed multiple areas of the dairy, meat, and egg industry—has recently grown from a few thousand members strong to close to two hundred thousand members, thanks to a rumour that Sullivan Sinclair has recently given his backing.*

*The content of their YouTube channel makes even the hardened carnivore shudder as they learn where their pork chops and Sunday roasts come from. We cannot confirm the rumours circulating that their sudden growth or success in breaking into mainstream media with their illegal videos is because of a wealthy benefactor, nor that the lawyers protecting them are associated with Sinclair and Sinclair Group. However, Sullivan Sinclair has become well-known for being more wolf than human, choosing to protect the creatures who can't speak over his own kind.*

*Sullivan Sinclair…the enigma.*

*According to* Times Magazine, *his personal wealth reached over ten figures last month thanks to breakthroughs and landmark sales. However, he is a man who has vanished from Big Pharma circulation. His board still reports to him, and he is still an active member within the science circles. However, he has not been seen as of late at functions or in city life.*

*Could it be the constant rumours of how much blood coats his hands keeping him away?*

*Could his lawyers have suggested he lay low after a recent charge of another member of his board going missing, only to be found a week later with his heart torn out?*

*Could he be dying and sampling his own medicines in private?*

*All we can say is Sullivan Sinclair is a monster when it comes to mankind. A well-known murderer, even if he's never been convicted. He is a man who is seemingly untouchable.*

Slouching in the velvet chair nestled in the office space off the bedroom, I chewed my cheek with worry.

I'd been booted from Sully's islands. I'd been running around like an alarmist, drunk on panic about his survival. I'd spent his money and remained obsessed with the notion of going back as soon as urgently possible.

Yet…

How was I supposed to turn a blind eye to what he'd done?

How could I accept that he might have killed his parents?

That he'd killed *people*—plural, not single.

That he bought girls and traded in sex and massacred men and attacked companies and earned a reputation for being an untouchable killer who only showed affection for whiskers and paws.

*God…does it make me a stupid, stupid girl to trust her heart over the ink online?*

To ignore the articles immortalizing his behaviour, warning me away with bold letters?

Could I honestly trust that he'd never hurt me in the same way?

*Trust…*

I curled my hands, hating the niggle of indecision and slight whisper of self-preservation.

*You're free.*

*You can go anywhere.*

*Do anything.*

*Go home, be safe, ignore a man who deserves to burn in hell.*

But…

Trust…

*Trust in your heart.*

*Trust in your own knowledge of him…not what strangers have written.*

Sully had sent me away, knowing full well that I had enough ammunition against him to go to the police. The internet had no mention of his Euphoria or goddesses. I could reveal every dirty, torrid thing he'd done.

Yet…he'd released me because he trusted me.

*Because he loves me.*

When Sully held me, he told me everything I needed to know.

He was a good person—despite doing bad things.

He deserved someone to fight for him—regardless of his past felonies.

Pika and Skittles loved him.

Cal respected him.

And I…

*I have enough sticky-taped faith that he will never hurt me…if he's still alive.*

I didn't know if I'd regret my decision. I had no idea how I'd find my way back to him or if this would turn out to be the most painful choice of my life. But I did know if I allowed online articles to sway my commitment to him—then I didn't deserve a happily ever after.

Sully had given me his trust.

Either way…I was going to break it.

And I'd rather break it by going back than by running away when he needed me.

*I don't care what you've done, Sully…I only care about what you* are.

Swallowing back my hesitation, pushing away the nonsense of leaving him to bullets and his brother, I scooted my chair closer to the computer and typed: *Sullivan Sinclair property purchases and locations.*

\* \* \* \* \*

Dawn.

I'd been up all night, going around in circles trying to find Sully's islands.

Not one hint. Not a single whiff of his location.

The more time passed, the more a chill crept through me that Sully was hurt. I couldn't explain it—I chalked it up to a racing mind and frustration at getting nowhere—but I had an awful, *awful* feeling that I was losing him, and there was absolutely nothing I could do.

*Sully…why the hell did you send me away knowing I can't get back to you?*

Temper gave me a new surge of energy.

My stomach growled, reminding me this hotel wasn't like Sully's villas. Breakfast would not magically appear, all organic and grown on *Lebah*. Here, I had to call. I had to accept a menu drastically slim on vegetarian options after a smorgasbord of deliciousness.

Ringing the restaurant, I ordered a bowl of muesli and local fresh fruit. Once my requests had been noted, I hung up and stared at the phone.

A phone.

I'd wanted access to one of these since I'd woken in my villa the morning after Sully gave me elixir. He'd made me sign a contract that I'd sleep with one-hundred-and-ninety-two men, and here I was, ignoring all that by fighting to go back to him.

Snatching the phone, I dialled for an outside line.

I rang my father over my mother.

Ever since their divorce, my mother and I had slowly drifted apart while my father and I grew closer.

A ring sounded in my ear.

*Ah, wait, I should've thought up a story!*

*What the hell am I going to—*

"Hello?"

I flinched, ready for his tears, his shock, his anger at my letter sent from the traffickers, the note I'd asked them to deliver on my behalf that I'd run away for love and not to worry. How ironic that it'd become real. "Dad…it's me. Eleanor."

"Ellie!" His bark of surprise hurt my eardrum. "Oh, my word. What are you playing at? Leaving it over a month before calling your old man?"

"Ha-have the police been looking for me?"

"Police?" My father, Ross Grace, cleared his throat in suspicion. "Why in the world would the police be after you?"

I frowned. "You weren't looking for me? You didn't get a note from the traf—" I cut myself off. "From Scott?"

"Scott? Who the hell is Scott?"

I sighed. He knew who Scott was; he just never approved. Not that he'd ever met him. I hadn't exactly reached the commitment stage of introducing Scott to my divorced parents. "You know full well who he is. The boy I was travelling with. The one you threatened to turn his testicles into earrings if he ever hurt me."

"You calling to tell me I have a new pair of earrings?"

I laughed under my breath. "No, Dad."

This was surreal. This was…*normal.*

My life had endured the biggest upheaval of my twenty-two years, and my father acted as if nothing had happened.

I felt adrift. No longer belonging to a boyfriend or parents who'd known the old me. Sully knew me. And I knew him.

*And he's in trouble…I know it.*

*Damn you, Sully, for making this impossible to get back to you!*

"Dad, I know I literally just called, but I have to go."

"So soon? But I want to know how your travels are. Where are you? What have you been up to?"

I swallowed against the truth, rolling my eyes at the absurdity.

*Well, Dad, I was sold by traffickers who didn't deliver my note like they promised. I fell in love with a man who rented my body to men your age, and now I'm about to lose my mind if I can't find my way back to him immediately.*

His world had stayed mundane while mine had strayed into magic.

I no longer belonged to him as his daughter.

I belonged to Sully as his…

Wife?

Goddess?

*Friend.*

"I love you, Dad. I'll call again soon. I promise."

"I love you too, Ellie Pie. Always will." A smile sounded in the silence before he gruffed, "Just tell me where you are, so I don't worry."

"I'm in Indonesia."

Privacy over Sully's and my unethical romance made me stay quiet on details but instinct overrode it. Previously, I'd vanished without a trace and had no way home. If I allowed that to happen again, I was the biggest idiot in history.

My father was my insurance policy.

He was common-sense and safety.

"I've been staying on a group of islands called Goddess Isles. They're owned by a man named Sullivan Sinclair. He owns a pharmaceutical company called Sinclair and Sinclair Group. If I…go missing for any reason. Please start there. I can't give you an exact location but tell the embassy or call the local police if you don't hear from me in a week or so, okay?"

"Ellie, what the hell—"

"Tell Mum that I'm okay. I'll call again soon!"

I hung up, my heart racing and mouth dry.

*Oh, my God.*

What did I just do?

*You were smart and told someone where you'll be. It's wise, Ellie.*

A fist knocked on my door, announcing my breakfast had arrived.

*Wise…but reckless.*

My father might bring more nightmares Sully's way.

*If he reads the articles I just read?*

I swallowed hard.

*Oh, God.*

A knock sounded again. "Room service."

I shoved aside my nerves of my father researching Sully's indiscretions and stood to answer the door.

I knew the truth about Sully, and I wouldn't let anyone change my mind.

I would eat.

I would hunt.

I would not give up until I found him.

*Don't die, Sully…please, please don't die.*

# Sullivan

# Chapter Fifteen

HER LIPS LANDED ON *mine—sweet with strawberry, sinful with lust.*

*I groaned and slipped my fingers into her long, delicious hair.*

*I loved her hair.*

*I loved her lips.*

*I loved* her.

*"I love you, Jinx." I fed my admission into her mouth, loving the way she gasped and shivered. I ached with the need to fill her. To cement how I felt about her with a physical bond as well as an emotional one.*

*"Come here." Plucking her from the sand where we lay watching the sunset, I rolled her on top of me. My fingers tugged at the bows of her bikini, removing the scraps of material hiding her perfect breasts and pussy.*

*She arched as I ran my nails down her back, grabbing fistfuls of her ass.*

*"Fuck, Sully." She tumbled onto my chest, letting me spread her cheeks, graphic and erotic, rocking her wetness against the straining erection between my legs.*

*She moaned, jerking as I drove up, hitting her clit.*

*"Put me inside you." I nipped at her ear, my balls tight and ready to fuck.*

*She shivered again as she reached between us, her delicate hand wrapping fierce and unforgiving around me.*

*I loved the way she touched me.*

*Firm and possessive.*

*Bold and sexy.*

*We hid nothing from each other. We didn't pretend we weren't obsessed.*

*We didn't fake our mutual desire.*
    *I growled as the first wet kiss of her pussy welcomed my tip.*
    *She cried out as I pushed her down my length, stretching her, taking her.*
    *My islands were no longer my paradise…she was.*
    *She was everything I wanted and more.*
    *A dream come to life.*
    *A manifestation come true.*
    *A girl I couldn't live without.*
    *I thrust up and—*

My eyes flew wide.

White haze and metallic fuzz on my tongue.

Throbbing heat in every limb.

A lacerating burn in my right thigh.

*What the fuck?*

Blinking, I tried to make sense of the scrambled existence of my mind.

It came to me in pieces.

Nightmarish pieces I couldn't compute.

Skittles dead in the sand.

My brother beneath me.

A harpoon within me.

Cal dying on my beach.

Corpses of my guards and the shitty situation of failure.

I groaned as a fresh wave of agony crippled me.

Handcuffs spread my arms as if I was on some sinner's cross, shackling me to metal bars. A cage surrounded me, biting into my back, consuming me like a python.

My heart shed off its sick sedation, granting me fury and fight.

I jerked against the handcuffs, jangling them nosily against steel. My ears rang as the noise vibrated around the villa.

A villa I recognised.

The one where disobedient goddesses spent a night or two.

I winced as yet another flare of agony crushed me, recognising with horrifying clarity that I was in Ace's old cage. The chimpanzee who I'd put to sleep after a life of misery. However, instead of standing tall and offering no place to stretch out, the cage had been placed on its side, trapping me while letting me lay horizontally on its painful bars.

I fought harder, clanking the handcuffs again. I flinched as a warning pain in the back of my hand ignited. A needle fed into my vein, fed by a tube, hooked up to an intravenous bag of liquid outside the cage.

The world spun.

The urge to vomit rose.

I gritted my teeth and looked down my body.

I still wore my black boxer-briefs and had been covered with a white sheet that'd fallen between my legs as I'd struggled. Tugging my right leg free from the sheet, the urge to vomit doubled.

A huge bandage wrapped around the meaty part of my leg. A bloom of red glowed in the centre. My skin around the bandage was a vicious scarlet, along with the rest of my leg down to my toes.

An infection had set in.

Wincing against the bite of metal beneath my back, I gritted my teeth, forcing my brain that couldn't quite shed off the sickening haze to work and work fast.

*I'm alive.*

*I'm sick and wounded.*

*I'm in a goddamn monkey cage.*

My nostrils flared as I kicked my legs, trying to scoot into a sitting position.

Pain.

Motherfucking debilitating *pain*.

Sweat broke out over my chest, granting the uncomfortable tangle of hot and cold from fever.

A phantom kiss pressed on my lips—residue from my dream. *Eleanor.*

Christ…had Drake chased after her?

How long had I been out?

Was she home yet?

Balling my hands, I jerked against the handcuffs. I needed to check. To ensure her safety all while mine hung in Drake's psychotic whims.

"I wouldn't keep moving so much if I were you. Your body underwent extreme trauma."

My head shot sideways, my gaze seeking the shadows.

Pure hate flared as Dr Jim fucking Campbell moved from the gloom toward me. He wore his usual cargo shorts and polo—a doctor enjoying his retirement instead of a highly paid surgeon.

I snarled, jumping to conclusions but instinctually knowing they were right.

Dr Campbell wasn't a prisoner of my brother.

He didn't jump when a guard entered.

He didn't cower as he came closer.

He moved with the acceptance of a man who'd become a goddamn traitor.

*"You."* I lay at his feet, chained and caged like a criminal. "You're the snitch." The handcuffs chewed into my wrists as I fought to wring his neck. "I should've fucking guessed."

He waited for my initial fury to pass, narrowing his eyes as I flushed with yet more sweat and slumped with hotter agony. Pushing his glasses up his nose, he did his best to plaster professional coolness on his face, all while guilt glowed in his watery eyes.

"Hated me that much, huh?" I bared my teeth. "Seemed even your obscene salary couldn't buy your loyalty."

He cleared his throat, rocking on the balls of his feet. "I don't hate you, Mr. Sinclair."

"You're fired."

He nodded with a grim smile. "I understand. However, you might want me to stay on for a few more days…for your own sake."

"I'll kill you the moment I get out of here." I rattled the handcuffs again, gritting my teeth against the metallic twang and the steady throb in my leg. The pain receptors over my entire body fought for recognition. Contusions glowed on my chest from fists. A small hematoma had formed around my left knee, courtesy of a kick, and blood spread in an ever-extending rose beneath the bandage around my leg.

My threat was fucking laughable.

Even if I wasn't imprisoned and trapped, I doubted I'd be a successful killer.

Dr Campbell pointed at my minced leg. "I removed the spear, sterilised the injury, checked that your thigh bone hasn't been compromised, stitched up muscle and flesh, and administered a strong round of antibiotics. Your system is robust from your active lifestyle and healthy diet. However, you're still fighting a fever caused by the infection from seawater and unsanitary metal." He swallowed, slipping into his medical role. "A wound such as the one you sustained can turn fatal if not carefully tended. I also suggest you restrict moving due to the swelling on your knee, bruised ribs, and possible concussion. You need to rest given that your…accommodations are not ideal. I did try to suggest you would recover faster in a bed, but Drake was insistent."

I glowered at him as if my eyes could reach through the bars and kill him on my behalf. "You have the gall to stand there and pretend you've done me a goddamn favour by stitching me back together? That I'm happy I'm alive after hundreds of animals were blown to fucking bits by my brother? That I'm *grateful* knowing Eleanor is unprotected and at Drake's fucking mercy?" My fury exploded. "You're the reason forty guards are dead, Campbell! You're the reason Skittles is dead. You're the fucking reason Calvin is—"

"Cal is alive." He held up his hand, stress etching his mouth. "I give you my word, Sinclair, Calvin Moor still breathes."

"You're lying." I froze, my chest pumping. "I saw him on the beach. His heart was giving out."

"He sustained two gunshots to his torso. One nicked his stomach and the other punctured his lung, but I was able to stabilise his condition." He looked over his shoulder at the guard posted by the door. "He's in my surgery. Along with…" He lowered his voice. "Your caique, the female…I scooped her from the beach when Drake summoned me to attend you. Her wing is fractured, but she's alive. She is recovering in secrecy beside Cal."

*Thank fuck.*

"And Pika?"

"Haven't seen him."

*Shit, he better be alive.*

Skittles was alive.

Cal was alive.

As much as I hated this bastard, he'd kept two of the most important things in my world breathing.

Eleanor would never have to know I'd been the reason Skittles almost died. I wouldn't have to live the rest of my life with Cal's ghost judging my every action.

I ground my teeth, cursing the weight of thankfulness as it slithered beneath my hate. "What do you want? A fucking thank you? They're hurt *because* of you. My islands have been infiltrated *because* of you. Eleanor and my goddesses are in danger because of *you*!"

He flinched, clasping his hands in front of him. "I owe you an apology, Sinclair. You're quite right that I now have to live with the knowledge that I am the reason so many guards—men who I knew on a first-name basis—are dead. However…" His jaw clenched. "I am not responsible for your goddesses being in danger. That's entirely on you."

"*What?*" The cage swam as I thrashed to get free. "You fucking hypocrite. You called my brother to kill me, and you stand there thinking my girls' lives are better off? How stupid do you have to be?"

Acid splashed up my throat.

Greyness feathered over my vision.

My leg switched from throbbing to beating like a war drum.

*Do. Not. Pass. Out.*

*Goddammit!*

I blinked, shaking my head and willing my heart to stop racing.

The doctor squatted to his haunches, his voice low and hushed. "Keep your voice down. The longer they think you're incapacitated, the more time you have to recover." He sighed. "In full disclosure, I patched Drake up too. The stab wound in his shoulder was shallow. The strangulation effects minor. A few stitches where you grazed him with a bullet. However, your punches did some damage. Regardless of your condition, Sinclair, you almost killed him three nights ago with your bare hands—"

"*Three* nights ago?" I groaned as adrenaline made me sick. "Three fucking days?"

"You were in surgery for a long time. Your body needed time to heal. Once you've eaten something solid, you'll regain your strength—"

"What sort of sick game are you playing?" I snarled. "Do you really think my life hasn't been drastically shortened thanks to your snitching? You betray me, yet you fix me. You welcome my worst enemy, and you fix him too. You have the fucking balls to tell me Cal and Skittles will survive, all while you condemn the lives of innocent women? Do you honestly think Drake will free them? Is that what this is about? You think he'll act merciful and stop my sexual trading? Bullshit! He's already enslaved them to a nightmare. He'll rape them until they beg to die. You just sentenced them to hell, Campbell—"

"You shattered the voice box of Calico and almost killed Neptune and Jupiter! That was my last straw, Sinclair! I'm a doctor. I swore an oath to *protect* and nurture, not repair what you break. And I didn't call him, alright?!" He flinched, lowering his temper. "Well, not directly. A coup was not my intention."

"Could've fooled me." I stiffened, ignoring the hiss of guilt for what I'd done to three goddesses who'd tried to murder the only girl who mattered to me.

He looked at the ground, genuine contrition on his face. "I only ever wanted to protect the girls you so callously turn into desperate whores. You've gone too far."

My hands curled, the handcuffs jangling. "You, as well as anyone, know how well they are treated. You're the head of their medical care, for fuck's sake. They're healthy and happy—"

"Healthy is debatable, and they're definitely not happy."

"Depends who you ask."

He scowled, a flicker of loathing on his face. "I *have* asked, and I don't like their responses. That's why I called your company. I told Peter Beck that elixir is far too potent. Long-term use is showing massive adverse reactions on the nervous system. I suppose Drake overheard somehow or got a hold of phone records. Who knows? But he contacted me and sounded legitimately concerned. I wasn't aware of the, eh…feud between you. My judgment of the matter was compromised because of my building worry over the girls. They're all suffering the same symptoms."

"What fucking symptoms? They're fine—"

"Heart palpitations, increased resting BPM, chemical stress, insomnia, anxiety."

"And you're blaming that on elixir? Symptoms that could be caused from anything."

"I'm telling you my hypothesis on a drug that hasn't been strictly monitored or tested that is now revealing severe side effects. Someone is going to die from it, Sinclair. Mark my words."

Metal bars bit into my back, driving my pain to a distracting level. I needed to sit up. I needed drugs to numb the agony so I could think straight.

Forcing my voice not to crack with discomfort, I hissed, "Let's ignore the fact that you went behind my back, enlisted the help of a psychopath instead of coming to me with your issues, and dumped us all in a clusterfuck that will only end with me dead and the goddesses that you're so concerned about being molested and left in far worse condition than I currently keep them in, and focus on a key couple of things."

He narrowed his eyes. "Okay…"

"Where is Drake right now?"

"He's completing the final sweep of the villas, looking for the goddesses you evacuated."

"Did you tell him where they are?"

"Of course not." He wrinkled his nose. "My duty is to them. I did this for *them*. I enlisted the help of a bastard all because Blossom, Sailor, and Jealousy won't last much longer if you continue—"

"What about Jealousy?" My heart rate increased, making the cage swim again.

If Jealousy betrayed me too, I honestly didn't know how I'd react. She'd been the closest thing I had to a female friend before Eleanor arrived. If she'd turned around and stabbed me in the back, then trust would be severely scrutinised for being the worst possible thing in the human psyche.

"Jealousy has been suffering the most." Dr. Campbell's face tightened. "She stayed quiet about the side effects. I only found out because she fainted in Divinity a few weeks ago, and I was called to attend. Her pulse, Sinclair, was two-hundred and thirty. That's excessively high. Two forty is usually the max before serious complications occur. Her heart palpitations took three hours to subside, despite the use of beta blockers and blood thinners. I fear she'll have a stroke. Elixir has scrambled her usual chemical pathways. Her nervous system is haywire—"

"If this is so serious, why didn't you come to me sooner?" My breathing turned shallow. "You know enough about me to know that I would've done something to help."

"I have tried to make you see sense, Sinclair. I warned you elixir was too strong."

"Strong is different from suicidal."

"Elixir will end up killing a girl one day because of your negligence. You can't keep playing god. I won't let you." He sighed, smoothing a hand over his thinning white hair. "Look, I made a mistake enlisting the help of your brother. When he offered to persuade your mind about ceasing the use of elixir, I shouldn't have agreed. I should've known anyone related to you wouldn't be of rational mind."

I snorted, squirming in my cuffs, trying to find a position that didn't end with my bones throbbing against metal. "I'm the sane one, Jim. You've just unleashed the devil."

He sniffed with a slight smile, a strained truce forming between us. "I'm beginning to see that."

I winced as my leg burned with pulsing fire. "If you're having second thoughts, you can try to remedy the situation by calling Peter Beck. Tell him I need reinforcements. Call the goddamn police."

"If I do…will you cease your enterprise? Will you release your goddesses? Will you destroy every single vial of elixir and swear never to make another drop?"

My hands curled as hate sprang fresh. "I don't bow to ultimatums, Jim."

"Then I can't agree to serve you any—"

The door smashed open, bringing starlight in from outside and the shadow of my cursed brother. "I hear you're alive and talking, Sullivan." Drake strode closer, stepping into the gloomy light of the lamp above me, his face a colourful patchwork of bruises.

Satisfaction battled back some of my pain. I'd done that to him. I'd almost killed him with knuckles and rage.

He looked me up and down, smirking. "You don't look so good, baby brother."

"Funny, I was just thinking the same about you."

Snapping his fingers, he barked, "Someone get me a chair."

Dr Campbell faded to the side, his upper lip curling with distaste for Drake. At least he still retained common-sense in that regard. He might have been the reason Drake had found my islands and learned what I'd created, but his intentions hadn't been betrayal. They'd been out of loyalty for girls I'd purchased and kept alive with no other attention than vague awareness.

*Doesn't mean he won't pay, though.*

He'd be punished.

Painfully so.

A human life was worth nothing to me because there was so many more to plague the earth.

Turned out, Jim Campbell was my opposite.

He fought for mankind. He viewed me as the enemy just as I viewed meat eaters as murderers.

Drake sat heavily in a deck chair that one of his mercenaries brought over. He waved him away a moment later. Campbell went too, free to come and go under Drake's command, slipping out the exit and hopefully going to tend to Skittles and Cal.

I needed them both alive.

*I* needed to stay alive so I could protect Eleanor from this creep.

Drake hissed under his breath as he rubbed his shoulder where I'd stabbed him. "Thought you were dead."

I hid my wince as I tried to inch higher, giving up when my pain levels threatened to make me black out. "Hoped you *were* dead."

He grinned. "Why would I be dead? You couldn't kill me even if I held the gun for you."

"Wouldn't be so sure about that, *brother*. Your bruises say differently."

He leaned forward, holding his side where the bullet had grazed him. "Where are the goddesses?"

I scowled. "Gone."

"Just like Eleanor Grace?" He clucked his tongue. "I'll find her. I'll find all of them."

My fever switched to ice. Thank fuck, he hadn't caught her. Three days was a long time to be unconscious. She could be anywhere by now. Back home with her family. Back travelling with her motherfucking boyfriend.

*You know she'd never do that.*

Jinx was many things, but most of all, she was loyal to a goddamn fault.

*Too* loyal.

*Shit, please tell me she's left Indonesia and isn't trying to—*

"I actually have a piece of news on the girlfriend front." Drake smiled coldly. "I found your favourite goddess. Seems she's been asking around Jakarta for your whereabouts. Reports say she's a little frustrated that you sent her away without a means of return."

I stopped breathing. "Leave her the fuck out of this."

"You can keep repeating that little demand, but we both know that's not gonna happen." Raking a hand through his hair, he added, "She's determined, I'll give her that. You've finally tricked someone into falling in love with you." He cocked his head, fluttering his eyes like a fool. "Isn't that cute? My baby brother has a woman. She could become my sister-in-law. It's only fair that I help her travel home so I can meet her, right?"

Metal clanged and twanged as I thrashed in my cuffs. "Don't fucking touch her!"

"Oh, I won't do that until she's here, Sullivan. I want you to watch when I fuck her the first time." He bared his teeth. "I'm guessing we won't have to wait too long. I gave her a pretty big fucking clue...and transportation."

*Shit!*

*SHIT!*

I kicked the sheet from around my legs. I ignored the trickle of blood from my bandage. I fought to remain human with the ability of speech rather than an animal with sharp teeth. "I'll give you the recipe for elixir."

"That's a given." Drake laughed. "You're going to give me the deed to your islands, your goddesses, your programs for Euphoria, and every ingredient of elixir. You're going to watch me drug your girl and suffer all while she begs for my dick." He stood and wrapped his hands around the cage bars, shaking it. "And once I've fucked her raw and everything that you own is mine...I'll kill you. I'll put a knife in your heart and put you out of your misery because I'm nice like that. I won't sentence you to a life knowing that she's mine. That I can take her whenever I damn well want. I'll be an only child and inherit everything that I was supposed to before you murdered our parents and stole from me."

The room darkened as my heart crashed and collided with my bruised ribs.

My blood boiled with utter fucking weakness of being trapped.

Eleanor.

*Christ!*

Drake put his fingers in his ears as the noise of my clanging handcuffs reverberated around the room. "Quit that. I need you alive and not having a fucking seizure."

I snarled.

I howled.

I ignored every splintering pain and nauseous roil.

I needed out.

I needed her.

I needed to kill my motherfucking brother before he broke the only person I ever loved.

*Eleanor...*

*Goddammit, forget about me...before it's too late.*

# Chapter Sixteen

THREE HORRIBLE ETERNAL DAYS.

Fifty-seven travel agencies.

Thirty-two hotels.

Twenty-three tour companies.

Eighteen cruise liners.

Eleven airlines.

Seven helicopter charters.

And five airports.

All with the exact same phone script: "Hello, I'm enquiring about a tour/flight/cruise/adventure that includes the destination Goddess Isles. It's located an hour or so helicopter flight from Jakarta."

"Hello, ma'am. I will see if we have such a tour/flight/cruise/adventure that includes Goddess Isles, please hold."

A requisite hold period where my heart would rabbit and stupid, idiotic hope would rise. Only for disappointment to crush me deeper and deeper into despair as they returned. "I'm so sorry, ma'am. We do not have anything suitable."

"Have you heard of Goddess Isles?"

"No, ma'am."

"Do you know of the proprietor, Sullivan Sinclair? He's an American who has chosen Java as his home."

"No, ma'am."

"Can you suggest someone who might be able to

charter/guide/find Goddess Isles?"

"No, ma'am."

"Do you have anyone else I can call? A sister agency/airline/company?"

"No, ma'am. Thank you for your call, ma'am. Good day."

*Argh!!!!*

I dug my elbows into the desk and dropped my face into my palms.

*Sully!*

I swear if I wasn't so fucking worried about him, I would be fuming wild!

How *dare* he agree to temporary?

How *dare* he fall in love with me?

How *dare* he pretend to *trust* me, all while knowing that I was powerless to return to him!

Three days!

Three fucking days!

Anything could've happened.

He could be dead and in pieces on the ocean floor by now. He could be wounded and dying without me by his side. He could be held prisoner by his brother.

Or...

And this was the worst part.

The sickening nerves and self-pity that kept me up at night, ensuring I hadn't rested properly since sleeping in Sully's arms with Nirvana splashing outside his bedroom.

He could have killed Drake.

He could've won the war.

He could be back to drugging goddesses and entertaining his smarmy guests.

He could have returned to his world...*without* me.

He could look at his credit card statement and see I'd spent an exorbitant sum on three nights in a five-star hotel instead of flying home like his staff had told me.

He could be laughing at me because I'd chosen to stay.

He could be pitying me because I couldn't damn well fly away without ensuring he was okay.

Even a cell phone number would be fine.

An email.

A PO Box, for God's sake.

*Anything* so I could contact him and find out if he was still alive.

I needed to hear his voice.

I needed to hug him and convince myself that the nightmares that found me when I couldn't stay awake weren't real.

That the images of him shot and injured weren't real.

That the fears of him bleeding out and dying on his beach weren't real.

That the terrors of Skittles and Pika being killed and plucked and roasted on a skewer *weren't real!*

*Dammit!*

I stood in a rush, and the chair that I'd sat on for the past seventy-two hours and called every tourism and travel firm I could find in Indonesia, shot backward on its wheels.

I'd exhausted my online searches.

I'd spoken to every single person who could possibly, maybe, slimly help me.

I'd even rang two police stations, enquiring if they knew of Sully Sinclair.

And I'd run into dead end after dead end.

I was in a maze with no way out. No clues. No hope.

Sully was hidden, and no matter how hard I tried…he remained unreachable.

*Fine!*

Sweeping from the office space, I ran to the bathroom. I was done being a hermit in my hotel room. I'd shower, withdraw some cash, and swap online hunting for physical.

I would door knock every damn backpacker, dive bar, and local transport.

I would bribe every bus, taxi, and motorbike driver if they'd ever heard of Goddess Isles. I would march into every pet store and request if they'd made bulk sales to an island called *Serigala*. I'd talk to veterinary clinics for medicine deliveries. I'd track down supermarkets and wholesalers about large quantities of goods sent to an island in the middle of nowhere.

I would do whatever it damn well took to find him.

I'd chosen to be loyal.

I'd chosen him as my future.

No way was I walking away just because he'd sent me away and slammed the door in my face.

*It's not permanent, Sully.*

*I'll find a way…you'll see.*

*And then, you and me? We're having a serious chat about commitment.*

\* \* \* \* \*

"Sorry, ma'am. We don't fly there."

"Sorry, ma'am. We don't sail there."

"Sorry, ma'am. There is no island by that name."

"Sorry, ma'am. We have never heard of Sullivan Sinclair or Goddess Isles."

"Sorry, ma'am. We did not make bulk pet food deliveries to a place called *Serigala*."

"Sorry, ma'am. We do not have vets who treat rescue animals in the Javanese Sea."

"Sorry, ma'am. We do not have records of sending non-perishable food to Sullivan Sinclair."

"Sorry, ma'am."

"Sorry, ma'am."

"Sorry."

*Sorry!*

*Don't tell me fucking sorry.*

*Tell me something!*

Exhausted tears ran down my face as I stumbled from the tenth market that dealt in spices and sweets. I'd had to return to ATMs four times to withdraw money for bribes. I'd wafted hundred-dollar bills beneath the noses of tour operators, greengrocers, and vets.

They all took the money.

Yet they gave nothing in return.

They either all lied spectacularly or…Sully had locked down his name, businesses, and address with military precision.

*What am I going to do?*

I didn't even know where I was.

I'd caught so many taxis, zipping north, south, east, and west, that I had no idea how to get back. I couldn't remember the name of the hotel I'd been staying at. I had no belongings apart from the small bag I'd bought to keep my cash and passport inside and the pair of white sandals I'd grabbed from a local stall.

I was homeless and frazzled, running on worry and adrenaline.

I couldn't keep up this level of franticness. But I also couldn't stop because if Sully was hurt…

*He can't be hurt.*

*I'd rather he be a bastard who turned his back on me than hurt.*

A bastard, I could reason with. I could convince him that what we had was special and worth fighting for. A dead man, I could not.

*God, please, Sully!*

The sun slowly sank behind skyscrapers and shacks, painting the sky crimson and tangerine. The humidity was different here. Stickier and polluted. My hair was limp and stuck to my shoulders. My feet throbbed from walking so much. And my body needed liquid and nourishment.

Plodding onward, stores shut for the day and workers conversed in happy Indonesian. A man bumped into me as he skipped from a convenience store, his hand holding a dewy, icy cola.

My mouth instantly craved wetness.

Stepping into the blast of air-conditioning, I beelined for the fridge, selected a sugary raspberry drink—desperate for one of Sully's nourishing thick smoothies—and grabbed a stale chocolate croissant from the shelf.

I hated eating these days.

I hated how everything tasted packaged and plastic-y. I missed nuts straight off the tree and berries right off the vine.

I didn't just miss Sully.

I missed his way of life, his ideology, his paradise.

More tears sprang to my eyes, and I angrily swiped them away as I handed over money for my pathetic dinner. The shopkeeper gave me a sympathetic smile.

I attempted to smile back, my gaze snagging on a prepaid smartphone.

New hope sprang ridiculously savage.

"I'll buy one of those too, please." Snatching the box, I asked, "Does it have internet?"

"Yes." The girl nodded. "Four gigabytes for one month, included in the price."

Shoving more money her way, I took my food and my phone and stumbled back into the muggy evening.

I needed a bench. A park. Somewhere to sit.

Ducking across a busy road, I followed the scent of salt.

The sea that'd once been my prison cell but now became the guard refusing entry back to its islands.

I'd already been down to the port this morning.

I'd walked the massive piers and padded over the litter-covered docks, catching the eyes of fishermen and exporters, attempting to ask them if they knew of Goddess Isles. I'd struggled with the local tongue, using Sully's name as a talisman that could somehow teleport me back to him.

It'd been utterly pointless.

But at least I felt closer to Sully sitting by the ocean, even if it was polluted and brown.

Finding a spot on a stack of shipping crates, accompanied by the pungent whiff of dead fish, I ripped at the phone box while eating my dried pastry. I followed the set-up instructions and then did something I probably should've done days ago.

The guy at the hangar had said no one could find Sully without an invitation.

Yet Drake had found him, and I doubted Sully willingly gave out his address.

*Therefore…there must be a way.*

*If no one will tell me…I'll find it myself.*

Loading Google Earth, I typed in Jakarta. From there, I zoomed out, I panned over the sea,  and I began the tedious search for forty-four islands all hidden far from me.

\* \* \* \* \*

I rubbed my tired and stinging eyes from staring at a bright screen in the dark.

Night had fallen.

My phone's battery had reached critical.

I'd tracked my way across the Pacific Ocean, Indian Ocean, and Java Sea. I'd squinted at land masses from some satellite that Google Earth used to spy on mankind, and suffered hope and disappointment, hope and disappointment, over and over again as one island was discounted, followed by another and another and another.

No archipelagos appeared.

No hints of coral reefs and utopian atolls.

Just endless water, blobs of fishing boats and cruise liners, and the never-ending blockade preventing me from returning to Sully.

Had he paid off Google Earth to hide his islands?

Was I blind and not looking hard enough?

Had I dreamed it all and been reduced to an insane girl sitting in the dark at a commercial port in Jakarta, reckless with her safety, stupid with her longevity, utterly obsessed with a man who'd sent her away…*permanently.*

*God.*

I dropped my phone into my lap and buried my face in my hands.

*This can't be happening.*

How had my life derailed so spectacularly without my permission, and now that I wanted what I'd been given, I couldn't damn well find it?

*How can he hide a nest of islands from everyone?*

How was that possible in this day and age?

Dragging my hands through my hair, I sniffed up tattered determination and grabbed my phone again. Sully had guests fly in and out. He released goddesses, for God's sake.

There *had* to be some mention of him.

*I'll try Facebook.*

Logging on, I went to put in Calico's real name, Sonya Teo, but my inbox caught my eye, habit making me click on that first.

Scott Martin's message bubble popped up from the night of my abduction. If I thought he cared about me, and that we were building a meaningful connection, I'd been a stupid idiot.

Scott Martin: *El, where the hell are you? It's late, and I'm drunk from those damn Irish and their super livers. I'm crashing on the bottom bunk tonight. When you get in, take the top. I'll see you in the morning.*

Scott Martin: *What the fuck, El? Did you sleep somewhere else last night? I saw that English twat flirting with you before you went into the kitchen to cook us dinner. You better not have been with him while I was too drunk to notice.*

Scott Martin: *This is getting rude. I've had to check out of the backpackers as we're catching the flight tonight for the bachelor party. I have your stuff…you coming or what?*

Scott Martin: *I'm at the airport. I've left your bag at reception of the backpackers. Poor form, Eleanor. If you wanted to end it because I refused to go to Asia with you, the least you could've done is tell it to my face.*

Scott Martin: *Look, I'm sorry. You okay? I'm getting a little worried. Just message me instead of giving me the cold shoulder. You're still welcome to come to the party. Message me when you get these, and we'll work something out. Let me know you're alright at least.*

Scott Martin: *Okay, I know this is a dick move, but…your profile is still showing active, so I know you're okay. Look, this isn't working. I have no interest in going to Asia. Ever. I've enjoyed getting to know you, Eleanor, but…feel free to chase your own destination from this point on. See ya.*

Wow.

How could I ever have felt guilty when I'd fought my attraction for Sully out of loyalty to that asshole? How could I ever, *ever* compare what I felt for Sully to the minuscule blip that Scott had been?

I wanted to feel something.

Rage. Injustice. Pissed off.

But all I felt was…nothing.

He was *nothing*.

His lack of concern while I'd been kidnapped and sold only added more panic to my desire to return to Sully.

Sully would *never* treat me that way. He would never forget about me so heartlessly.

*He sent you away, remember?*

*Only to keep me safe!*

My heart rabbited.

He'd sent me away to keep me *safe*.

He'd given me no option to return so he knew I would *continue* to be safe.

*But what about him!?*

He'd held me and kissed me, and I'd felt his love, his regret, his pain.

He'd known something bad would happen.

He'd protected me by giving me up.

He'd sacrificed us because he loved me.

*God, I can't do this anymore!!!*

Regardless of safety or sanity. Despite the impossible task.

*I need to go back.*

He would've come for me by now. He would've appeared at the end of the street or pulled me into an alley if he'd won against his brother—because if he felt a tenth of the pain caused by our separation that I did…*nothing* would've kept him from chasing after me.

That wasn't ego.

That was inevitability.

The only reason he hadn't was…*he's hurt.*

*Sully!*

Launching from my chair of crates, I opened a tracking app and installed it on my phone. While I sped down the dock, I called my father.

It went straight to voicemail.

It didn't matter.

I only wanted to update my insurance policy.

The answer machine beeped, and I rushed, "Dad, the man I mentioned, Sullivan Sinclair? He's in trouble. I'm travelling to a set of islands that isn't on any map. There's no airport code or address. All I can give you is this phone number and a tracker app that I've installed. Trace the call, Dad. Give my location to the police. I don't know how I'm going to find my way there, but I will. I have no choice—"

I slammed to a stop as a pallet loader drove past, cutting off my race down the dock.

I went to travel around him.

I opened my mouth to give more details to my father.

But then, I froze.

Fate.

Glorious, mercurial *fate*.

It'd just given me a way back to Sully.

A blatant clue that'd driven directly into my path.

The boxes stacked high on the pallet loader held a distinguished, solemn SSG.

Sully's logo.

Sinclair and Sinclair Group.

And the boat they were being loaded onto?

My chariot back to him.

# Sullivan

# Chapter Seventeen

"ARE YOU QUITE DONE?" Drake snapped as my rage petered out thanks to fever, agony, and nausea.

*Eleanor!*

*Stay the fuck away from here!*

I couldn't catch a proper breath. My leg drained me of every awareness and energy. My mind fixated on Jinx. On the horror that I couldn't fucking protect her. That I'd failed her. I'd failed fucking everyone!

Drake snapped his fingers, summoning two mercenaries as the ringing of my handcuffs fell silent. "Let's get started. Don't have all fucking night."

My hate reached critical levels, blistering through me and feeding me false power.

I glowered as a man dressed all in black brought over a foldable table, and another man deposited a box on top. The weak glow of the light above created shadows and sinister promises.

I stopped fighting.

My eyes locked onto the box and the contents that I was highly intimate with.

Fresh agony swamped me. My back arched as metal bars bit into me. Blood trickled once again down my thigh. If I kept struggling, would I eventually get free or would I fail Eleanor faster than I already was?

Breathing hard, covered in pain-sweat, I growled, "Crawling over my island and helping yourself to my Euphoria supplies, *brother?"*

Drake nodded, his hands diving into the cardboard and placing the smaller packages in a line up on the table. Each one had a purple orchid stencilled on the top.

A big fuck-off hint what the main ingredient was.

A cocky decision on my end, yet my witless brother hadn't realised the clue staring him in the goddamn face.

"Found your playroom. Couldn't figure out how to load a fantasy, though, so that's another thing you'll have to divulge, along with telling me how this stuff works." He ran his fingertip over the lids. "Seeing as we have time while waiting for Eleanor Grace to arrive, how about we do an experiment?"

I held his stare. "I've already tested and perfected the sensors. They don't need further experiments."

"Oh, these do." He picked up the oil, sloshing glittery liquid in its bottle. An oil specially crafted to distort the sense of touch while in the virtual reality hallucination. "Let's just say, I've tweaked them. Made them better."

I didn't ask what he'd done.

I wasn't an idiot.

Whatever he'd done would guarantee pain.

That was his MO.

Torture, then torture some more, keep torturing until death.

"I helped myself to your supplies while you took a nap, but I couldn't find your stash of elixir. Where is it?"

I bared my teeth, cursing the rush of sickness originating from my harpooned leg. "Don't have any left."

My patience was a big fat fucking zero.

The wire beneath me, the handcuffs biting me, the threat of Eleanor's life? It'd put me in a right shit. The only thing stopping me from killing him was a cage and these handcuffs. My injuries wouldn't matter the second I got close enough to slaughter him.

His temper flared, his forehead trying to furrow but struggling thanks to Botox. "Bullshit, where do you keep it?"

"It's true. My supplies are gone."

It was bullshit.

Kind of.

I had three vials left in my apothecary cabinet in my office.

But that didn't include the entire box that'd just finished cooking in my lab on *Monyet*—another island named in Indonesian for monkey. An ode to all the primates that'd died in the quest for useable drugs. An island that was my most heavily fortified, hidden, and priceless jewel in my empire.

"Still a terrible liar, Sullivan."

I smiled savagely. "What can I say? I detest thieves."

"A thief? Me?" He chuckled. "Just taking what's rightfully mine."

"And I'll take your life for this."

He clucked his tongue. "You've created a fantasy, and now, you're believing in one." Unboxing the rest of my VR sensors, he lifted out eye lenses, fingerprint deceptors, nasal stick, taste scrambler, and earplugs. Unlike my carefully designed stock, these had been tampered with. The contents were different. The colours all wrong.

Raising his eyebrow, he sighed as if he'd rather just be resting than preparing to torture his own flesh and blood. "Ah well, first things first."

My stomach clenched as he snapped his fingers at a mercenary who came gingerly toward my cage. Drake passed him a key, and the man swallowed as he inserted it into the lock and opened the gate.

One imprisonment down.

I rolled my wrists in the handcuffs, hissing as my torn skin oozed blood. Pain gathered on top of pain, but I ignored it all.

I had to stay lucid for this.

I had to survive this because I fucking refused to fail Eleanor again.

Drake took the key back from the guard and replaced it with the skin oil. His blond minion wrapped his fist around the bottle.

Drake arched his chin at me. "For the next few hours, you are my own personal guinea pig. You liberated all those animals in our labs. You feel such *empathy* for the rats and vermin that were born for that very fucking purpose. Therefore, you will become them. You get to feel how they did, baby brother. You get to have your skin burned, eyes blinded, and veins pumped with concoctions."

Reaching through the bars, he patted my head like I was some doomed beagle ready for a scientist and their syringe. "Rather poetic, no?"

I tore my head away, snarling, "You're a sick sonovabitch."

Nodding at the mercenary, he said, "Pour that oil on my brother. He won't bite."

I snarled as the guy ducked to enter the door. He legitimately looked afraid about climbing into a small cage with me.

He should.

My arms might be restrained, but my legs weren't—even if one had a massive hole in it.

Drake pulled up his chair and sat as if I was his favourite brand of entertainment. "Maybe we'll get you spouting the recipe for elixir before Eleanor arrives. If we get business out of the way, we can focus on pleasure the moment she lands."

I fucking *hated* her name on his tongue—I wanted to rip it from his godforsaken mouth for ever mentioning her.

I had a tally.

A tally on every infraction Drake had done to me since I was fucking born. I owed him a lifetime of torture for what he'd done to *Serigala*, to my animals, and to Jinx. I had an entire notebook requiring savage reciprocation, and I couldn't fucking do a goddamn thing as the guy bent and poised over me, the bottle tipping to pour oil over my bruised and broken body.

Drake had taken away my ability to deal with this as a man. He treated me like a creature…so I'd become a fucking creature.

I didn't wait to strike.

I just did.

Kicking out, I scissored my legs around the guard's ankles, dropping him to the floor. The oil splashed onto my belly, burning, bubbling—a form of acid chewing through my flesh.

I bellowed with agony as he cried out and bounced off the metal wire, then screamed as I wrapped my thighs around his throat and squeezed.

I fucking *squeezed*.

I locked my ankles and crushed his goddamn windpipe.

"Ah, for fuck's sake." Drake clapped his hands in impatience, signalling for reinforcements. "All of you, it seems this is gonna be a team affair. Stop my brother from murdering your colleague and get some rope for his legs."

Three mercenaries jumped from the shadows. One went behind me and shoved his hand through the bars. I tried to bite him, but he managed to grab a fistful of my hair, jerking my head back.

The guy between my legs turned blue, his eyes bugging as I shoved him closer and closer to death. He scratched at my thighs, making me bellow when he clawed at my wound.

I squeezed harder.

His eyelids fluttered closed.

Two mercenaries climbed into the cramped cage with me, kicking at my guts until I couldn't ignore the pain anymore.

*"Fuck!"* I let my victim go.

I breathed hard as the two men carted their colleague's lifeless body from the cage and dropped him at Drake's feet.

They didn't revive him.

Instead, they entered the cosy quarters I'd found myself in and wrapped a heavy rope around each ankle. Only once they'd tied me to each side of the cage, spreading me, making me utterly defenceless did the redhead one leave to deal with the unconscious guy.

A dark-haired one grabbed the abandoned oil bottle.

He gave me a nasty smile and squatted between my spread legs, pulling out a knife from his commando boot. "Not so scary now, are ya?" With our eyes locked, he tipped the oil down my chest, rivering over silver scars courtesy of a younger Drake, dripping into fresh scratches from our beach battle, stripping flesh from my bones with corrosive and caustic agony.

My vision went red.

My back arched.

I howled.

The last thing I heard as I tripped into deeper hell was my brother muttering, "Put in the lenses. Let's see how he likes being blind."

# Chapter Eighteen

I STOOD ON THE bow of my chariot.

I clung to the railing as the sun rose in all its tangerine and golden glory, shining its glow on the cluster of islands on the horizon. Sun spiels painted heavenly spotlights on Goddess Isles.

Islands that were invisible to the outside world.

Islands that housed a man I adored.

*I'm home.*

Tears sprang to my eyes as the small cargo ship chugged its way closer and closer. I swayed with the waves beneath the hull. I fought the urge to fall asleep while standing.

I'd never been so exhausted. So drained. So fraught.

Not even when I'd been sold.

When I'd been kidnapped, my worry had only been about me. My fear nursed around my heart for my own mortality. This time, my worry had extended outward. A thousand strands of concern all straining to find Sully, all failing until fate had decided I was worthy of going back.

I turned and looked at the ratty boat that'd sailed me throughout the night and the mismatch crew who'd been my champions.

Intan, the teenager who'd been driving the pallet loader, had been my ticket home. I'd chased him all the way to the boat tether where he deposited the boxes with Sully's logo onboard.

He hadn't seen me.

I'd pulled out a fist of money, ready to bribe and cajole, only to freeze beneath the stare of a sea-weathered captain as he popped out from the tiny cabin above.

Our eyes had locked.

Something sinister slithered down my spine.

A harbour breeze sprang up and danced in my dress with warning.

If it'd just been him on that boat, I would've heeded the ominous sinking in my belly and admitted that not everything was fate's design. But a girl appeared and kissed his whiskered cheek.

A granddaughter perhaps?

A girl dressed in the subtle olive uniform of the gardeners on *Lebah*.

It was another sign. Sully's staff and his supplies. If I didn't grasp this opportunity, I might never get another.

Something had happened to Sully.

I knew that in my bones.

I was past the rational stage of what I could do to help.

I gave up believing I was some Amazonian warrior with talents to free him.

I was just a simple goddess in love, willingly putting her life on the line because Sully had done the same for her.

Intan smiled and came toward me, holding out my phone. His young, tanned face was the epitome of innocence while the salt-cragged captain still set my teeth on edge. "Here. Charged."

"Thank you." Taking it, I checked the connection. No bars. No service. Would my dad be able to track me without cellular towers to guide his way?

I was walking into danger, but I had an army coming...*I hope.*

"Grandfather say dock no big. We get closer. You swim."

I looked past Intan to the old man in his cabin. A man who'd never taken his gaze off me the entire journey. Every now and again, I'd catch guilt in his black stare, followed by pissed-off acceptance.

Something wasn't right about him.

I wasn't an idiot. I knew I should heed the vibe he gave, whispering harsh with warning. But his grandkids had been a buffer between us, and my priorities overshadowed my concern.

Besides, Intan had been nothing but sweet to me, sharing his packed dinner of rice and watermelon, charging my phone when it died an hour into the cruise, staying up with me to stargaze—even though exhaustion made my words slur and my heart skip with nervousness. He'd kept me awake, chattering in a hiccupping blend of English and Indonesian.

He'd been the one I'd approached first. After he'd deposited the pallets onboard the tatty boat that waited like an old family pet—a pet that probably had arthritis and kidney issues—I'd ignored the old man above and stepped in front of Intan, holding out two thousand dollars. "I know where you're going, and I know who those boxes are destined for. I want to come with you."

He'd turned off his loader and tiptoed toward me as if the money would suddenly vanish. His mouth had fallen open, his cheeks covered in pimples and his chin cute with a dimple. "You want go *Lebah*?"

I'd nodded. "I'll pay."

His shorts were torn at the bottom, and his t-shirt held a few nibble holes. He wasn't rich and was obviously well-acquainted with hard work. I'd wanted to offer more. I'd wanted to hand over Sully's credit card if he agreed to give me a lift.

The old man and the girl in Sully's gardener uniform had yelled down to the dock, muttering in Indonesian to Intan. I'd braced myself. So, so sure that the old man would forbid such a trade.

But surprisingly…he was on my side.

He'd silenced the girl who'd shaken her head and waved her arms aggressively in my direction. He'd nodded at Intan and narrowed his eyes my way. He'd said yes without knowing anything about me, which set off more alarm bells, but I was far too grateful to care.

"Money good for grandmother." Intan grinned as we sailed closer to Sully's islands, patting his short's pocket where the cash had found a new home. "She need…medicine. No long live. You help. Help lots. Grandfather not happy. Very sad."

I smiled. "I'm glad the money can go toward helping your grandmother. Hopefully, she gets better soon, and your grandfather is happy again."

Intan smiled, then stiffened as his sister stormed toward us. She hadn't spoken a word to me since I'd climbed aboard and we'd set sail from the busy harbour, past paint-peeling boats, fishy fishermen, and into the open waters in the dark.

Unlike Intan, who worked as his grandfather's strength and agility, she was hitching a ride to her employment. Two weeks on and four days off. She had the best green fingers in her family and had been hired by Sully's head horticulturist—according to my midnight conversation with Intan.

"Why you go back?" She crossed her arms, her petite frame and face almost identical to her brother. "You free."

I narrowed my eyes. How much did she know of Sully's business and his goddesses? Did she know that the women who lounged around all day and ate the food she painstakingly grew actually paid for that luxury with forced sex?

Not waiting for me to reply, she snapped, "Grandfather say you dead woman."

I flinched. "Why would he say that?"

"You curse on boat. Should never bring."

"How am I a curse?"

She shoved a finger at the sky, pointing at the gathering black clouds smothering the pretty dawn. "Storm coming. You cause."

My back prickled with temper. I deliberated using up energy I didn't have to argue with her, but a crackle of lightning flashed just before the soft boom of thunder echoed in the distance.

Raindrops fell almost in slow motion, plopping onto the weathered deck, leaving behind wet spots as if the boat caught a strange kind of nautical measles.

"We're almost there. I'll be off your boat soon."

"You get off boat. You die."

I scowled. "I won't die."

"Grandfather say so."

I looked over her shoulder, peering at the old captain. He pinned his black gaze on me through the salt-etched windows of his cabin, wrinkles deep-set around his cheeks and forehead, his lips thin and jowls hinting he'd lost weight he couldn't afford. He looked as if he regretted bringing me, his determination faltering.

Goosebumps spread over my arms.

*Does he know something I don't?*

Was this not fate's doing...after all?

Had *Drake* arranged this?

I swallowed hard.

After all my searching, I'd been owed a break. But what if this lift was far too coincidental to be real?

*But if someone is puppeteering my journey back to Sully...it doesn't change anything.*

I would still have taken the offer.

I would still have leaped aboard with reckless thought to my safety because Sully was hurt. He'd given me his credit card to track me. If he'd been of able body and free to chase me...he would have.

The fact he hadn't meant I had to do the chasing because who the hell knew if he was even alive?

My heart galloped with fear.

I'd returned by impossible means. I had a girl promising my death if I leaped overboard. I had instincts that agreed with her and common-sense that told me to stay with this family and sail back to Jakarta.

But...

I also had the highly inconvenient disease of being in love, and being in love made people do stupid, *stupid* things.

Locking gazes with the girl, I said sternly, "If your grandfather brought me here on behalf of someone...if he's regretting that choice because he fears I might be in danger, please tell him to call for help. I have no cell service. I have no idea where we are. I think your employer is in danger, and I can't do this on my own."

Her eyebrows knitted together as if shocked I'd faced her hints head-on or possibly struggling to understand my rabid tongue. "Please...just tell the police that Sullivan Sinclair is in danger. I'll give your grandfather more money for his wife. I'm sure Sully will pay whatever expensive treatment she needs *if* he helps him."

"Call police?" She shook her head. "No police allowed. Rules."

"I'm sure we can break that rule this one time."

"I get fired."

"You won't." I went to touch her, to squeeze her arm and march her into the captain's cabin to use the radio and summon every law enforcer and agent available, but Intan shoulder-bumped his sister out of the way, handing me a plastic bag. "Keep phone dry when swim."

"Ah, good thinking." I took it, slipping my phone inside and wrapping it up tight. "Thank you, Intan."

His sister's face scrunched up with dislike. "You crazy."

My fear blended with temper, making me snappish just as Sully's main island came into full exquisite view. With fresh raindrops bouncing off palm leaves and the golden-silver beach dappled with wet diamonds, I felt the most incredible *longing*. The deepest, rawest connection to a land that I'd chosen for my home.

My feet begged to sink into the sand. My nose flared to smell coconuts. And my heart...God, my heart physically ached with a hundred worries over Sully.

*Where are you?*

*Where are Skittles and Pika…Jealousy and Cal?*

No birds flew or sang.

No guards patrolled or goddesses laughed.

The island looked abandoned and in mourning.

Ice slithered through my veins. The vacantness of the island was wrong. The quietness was wrong.

*Everything is wrong.*

Something bad had happened.

I wasn't making this up.

I was willingly putting myself in danger because I'd been right, and Sully needed my help.

*Shit.*

My heart stuttered with rapid palpitations, finally realising just how crazy this was, recognising that I didn't have a choice, understanding that if I did this…it might be the most fatalistic thing I'd ever do.

*It's now or never.*

The boat's engines coughed like a bad smoker, the chug of diesel ruining my shield of surprise. If I had any hope of being successful, I had to be as stealthy and as sneaky as possible.

Gritting my teeth, I marched past the two siblings and straight toward the old captain.

He baulked as I entered his cabin, the interior smelling of mildew and fish scales. "Sail away. Don't let them hear you." Pointing at his decrepit radio, I added, "Call the police. You have to call them. You know more about this than you're letting on, and I hold no ill will toward you for bringing me back if someone paid you. I *wanted* to come, but I also need you to radio for help." Clutching my plastic-wrapped phone, I did my best to clutch my courage too. "I'm leaving now. Please…do as I ask."

He raised his hand as if to stop me, but it was too late.

Smiling at Intan, nodding at his stern sister, I ran to the side and vaulted.

I tumbled overboard.

I fell and fell.

I sliced through the sea and deep into the warm embrace of Sully's empire.

* * * * *

Rain battered me as I snuck from the shallows and ran up the beach to the undergrowth.

Breathing hard from my swim, cursing the heavy material of

my dress as it clung to my legs, I dug a shallow hole under a glossy leafed bush and shoved my cell phone into it.

Hopefully, the plastic bag would protect it from the rain and the drenching of my swim.

Hopefully, Sully had his own network that would report my location back to my father if the old captain didn't heed my request. The phone had become an amulet of protection. A beacon of hope that I had to protect to ensure artillery could find us.

Pushing a handful of sand over the device, I shook with adrenaline. My ears strained for voices, hoping for victory but all too aware violence lurked instead. Creeping away from the openness of Sully's beach, I turned my back on the helipad and purple orchids, and faded deeper into the manicured forest.

My heart found a new home in my throat, beating rapidly, quaveringly quick as if afraid its regular drum would wake up evil spirits lurking within Sully's shores.

*Stay low.*

*Stay hidden.*

I travelled for a while, past Jealousy's villa. Past mine. Doors hung open and furniture had been displaced, footprints masculine and mean in the pathway leading toward Divinity and the main guest hub.

I avoided areas of traffic, catching the scents of gunpowder and blood.

Where were Sully's guards?

I'd heard him and Cal discussing evacuating the guests and goddesses…but *where are the damn guards?*

My hands curled to hit someone. My fear was drowned out by aggression.

*Sully…God, Sully, please be okay.*

I would take on an army for him.

I would slaughter his brother for him.

I might be a girl.

I might be biologically weaker in physical things.

But I wasn't a coward.

And I wasn't afraid.

A threat danced on the breeze.

A warning hissed through the trees.

My skin prickled and hair stood up as fresh power commanded my legs to *run.*

Balling my hands, I ignored the urge and ducked behind a

bush instead.

Running would be idiocy. They might hear me crashing through the foliage. Keeping my breathing shallow, I did my best to be the perfect spy—the sneaky snake waiting to strike.

Thunder cymballed directly above, coating the morning in lightning and tossing a monsoon onto my head.

I shivered as I did my best to stay smart; even though I'd been ridiculously moronic to return.

I honestly didn't know what to do.

Did I travel to Nirvana and see if Sully was trapped there? Did I head to his office and see if I could call for help? Should I try to swim to *Lebah* before I got caught?

*Are you so sure Sully is still here?*

Sitting in the downpour, rain blurring the world with blues and greens, I felt as if I was the only person alive.

My stomach tightened, worrying about Skittles and Pika, but with how heavy the rain fell, it made sense that no birds flew. They'd be at the mercy of water missiles.

Tropical peace tried to lull me into a false acceptance, but regardless of the emptiness of Sully's island, I couldn't shed the sensation of sinister.

*Something isn't right.*

*I need to find him…now.*

Sighing hard, I pushed back my sopping hair and continued onward.

I'd kicked off my sandals during my swim and twigs dug into my soles as I did my best to stay silent. Travelling deeper into the island, I stopped at the main fork. The fork where Sully had driven inside me, high on elixir, and shoved me face-first into forever.

*Dammit, Sully, where are you?*

A twig snapped loudly beneath my bare foot.

I flinched and froze.

The air didn't change.

A threat didn't materialise.

I kept going.

I kept going until I stupidly began to relax in my hunter prowl.

I neared the undergrowth surrounding the god-awful villa where Sully's lab cages were housed.

The whiff of cigarette smoke made my nostrils flare.

Signs of life.

The harsh cough of a man.

*Turn around!*
*Now!*

Backing up, I scurried deeper into the jungle, my heart chugging wildly.

Was he there?

Had they imprisoned him in the very same cage he'd locked me in after he'd dragged me back from *Serigala*?

My mind raced.

If he was locked up, how could I free him?

How many men were in there with him?

My thoughts were too focused on a jailbreak. My attention internal instead of external where danger lurked.

It was my fault.

My stupid, idiotic fault that I forgot men had a body that permitted them to piss wherever the hell they wanted.

I brushed aside a large banana leaf, my thoughts on returning to the beach and waving down the police that were hopefully on their damn way, and came face to face with a man holding his cock, spraying a stream all over a shrub.

*Oh, shit.*

Shock hit me with an icy slap.

Our eyes locked. Surprise mirrored. His mouth opened.

And I ran.

I vaulted over vines and roots, bolting as far away from him as possible.

His shout behind me ignited tears and pure hate for myself.

*God, Eleanor!*

*How could you be so fucking stupid!*

I twisted and parried around palms and heliconias, missing the green flutter of a tiny parrot who'd adopted me. Missing the strict rules that'd kept goddesses in line but provided trustworthy protection.

"Karl! *Get her.*"

Rain fell harder.

I ran faster, harnessing the weightlessness of wind, bolting from the undergrowth and racing down the sandy pathway.

*Run!*

I raced and raced.

I galloped toward the horizon where rain blurred distance and time, almost reaching freedom.

So, *so* close.

Waves slapped on the shore with urgent welcome.

*Faster!*
*Faster!*

A man stepped out of the undergrowth, directly into my path. A gruesome, ghoulish enemy.

His eyes popped wide as my dress slapped around my legs and my hair glued to my skin. Widening his stance, he spread his arms, blocking me from bolting down the path to the awaiting beach. His crooked teeth gleamed, his dark eyes glowered, his hair plastered on his forehead as rain continued to pummel.

I skidded with speed, ready to slam to a stop and run the other way. The other man had gained on me, crunching through the undergrowth like a lumbering wildebeest.

I was trapped.

It was a split-second choice.

Reckless and crazy but my only hope.

I dug my toes into the sand and ran straight toward the bastard waiting to snatch me. I ducked past him and almost ran headfirst into a palm tree, crushing three orchid plants as I bowled through the neat border of the path, leaving him behind with an almost comical expression of surprise.

The sea.

*Run!*

I galloped down the beach.

The tide bounced and splashed with raindrops, freshwater blending with salt. Two worlds. Two deaths. One hope.

I ran and *ran.*

I tripped and kept running.

Launching myself into the water, I waded, leaped, and dived beneath the warm surface.

My lungs burned as I kicked with fury, swim, swim, swimming.

Popping up for air, I focused on the island in the distance.

*Lebah* wasn't far.

I could swim it.

*I can.*

Something wrapped around my ankle and tugged me underwater.

I choked and kicked, thrashing like a shark on a line.

My foot connected with something solid.

A man grunted.

A pair of hands wrapped higher up my leg, pulling me back, reeling me in against my will.

I kicked again.

I screamed underwater as a second pair of hands wrapped around my waist, plucking me from the depths and back to a miserable world.

Clutching me to his chest, the man laughed as I continued to fight and kick.

With a grunt, he trapped my arms, pressing a rancid kiss against my ear. "Hey, gorgeous. Where did you appear from? My dreams?"

I tried to bite him.

I kicked and head-butted him.

*Jackass.*

Fisting my breast, he raised his voice. "Go tell Drake we have a visitor. I'll entertain her while you do."

The other man with a shaved head and cruel eyes glowered at his colleague. "I'm not leaving. You tell him. She's mine."

"Bullshit." He pinched my nipple, making me jolt. "I caught her."

I growled and squirmed.

I used up every shred of energy I had left after days of terrible sleep and stress.

"I saw her first. She practically ran onto my dick."

"You can have seconds."

"You'll have seconds too. Drake wants firsts. He warned us."

The guy froze behind me, deliberating. "Fine. I won't touch her. Not until Drake's had his fill."

My muscles burned with lactic acid.

My heart pumped frantically.

And adrenaline quickly switched to powerlessness.

I continued to fight as the man lugged me from the sea and up onto the sand.

But I was pathetic in my attempts.

Exhaustion had caught up with me.

And I had to make a new choice.

As much as I wished otherwise, I'd lost.

*For now…*

I'd returned with this inevitability lurking in the back of my mind.

I'd been prepared to pay this cost if it meant I'd be taken to Sully.

I had to be smart.

I had to save my energy for when it truly mattered.

It went against everything fundamental inside me, but…I stopped fighting.

I didn't say a goddamn word.

I reverted to the antifreeze that had kept my temper in check in Mexico.

I stood regal and untouchable as the second man took off up the beach, snarling, "Don't move. I'll go tell Drake his visitor has arrived."

# Sullivan

## Chapter Nineteen

"SIR."

I groaned.

Pain tried to shove me back under, but familiarity forced me awake.

*Cal.*

Cal was here, and his sarcastic 'sirs' had to be reprimanded. There were only so many passes I'd give him. Otherwise, he'd start thinking he could force his opinion on me all the damn time.

"Sir…she's arrived."

I battled past the agony that'd become a cloying blanket. I groaned again as I stupidly tried to move. The daggers in my shoulders from being handcuffed, the stabs in my legs from being tied, the thousand metallic bites along my back from the cage, and the feverish infection in my leg.

It all pushed me down, down, down.

*She's arrived…*

*Fuck!*

My eyes shot wide. My lips inhaled a torn breath. Aliveness crippled me as my heart did its best to cleave its way from my chest and charge to wherever she was.

*She…*

*She's arrived.*

*Eleanor.*

**FUCK!**

I jack-knifed, clanging my handcuffs against wire, bellowing as my wrists began to bleed all over again from struggling to get free.

For hours, I'd been Drake's plaything.

All night, he'd kept me in the excruciating role as his own personal guinea pig.

Around dawn, my system had given out, and I'd fallen unconscious. I'd been glad. Thankful to no longer feel the agony of my chest where he'd burned away the top layer of skin with his acid in my Euphoria oil. Grateful to no longer have to smell the stench of the nasal deceptor smeared beneath my nose, replacing my serum with a putrid form of bleach and sewer, making me gag until my ribs threatened to crack, one by one.

I'd managed to survive everything he did to me.

I even bared my teeth and promised him a slow death as a mercenary shoved finger sensors onto my every digit, replacing my flesh-approved adhesive with finishing nails.

As each nail dug into my fingers and more blood dripped, Drake grew drunk on his power over me.

I was his lab rat.

I had better endurance than a mouse.

I had a greater body area than a chimp.

He drove me to my breaking point, all while I saw past his pompous power.

He might laugh as his minions drew my blood and turned me into a grotesque experiment, but his debonair attitude and psychotic glee couldn't hide the truth blazing bright between us.

When I'd felt it, I'd laughed.

I'd choked on spit and coughed on agony, but I'd *laughed* because I finally understood why he'd been such a cunt all my life. Why he bound my legs and arms, threw me in a cage, and let others torture me instead of doing it himself. Why he was here, stealing my shit, believing he could take everything I held dear.

Drake Sinclair might be the older brother.

But he was fucking *terrified* of me.

Afraid of his baby brother, trapped in a cage, and driven to insanity by pain.

I saw it in his eyes as he commanded poison to be poured down my throat that'd made me vomit until my guts churned in absolute misery.

I heard it in his voice as he'd ordered earplugs that'd been soaked in chilli to be driven into my ears, firing agonising pathways into my brain.

And once I saw it, our dynamic changed.

He might be the one in charge. He might kill me before I ever saw the sun again…but thanks to his fear of me, *I* was the one with all the power. I was the one who would survive because I was the stronger one, the worthy one, the invincible one.

So…I'd clenched my teeth and taken it.

I'd withheld any sound of discomfort until the final experiment.

He'd put the lenses in last.

He'd chuckled as three guards held me down and a fourth placed a tampered lens over my pupil.

I'd howled.

I couldn't help it.

A harpoon to the leg was nothing, fucking *nothing*, compared to the convulsive crucifixion of what he'd done to my eyes.

"Like what I've done with the formula?" he'd snickered, yelling over the din of my handcuffs clanging, the cage groaning, and my motherfucking howl.

One lens was enough to break my brain, but when his men put in the second, I lost it.

I didn't remember what I was, where I was, why this was happening.

I couldn't rub them, remove them, couldn't cry.

I'd passed out in a body slam of suffering only to blink now and…

See nothing.

*Fuck!*

"I didn't hear the boat pull up." Drake's voice sounded to my left, slightly raised to combat the rain pounding on the villa roof.

I blinked back blackness.

I strained to see colour, shapes, life.

I couldn't see a fucking thing.

No light.

No shadows.

No hint of cages or paradise.

*Nothing.*

I teetered on the precipice of giving in to the horror and the stubbornness of not accepting such a disability.

*It can't be permanent.*

I balled my hands, feverish sweat covering me head to toe as a mercenary said, "She must've swum ashore. We caught her trying to swim away." The man's voice curved with a smug smile. A smile that was visible in my mind. A smile that brought disaster and death right to my stupid, pointless heart. "She's feisty. Put up a fight but hasn't said a damn word."

My mind flooded with images of a girl who'd stood up to me from the very first moment I'd met her. The trafficked slave who'd stared at me like a priceless fucking queen.

*Christ, Eleanor!*

*Run away, Eleanor!*

*What the fuck are you thinking, Eleanor?*

I struggled in my binds, claustrophobic and driven to madness. My eyes burned, remaining as sightless and as useless as the rest of me.

"How do you know she swam ashore?" Drake asked.

"Just a guess, but she's wet, so I'm guessing she swam from somewhere. Then again, it is pissing down out there."

"She's wet, huh?" Drake's disgusting chuckle made violent rage burn through me.

*Fuck him.*

*Fuck ALL of them.*

"So her ride kicked her overboard, or did she jump?"

"How the hell am I supposed to know?" a mercenary grumbled. "I don't know the logistics, Sinclair, only that she's here."

She was supposed to be *safe*.

She was supposed to stay away.

She was supposed to fucking run!

A grunt fell from my control, making Drake chuckle as his footsteps came closer. "Hear that, Sullivan? I think we have a visitor." He rattled the bars of my prison, sending sound waves through my chilli-blocked ears and making my body flinch.

Everything was more intense without sight.

My body scrambled and instincts a mess.

The rustling of his clothing as he squatted by my head made me twitch. I could no longer tense before a blow or prepare for a strike. I couldn't see what the hell would happen.

He had me at my most vulnerable, and he fucking knew it.

He tapped my cheek, making me recoil and blink agonising blind eyes. "Do you want to say hi, baby brother? Think she'll find you a fucking turn-on in your current broken condition?"

I bared my teeth. "Touch her and I'll rip your cock off with my bare hands."

"Promises, promises." He patted the top of my head. "Tell you what, I'll go welcome her. You're in no fit state for company, and you need your beauty rest." He lowered his voice to a whisper, ensuring it slithered through my skull and made me snarl. "I'll be gracious…I promise."

I struggled in my cuffs and rope, activating bruises and blood, agony and torment. "I'll give you the goddamn elixir recipe. I'll sign whatever you want."

"Maybe later, Sullivan. Right now, I have a date."

The sound of his shoes was the worst goddamn thing I'd ever heard.

The slam of the door closing was the guillotine on the end of my life.

Eleanor…

*Run!*

# Chapter Twenty

THE THUNDERSTORM CEASED ITS downpour just as Drake Sinclair appeared at the top of the beach. Raindrops transformed to a gentle drizzle, clouds switched to grey, and muggy humidity sprang back into existence.

I'd tried to escape, but the guard who was holding me outweighed me and outpowered me ten to one. I struggled again, wriggling and furious, as Drake walked down the beach toward me, flanked by two men in matching black combat uniforms.

For a millisecond, my heart was confused.

The way he moved reminded me of Sully. The svelte prowl, the masculine stride. But that was where the similarities ended. Both had dark, thick hair, but Drake kept his trimmed to his skull while Sully's was untamed with bronze tips. Drake's eyes were blue but not ravishing sapphires like Sully's…more like a murky puddle. Sully's lips were full and shapely, a sinful mouth that made cursing decadent and kisses depraved, while Drake's were thin and permanently pursed as if he'd smelled something offensive.

The more I studied him, the more I saw differences instead of family resemblances. Sully had a natural weathering around his eyes, granting him a distinguished sex appeal. His nose was straighter, his cheekbones sharper, and his five o'clock shadow etched his jaw with delicious danger.

Drake, on the other hand, looked…strange.

His forehead didn't hold laugh or frown lines. His eyes stretched with no wrinkles. The skin around his lips and down his neck shone from cosmetic enhancement.

Sully looked thirty-three. He embraced every bit of his age, and it made him undeniably attractive. Drake had attempted to harness aging and reverse time, and instead, he'd made himself a caricature. An evil villain who played his part far too well.

"Hello, Eleanor Grace. What a pleasure to finally meet you." Drake bowed and narrowed his eyes at the man holding me. The guy released me, shoving me at Drake.

I stumbled and bared my teeth, recoiling from his body before touching him.

His hand lashed out, catching my wrist, bringing my knuckles to his lips and kissing them as if this was some rehearsed tea party. "I see why my baby brother has fallen madly in love with you." His gaze travelled over my figure, highly visible thanks to my dress plastering itself to my curves. "Nice tits, nice hips, and I've heard you know how to beg for cock." He chuckled. "A perfect woman."

God, the urge to scream at him became almost unbearable, but just like the traffickers in Mexico, this man was *nothing* to me. He was chewing gum under a table, a cigarette butt in the gutter. He was utter trash, and I wouldn't waste one damn word on him.

His eyebrows flared toward his trimmed hairline as his fingers released me. "Shark got your tongue, Eleanor Grace?"

I bit my tongue for good measure.

"Or do you prefer Jinx?" He licked his lips, reaching out to cup my breast.

I was free.

I had no shackles or binds.

I could shove his touch away and run.

But that would trigger predatory instincts for him to chase. That would end with me pressed against a palm tree and raped. Instead, I chose to stand up to the monster trying to intimidate me with pure, infuriating silence.

Sully was the only one who'd shattered my temper. He was the only one deserving of my voice. He was *worthy*, unlike this lacklustre imposter—this shameful older brother who thought he could invade and pillage with no consequences.

His hand squeezed my breast painfully. "I don't like being ignored, girl."

Inhaling hard, I gritted my teeth with no reply.

"Shy?" He grinned, pinching my nipple, then frowning when I reacted with absolute zero fucks. "That'll change when I feed you elixir."

I stiffened.

Did he know where Sully kept the vials?

Did he have some in his possession?

I swallowed hard, terror siphoning through my blood at the thought of being drugged and fucked by him. To violently hate him all while he violently raped me.

*No.*

*Hell no.*

"That got a reaction." Drake's muddy blue eyes twinkled with violence similar to the violence I'd seen in Sully. Only, Sully wielded his like a sharp-edged sword, hidden in a scabbard and only swung with utmost precision when necessary. Drake, on the other hand, used it like a club, bashing around like an ignoramus.

"Fancy sleeping with the better version of the Sinclair brothers? I promise you, I'm a better lay than Sullivan." He stepped into me, shoving his thigh between my legs. My sodden dress acted as a chastity belt, refusing to part enough for him to drive his crotch into mine.

I tipped my head, arching my chin.

*Sully…*

I needed to figure out how to get away from this asshole and find Sully before he made good on his threat.

Dropping his hand from my breast, Drake scowled. "You're not at all what I expected. Frankly, you're boring me, and I'm not a nice guy when I'm bored."

I narrowed my gaze until my eyelashes shadowed my vision. I hoped hate dripped from every inch of me. I hoped disgust and repulsion cloaked me, so he knew just how much contempt I held for him, how little cooperation he'd earn, and how quickly I'd kill him if I got the chance.

With my stare so sharp, I noticed things I hadn't before, and a small sweep of victory tugged up the corner of my mouth.

Drake's face wasn't as Botox perfect as I'd assumed.

His nose was swollen and coloured with a shade of purple, black bruises ringed his left eye, and the corner of his mouth was puffy. Come to think of it, he moved stiffly, guarding his side while a bandage on his shoulder peeked out from his black t-shirt.

Sully had hurt him.

Triumph filled my heart. Pride followed.

Whatever this bastard had done to Sully…Sully had fought back.

Fear iced my blood.

Had he fought too hard?

Was he still alive?

*Sully…dammit.*

My patience reached snapping point. My lips trembled to part with a torrent of profanity, but I bit them back.

Drake's only purpose was to take me to Sully.

That was all I wanted.

Then he could die, painfully. Very, *very* painfully.

"Did you appreciate my lift?" Drake smirked.

I glowered.

"Aren't you going to say thank you? Without me, you wouldn't have found your way back."

I glared.

"I bet you'll speak to me when I shove my dick inside you."

I bared my teeth.

He chuckled with an edge of frustration. "Don't want to talk to me? Fine." He smiled, cold and cruel. "I know someone who would *love* to talk to you." Leaning forward, he planted his hands on my hipbones, dragging me flush against him. "I must warn you though…he's not the man you remember. I gave him a little lesson on sibling insubordination."

*What the fuck did you do?!*

I swallowed back my scream, but I couldn't control my physical reaction.

My hand whistled through the air and sliced across his cheek.

He stumbled backward; his pain tenfold thanks to previous injuries beneath my new one. "Fuck!"

While he nursed the handprint I'd left on his bruised face, I held up a one finger salute.

*How dare you!*

*How fucking dare you hurt him!*

My silent curses ricocheted in my ears, and once again, I went too far—just as I'd pushed the limits with the Mexican guard who'd wanted me.

Drake launched himself at me. "You little slut!"

He wrapped his arms with tight captivity around me as his teeth latched around my throat. He bit me. He made me struggle. And his disgusting voice slithered into my ear. "Be as stubborn as you want. Be as stupid as you need. Piss me off, I dare you. Fuck me off, and you'll be screaming my name while I'm cock deep inside you. Hate me? I don't fucking care. Thanks to my brother, he's created a drug that makes you a whore, and according to his doctor, your heart has the risk of being overloaded, your system overwhelmed, and there's a very high chance you could die while I take you."

Dragging his tongue up my cheek, he hissed, "I like the thought of that. That I could fuck you to death. That I'd be the last one you saw, heard, touched. That you'd die belonging to me, not him. And the best part...I'll make him watch. He'll be there as I fuck you. He'll watch it all, knowing that you are mine and not his."

Wrapping his awful arm around my waist, he kissed me.

I bit him.

*Hard.*

I bit him for disrespecting me and for disrespecting Sully.

I'd bite his cock too if he ever tried to sleep with me.

I'd bite his balls clean off and spit them into the sea.

He lurched back.

His palm connected with my cheek in a five-finger blaze.

His finger went to his lip, smearing the bead of blood that my teeth had punctured.

His eyes met mine.

My cheek smarted.

I balled my hands and kept my spine rigid.

I couldn't bite my tongue any longer.

I'd reached the end of my limit.

*Don't do it, Eleanor.*

*Don't give him what he wants.*

I'd been able to ignore the traffickers.

But I hadn't been able to ignore Sully.

And I couldn't stop myself from defending him.

Looking straight into the eyes of Sully's cad of a brother, I snarled, "Is that meant to scare me? Am I supposed to tremble and obey?" My nose stabbed the sky with regality. "How can I be afraid of a stupid boy who thinks tearing the wings off butterflies makes him strong? A boy who never grew up; an idiot who thinks Botox will hide his ugliness."

He froze, dropping his hand and rubbing his blood into his skin. "She speaks."

"She bites, too."

"She behaves if she wants to stay alive." Grinning as if our threats were flirts, he wrapped his fingers around my throat. He squeezed my larynx, activating bruises from Calico's attempt at murdering me, and the strangest, scariest thing happened.

A few times on Sully's islands, I'd had moments of premonition: bathwater puddles revealing that Sully would forever change me. A parrot chirp hinting at a man behind the monster. A kiss without sensors or masks delivering my destiny.

And now, a brother who gave up the secrets of their joint childhood.

Sully was a control freak because he'd had all control taken away when he was a boy—by this man. He had no faith and broken trust because his brother had physically punished him every time he'd tried.

My heart spasmed as things fell into place—Sully's many long-ago scars. His torment at falling for me. His denial of our closeness.

The last person he'd been close to had been his family, and they'd done unspeakable things.

"You hurt him," I hissed. "You scarred him."

His eyebrows tugged down—or as much as they could with chemicals preventing facial movement. "I've hurt him all my life." He jerked me closer, his fingers twitching around my neck. "But I haven't been able to hurt him nearly as much as you have."

He laughed softly, sounding like a psychotic boy with a box of kittens, lighter fluid, and matches. "You've been able to create a pain deeper than I ever managed. You'll be the one to kill him, Eleanor Grace…not me, and I can't wait to watch you do it."

\* \* \* \* \*

Blood.

Bright vicious crimson.

It was all I could see.

All I could smell.

Blood.

*Sully…God, Sully.*

I tripped as Drake dragged me over the threshold of the villa and dry-heaved as he carted me to stand beside Sully's cage.

The same cage I'd spent a night in.

A cage that'd been flipped on its side to give enough horizontal room for the tall man within it.

"Eleanor?" Sully spasmed the moment he heard my footsteps. His gorgeous, powerful body jerked to get free. The metal ring of handcuffs clanged as he struggled, slowly at first as if he had no strength left, then faster, crazier. *"Eleanor?"*

*His eyes.*

*God…what's wrong with his eyes?!*

Drake snickered beside me, staying silent while his brother danced on the border of life and death by his feet.

I'd never seen anything so spiteful, so tyrannical, so inhumane.

A sob caught in my throat as I fell to my knees.

Sully's beautiful blue gaze was a morbid black, staring at nothingness.

Drake let me go, his snicker morphing into a self-congratulatory chuckle as I crawled over the floor, shoved my hand through the bars, and linked my fingers with Sully's.

The second I touched him, he broke.

His face twisted, his head tipped back, and his lips parted in the most heart-stopping, belly-stabbing howl. ***"FUUUCK!"***

The chemistry between us. The connection. The bond.

It *hurt.*

It hissed from his skin to mine. It electrified, it condemned, it hummed along its conduit with a lick of lust and love—a link that shared our pain, our promises, and every other pitiful thing we'd become.

"Eleanor…*Jesus Christ.*"

I clung to his hand, bowing to kiss the dried blood flaking from each finger, frantically pulling out the nails that'd been driven into his pads.

Blood.

So, *so* much blood.

I couldn't speak.

I couldn't breathe.

All my fight.

All my bickering, feuding challenge died a miserable, despairing death as I drowned beneath crippling grief. "Sully…"

He shook his head, shaking the cage around him. "This isn't real. You can't be here. You. Can't. Fucking. Be. Here."

I pulled out the last nail of his left hand. He didn't even flinch, as if his threshold for pain had been crossed hours ago.

"I'm so, so sorry." I kissed him. I kissed his knuckles, his palm, his fingers. My lips stained red from his blood as my tears splashed onto his feverish skin. My gaze stuttered over his body, unwilling to look, violently sick at what Drake had done to him.

His chest oozed with plasma and blood. His wrists lacerated

from the handcuffs, his ankles bleeding from the ropes. A large bandage hugged his thigh. It might've been white, once upon a time, but now it'd soaked into a rusty carmine.

"What were you thinking coming back?" His voice cracked with misery; his eyes unseeing. "How can I survive now that you're back?"

I reached through the cage, straining to touch his face.

I couldn't reach.

It *killed* me that I couldn't reach.

*I have to touch him.*

*Have to kiss him.*

*Have to help!*

A sob crawled up my throat and broke free. A sob born from seeing the worst thing of my life happen to the most important person in my world.

I couldn't do it.

I literally couldn't cope.

I couldn't live in a world where men like Drake could kill hundreds of animals with a single bomb, then torture his own flesh and blood for days.

*I...I can't.*

My mind fractured.

I lost all links to my girlhood, to goodness, to grace.

I became feral.

Single-minded.

One purpose.

*Him.*

*Help him.*

*Now!*

I screamed as I scrambled at the cage, desperate and frenzied to get to him.

My ears rang from my sobs.

My gaze stung from my tears.

And I snapped.

*I can't touch.*

*I can't help.*

*His eyes.*

*His body.*

*Fuck!*

I swooped to my feet, and I threw myself at Drake.

His smug smile tumbled as we plummeted to the ground. I slapped and scratched; I hit and punched.

I couldn't see to strike.

I didn't plant strategic fists.

I just couldn't contain the violence.

The hunger.

The *rage*.

I vaguely heard someone screaming.

Felt someone tugging.

I went weightless as I was hauled off Drake.

Commotion bellowed around the villa.

Sully's shout, Drake's curse, men's panic.

As quickly as I'd entered the black stupor of mania, I slammed back into my body.

I hissed with a fire that lived in every artery and vein.

I trembled with hate that screamed to hit, maim, and *kill*.

"Eleanor!" Sully's gaze couldn't find me. His face twisted in my direction; his sea-glass blue eyes utterly destroyed.

My legs gave out again as I stared into the black pupils and red soreness of Sully's blind stare. Sweat drenched him as he fought his imprisonment. More blood poured, diluted by his sweat, rolling in thick droplets off his body.

And the opposite happened.

My fire turned to ice.

To snow and sleet and blizzard.

Balling my hands, I shoved off the two men holding me and strode to Drake where he nursed four deep scratches on his cheek.

He snarled as I approached, but I didn't fucking care anymore.

I wasn't afraid of this bastard.

"Get him a doctor. *Right now*."

He narrowed his eyes. "Commands now? A breakdown followed by demands?" He snapped his fingers at the men lurking around me as if I'd decimate them all. "Tie her up."

A redheaded man headed toward the perimeter of the villa, returning with a length of rope.

I didn't flinch as he jerked my hands behind my back and began tying. Ignoring him, I hissed at Drake, "He's dying."

"Do I look like I give a shit?" He wiped his cheek with the back of his hand.

"Eleanor. Shut up. You're going to get yourself fucking killed!" Sully continued fighting in his cage, costing himself valuable energy he didn't have.

It pissed me off.

It angered me that he was so reckless with his life when he'd burned through so much of it without me. "Stop *moving*, Sullivan!"

I used his full name.

I injected venom into my voice.

He paused, his throat worked, his blind stare seeking mine again.

My stomach spasmed. Tears clogged my throat, and sobs begged to release.

*He's blind?*

*Don't focus on that.*

I couldn't focus on that.

*Not yet.*

*Not yet!*

"Get him a goddamn doctor!" I stepped toward Drake, forcing the guard still tying my hands to trip with me.

Drake crossed his arms, narrowing his eyes. "Never thought I'd see the day." He looked me up and down with loathing. "You *are* in love with him. Thought that was just a joke."

"Of course, I'm in fucking love with him, you bastard!" I squirmed against the rope.

Too tight.

Too restrictive.

"Eleanor. For fuck's sake, just be *quiet*," Sully growled. "Don't give him any reason to—"

"If you love him, prove it," Drake snapped.

I froze. "Prove it how?"

Sully snarled, "Shut *up*, Jinx—"

"You want him to have a doctor…and I want…" His lips spread in an apocalyptic smile. "And I want what he's had." Grabbing a handful of my semi-dried hair, he murmured, "Show me how Euphoria works, Goddess Jinx. Take the elixir. Beg me to fuck you like a whore. And I'll agree to bring in Dr Campbell to keep my baby brother alive for another day."

"No. No fucking way." Sully thrashed harder, the handcuffs ringing so loud. "Leave her the fuck out of this, Drake! Use another girl. Any other girl. I don't care. Just—"

"I'll gag you if you keep talking, you little cocksucker," Drake muttered. "Be quiet, the adults are talking." His washed-out blue gaze landed on mine again. "Do we have a deal, Eleanor Grace? Your body for his. I break you while the doctor fixes him. I'll even be generous and give you two the day to recover." He laughed softly. "After all, you've had a long journey, and Sully…well, he hasn't had much sleep lately."

I looked at Sully as he arched his neck and bared his teeth like a demon trapped in hell.

Bile washed up my throat.

Drake had blinded him, tortured him, broken him.

I wouldn't allow him to hurt Sully again.

This was why I'd come.

I'd come to help.

To shield him.

To hope upon a wishing star that love would triumph over evil.

I swallowed hard and nodded. "Deal."

Drake grinned.

Sully howled.

And I was marched to his cage and tied to the bars.

*So close.*

*Not close enough.*

A clock began ticking loudly over our heads.

A countdown where Sully would get treated, and I would get molested, and our sorry little love story was over.

# Sullivan

# Chapter Twenty-One

"I CAN'T TREAT HIM while he's tethered," Dr Campbell muttered. "Uncuff and untie him."

I gritted my teeth, my ears burning from the chilli earbuds, my heart in pieces thanks to goddamn Eleanor.

I could *feel* her.

Her every breath.

Her every heartbeat.

Her very aliveness sent a shimmer of connectivity to my soul.

For a man who traded in myth and misery, I had pretty black and white views on what was possible and impossible.

Possible were fantasies coming to life because of technology, computer coding, and advancements in sensory deceptors.

Impossible was feeling so deeply for someone that evolution opened new senses.

Impossible was *feeling* her as if we shared an intricate spiderweb, and she kept triggering a strand twined directly around my heart.

*Fuck, Eleanor.*

She was here.

She'd sold herself to heal me.

She'd sacrificed everything she was…*for me.*

My teeth threatened to turn to ash as I tensed in my binds.

If I didn't already love her, I'd be hers for the rest of my godforsaken life.

How had I ever doubted what I felt for her?

How could she put my health over her own safety?

*She can't.*

I couldn't let it happen.

No matter what she said or what Drake expected, I wouldn't let him lay one goddamn finger on her. I didn't know how I'd stop him, but I would.

For now…at least she'd bargained us some time. A full day. If she could get free, then I'd happily face the rest of my sorry existence knowing she was out of his reach.

"He stays tied," Drake barked. "Not debatable."

"Don't you get it?" Campbell said. "You don't need to tie him anymore. You have the best restraint there is." His clothing rustled as he moved closer. "*Her.* As long as you have Eleanor…Sinclair isn't going anywhere."

"Not happening," Drake snapped.

"His wrists and ankles are infected," Eleanor hissed. "You promised he would be treated. That includes *every* injury, not just a few."

I groaned.

Why did she have to be so stupidly brave?

Why couldn't she have forgotten about me? Hated me? Left me?

"I agree," Dr Campbell said. "If I'm to tend to his fever and wounds, I need access to all of them. There's no point only treating—"

"Fine!" Drake growled. "Henry!"

Heavy footsteps fell, moving a stranger closer. "Aim your gun at Eleanor. If she so much as moves, shoot her. Hear that, brother? You fight back, you try to escape…she dies before you're even out of the cage."

My stomach roiled, but I kept silent.

Frankly, I hovered on the dangerous edge of passing out again. I didn't have the energy for another battle—intellectual or physical. The stress of having Jinx beside me had amplified my fever and increased the pain in every limb.

I needed to gather my strength if I had any chance at saving her.

He took my silence as obedience.

Clearing his throat, he yawned. "Know what? If we're having a little break before more games begin, I might go have a snooze myself." He chuckled. "Might shoot a few of the squirrels in your palm trees, Sullivan. Have a roast rodent for lunch."

*You motherfu—*

My hands balled, and once again, I resisted the urge to reply.

Eleanor sniffed, her temper a buffet of air even if I couldn't see her cheeks pink or grey eyes turn into thunderclouds. "Don't you *dare* kill any more creatures, you sick sonovabitch."

Drake laughed. "But I'm hungry."

"Eat a damn vegetable!"

He laughed harder. "God, you two were made for each other. Matchingly pathetic." His footsteps faded toward the doors. "Men, stand guard. I'll be back tonight. I expect both my brother and his little goddess to be exactly where they are when I return, got it?"

A murmur of acquiescence as fresh air entered the villa, then vanished as he opened and closed the door.

Eleanor inhaled heavily, her presence electrocuting me, granting much-needed stamina. When she'd touched me before? Christ, my heart had almost given out. I'd never been superstitious, but touching her had been like touching an angel— willingly placing my life into her divine power, ready to transcend this shitty body and shitty situation.

I'd failed my animals.

I'd failed her.

Death could delete all of that in one instance.

"Are you okay, Sully?" Her gentle question poked my temper awake.

I loved her.

I fucking *adored* her, but she'd disobeyed me. She'd returned, despite the difficulty of finding my islands. And now, she was trapped because of me.

Drake would hurt her...because of me.

Everything she'd endured was because of *me!*

I groaned, my blind eyes throbbing in agony. "You don't get to ask me that question, Jinx."

"What?" She twisted to face me, the rope hissing against my cage. Every sound was louder, every sense straining to compensate for lack of sight. "What the hell does that mean?"

"It means he's blaming himself...as he should," Dr Campbell answered on my behalf. "He's finally earned a conscience where humans are concerned. You've taught him that it's fine to have empathy for animals, but it's hypocritical not to care for his own species."

I bared my teeth in his general direction. "You're saying I

should let men like Drake live? Men like you? Men who betray—"

"I'm saying every animal—man *or* beast—has good and bad in them. It's not up to you to play god." A creak of the floor sounded as he stopped outside my cage. "Open the door. I need to evaluate my patient."

"You're going in there with him?" a mercenary asked.

"I am." Dr Campbell aimed his next question at me. "You won't hurt me, will you, Sinclair? After all, I'm here to keep you alive."

My anger boiled.

He was the reason this had happened.

I owed him for the death of all the creatures who'd died on *Serigala*.

But…I also needed him.

I needed his help to protect Eleanor.

For now.

"I give you my word, I'll behave."

"Good. Release his binds," Dr Campbell commanded. "And unlock the cage."

The screech of the cage door opened. Two seconds later, hands touched my ankles, unthreading the rope until my legs were free.

Instinct ordered me to snatch and strangle, but I restrained. Jim was right; Eleanor was the biggest set of handcuffs I needed. Knowing that my actions increased or decreased her lifespan was enough for me to lie there perfectly still while a guard unlocked my right handcuff and then my left.

*Sit up.*

*Sit up!*

The urge to get off the wire bottom was unbearable. I jack-knifed up, groaning in misery and absolute relief.

My spine rolled. My legs bent. Pain swarmed.

I almost passed out, clinging to awareness with difficulty.

I'd never thought sitting would be so rewarding.

Vertigo found me, sloshing my insides as my head pounded. My leg passed painful and entered a realm of burning hellfire. I was hot-cold, hot-cold, jittery and shivery.

I was weak and beaten and so fucking fucked off that all my control had been stripped away.

"I'm coming inside, Sinclair."

I nodded, backing up and creating space in the cramped prison for a visitor. Bumping into the wire behind me, Eleanor gasped right by my ear.

*Fuck.*

I couldn't control it.

The need.

The paralyzing thirst to touch.

My hands fumbled against the bars, slipping through and finding her.

*Holy shit.*

The chemistry that'd overrode Euphoria and elixir—the spark of power that only grew stronger the deeper I fell—crackled in my bleeding fingertips.

She gasped, feeling it too. Our bodies in-sync. Our bond unbreakable despite how much I hated that she'd come back.

My head bowed as my fingers found her cheek.

Her breath caught as she kissed my thumb, her skin so soft, her hair still damp from the rain. "Goddammit, Eleanor." Bringing her face toward me, I closed my useless eyes, focusing on the tingly proximity of her rather than my broken sight.

"I'm here," she whispered, her breath feathering on my lips just as I found her mouth.

I kissed her.

I convulsed with sorrow and sadness as her familiar taste and comfort slipped through my bleeding body and into my heart. My skin prickled. My chest squeezed. My nose, even scrambled by bleach and stench, recognised her subtle delicious fragrance.

She smelled like my sea.

She smelled like me…an extension of my sex and soul.

A loud twang sounded, ripping us apart. "No kissing!" the mercenary snapped. "No touching."

"Leave them be. They're both dead tomorrow," Dr Campbell muttered, his body brushing against my legs as he set down his medical bag, the leather creaking in my ears.

It hurt me worse than any torture Drake had done, but I released Eleanor and sat back in my cage. I fought the curse of her, the jinx she'd put on me. If I'd known this would be our ending, I would've denied my need for her.

I would've set her free the second she appeared.

"Sully…"

"Don't." I pinched the bridge of my nose, doing my best to shove away my debilitating pain and stay awake. Sitting up stole the rest of my energy. Nausea climbed up my gullet. I hated the blackness of my world—the unknown threats lurking right outside. "How many men are in here with us?" I asked the doctor.

His clothing rustled. "Three currently, but another two are outside."

"Can you take the pins out of his fingers?" Eleanor's voice wobbled. "They're still stabbing his right hand."

I splayed my fingers, seeing nothing. I'd gone past sensation. I'd blocked out the discomfort to focus on the worst parts.

Campbell lowered his voice, slipping to an audible I might not have heard if I still had sight. "Sinclair...I've brought a few of the noncompliant serums and pharmaceuticals. Do you give me permission to administer?"

My mind raced. After years in the business of drug manufacturing, we had crates of failed experiments and unapproved medicines. Some were rightfully denied—causing worse side effects than the original problem. But some...some were just too potent to be approved.

Those would decimate the industries and cause anarchy in the public sector because to them...they were miracles. Drugs that could work in a fraction of the time as others. Creams that could reverse damage in a few hours. Nanobots injected in a fluid that could knit flesh together from the inside out faster than any surgeon.

I had no idea he had a stash on my shores.

Gritting my teeth, I nodded. "Use whatever you want. I need to be able to walk. To see. To fight."

He cleared his throat, taking my right hand and using a pair of tweezers to remove the nails holding the fingerprint sensors against my flesh. "There might be side effects that we can't foresee."

"I'm aware."

Eleanor sucked in a breath. Following our conversation, she understood the risks but wisely stayed silent.

Removing the final nail, Campbell sighed and settled into his task. "In that case...let's begin."

# Chapter Twenty-Two

I NEVER TOOK MY eyes off Dr Campbell as he pulled the buds from Sully's ears and threw them away in disgust. "Chilli in someone's ears? He's a madman."

Sully winced. "I told you I was the sane one."

My trust was a shattered thing by my feet.

Was Dr Campbell part of this war or had he been caught in the middle of it?

Who was our enemy, and who was loyal?

"Is Cal still alive?" Sully murmured, keeping his voice too low for the guards to hear.

The doctor nodded. "He's made it through the past few days. He's getting stronger but still hasn't woken."

*Cal?*

*What happened to Cal?*

Sully nodded, flinching as Dr Campbell cleaned his face, throat, arms, and hands with antiseptic wipes, smearing away as much blood and sweat as he could. "The massacred guards? Are they rotting on my beach?"

The doctor blanched. "No, he dragged them out to sea. There's no evidence of what happened."

Sully sat unmoving, callous. "And Skittles?"

*Skittles?*

My heart fisted. "What about Skittles?"

Sully's shoulders tensed. He didn't reply, allowing the doctor to speak. "She's recovering too. Her wing will mend."

"Her wing?" I blurted.

"She broke it," Sully muttered. "Trying to defend me." His jaw clenched; the cords of sinew visible in his neck as he struggled with the truth. "I'm sorry, Jinx."

"Sorry?" I struggled against the rope trapping my hands. I needed to touch him again. It was the only thing that made sense. The only thing that calmed my heart even though it existed in a hopscotching, hiccupping mess. "Don't apologise. She loves you. She—"

"I put her in danger. Just like I put you in—" He hissed between his teeth as the doctor stabbed the back of Sully's hand, inserting a new needle and bag of antibiotics.

"This is concentrated. I don't like your fever, Sinclair. We need to lower your temperature if you're to stay conscious."

I bit my lip, forcing myself not to ask questions about Skittles and the drugs that Sully had agreed to take. What sort of side effects? How deadly could this be?

For the next fifteen minutes, I stayed silent while the doctor did his best to put Sully back together again. I watched as he smeared black cream over the bloody abrasions around his wrists and ankles.

I flinched as he patted the raw flesh of Sully's chest with a green goo that made his back bow with an influx of agony.

Two colours that I'd never associated with healing before. Black and green. Poison. Dangerous. Wrong.

"Take these." Dr Campbell took Sully's hand, popping four pills into his palm. He waited for Sully to place them on his tongue before passing him a bottle of water from his bag.

Sully downed the entire thing.

"Shit, I should've remembered sooner." Pulling free two tin-foiled wrapped sandwiches, the doctor passed one to Sully and placed one on my lap through the bars. "It's simple salad and egg. The only ingredients I could find in the kitchens with the staff evacuated."

Sully ripped at the foil, wolfing the food down. "Seems you've thought of everything. Guilt's a bitch, huh?"

The doctor scowled. "I told you it wasn't my intention to cause more pain. I just wanted to protect the goddesses."

Sully snorted, wiping crumbs away from his chin.

I eyed mine.

With my hands tied, I had no way of eating. Not that I had an appetite. My nose reeked of antiseptic and Sully's blood. But I was sensible enough to know I'd need the energy later—if I could figure out how to eat it.

My mind dared skip into the future, to fixate on the deal I'd made with Drake.

Sully was being cared for…but I would pay the price of that luxury.

When Drake returned, I'd be forced to drink elixir for the fourth time and lose myself in the haze of desire. I would have to give myself to another man…all to save the one I loved.

Tears prickled. Fear rose.

*Don't.*

*Just don't.*

Sniffing back helplessness, I kicked the sandwich off my lap and swallowed down my nausea. I almost threw up as Dr Campbell turned his attention to Sully's leg.

Sully stiffened as he unwrapped the bandage, snarling under his breath as the sodden material pulled at the wound.

Light-headedness hit me as the full carnage of his thigh appeared.

*Oh. My. God.*

What had Drake *done* to him? Shot him with a fucking arrow?

Tears spilled, despite my commands not to. I sniffed and trembled as the doctor inspected the stitches holding Sully's leg together and poked around as if it was a chewed-up piece of meat that had no feeling.

Sully swayed as the doctor grabbed a huge, wicked syringe from his bag.

He looked up, searching Sully's face, unable to catch his blind eyes. "You might want to lie down for this."

Sully swallowed hard. "What are you going to do?"

"Your stitches have pulled away in some areas. There's puss which indicates the antibiotics aren't working as quickly as I'd like. You've agreed to the less mainstream methods. I intend to administer them."

"Ah, fuck." Sully gingerly lay down on metal wire, his eyes closed and face tight with pain. His hands balled as Dr Campbell repositioned himself between Sully's spread legs and inserted the nasty looking needle directly into the wound.

Sully bellowed. His body spasmed.

He fell lax into unconsciousness.

The doctor looked up, waiting to see if he'd wake. When he didn't, he muttered, "That's for the best. I can work quicker with him no longer aware." Injecting him again, he continued inserting and depressing the plunger until the silver liquid had evacuated the syringe and vanished into Sully's flesh.

Next, he pulled out a needle and surgical twine, embroidering new stitches on the areas that'd pulled out of his skin. Finally, he squirted a skin adhesive, gluing Sully's leg as well as stitching it. "That should hold…as long as he doesn't do anything stupid."

My sandwich lay forgotten on the floor.

I clamped my lips together, fighting the urge to vomit.

Tears cascaded faster as I studied the mangled man in the cage.

I didn't care about my own predicament. I didn't fret over my payment with Drake.

All that mattered was *Sully*.

He was still the majestic magistrate of this paradise, but he'd paid for that title with every drop of blood he had. Every molecule of pain. Every shred of sanity.

"The harpoon really mangled his thigh," the doctor muttered, wrapping a fresh bandage around Sully's leg.

*Harpoon?*

My heart cracked; I slouched in my rope.

*I'm too late.*

If only I'd arrived sooner. Found him quicker.

Dr Campbell looked up. "I know he's going to attempt to walk on this. I know he doesn't really have a choice…but I can't guarantee he won't have a permanent limp if he does, even with the nanobots knitting him together."

I bit my bottom lip and didn't speak, too green and terrified to reply.

He returned to work. Once he'd secured the bandage, he crawled toward Sully's face and peeled open his eyes.

He winced. "He's right. I am guilty of this. What a fucking bastard to do this to his own kin—to anyone."

Swallowing hard, clammy with sickness and full of pain for what Sully endured, I stuttered, "What…what did he do to him? Is he blind?"

"Whatever he did, the sclera is irritated, and his cornea is black. His pupils don't dilate with light. I've never seen anything like…wait." He narrowed his gaze, leaning forward. His hand trembled as he pulled Sully's eyelid higher and touched his pupil.

A black contact lens stuck to his finger, pulling away and revealing an angry purple-blue iris.

"It's just a blockage." He smiled weakly, hope flaring over his face. "A simple barrier…a curtain if you will." Peering at the lens on his finger, he added, "A lens that blinds instead of enhances."

I couldn't speak.

I could barely contain the rage toward Drake and the relief for Sully.

The doctor gave me another half-smile before returning to his task. Removing the other lens, he applied three drops of something into each eye before sticking thick cotton pads over Sully's eyelids. "If he wakes, tell him to keep the padding on for as long as he can. The more time those drops have to work, the better his chances at seeing."

I forced myself to ask, "Will he have his full sight again?"

He shrugged, pulling out another syringe, this one full of golden contents. "Time will tell. He'll be hazy for a few days. There are scratches and traumatised blood vessels, but I am hopeful it's not a permanent disability." Inserting the needle into Sully's bicep, he plunged the golden liquid deep and wiped at the bead of blood left behind.

"What did you just give him?"

He sighed. "Something that would never pass clinical trials but has proven to be miraculous for those on death's door."

Goosebumps spread over me, prickling my skin. "What do you mean?"

"I mean…whatever you two face tonight…that should grant him the power he needs to endure it."

"Will…will he be okay?"

He nodded. "He'll stay alive…until Drake decides otherwise."

*Alive.*

*He'll stay alive.*

It was a magical incantation to incapacitate me.

I'd fought for so long.

I'd searched and called; I'd bribed and threatened.

I'd spent almost four days ignoring sleep and sustenance so I could get back to Sully and hear those very words.

*He's alive.*

*He's okay.*

I couldn't fight it anymore.

*He's okay…*

I bowed my head as exhaustion crept over me.

The guards had drifted toward the exit, three of them sprawled in chairs and gossiping like old women.

The immediate danger had been removed…for now.

Sully had been treated.

He was asleep and doing exactly what his body needed to heal.

*He's alive…*

My eyelids fluttered downward, feeling heavy and determined to rest.

*He's okay…*

I folded forward, held by a rope, dragged into the darkness, out cold before the doctor had finished.

* * * * *

"Eleanor…"

*Sully.*

My eyes shot wide. My heart kicked awake. I moaned as aches and stiffness shot down my back—my spine did not appreciate my slouched imprisonment.

"Are you okay?"

I laughed sadly. "You're asking me if *I'm* okay?" I watched Sully's every move as he struggled to sit upright, wincing and hissing. His body was no longer the sleek, invincible man I'd been sold to but a pieced together king who'd been overthrown. "What about *you*?"

"What *about* me?" His lips thinned as he swayed, his forehead furrowed as he fought the residual unconsciousness and pulled out the drip from the back of his hand. His fingers strayed to the cotton over his eyes. "What the—"

"Leave them on. Let your eyes heal."

He stiffened. "Did Campbell figure out what Drake did to me?"

"He removed the lenses blinding you. He believes they were tampered with to ensure no vision was possible."

His chest rose with harsh hope. "I'll be able to see again?"

*I truly, truly hope so.*

"If you leave the drops in for as long as you can…he believes you should, yes."

"Thank fuck for that." He bowed his head, dipping his fingers through his bronze-decorated hair. The tips of each pad held a small scab where they'd healed from the pins driven into his flesh. The skin under his nose still gleamed red and sore; the insides of his ears had streaks of blood from the earbuds and the rest of him…

*Don't look.*

My heart couldn't handle the pandemonium his body had become.

*Focus on his face. His lovely, lovely face.*

*That's enough…for now.*

Sully shifted again, the metal cage creaking in protest. "Is it dark?"

I licked my lips, looking out the window high above the stack of dog, cat, and mice cages. "Dusk is falling."

"Shit, how long have I been out?"

I shrugged, activating more aches. "Seven hours or so? I'm not sure. I slept too."

"Goddammit!"

"Don't yell…save your strength." Tiredness and tragedy wobbled my voice. "It's fine. Drake hasn't returned, and the guards are outside having a smoke. It's just us…"

His fists curled, his nostrils flared, his rage was palpable, leaking through the bars. I understood his anger, but it cost so much energy to be mad. Energy he didn't have.

"Sully…please, relax."

"*Relax?*" He bared his teeth. "How can I relax knowing you're here? How the hell did I sleep seven *fucking* hours when your life is in my hands?"

"My life is in *my* hands. I came back of my own accord—"

"You came back when I told you to stay as far away as possible."

"You didn't. You agreed to temporary all while you lied to my face," I snapped, skating my gaze to the exit and the locked door between us and the mercenaries. I didn't know when they'd left, but I supposed they figured two unconscious people who were tied and caged weren't going anywhere fast enough to warrant sitting inside all day.

"I'm not debating this with you," he growled. "You never should have come back."

"Never?" I struggled to suck in a breath. "You could have survived never seeing me again?"

"Of course not. It felt like I died the moment you took off."

"Well then, you're welcome."

"Christ, you test me. You're not getting it. I love you. Do you understand that? I fucking love you more than anything and anyone, but having you here? You've ruined me because how the hell can I protect you? How can I stop him from touching you, fucking you, hurting you? How the goddamn *fuck* am I supposed to protect you when I'm shackled, wounded, and blind?"

"I'm not asking you to—"

"Just as I didn't ask you to throw your life away for mine!"

I struggled to get my temper under control. This wasn't how our reunion was supposed to go. We shouldn't be fighting when he'd just woken up from being pushed to the brink, while he lay upon the stains of shed blood, while we honestly didn't know how long our lives would last. "Sully…I had to come. I didn't have a choice."

"You did. You *did* have a choice. You could've chosen to obey me. At least you were out of his reach."

"He would've found me if he wanted to. He knows my name. I would never have been safe."

"Goddammit, why do you have to be so smart?" He threw his head back, his throat working as he swallowed. "Why can't I win with you? All I wanted was to keep you safe. You are my top priority. My *only* priority. Yes, he could have found you if I failed to kill him, but you would've been surrounded by society and other people. You would've been a hell of a lot safer than here!"

"Hush." I attempted to give each other sweetness and forget the sour. "It's not worth arguing about. I'm here. We're together. We can—"

"Damn you, woman." His voice filled with a painful huskiness. "You've betrayed me in the worst possible way."

"Betrayed you?" I sucked in another thin breath, my temper heating with injustice. I'd known he was stubborn. I knew we had similar fiery responses, but I didn't think he'd be stupid enough to burn through whatever energy sleep had given him with accusations and slurs. "It's not betrayal…it's loyalty."

"It's *insanity*."

"It's *necessity*!" I twisted to face him as much as my binds would allow, glaring at the cotton over his eyes and the bruises shadowing his tanned skin. Just looking at him and imagining the torture he'd endured drowned my heart and made tears spring.

He was angry with me because he was afraid for me.

And I was angry with him because I hated that he was hurt.

Our rage wasn't meant for each other, but that bastard who'd done this to us.

*Damn you, too, Sully.*

*I didn't ask for this.*

*I didn't ask to fall so stupidly hard that I'll literally do anything to keep you safe.*

I sniffed back my sadness, forcing myself to remain as silent as I could. He couldn't know I was crying, couldn't know I churned with compassion, pity, and a decent dose of regret.

I should've come here with an armada.

Instead, I'd come alone and failed spectacularly.

*Stop crying!*

But he heard me.

Of course, he heard me.

"God, please don't cry," Sully whispered brokenly. "I'll lose it if you cry."

I laughed weakly as I rubbed tickling droplets from my jaw with my shoulder. "You can hear me?"

He shrugged helplessly, his lungs exhaling our fight and making him soft, gentle…kind. "I've always been aware of you. Now that I can't see…I'm hyper attuned to your every breath."

I wanted to say something.

Something profound and promising. Something that would give him back his pride, his power, his hope.

But…I had nothing.

All I wanted to do was crawl into his arms and kiss him until we both either died or help arrived.

*Help.*

"Sully…" I glanced at the exit, my tears drying. Still no guards. Still alone. I lowered my voice for good measure. "I told the captain who dropped me off to call for help. His granddaughter works on *Lebah*. I think he accepted Drake's bribe to bring me here but regrets it. He might call on our behalf…I hope anyway. I also installed a tracker app on a burner phone and told my dad to call the police, the consulate—anyone in a position to help us with the coordinates. I don't know if I have reception out here…but I tried."

He froze.

I added quickly, "I told him your name. I…I hope you don't mind."

I was almost grateful he couldn't see me just yet. I didn't have to hide my worry or pretend to be stronger than I was. I'd done my best…*but it might not be good enough.*

Silence fell for a second before he chuckled darkly. "You told your father about me?"

"I told him you needed help."

"Did you also tell him I bought you? That I paid money for your body and ended up stealing your heart?"

I shook my head, my hair catching on the bars behind me. "No...but he'll hear in my voice that you're special to me. That you're...the one."

He groaned. His body stiffened and face twisted. He sniffed as if he couldn't believe what I'd told him before clearing his throat and murmuring, "If we survive this, Eleanor Grace...I'm going to fucking marry you."

Goosebumps shot over every inch of me. I shivered. I smiled. "Is that a proposal?"

"It's a vow. You've somehow claimed my entire useless heart. I let you go, Jinx. I watched you fly away like so many of my rescues...but you came back. You came back despite impossible odds...therefore, I'm keeping you. You don't get a choice anymore."

Overwhelming heat and need licked through my veins as he lugged himself into a better position and reached through the bars for me. The cotton on his eyes hid his penetrating stare. His lips were cracked from lack of hydration and abuse, and his five o'clock shadow bordered a beard. He looked as wild as the animals that would've inhabited the cage before him.

His fingers moved hesitantly as if afraid to hurt me in his quest to find me.

I moaned as he cupped my cheek.

He let out a heavy sigh, caressing me with a shaking touch. "It's killing me that I can't see you." His forehead pressed against the bars. "I'm sorry I'm the cause of so much misery." Curling his fingers against my jaw, he pulled me toward him, kissing me through the metal, running away from our entrapment and the colossal unknown in our future.

His tongue licked my bottom lip.

I parted for him.

He dipped inside my mouth, his breath hitching as I welcomed.

We gave each other the sweetest kiss we'd ever shared. A kiss of hellos and goodbyes, apologies and arguments. We kissed like lovers, all while we were lab rats trapped at the mercy of a mad scientist.

How long until the police arrived?

Would they come by boat or helicopter?

*Will they get here before it's too late?*

Pulling away, Sully's touch dropped to the rope looping around the bars and tethering me tight. "Are we still alone?"

I licked his taste from my lips, nodding. "Yes."

"Can you see anything we can use as a weapon?"

I scanned the villa, empty apart from towers of cages and horrible history. "No."

His fingers worked the rope, tugging on different areas, attempting to free me. He was just as capable missing a sense as he was at full power. He'd endured so, so much, yet he wasn't complaining or giving up. In fact, his skin flushed with a healthy colour beneath his bruises, the swelling in his leg looked less angry, and the rawness of his skin around his wrists, ankles, and chest were all—

"Oh, my God." I gawked closer. "Your injuries…they're—"

"Better?" His lips twitched. "Yeah, they're not hurting nearly as much either."

"How…how is that possible?"

His forehead furrowed as he continued to fumble with my rope. Up close, I noticed the skin around his wrists still oozed, but the flesh was a healthy pink. Tissue had already begun covering with new cells and blood supply.

He cursed under his breath, tugging the twine harder. "A hazard of my line of work." Bending in half, he attempted to gnaw at the cord around my hands. "We stumble upon miracles as well as disasters."

"And you happen to create a cream that heals in a few hours?"

"A few days for full granulation, but yes, substantially faster than anything else on the market." He cursed again, his fingers brushing my hands as he continued to work the rope. "I'm assuming Jim gave me Tritec-87 while I was out. Did he inject me with something?"

"Yeah, a few jabs in your leg and one giant syringe of golden liquid in your arm."

"The ones in my leg will help stitch my inner muscles together. The golden one we cooked completely by accident…well, not entirely by accident." He sniffed with satisfaction as my left hand slipped free.

"What does it do?"

"We found a substitute for morphine from a rare plant in Borneo. We blended it with adrenaline and low-level opiates. The results are muted pain, improved stamina, and strength to survive if you'd say…fallen down a cliff or gotten hurt on a trail."

I stretched my arm, wincing against the tightness in my

shoulders. "And you didn't sell it? Sounds wonderful. A second lease on life when you're so close to death."

He sucked in a breath, his voice switching from informative to cagey. "It never got approved…for legitimate reasons."

"What reasons?" My right hand fell from the rope as he freed me. I twisted to face him fully. My heart bucked as he bowed his head, his jaw working. "What reasons, Sully?"

He swallowed. "The side effects were…complicated."

I grabbed the bars, wrapping my hands so tight my knuckles went white. "*What* side effects?" An awful forewarning clouded over me. I wanted to reverse time and snatch the injection right from the doctor's hands.

"Heart failure in some. Stroke in others. Coma for a few days in the majority."

"Holy God." I leaped to my feet, stumbling as blood shot down my legs, granting pins and needles. "How long? How long until that might happen to you?"

He spread his hands and his eyebrows tugged so low the tape over the cotton stuck outward. "A typical dose lasts about forty-eight to seventy-two hours before the host's system overloads."

"So…you're telling me he injected you with a super drug that allows you to ignore everything you've already gone through? That it tricks your mind into believing you're not hurt and drives you closer to a grave with every passing moment?" I grabbed the locked padlock to his cage, yanking it with terror. "My God, Sully. What the hell were you *thinking*?"

He shrugged. "I don't care what happens to me at this point. I needed to be strong to protect you. With every hour that passes, I'll increase in energy. It's a stacking effect. By the time I've burned through everything I have left…Drake will be dead and—" His lips snapped shut, and his face shot to the side.

He bared his teeth and snarled, "Run, Jinx. Someone is in here with us. *Go!*"

# Sullivan

# Chapter Twenty-Three

MY HEARING HAD BECOME acute.

A so-called side effect of not having sight.

The barest of noises.

The faintest of sounds.

And I heard it.

I wished to fucking God I wasn't locked up, so I could place myself in front of Eleanor and keep her safe, but at least she was free. At least I'd given her a warning.

"Go, Eleanor."

"I'm not leaving you!" she whisper-hissed.

The noise came again.

Was it Drake?

No...too light of foot.

Was it a mercenary?

No...too swift.

"Who's there?" I balled my hands, primal instincts crawling through my blood. I already felt stronger than when I'd first woken up. My fever had broken, and I could ignore the steady throb in my stitched-together leg. The rest of my injuries had become inconsequential. Simple scratches that didn't require attention.

Despite the ending that awaited me—the possible fatal aftermath of my Tritec-87 concoction—I embraced the sensation of power. I welcomed back the use of limbs that'd become a hindrance rather than a help.

"Who the fuck's there?" I growled.

"Shush!" The soft noise came again, the faint scrape of wood followed by a soft thud in the shadows. "It's me."

"*Jealousy?*" Shock rippled through me. "What the hell are you doing here?"

Fuck, Cal would be pissed if he knew she'd put herself in harm's way. I'd seen him watching her. I knew things he hadn't divulged.

Eleanor's inhale quickened my heart, making me insanely aware of her.

"I saw the boat," Jealousy said. "And I couldn't stomach sitting around another day not knowing if you were okay. So…I swam here."

"You swam?" Eleanor asked. "On your own?"

"I didn't tell anyone I was going. Arbi wouldn't have let me." Her voice softened. "I had to try. I knew the moment the boat appeared that it was you, Jinx. You're too pig-headed and besotted to leave for good."

Eleanor's voice teased with a smile. "Well, thank you for putting yourself at risk." The pad of bare feet paced in front of my cage. "We need to find a key. Even a piece of metal to work the padlock."

"Forget about me. Leave. Swim back to *Lebah*." I searched for Jealousy in my current blackness, settling on speaking in her general direction. "How did you get in here? Take Eleanor and go."

"I came in through the window at the back, but two men are smoking outside now. It was only luck that kept me hidden."

"Well…luck will continue to aid you. Take Eleanor to the beach and swim away."

"We've discussed this," Eleanor clipped. "I returned to get you. If I leave…*you* leave."

"I'd be happy to, but right now, it's not fucking *possible*."

"Then I'm not going." Her feet scurried faster, ducking to the corners of the villa and coming up empty. "No keys. No metal wire or tools to get you free."

"That's why I'm telling you to *run*."

The tingling awareness of her heated me as she stopped outside my cage. "Did I run the last time you asked me? Did I run when you attacked me high on elixir? No. I didn't. So stop asking me to because you'll just get shitty at my reply."

"Christ, you're—"

"Annoying? Yes, I know." The two goddesses drifted away, moving around the villa in a choreographed hunt. Five minutes later, Eleanor asked, "Anything?"

"No. Nothing. Not even a hairpin or paperclip." Jealousy's sweet voice came from somewhere in the distance.

"Shit."

Eleanor's curse lodged like a rock in my belly. I balled my hands. "I keep telling you. Run! While you still can."

They flat out fucking ignored me. Eleanor asked, "Do you know where Drake is?"

Jealousy answered with hesitation. "I saw him, eh...having a barbecue by the main restaurant hub. He...um, skewered a few squirrels and a couple of herons. A few men dressed in black ate with him."

"For fuck's sake!" I ran both hands through my hair, digging nails into my scalp. How many more of my creatures would that motherfucker kill?

"I told Arbi we should radio for help...but he's too literal and obeying your rules, Sullivan." Jealousy's voice moved closer toward me. "You're adamant no police. Ever. So...he's refusing to call them."

I pinched the bridge of my nose. "He's loyal but not forward thinking."

"I tried to call them myself, but I couldn't get access to the radio network, so I—"

The door opened.

Fresh air spilled into the space.

Screw being blind. Fuck letting the drops heal my eyes.

Tearing at the tape and ripping off the cotton, I blinked. Blackness.

Just utter fucking blackness.

"Well, well, seemed Henry was right...we have a second visitor." Drake's oily voice snaked toward us. "Look what the sea spat out."

I rubbed my eyes, begging them to work. Desperate for sight, shadow, shape. *Anything.*

His shoes grated on the floor as he turned to Eleanor. "How did you get free?" His anger boiled. "Why is no one inside here as I fucking requested?"

A man I couldn't see muttered, "They were out cold. It got too hot and stuffy. Figured they couldn't go anywhere, so we—"

"I hired imbeciles," Drake muttered. "Shut up. I don't care.

Do your job, or I'll end your purpose on this earth, got it?"

I blinked again, my heart rate manic as the first threads of light broke through the dark.

A soft feminine shout sounded in Jealousy's vicinity. "Stop!"

"Don't fucking touch her!" I grabbed the bars, wishing I could pry them apart and leap from this goddamn cell.

Drake laughed. "I love how you're still giving orders, brother. Ah well, despite the lax security, it seems I have two goddesses to play with tonight."

More light spieled through my vision, crackling like old paint, ripping back moth-eaten curtains.

Eleanor's curse whipped my head toward her.

Her short scream made my mind drip motherfucking red. "GET YOUR HANDS OFF HER, YOU FUCKING SONOVABITCH."

"It's okay, Sully. I'm okay."

Goddammit, how dare she make me this privileged, this wretched, this *powerless*.

My head ached as my eyes did their best to focus past the cloying haze. "Just let her go, Drake. You win, alright? Let both girls go and I'll sign whatever deeds you want. I'll give you the schematics for Euphoria, the codes, the programming, the sensors. I'll give you the recipe for elixir. You can have all of it...just let them fucking *go*."

He didn't reply, leaving me floundering in the light crackled dark.

Eleanor gasped, her body rustling with fight. "Don't!"

My heart pounded with panic, amplifying the Tritec in my blood, granting me a surge of strength that would demand the worst kind of payment at the end. "Don't touch her!"

"You're no longer in the position of command, Sully." He kicked my cage, making me jolt. I hadn't felt him come near. My instincts were scrambled by Eleanor. Every cell homed in on her. Every scrap of awareness and survival had locked firmly onto our electric connection. "I'll take you up on that generous offer. However, I have to sample the merchandise, don't I? Oh, and FYI, your resident squirrels are delicious. They taste like nutty chicken."

"I'll kill you, you—"

"What am I holding up, Eleanor?" Drake projected his voice a bit louder, cutting me off and waiting for a reply.

Eleanor took her time, either refusing to obey or debating

other choices. Finally, she clipped, "You're holding up a vial of elixir."

*Ah, fuck.*

He'd raided my office then.

He'd found the last three vials on this island.

"Know what that means, baby brother of mine?" Drake snickered. "It means I hope you two had a good sleep because tonight, I get to sample what you've been having. I get to fuck a goddess. And you're going to watch…everything."

# Chapter Twenty-Four

WE MADE A SAD procession.

Two goddesses, one god, one devil, and four hobgoblins.

Drake led the way, his boots kicking up sand while Jealousy padded in front of me, barefoot in just a black bikini. Swimming here hadn't exactly equipped her with a wardrobe fit to hide her curves from evil men.

My palms clasped together, my wrists once again bound; faint bruises from the last imprisonment ached beneath the new. At least this time, my hands were in front of me, instead of behind. Jealousy's too and Sully's.

All trussed up like cattle with guns aimed at our heads, marched from our cages and down sandy laneways to our demise. Stars peeked between stencils of palm leaves. A flash of emerald hinted Pika chased us from afar, and the chorus of cicadas, frogs, and bats did its best to still masquerade as a paradise but failed.

Thanks to Drake, he'd infected this Eden with his monstrosity. He was Lucifer himself, undoing all the good in the world.

Sully's harsh breath tickled my nape. His rage was a thick vapour, seething with condemnation, sharp as a scalpel and searching for the tiniest opportunity to murder his brother.

Glancing over my shoulder, I flinched as I looked into his red-rimmed eyes. I wished he hadn't taken the cotton off yet, but I understood why. He'd wanted to see.

*But...he can't.*

My heart bled when Sully kept his fractured stare directly ahead, not noticing I studied him. His back remained rigid, his hands clasped with white knuckles and rope chewing into newly knitted skin. Clad only in black boxer-briefs, the damage done to him remained on display like a dreadful tapestry. However, even with the bandage around his thigh and the terrifying blankness of his defective stare, he was still a thousand times the man the guards and his brother were.

He moved with an untouchable fortitude, a brooding vigour that guaranteed vicious violence the moment my life wasn't in the crosshairs.

I bit my lip as he stumbled, a slight limp from his leg as he followed in my footsteps, blindingly linked to me through our heart-knotted strings.

Jealousy grunted with anger as we travelled around the bend and Euphoria appeared.

My heart kicked up sick speed.

Drake had found Sully's elixir.

He'd traded a doctor for my body and because I loved Sully with all my loyal soul, I'd entered into a covenant that would ruin me.

Sully growled as our feet connected with the decked steps, climbing the short distance to the large cathedral-inspired doors. His shoulders bunched, and his temper was no longer a vapour but a polluted nebula gnashing its jaws to get free.

*God...think.*

*Hurry.*

If we entered this place—if Sully was made to listen while his heinous brother raped me...he'd die. He wouldn't permit it. He'd do whatever it took to protect me...even if it meant being shot.

I needed to talk to him.

To tell him in explicit terms that I didn't return to watch him be killed. Whatever was about to happen would happen with him staying *alive*. He owed me that. He'd already gambled with his longevity by taking a drug that may or may not take his life in payment.

"Sully...don't be stupid," I whispered as we entered the foyer of the high swept, roof thatched church of Euphoria.

He grunted a savage response, sending goosebumps beneath my rain-crinkled dress.

Drake didn't stop our little train until we entered the

playroom where a harness hung from the ceiling, cupboards with fantasy props ringed the bare space, and a glass-frosted door led to a bathroom where Sully had kissed me for the first time.

My lips tingled in memory as Drake spread his legs and snapped his fingers. The guards with their guns came to a stop, forcing us to halt. Sully's temper grew until it touched the vaulted ceilings and slithered across the tiles.

I trembled in worry.

*Please, Sully…*

If Drake gave me elixir, that was protection in itself. If there was no way out of this nightmare, at least elixir would shield my mind and leave my body a nymphomaniac shell. Sully, on the other hand…he'd suffer my every moan; my every beg would break his heart.

I flinched, brushing my shoulder with his.

He stiffened, his jaw clenching as a spark crackled from him to me. A promise that I was still his, and he was mine…throughout sickness, death, and Drake. His face turned to mine, his eyes narrowed and a painful red. However, amongst the sore seeking, he managed to catch my gaze and hold it.

My knees threatened to buckle. Tears sprang in relief.

*You can see…*

He nodded slightly as if he'd heard my question, as if our connection allowed telepathic communication.

"Right." Drake clapped his hands, ripping our moment apart. "It's playtime, ladies and gents, and this is how it's gonna go." Pointing at the guards all aiming guns at us, he muttered, "If the girls run, shoot them. If my brother does anything idiotic, shoot him but don't kill him. I need what's in that brain of his before he's allowed to die." He chuckled coldly. "He also has a show to watch. I'll give him some pointers on how to fuck a woman."

Sully bristled beside me, a vibrating snarl in his chest. "You planning on fucking in front of your men, Drake? Euphoria works on corrupting the mind. You won't be here, but your body will. They'll see every shudder of your flabby ass."

Drake gritted his teeth in a tight grin. "We all like pornography, baby brother. They can watch to ensure you behave." His puddle blue eyes met mine, and his lips twisted into a smirk. "Now, Eleanor Grace…come here."

A guard grabbed my elbow, dragging me away from Sully.

And Sully let go of his leash.

Even with imperfect eyes and bound hands, he still moved

like the immortal ruler of this island. One second, he stood stoic. The next, he charged past me and threw himself at Drake, knocking both of them to the tile.

With his hands tied, he used both in a single strike. A heavy club of knuckles crunching right into Drake's cheekbone. "I'll fucking kill you before you touch—"

"Get off him!" Three of the guards bolted to the grappling brothers, jerking Sully off Drake and kicking his legs out from beneath him to slam him to his knees. Sully howled as blood bloomed through his bandage on his thigh. Three guns wedged against his skull as he kneeled, panting and snarling, a true wolf hidden within a human skin.

The fourth guard continued trapping Jealousy and me, his attention on the chaos, but his weapon sweeping between us.

Drake cursed and shoved himself to his feet, touching his swollen cheek and smearing the streak of blood from his perforated skin. "That's the last time you touch me, cocksucker."

Sully seethed on the floor, his chest drenched in sweat from pain and adrenaline. "The last time I touch you is when I take your godforsaken life."

Grabbing a handful of Sully's roguish hair and yanking his head back, Drake spat directly into his face. "I'm tired of your bullshit, Sullivan. I'm tired of being *nice* to you. You just ensured I'm not just gonna fuck your girl tonight, but I'm also gonna kill her all while she rides my dick. And the best part? She'll be so fucking high on whatever you've created in your special little labs that she won't even care. She won't remember you. She won't miss you. She'll thank me for giving her the best fuck of her miserable little life."

Sully punched Drake square in his guts.

Two guards punched him in return.

"Stop!" I dashed forward, earning a gun to my temple. "Stop it. Just...leave him be and I'll—"

"Hear that, Sullivan? Your whore is begging for your life. She's fighting your battles for you because you're a worthless piece of shit and always have been."

Turning his back on Sully, Drake commanded, "Bring her here. *Now!*"

The guard dragged me away from Jealousy and across the sandstone tiles, dumping me in front of Drake as the three men ringing Sully kept their guns digging into his nape, making him bow forward, his bound hands between his spread legs, blood oozing through his bandage, and his eyes sparking red and blue fire.

He'd never been so inhuman, so consumed with nefarious wrath.

I trembled as Drake grabbed the rope around my wrists and untied me. "Do you like watching him be hurt, pretty Jinx?"

Gritting my teeth, I swallowed back the temptation to return the favour of spitting in his face. "What do you think?"

"I think you're a temptress and a fighter. I think you're not above using your body to get what you want. I think you'll do whatever it takes to save him…even if it means sacrificing yourself."

I balled my hands. "You know nothing about me."

"Oh, no?" Arching his chin at the guards ringing Sully, he barked, "Shoot him in the foot."

Spinning around, I ran as fast as I could. I leaped through the sky and landed on Sully's lap. He grunted as I hurt his stitched leg. He shuddered as I shouted with every passion and pain in my lungs. "*Don't!*" I glowered at the men with guns. I straddled Sully and stared them down. "Don't you dare!"

Drake's applause filled my ears, his laughter sent sickness washing through me. "Thanks for proving my point, Jinx." Snapping his fingers again, he barked, "Bring her back here. Don't shoot my brother."

It was the worst pain imaginable being torn from Sully's body. Removed from his heat, his power, his love. Our eyes locked, even as I was dragged away and shoved back into my position in front of Drake.

Sully hadn't spoken a word, almost as if he couldn't remember how to articulate, too consumed with the feral savagery of ripping out his brother's throat. His nostrils flared with every breath. He never surrendered even as the three guards once again dug their guns into the back of his head, making him fold over his knees.

Jealousy padded toward me and Drake, the only one of us with some margin of freedom. She stopped beside me, staring at Drake with a coldness I'd never seen on her. A familiar hate that said she'd known men like Drake before. That she'd endured her own torment and come out the other side intact.

Her voice snipped with disgust. "I'm tired. I'm hungry. I'm not feeling very well, and I'm sure I speak on behalf of both my master and my friend that no one wants any more bloodshed."

"Jealousy…" Sully growled. "Shut up."

She didn't look at him, keeping her stare pinned on Drake. "Sullivan won't be cooperative, no matter how many guns you point at him. He only cares about Eleanor, so unless you've figured out how to work Euphoria on your own, you need someone else to help you."

"*Jess!*" Sully bellowed.

*Oh, God, what is she doing?*

Drake smirked. "And I suppose you know how his virtual reality works?"

Jealousy flicked me a look, hiding her loyalty or her deception, I didn't know. "I do. Sullivan regularly trusted me to load a guest's program and insert a goddess into his VR."

My heart hammered as I whispered, "Jealousy, please…"

"I'll show you. I'll load you safely into any program already cyphered by Sullivan…if you promise to leave Jinx alive once you've had her."

Sully stayed silent, his anger pulsing behind me.

Drake snickered. "And why would you do that? You're in love with her too?"

"She's my friend. I don't want her to die just because you have a feud with your brother."

"Jealousy…*Jess.*" I reached with my unbound hands, touching hers. "He'll kill all of us, or make us wish he had. Don't bargain with him—"

"Done," Drake snapped. Reaching for Jealousy's rope, he released her and smirked. "Show me."

Jealousy swallowed hard and padded toward the cupboards hiding the trolleys stocked with sensors and reality distorters. Sully groaned under his breath as she wheeled one toward me and flicked me an unreadable look.

*What the* hell *is she doing?*

"Jinx…" Her voice cracked, but she arched her chin and cleared her throat. "Can you remove your dress…please?"

Sully snarled, "For fuck's sake—"

"*Quiet*, unless you want another hole in your leg," Drake yelled. He waved his hand at Jealousy. "Continue. I like where this is going."

I shuddered as Jealousy moved toward me, resting her hands on my shoulders and plucking at the straps of my dress. Her lips touched my ear; her whisper slipped into my being. "Please…just trust me."

Whipping back, I narrowed my eyes. I needed to know what she had planned. What was her end goal? What did she think this would achieve other than Sully's last life force on the floor?

Her hazel gaze held no secrets or sins as she stared at me with imploring need, risking herself so I would risk accepting her help.

Slowly, I nodded and gathered the hem of my dress. Without a word, I pulled it over my head. I had nothing on underneath. I'd left Sully's shores in this dress. And I'd returned within it. Now, I stood naked in front of too many men and a woman I didn't entirely have faith in.

Drake sucked in a breath. All the men did.

Sully growled, and my nipples pebbled with nervousness.

Jealousy didn't pause. Grabbing the earbud box, she quickly adorned me with the hearing deceptors. Her hands quick and feminine compared to Sully's possessive paws.

I bit my lip as she ran the scent stick under my nose, stuck fingerprint pads into place and struggled to be as gentle as she could placing lenses into my eyes.

Sully made a noise as I bent my head back, permitting her to obscure my vision and prepare my sight to see a different world than this one. At least these lenses weren't tampered with. At least I still saw, if through an unwanted film.

Drake crossed his arms as he studied everything Jealousy did. A student learning a topic he wanted to excel at so he could steal every original idea and copyrighted magic from his brother.

I stiffened as Jealousy tipped oil into her palms and caught my gaze. With our eyes locked, she rubbed the silky liquid into my chest, over my breasts, along the planes of my stomach and then ducked to rub over my hips, thighs, and legs.

I couldn't help it.

I glanced over at Sully, jolting on the spot as I caught his hungry stare.

Even with disaster surrounding us and monsters threatening to ruin us, he still cherished me. He still thirsted for me, wanted me, and couldn't prevent his body's obsession with mine. He bit his bottom lip, his stare touching me in intimate places, his presence preparing me for sex even though it wouldn't be with him.

*I hate this!*

I hated that I had no way to stop this. I hated that a woman stroked my skin and not him. I hated that, unlike the other times I'd been inserted into a fantasy…this time, it wouldn't be Sully. It wouldn't be the man I loved hiding behind a mask and lies.

I couldn't look anymore.

Dropping my stare, I balled my hands as Jealousy finished coating my back in oil, then dropped the empty bottle on the trolley and wiped her hands with a cloth. "She's ready."

"Not quite." Drake smiled a wolfish, rabies-infected grin. "My turn."

Jealousy huffed but obediently opened fresh boxes of supplies.

"Not you," Drake sniffed. "Her." Taking my hands, he placed my palms against this chest.

I shivered with revulsion.

"Undress me, Goddess Jinx."

"Christ, *stop!*" Sully fought the three guards blocking him in a blast of power and fury.

For a second, he won. He stood and shoved two men to the ground.

But his victory was short-lived, paying for his outburst with heavy punches to his head and kicks to his already injured body. Falling back to his knees, he groaned as Drake pinned his nasty stare on me. "Undress me, or I shoot him."

Jealousy murmured, "I'll do it—"

"No, *she* will." Drake let my hands go, cocking his head to see what I'd do.

Jealousy's hiss mimicked the one snaking around my chest— sick frustration that men could dictate our existence. Inhaling hard, I kept my chin high even though my heart was one giant mess of gristle and grief.

"Don't be a martyr, Eleanor," Drake murmured. "Don't think you can cause mischief and stop this. Do as I say, and everyone stays alive tonight." Planting his hands on my naked waist, he smiled. "You'll prefer me, I guarantee it."

"Doubt it. I find you repulsive."

His eye twitched beneath the perfectionism of Botox. "You'll change your mind. Now, undress me. Otherwise, Sully can have a few fingers removed. For every delay you cause, he'll lose an appendage. I need him alive...not intact."

Everything he said aimed to break me. Every part of him thought he could crush me into his control.

*No.*

*Just no.*

I didn't just find him repulsive, I found him lacking in every way.

*He's nothing.*

*Just like those traffickers.*

*Just like Scott.*

*Nothing.*

*And he's standing in the way of everything.*

I didn't beg.

I didn't cry.

I didn't run.

*Sully…*

I ripped off Drake's t-shirt like he was a naughty toddler and I was his mother about to spank him.

Drake grinned like a bastard as I yanked at his belt and unzipped his jeans. "Like what you see, Sullivan? Her hands are fucking Viagra."

Sully jerked and fought so hard, another guard found himself on his ass with a punch to his nose. The other two men leaped on Sully, once again beating him, striking him—

"Stop it!" I yelled.

The men stopped, leaving Sully breathing hard on his knees with his hands bound and blood soaking brighter through his bandage. "I'm fine, Sully." I pulled down Drake's trousers and boxer shorts with no emotion whatsoever. "He has the smallest cock I've ever seen."

Sully groaned.

Drake slapped me.

I spun to the side with his violence, wincing against his finger thorns and poisonous palm.

"You'll regret that," he hissed, kicking off his boots and stepping out of his jeans. He didn't care four guards and his brother saw him naked. He didn't care those same guards drooled as they looked at me, bulges in their pants disgustingly obvious.

What was his plan here?

Did he honestly think he could insert himself into Euphoria and the guards wouldn't try to join in? That they would stand by like good little soldiers all while he fucked me?

My skin went snowy cold.

If he gave me elixir, I'd be a temptation too hard to ignore.

I wouldn't care who joined.

Was that why Jealousy had been included?

To be the distraction while their boss got his kink on?

Drake grabbed my hair, dragging me closer and shaking me.

"Sensors, Jinx. I'm sick of waiting."

Every second I could prolong this gave more time for help to arrive.

Had the boat captain called the police? Had my dad done what I'd asked?

"Fuck it." Drake grabbed the earbuds and stuffed them into his ears, followed by a quick slash of nasal scrambler under his nose. Fumbling with the lenses, he awkwardly plopped one over his right pupil and then his left. Squinting against the discomfort, he shoved a bottle of oil into my hands. "Do it."

Jealousy glanced at me, her chest heaving in her black bikini. She seemed wound up, like a music box cranked too tight, the fragile ballerina about to dance into suicide.

Why did she look so tense?

What scenario ran through her mind while mine continued to fumble for a solution?

She nodded at me once, her eyes flaring with encouragement.

Ignoring the laceration in my heart, my stare found its way back to Sully. He'd been forced to bend deeper from three guns wedged against the back of his skull.

*Dammit!*

I wanted to drown Drake in the cursed oil. I wanted to pour it over his head and then set him alight.

"Fuck, you're disobedient." Snatching the bottle, Drake poured the entire contents into my hands then slapped my touch on his naked chest, forcing me to rub it in.

I recoiled.

Sully growled.

And Drake commanded the guard trapping Jealousy and me, "Grab the vials and my brother's cell phone from my pocket." He raised his eyebrow at the floor where his clothes were strewn.

The man ducked and fossicked through his pockets, coming up with a cell phone and three tiny vials of sorcery.

"Give them to her." He pointed at Jealousy.

Jealousy took the offered gifts. The second her fingers curled around elixir, a darkness fell over her. A shadow that seemed to suck her down into whatever trickery she'd planned.

"Load a program," Drake snapped.

"What do you want?" she asked quietly, carefully, her thumb flitting over the phone and bringing up the app I'd seen Sully use.

Sully's growl filled the room. "You do this, Jess, and I'll kill you myself."

She ignored him, scrolling through fantasies. "Underwater? Flying? Sacrifice? Forbidden sibling? Abusive teacher? Shared woman? S and M club?"

"That one," Drake nodded, licking his lips, his cock swelling with anticipation. "BDSM with as many toys as possible."

Jealousy swallowed hard and nodded, pressing a line of code and flinching as a *'Load'* button popped up. "It's ready."

Drake smiled like the devil. "Pass me the elixir."

"Don't you fucking dare!" Sully snarled. "Have Jealousy, the traitor. Fuck her. Take her however you want. Just leave Eleanor—"

Jealousy fisted all three vials, carefully placing one into Drake's eager palm.

She caught my gaze.

I bared my teeth.

She shrugged slightly, but instead of apology, I saw fierce determination.

Had she hated me all along?

Had this been her plan?

To become indispensable to someone who would keep her? Who would put her in the position of power she'd told me she always wanted? The gatekeeper of hallucinations and madam of trapped goddesses.

Betrayal burned through me. "How could you—"

"Time to play, Jinx." Drake grabbed me, wrapping his hand around my nape and jerking me into him. Our bare flesh slicked together with oil. His hard cock pressed against my belly.

*No!*

I squirmed and fought.

It wasn't enough.

He fed the nasty, abominable bottle past my lips.

I fought harder.

Fuck, I fought.

He tipped it upside down.

Elixir splashed onto my tongue with its nauseous takeover.

I turned wild.

I kicked and scratched, punched and struck.

"Christ!" Sully's howl filled my ears.

I tried to spit out the fragrant sugary drug.

I hit him.

I kicked him.

I almost got free.

But he was Sully's brother after all, and he did exactly what Sully had done to me at the beginning of our story.

His palm slapped over my mouth.

His fingers pinched my nose.

He suffocated me…

killed me…

destroyed me…

"Fuck this!" Sully's roar bounced off the walls. A gunshot rang. A bang ricocheted.

Greyness drowned me.

Lungs clawed me.

I had no choice.

I gagged.

I moaned.

I swallowed.

# Sullivan

# Chapter Twenty-Five

I WAS A SCIENTIST—not because I'd been born into the lineage, but because I had an obsessive need to chase the impossible. I didn't accept that a human body was at its full capacity in its current pathetic state.

I believed we were a battery—a machine working at thirty percent—and all we needed was a compound or chemical…something to trigger a new state of being. A stronger state, an *invincible* state.

Medical advances had gotten me closer to that goal.

Trials and failures had inched me closer to achieving what no one else had before.

But it was fury that shattered the threshold of evolution.

Seeing Drake touch her.

Drug her.

Rub his *cock* on her.

Yeah, it was the best narcotic, stimulant, and biological enhancement I fucking needed.

Three men were nothing.

Their weapons were nothing.

Life was fucking *nothing* if he hurt her.

My body moved of its own accord, sweeping from kneeling to standing and choreographing a war that I disassociated with.

My entire mind and whole heart were already across the room with Eleanor. I didn't feel the crunch of my knuckles as they ploughed into someone's face. I didn't hear the crack of their bones as I kicked a man's ribs and sent him sprawling to the floor.

I didn't feel their retaliation or the stitches pulling my flesh, nor the hot gush of fresh blood.

My eyes had found their target.

Drake.

*Motherfucking Drake.*

He fought Eleanor as she turned into a cyclone in his arms. She scratched and clawed, she screamed and went crazed, knowing as well as I did that she had a few short minutes to get away. A few measly minutes to run before she'd spread her legs, welcome the devil, and fuck whichever man would have her.

*No.*

A simple word. A ruthless voice in my mind.

*No!*

*She's mine.*

A bullet zinged past, missing me by a fraction.

I shoved my bound fists into a guard's neck, making him gag for air.

I fell to my knees as two men landed on my back, crushing me.

My eyesight still flickered with black clouds and grey paint. Shadows danced over clarity, leaving my other senses working at maximum. My sight had returned in spurts, teasing me with slow recovery.

But even lacking vision, I was still dangerous.

Tritec licked through my blood, granting false power, making me otherworldly in my strength.

Shoving the two guards off me, I round-housed one and sucker-punched the other. I didn't wait to see if they'd fall. I strode toward Drake holding my woman, snarls tumbling from my throat, sounding exactly like the wolf I was nicknamed for back in society.

Drake's naked cock branded her back as she struggled in his embrace.

I would kill him slowly.

*Painfully.*

I crouched and prepared to attack, but Jealousy moved, inserting something into her ears, catching my sniper attention.

Crimson fog descended over my broken vision.

*Her!*

She betrayed me.

Betrayed Eleanor.

Betrayed Cal.

*She deserves to die.*

I ran for her instead.

A mercenary grappled me to the floor.

I spun onto my back and fought him, striking his nose and snapping gristle before he could wrap his hands around my throat. He choked on blood, and I kicked him away. I shot to my feet again; no injured leg or half sight would stop me from killing Jessica Long and making her pay.

Her gaze flared wide as I stalked toward her, my trajectory once again foiled as three men tackled me. I fought them, all while my attention stayed on her. While Drake restrained my woman, and Jealousy waited for me to kill her, she gave me the saddest, sweetest smile and tore off her bikini.

Her breasts, her pussy, she stood there stark naked as I howled and punched the men restraining me. Harder, faster, crueller. I drove them all closer to death with sheer brutality.

Another bullet let loose, wedging into the floor and erupting a plume of tile dust.

Eleanor let out a tattered moan.

*She's slipping.*

*Sinking.*

*Hurry!*

I bellowed and struck with every fury inside me. Men dropped away, nursing their injuries, their commitment to pain not nearly as loyal as mine. If I lost, it would mean sacrificing everything. If they lost, they just voided a paycheque.

They couldn't win.

It was impossible.

Kicking them away, I had a clear path to murder Jealousy.

She flinched and darted toward Eleanor and Drake, inserting herself into the sexual friction of their war. She rubbed at her eyes as if something burned.

My gaze locked on Eleanor, hating the torture on her face, the need in her body, the fidelity in her stare as she saw me. "Sully...I can't—"

"You can." Words were thick and foreign in my mouth. "*Fight it.*"

Her face scrunched up as another gun fired. I ducked as a bullet grazed my shoulder blade, stinging like a wasp. Spinning around, I struck the bastard with both hands, the rope doing nothing to prevent my ferocity.

"Fuck off, Sullivan," Drake sneered, his hands grabbing Eleanor's breasts, a scene of fornication as he gyrated his hips into her ass. "She wants me...not you."

I lost it again.

Red miasma.

Black infection.

I let loose on the mercenary who stupidly tried to stop me. I beat him until his face was unrecognisable, all while my attention fixated on Jealousy as she tipped her head back and shot a vial of elixir down her throat.

My eyes narrowed, second-guessing my flickering sight.

Why?

*Why would she—*

With a heart-breaking sigh, she uncapped the third and final bottle of elixir. Bringing it to her lips, she braced herself, then upended it. Tossing the empty vial away, she rubbed provocatively against Drake's side.

"Want to join, huh?" Drake shuddered as her right hand went behind Eleanor and grabbed his cock. "Fuck..." His gaze snapped closed as his body jerked.

"Jess...what are you—*Oh, God.*" Eleanor curled into herself, stopped by Drake's hands on her breasts, sweat gleaming all over her as she continued to fight the insidious need for sex.

Jealousy swooped up on her tiptoes and planted her lips on my deplorable brother.

He groaned, his hands still clinging to Eleanor. His hips rocking, feeding his cock into Jealousy's fist, rubbing himself against both women. He went to pull away, but Jealousy wriggled closer, she pumped his erection, entrapping him within her spell. Eleanor was sandwiched as Drake returned her kiss, his hands kneading my woman's breasts, the three of them writhing in a threesome of fucked-up eroticism.

Jealousy kissed him harder, her cheeks hollowing as she fed the third vial of elixir onto his tongue.

I waited for him to spit it out.

To strike her down.

But...he swallowed.

He returned Jealousy's lust, opening his mouth, their tongues lashing with sin and spit. Jealousy moaned as her elixir reached a fever, throwing herself into it while Eleanor still battled hers.

A mercenary punched me in the jaw.

I howled and returned the favour, refusing to look away from the sinful scene before me. My heart thundered as Jealousy held up her left hand.

She still held my phone.

Still poised her thumb over the *'load'* button.

*Oh, fuck—*

I stumbled in my haste.

*Don't!*

Riding Drake's leg, giving herself entirely to the unfightable lechery, Jealousy moaned again and tapped her thumb against the screen.

I was too late.

Her spine bowed.

Drake's body jerked.

Eleanor cried out with carnal hunger.

All three of them fell.

A tumble of nakedness and need, blinded and overloaded by the Euphoria loading system.

*Eleanor!*

A mercenary pressed a gun to my head. "Quit fucking moving!"

Eleanor remained sandwiched between Jess and Drake.

No one moved.

And I didn't care anymore.

If Eleanor was loaded in that fantasy, I had seconds to remove her. A few precious seconds before my brother fucked her. No one on earth would stop me. No man. No animal.

*No one!*

I spun and struck his wrist.

He howled.

The gun smashed and skittered across the tile.

Diving for it, I turned off all my pain, snatched the weapon, found the trigger, and fired.

One, two, three, four.

Four men.

Four bullets.

For once, my aim was true.

Two lodged in their chests, one in the head, and one in the redhead's hip. He screamed and scrambled away from me as I climbed to my feet and braced over him. With no fucking mercy, I pressed the trigger point-blank into his skull.

A spritz of brain and bone soaked my pristine tile. Men had become corpses, and I was finally alone.

Tripping forward, thanks to the weakness in my harpooned leg, I crossed the distance to the paused orgy and wrapped my fists around Eleanor's ankles. Yanking her from the prone bodies of Jealousy and Drake, I pulled her until her bareness no longer touched theirs.

Jealousy twitched, her eyes flaring wide as the virtual reality kicked in and delivered her into the fantasy. Drake groaned as he blinked too. Both of them were no longer in this world, but the BDSM club that I'd coded a few years ago. A raunchy, vulgar setting where a labyrinth of playrooms, dungeons, and toys would ensure my brother's every sick wish was fulfilled.

But he wouldn't fucking fulfil them with Eleanor.

Eleanor curled around herself, her arms hugging tight, wetness glistening down her inner thigh.

*Shit, hurry!*

Snatching my cell phone, forgotten beside Jealousy, I brought up the cypher and scrolled through the individual lines of code. Each goddess had their own unique identifier, a sequence already created for ease of VR insertion and activated by the eye lenses.

My eyes darted over the text, searching for Eleanor's code, ready to delete it from the fantasy and free her.

Only...

There was no code.

Only Jealousy's existed.

I looked up, my heart skipping a beat.

*What the——?*

I thought she'd *betrayed* us. I thought she'd finally shown her true colours, just as so many people I'd trusted in my past. Instead, she'd sacrificed herself so I wouldn't have to watch Eleanor be raped by my sibling and earn a bullet in my brain when I snapped. She willingly slept with my brother, all while I knew about her feelings toward Cal.

*She took elixir...even knowing how it affects her heart.*

*Shit.*

Not only had Eleanor given me a gift of absolute devotion but Jess had too. She'd put her very life and happiness on the line.

How could I ever repay her? I owed her an insurmountable debt.

"Sully..." Eleanor's gorgeous grey eyes snapped open, smoky with lust. "I can't...I need...*God!*"

Her moan snapped me from my shock.

I owed Jealousy the biggest fucking apology.

But in that...I was also too late.

The fantasy had fully loaded. They were no longer here but there, and that was where they had to stay until the end.

I'd broken the farm boy hallucination with Eleanor when we'd removed our sensors, but only because I was the creator. I could manipulate from inside the falsity, sneak in and out through a back door.

My guests and goddesses weren't so lucky.

It wasn't safe to pull the plug now. Just like my elixir, Euphoria was far too potent. After previous attempts of cutting a session short had ended in brain damage, I'd learned that the only way out of the illusion was to fall asleep by natural means or to physically have an escape hatch programmed into the illusion.

Only two ways to break it, and this particular mirage didn't have an escape.

My brother's hips pumped air, seeking relief. Jealousy's hand went between her legs as she sought the same thing. They writhed in lewdness, clinging to each other and knotting body parts. Their mouths slammed together, their hands touching everywhere at once.

"God..." Eleanor's hand cupped her pussy, her gaze locked on Jealousy as she climbed over my brother and straddled him. Eleanor shuddered as Jealousy's gaze flared wide, seeing something Eleanor and I couldn't see while her body was stuck in a room that'd become a grave for four mercenaries. Her arousal thickened the air as she grabbed Drake's cock, angled him up, and sank down.

They groaned in unison.

They clawed and thrust.

Eleanor cried out, her skin flushed and eyes turning hazy with intoxication as her fingers dipped inside herself. She quaked and bit her lip as Jealousy screamed and shattered through her first orgasm. Drake followed a second later, his roar making Eleanor whimper and bow her head.

With utmost desolation and dirty desire, she crawled to the two having graphic sex. "I'm sorry. I can't...I—"

She couldn't fight her need anymore. *I'd* done this to her. *I'd* done this to Jealousy and every fucking goddess on my island.

*Shit!*

"Eleanor...stop."

Clutching my phone, I stood over her, my entire worthless soul hurting for what I'd made her become. Jealousy's groan throbbed in my ears. I turned hard from the sounds of wet sex and wanton abandonment. The urge to take Eleanor there and then made my balls tighten.

She was primed.

So fucking primed for me.

I needed to tend to her, to be the antidote to her suffering, but I also couldn't stay here. I needed her off this island.

*I need her safe.*

Once she was safe and I had a legion of men ready to slaughter my brother and his mercenaries, then I'd fuck her. I'd give her as many goddamn orgasms as she needed.

Tearing at the rope around my wrists, I made short work of the knot and tossed it away just as Eleanor touched Jealousy's ankle.

"Come on." Ducking, I gathered her feminine weight in my arms. She screamed as if my touch on her body was too much. Her nipples turned to diamonds. Her lust trickled quicker down her leg.

She nuzzled into me, wriggly and wanting as I tried to hold her against my chest.

Bruises and aches, stitches and sore vision—I ignored it all as I marched away from my brother and Jealousy as he flipped her onto all fours and plunged back inside her.

"No. Wait. I want—" Eleanor scratched me, tears rolling agonisingly down her cheeks. "Sully, I need to come. I need—"

"I know. Just…wait a little longer. Fight it a little longer."

"I can't!" She wailed as I paused by the exit and looked at the gun abandoned on the floor. It would be so fucking easy to shoot my brother while he no longer existed in the same universe as me.

I could blow his brains out while he played in some BDSM dungeon.

But…if I shot him, I'd kill Jealousy.

Two bodies linked through a program warping their neurons.

After what she'd done for me?

After the way Cal looked at her?

After the sacrifice she'd made for Eleanor?

I couldn't.

I would never hurt Jess again.

Hoisting Eleanor higher into my arms, I strode over the threshold of Euphoria and prepared to rescue my woman.

Only once she was safe would I come back.
I'd come back and save Jessica.
I'd give her, her freedom.
I'd place my debt at her feet.
I'd try to repair everything that I'd done wrong.

# Chapter Twenty-Six

I NEEDED, NEEDED, *NEEDED*.

I'd tried to remain sane.

I'd tried to fight the repugnant pull of elixir.

I'd done my best not to be a slut while Sully fought the guards and turned murderer.

But I wasn't strong enough.

Something was wrong.

Something was terribly, terribly wrong.

I needed to come; that was undeniable. I was beside myself with pain—that was irrefutable—but my heart…my heart couldn't figure out a healthy rhythm anymore.

The longer I denied myself—the harder I fought the ratcheting, climbing, tightening mess my body had become, the more my heart coughed and tripped.

I cried out again as Sully's touch ate into me with acid and delight. Having him so close physically branded me. He felt like fire. Cinder wrapped around me, gunpowder trickling through me.

It hurt. It hurt so, *so* much.

"Arbi, it's Sinclair. Call the fucking police." Sully tripped and limp-jogged down the sandy pathway, my body jostling in his embrace. He wedged his cell phone against his shoulder, barking commands at his third-in-charge. "Don't care. Do it. Do it now." Allowing the phone to fall from his hold, he picked up his punishing pace.

My mind flew back to Euphoria where Jealousy was given a

cure. The image of her slipping onto a cock made me moan. Envy filled me as my core clenched around nothingness.

I didn't want Drake, but I wanted what she had.

I *needed* what she had.

I needed it because I couldn't survive the compressing, contracting agony of every cell. My stomach, my chest, my core, my clit. They'd filled with toxin that I had no vaccine for, no way of curing on my own.

*Come.*

*You need to come.*

It'd gone past salacious hunger and slipped into life-threatening.

I needed to release.

To shatter the bone-cracking pressure.

*I need—*

"Eleanor. Please…fight it." Sully carried me farther from Euphoria, bats flitted around us, night insects serenaded us. No tiki torches flickered, leaving us at the mercy of the scattered solar lanterns and the Milky Way above.

My spine bowed in his arms as things turned unbearable inside me. I panted and gasped, my mouth wide for air as my heart slammed violently against my ribs.

I battled lust, but I also scrambled to stay clawing to life.

I'd never felt this way before—never had such a nightmarish blend of death and desire.

"Sully…I don't feel right."

I wanted him inside me.

I *needed* him to fuck me.

It wasn't about sex anymore.

It was about keeping me alive.

"Sully…" I squirmed in his arms, desperate to kiss him, trying to capture his lips as he clutched me close and continued half-running, half-limping down the laneway. "Please…you have to help me."

"Give me more time, Eleanor." He tripped, cursing with a vicious tongue. A tongue I needed in me, on me, tasting me, corrupting me.

I curled into a little ball as an orgasm wrapped itself tight around my core. The blood-red eyes of those nasty little demons were back, slicing my womb with savage teeth—a seething mass of yearning.

We appeared at the fork. The same fork where he'd fucked

me against a tree, on my knees, on my back. "Sully!"

I couldn't be denied much longer.

I'd been a good girl.

I'd fought against Drake as he'd kneaded my breasts. I'd ignored Jealousy as she'd rubbed against me. I'd kept my hands to myself and not self-administered a release.

*I've been good.*

*So please, please give me bad!*

Struggling to breathe, I wriggled my hand between us as Sully continued his ruthless staggering march. I fisted the iron rod between his legs, the tip slippery with pre-cum, popping out the top of his black boxer-briefs.

The stupid fingerprint sensors tried to scramble how delicious he felt. My eyes were hazy from the lenses. My skin slippery with oil I didn't need. I'd been prepared for a session to be fucked and taken…and instead, I'd only been given refusals and rejection.

Tears tracked down my cheeks.

I was pitiful.

I was pain.

I was pathetic as I rubbed him with an invitation he didn't want. "Please, Sully. I can't survive this much longer."

He stumbled, his jaw locking as he looked down into my sweat-flushed face. "Eleanor…" His forehead furrowed into thick tracks. "I need to get you safe. Stop touching me."

My smoking, malfunctioning heart faltered. "You don't want me?"

That killed me.

*Annihilated* me.

Thick torrents of desolation spilled over as I lost myself deeper to elixir.

*He doesn't want me.*

*He can't help me.*

*He's immune.*

I sobbed as my other hand went to my breast, squeezing and massaging, my fingernails digging punishingly into my nipple.

Sully groaned and kept running, jostling me in his arms, not caring about my disease or interested in granting me medicine.

I cried harder as my right hand squeezed him and my left dove between my legs.

I screamed as I thrust two fingers inside, rubbing my clit with my thumb, humping air, horny and hungry, a madwoman in his arms.

*If he won't help me…I have no choice.*

"Fuck, Eleanor!" He tripped again.

I didn't care.

If he dropped me, I could writhe on the sand. I could dig my heels into the ground and spread my legs as I—

"Oh, *yes*…" My first release, the most painful release, shot like a bullet from my heart. Its trajectory pulverised ribs, ricocheted around my core, suffocating me with wave after wave of indecent demented pleasure.

Nothing else mattered but that.

Nothing else compared.

*It's not enough.*

I'd forgotten why we were running.

Why he was broken and bloody.

*Just take me.*

*God, please,* please *take me.*

As the final clench of my release left me hanging in his arms, I sniffed back my tears with determination.

I had a man.

He might be oblivious to the hissing hunger between us, but I wasn't.

I lived within it.

I was it.

*I'll show him.*

Wrapping my fingers around his neck, I smeared my spent pleasure against his nape, and tugged at his thick dark hair. I rose in his arms and captured his earlobe with my mouth. "I need you to fuck me, Sully."

"Goddammit." He tripped again, his arms squeezing me tight. "Christ, you're destroying me. Fight it!"

*Fight it?*

Impossible.

My tongue licked his ear and down his throat.

My teeth sank into his neck.

His chest heaved with breath. His arms spasmed.

I bit him harder, licking the feverish metallic salt from his skin.

My hand dove between us, finding his cock again.

Hard.

Rock hard and straining against its entrapment.

"Stop it!" he growled, breaking into a staggering run, making me jerk. My teeth sank deeper into his neck for purchase, and my hand wriggled farther into his underwear, finding the throbbing weight of his balls.

He stumbled.

We fell.

He collapsed to his knees, barely holding onto me as my feet hit the sand and every desire and wish and need rose to unbearable levels.

"Fuck me, Sully. I need it." I scrambled from his embrace, straddling his lap and ripping at his boxers.

He grabbed my biceps as I angled his cock, attempting to spear him inside me.

"Eleanor!" He shook me, holding me upright, preventing me from sinking down. "We can't do this. We don't have the time."

I cried again, beside myself with pain.

I *needed* him.

Couldn't he see that?

Couldn't he hear my crazy, chaotic heart?

Tears came again, possessive tears, jealous tears, rejected tears. "I *need* you." I gawked at his cock. I licked my lips at the proud tip and angry veins. Something stabbed the centre of my chest as air turned to cyanide in my lungs.

*Please.*

*Can't you see...*

*I'm not well.*

*I'm dying.*

*I need you!*

I tried to kiss him.

I fixated on his mouth.

*Kiss me.*

*I'll come from a kiss.*

*Please!*

He shook me harder. "You will die if we stay here. I will die. We will all fucking die. Is that what you want?"

I tumbled into him, rubbing my head against the crook of his shoulder like a cat in heat. "I don't care. I'll die if you don't fuck me."

"You're being dramatic. You won't die."

"I will!"

"You won't!"

I tried to sink down again, snapping my teeth at his strength. "*You* did this to me. You created this."

"You're right. And that's why I've decided to destroy every

vial of that fucking elixir." Shoving me away, he stood on shaky legs and bent to grab me. "It's pure suicide."

I lay back and spread my legs. I blatantly, indecently rubbed my clit. I gave him a show, revealing everything.

I begged and pleaded and cajoled. "Please, Sully. I...I..." My teeth pinched my bottom lip as a second orgasm got lost and went to my heart instead. It tingled and prickled, feeling like a thousand stinging needles.

*Please!*

I knew I needed to come, but I...I couldn't...

*Please!*

"Goddamn you, Eleanor." Sully dropped back to his knees. With one arm around my waist, he pulled me into him. A second later, his large hand cupped me, and three fingers thrust inside me.

I screamed.

I couldn't help it.

His mouth clamped over mine, hiding my cries, silencing me with a vicious kiss. He wasn't teasing or tame; he didn't give me time to swell or enjoy the steady sinful build-up. He might not let me have him, but he fucked me with his hand, driving into me, making me bow into his control.

My mouth opened, and my belly spasmed as my second orgasm figured out where it belonged, racing to my core and splitting me in two.

His tongue plunged deep into my mouth, keeping time with his fingers, consuming me, wounding me, wringing every clench of my climax to the end.

The second I went from stiff with pleasure to lax with relief, he withdrew his fingers, pushed me away, and shoved painfully to his feet.

Bending down, he held out his hand. The same hand that'd just been inside me. Threads of desire glistened over his three fingers, thick and condemning, making me shiver with shame, then melt in carnal craving.

"Come. We need to go. Now. Before you suffer again."

My hands ran over my breasts on their own accord, gasping as I squeezed hard. "I'm already suffering."

"Fight it." He grabbed my wrist and hauled me to my feet.

Rearranging his boxer-briefs, half of his massive cock straining out the top, he broke into a limping run. I tripped and ran beside him, my breasts bouncing, my hair wild, my lust trickling thickly down my inner thigh.

The friction of the sand on my feet.

The lick of air on my skin.

The raw violence emitting off Sully.

It was a complex cocktail full of desire and demented danger.

My heart once again couldn't cope.

It skipped and pitter-pattered.

I folded in half as my core crippled me with need.

Sully never let me go, dragging me behind him like his captive. A captive who he had no intention of sleeping with even though she'd begged.

I tried to touch myself.

I tried to give in to the rapidly clawing new release, but his pace wouldn't allow me. He kept going, ignoring my whimpers and cries, his erection staying trapped and unsatisfied against his stomach.

"Sully. I can't!" I moaned as we broke onto the beach, leaving the pathway and its tunnel of jungle behind. "I can't. I'm breaking—"

"You're breaking *me*, Jinx." He scooped me into his arms again, sending me into wanton drunkenness. "Fight it harder. Give me a little more time." He struck off into a limping lurch, running for the sea.

Each jiggle.

Each smash of our skin.

It drove me *insane*.

My system was primed, my thoughts drowning in sex. I hadn't reached the second stage of elixir yet, and shame did its best to stop me from being this rabid feral beast.

I didn't want to be this unhinged creature.

I didn't want my heart constantly threatening to cease.

*Stop it!*

*Do what he says and fight!*

But his skin was too hot. His smell too rich. His cock so close with temptation.

My lips found his throat again, making him stumble. I tried to get my hand between us, to fist his erection and break him into fucking me right here beneath the black velvet of a sky that would keep our sordid secrets.

I wanted to be spread-eagled as he feasted on me. I wanted to arch my back as he thrust into me. I wanted to be used, abused, taken, devoured.

I bit him hard enough to break his skin, tasting fresh blood mixed with old. I hurt him. I hurt him even though he'd been hurt so much before. And I would continue to hurt him until he gave in, until he filled me, took me—

"I can't do this anymore!"

"You have no choice!" he snarled, leaving dry land behind with me clutched in his embrace.

Water splashed my back and ass as Sully left the shores of his invaded paradise and waded into the sea. He hissed with pain as saltwater lapped at his raw ankles, wounded leg, and every other cut and graze he'd earned in his battle with his brother.

I tried to put his welfare first.

I truly, truly did.

I attempted to be my usual rational self.

*Fight it!*

But the second I thought I had control over myself, I slipped. I fell. I didn't care that his chest still stung with soreness. I didn't care his fingertips had scabs from being pierced with nails. I didn't care that his leg had been speared with an agonising harpoon.

All I cared about was his body in mine.

He'd survived all that.

He could survive giving me what I needed.

Sully groaned as water lapped over his waist, his pain vibrating over the sea.

A flash of worry came and went.

He was bleeding.

He was heading to open waters.

Sharks.

Sharp teeth.

Death.

*Who cares?*

*You'll die if you don't come.*

I gave up trying to beg and turned vicious instead.

Thrashing out of his arms, I squirmed until he let me go as deep water cradled me.

He grabbed my wrist. "Swim with me. The sooner we're on *Lebah*, the sooner you're safe." Pushing off from the bottom, he struck into a powerful swim, keeping hold of me and dragging me beside him.

Water cascaded over my head as I sank, then broke the surface again. My hair streamed behind me, the ocean teased me, and the blistering need to orgasm made me so *unbelievably* selfish.

I climbed onto his back, twining my arms around his waist

and finding his cock.

He choked and sank.

His hands shoved mine away, his feet kicking for the surface.

He tried to push me off him.

And I did the most unforgivable thing.

I wrapped both legs around his, ruining any chance of buoyancy, sinking us like a stone.

# Sullivan

# Chapter Twenty-Seven

FUCK EVERYTHING THAT WAS fucking holy.

*She's going to kill us.*

Either on land or sea by sex or gun, she'd just signed our death warrants because how the hell was I supposed to save her when she didn't want to be saved?

Drake would be occupied for hours. Jealousy had sacrificed herself in Eleanor's place. I'd killed four of his guards, but who knew how many were left.

The fact we'd gotten this far was a goddamn miracle.

I ran on the dregs of energy.

Tritec-87 had granted me accelerated healing and strength, but not enough to fight a demented creature thirsting for sex.

Every muscle fought a battle of sickness and salvation. My body needed nutrition and stamina. My eyes needed more medicine and rest. And my peace of mind needed to get Jinx off this goddamn island before it was too late.

But no.

She had to be drugged and as high as a motherfucking kite with lust.

And it wasn't her fault.

It was mine.

I took full responsibility for this rescue disaster.

But I still cursed her inability to fight it. Still hated that she'd fed me elixir and shown me what sort of agony she drowned in. That I'd experienced the shame, the pain, the unstoppable drive for sex first-hand.

Of course, she couldn't fight it.

I hadn't been able to.

No one on this planet could win against a drug carefully designed to hijack the mental and nervous system of its host.

My lungs burned as we fought beneath the surface. She was like a fucking octopus with her hungry tentacles and eager hands. She'd hate herself for this. This wasn't her. She'd curse every heartbeat because she was the sweetest, most caring person I knew.

I forgave her delays and demands even while I cursed her.

But her actions would kill us...

And I couldn't permit that to happen.

I couldn't let her be her own worst enemy.

Her legs tangled tighter with mine as she tried to swim around me. I kicked for the surface, breaking the seal and dragging a sharp breath into my lungs just as her lips wrapped around my cock.

*Holy shit—*

She sucked.

Hard.

She willingly drowned herself by blowing me.

*Goddammit!*

Dipping beneath the surface again, I pushed her mouth away, wincing at the threat of her teeth. She gasped as I yanked her from the depths. Water poured over her head, her hair rippled with the blackness of the tide. Her grey gaze reflected starlight with a manic kind of misery.

She'd never looked more stunning or so sad.

My chest ached for her. My cock throbbed for her. I cupped her cheeks as tenderly as I could, and whispered, "Please, Eleanor. Give me an hour. Swim with me. Ignore it. The minute we get to *Lebah*, I'll fuck the ever-living elixir out of you. You have my word—"

Wrong thing to say.

She pounced on me like a water nymph.

We both plummeted beneath the surface again as her legs wrapped around my waist. She became an anchor, a snare I couldn't get free from. Her pussy rubbed enticingly against my cock, making my hips thrust instinctually.

My bad leg bellowed as I kicked toward the surface. I did my best to focus on survival while her only capacity was for sex. I grunted as she worked her way up, looping her arms over my shoulders and pressing her clit against my cock.

Christ, she was hot. Hot and bothered and miserable.

"Eleanor. Stop—" I spluttered with a mouthful of salt as she totally ignored me and clawed my shoulders with greedy hands.

"I can't stop. I'm sorry. So sorry!" She arched her hips, seeking the tip of me, trying to angle us together to copulate.

I hated that I was hard.

That even though I fought with every part of me to get her to safety, I still wanted this mad woman.

"Jinx…stop—*ah, fuck.*"

I bucked.

I groaned.

I no longer had any worries in my head as she slid me deep inside her. My belly clenched as natural needs took over. I drove upward even though I had no purchase to push against. Just water around us and a reef beneath us and sharks most likely circling me for dinner as my blood once again rang the dinner gong.

The level of insanity that she'd become made me doubt we'd ever get free. But for a blissful, brutal moment, I gave in as she locked her legs around my waist and sank down my final inches.

She shuddered with desire amplified by a million percent. Her pussy fisted me as she came just from having me inside her.

"Yes. Oh, God, *yes!*"

Her inner muscles milked me. She came over and over. Her breath caught; her torture tangled with despair as she was consumed by ecstasy.

Ecstasy that could very well be our demise.

I held her up the best I could until the end of her climax. I fought the need to chase my own, focused on getting her to safety rather than indulging in something that could get us both killed.

Pushing her away, I winced as we disengaged.

She cried out, granting the salty sea her tears, adding drop by drop. "I'm sorry, Sully. I'm *so* sorry." She dug both hands into her hair, yanking as if she could pull the elixir out by its root. "I'll—I'll fight it. I will. I'll fight—" She moaned again as a rogue wave bashed us together, sending our legs sliding together with eddies. "Ah, God."

She attacked me.

I wasn't prepared.

She dragged me below the surface again, sinking us to the bottom where predators hunted.

Her feminine lubrication smeared over my leg as she rubbed herself against me. The moisture of desire so different to the moisture of the sea.

My own release snarled in my balls, making me a traitor to our escape.

As we sank, I fought her. I attempted to lock her hands together so she couldn't touch me. I tried to keep her away with a foot planted in her belly. But she was like a siren who corrupted men. A medusa of the sea with tricks and triumphs, sinewing around me quicker than I could untangle her.

My lungs began to hurt.

My ruined, hazy eyes locked on the midnight sky far above us.

Eleanor jerked in the beginning of a suffocation death dance. Her body at the mercy of lust when all her vitals wanted was air.

She was me when I'd almost drowned in Nirvana.

*Fuck.*

She'd been the mermaid to save me. She'd brought me back to life. Damned if I'd fail her when given the same test.

Grabbing her throat, I squeezed until she clawed at my wrist rather than my cock. Keeping her locked at arm's length, I kicked for the surface as fast as I could. She jolted again, her mouth spread wide as she tried to drink seawater.

The urge to do the same crippled me. The relief as we broke into air was immediate.

I inhaled gusts of fresh oxygen and she choked up salt, coughing and crying, her hair roped in seaweed coils over her face.

Not giving her time to recover, drained of all energy and unable to face her attack again, I turned back toward the shore.

I grabbed a handful of her hair, keeping her strewn behind me as I swam with the final effort I had left.

By the time my feet hit the shallows, she'd recovered from her brush with death and moaned for life again. She crawled up the beach on all fours, her ass high, and pussy swollen to be taken. I collapsed to my knees, cursing every fucking deity that'd given me this disaster.

She'd been there for me while I'd been in the height of my musk. Despite the danger and the imminent threat on both our lives, she currently suffered a curse she couldn't wake from.

What sort of man was I to let her suffer any longer?

She'd suffered so fucking much at my hands already.

Almost as if she'd given up hope that I'd help her, she flopped onto her back and brought her knees up. Wedging her heels into the wet sand, she spread her legs and pressed her entire hand against her pussy.

Her eyes closed and spine bucked, and I couldn't fucking do it any longer.

Crawling to her with blood gushing through my bandage and every part of me screaming for cures, I swatted her hand away and dropped to press my face against her.

I feasted.

The second my mouth latched onto her pussy, she turned into the sister of Hades. A goddess who wore the souls of men as her empress gown while that damn invisible crown of hers glinted with the gruesome remains of the hearts of her victims.

She dug her nails into my hair, dragging my face deeper between her legs. She thrust up, panting, hyperventilating as I speared my tongue deep, deep inside her.

My lips spread over my teeth as I fucked her with the entire length.

She sobbed as my nose bruised her clit, and I gave up trying to catch my breath. Instead, I willingly drowned on the clean, sea-washed scent of her.

Her fingernails dug into my scalp as her fourth release slammed through her. Her legs tried to scissor together, crushing my head and making me punish her with my teeth. I bit her clit as she throbbed and shuddered, milking my tongue until my hips thrust into air, caught up in her magic, desperate to fill her.

She hadn't finished coming before I reached my limit.

Ripping my mouth from her, I leaned back, grabbed her hips, and flipped her onto her belly.

As gentle waves lapped up the shore, I plunged my entire throbbing length inside her.

She screamed.

"Quiet!" I clamped my hand over her mouth, driving her cheek into the sand, not caring that her hair became tangled with the stuff. I held her down, prone for my taking as I punished her for making me do this.

We should be halfway to sanctuary by now.

I should be getting reinforcements for Cal and Skittles, and sending an army to save Jealousy and my empire. Instead, I was fucking a demented goddess on the shores of my island that wasn't paradise but the worst illusion imaginable.

This was hell.

And I was the devil who'd corrupted this girl to the point of becoming a succubus. A succubus custom-tailored to drip me dry from sanity, health, and everything else I held valuable as a man.

I closed my burning eyes, cutting out her fuzzy form as I continued fucking her, harder and deeper, dropping all my barriers and not caring in the slightest if I took her too roughly.

There was no such thing as too hard while in the clutches of elixir.

She might not be able to walk after this…but this was what she begged for.

Her fifth release started in the caverns of her and quickly fanned out with mind-scrambling ripples. She moaned behind my hand, her eyes closed and face flushed as I drove again and again. She came on the heels of her last orgasm, sobbing as her entire body betrayed her.

I went with her.

I choked on my growl, trying to stay silent as I pumped my load into her and died with pleasure. My release was brutal and blinding, cruel in its intensity and condemning in its whispers to run.

The second I finished, I withdrew, somehow pushed to my feet, and plucked her from the mess of our ruin. Breathing hard and dripping cum, I snapped my boxer-briefs into place and dragged my broken woman into a run.

# Chapter Twenty-Eight

I WAS MOVING BEFORE I fell from my climax's clutches.

I didn't know how my legs found coordination to move but they did, hauled forward by Sully's vicious grasp.

He jerked me up the beach and down a path I hadn't explored before.

The guest area.

Villas for billionaires and princes instead of lowly purchased women.

A cough and a curse sounded behind us.

Company.

Sully froze, dragging me close and looking over his shoulder.

"Ah, fuck." His face resembled an animal on its last-ditch for freedom. "*Fuck!*" Throwing himself into a painful lurch, his bleeding bandaged leg left a trail of droplets in the sand.

I saw his blood.

I witnessed his pain.

I felt his panic.

But all I cared about was having him again.

My heart rate was berserk.

My loyalties all scrambled.

I'd tried to stop it, and I couldn't.

I'd done my best to find an antidote that didn't include sex, but there wasn't one.

I was the villain in this because Sully had tried to rescue me, and I'd been the one to drag him back. Drag him back into a nightmare where death welcomed us with open arms. If he'd attempted to swim across to *Lebah*, I would've drowned us.

And that confession prevented me from entering the uninhabited stage of elixir. I found no release in letting go. I entered no freedom for accepting my drunken needs. I merely sank deeper into misery, gasping with an irregular heartbeat, crying over my weakness to ignore synapses and systems that had become the worst kind of enemy.

Sully tripped and limped, ignoring the fact that his leg once again needed severe medical attention. A villa existed up ahead. Luxury accommodation that could perhaps protect us while I continued to destroy us.

"Come on." He broke into a haggard sprint, dragging me with him.

I fell even more in love with him.

This man.

This insanely wonderful, protective man.

He could've left me behind.

He could've turned his back on me and gone for help.

Elixir would've kept me free from whatever happened to me.

He could've claimed back his island, his fortune, his goddesses if he'd only forgotten about me.

But he hadn't.

No matter what I'd done to him.

No matter how aggressive and wild I'd been in my lust, he'd never even thought about abandoning me. He'd pulled me to shore in the middle of my haunting heat. He'd given me what I'd needed all while our freedom sifted through our fingers. And he'd threaded his life with mine, ensuring that if I died, he died.

We'd both die.

*I love him.*

*I owe him.*

If we survived this, I would marry him and promise him anything. I would sign my life into his care. I would sell him my very soul. I would vow to obey, cherish, care for, and adore him for as long as we both may live.

*If he still wants me after this.*

*I'm so sorry, Sully.*

Throwing me into the villa, he slammed the door behind us.

His chest pumped air, his muscles etched in stark relief. Even covered in wounds and blood, he was still the most staggeringly handsome man I'd ever set my eyes upon.

*Oh, no.*

My short siesta of love rapidly mutated into lust.

I didn't just love him. I needed him... *now.*

I buckled, wedging a fist in my belly.

*No.*

*Not again.*

I'd had a reprieve.

A short reprieve but one that'd lasted longer than all the rest. But...

I was slipping, sliding, falling.

I went from sane to insane, grateful to gluttony.

I backed away from him, stumbling through the airy foyer and into the lounge of a guest's villa. Similar to a goddess's accommodations, the ceiling was vaulted with thatched roof and exposed rafters. A large TV sat on a sidebar, acting as a partition to the office area overlooking the private beach. A white couch with teal cushions and a dining table with a bowl of fruit by the window all welcomed.

The bedroom waited to the right, a set of double doors announcing a grand entrance for the extra-large bed, pristine mosquito net, and large seagrass woven mat.

I wanted to see only furniture.

I forced myself to focus on material things.

But in my current predicament, I only saw places to fuck.

I could be ass up over the coffee table, bent over the couch, plastered against the window, or on all fours in the foyer.

I shuddered as every cell demanded I do something about the crawling, consuming hunger growing rapidly once again. I was in a famine. An utmost famine for orgasms and touch.

Looking up at Sully, I shook my head in shame. "I can't...I can't stop it."

"I know." He came toward me, gathering me in a tight embrace.

It was the worst thing he could do. The best thing he could do.

I tensed and tingled in his embrace.

Our connection vivid and vibrant. Our lust vicious and violent.

Seemed there was no pleasure without pain, no softness without aggression.

I wanted both.

I wanted it all.

I wanted him forever, but only if he filled me, fucked me, promised to be mine for eternity.

"Sully…" I groaned as my fingers disobeyed me and crept between us. I hunted for his cock; I struggled to open my legs for his taking.

His arms tightened, imprisoning them unforgivingly by my sides. "Just breathe, Eleanor. Breathe. Don't move. Don't make a sound."

The warning in his voice tried to slap sense into me, but I was too swept away by lunacy. I moaned again, jolting as the sound of the front door being kicked in smashed around us.

"Shit." Sully spun around, shoving me viciously behind his back.

I battled with self-preservation and the damning world of need.

I blinked as three men entered the villa, their lips tilting into smug smirks. Two dark-haired and one copper, they wore matching black cargos and t-shirts.

All three held their guns pointed directly at Sully and me.

The vulnerability of us was acute when faced with fully clad mercenaries.

I wore nothing, and Sully had retained his black boxer-briefs, sandy and drenched from the sea. His only other wardrobe was a blood-stained bandage that made him appear easy prey.

"Get the fuck out," Sully snarled.

The men laughed, eyeing us up and down. "Well, well…tried to run from Drake, did ya? Steal his fuck toy too by the looks of it." The copper-haired man stepped to the side, peering at me hidden behind Sully's back.

I bared my teeth.

I attempted to be normal.

With every fractured heartbeat, I tried to wake myself up. To accept the seriousness of this situation. To be smart! But each time I caged my sinister libido, it sank venomous fangs into my veins and amplified.

*I need—*

*You don't!*

I swayed behind Sully, losing myself, defeated and doomed.

"Is she naked?" A guard grunted, smiling sickly. "Willing to share, Sinclair?"

Sully vibrated with loathing. "My brother is in Euphoria. I suggest you go find him."

"Oh, we know where he is. We watched him fucking that wet little minx for a while." They chuckled as one. "We also shoved aside four corpses…and decided to come find the culprit."

"Leave," Sully hissed. "Drake got what he wanted. He can have everything for all I care."

"See…that's where I think you're wrong," the one with a scar on his cheek muttered. He pointed the gun over Sully's shoulder, aiming for me, making my inner muscles clench with sick sensual need. "I think he wanted *her*." He grinned. "And it looks like she wants something herself."

My knees buckled as my core clenched.

Sully held me up, his fingers biting into me.

His touch felt strict, severe…sexy.

My mind was petrified. But my body? It was impatient, thirsty, irritable.

I moaned as an indecent wave of lust lashed around my belly.

Sully struggled to hold my weight as I crumpled against his back.

I battled with the need to orgasm and the self-preservation not to show how unhinged I was.

This was dangerous.

This wasn't a fantasy or illusion.

These men were *real*.

They were real, and their guns were real, and their threat toward Sully and me was horrifyingly real.

*It's real!*

My lenses, fingerprint sensors, and oil had all washed off in the sea. I hadn't been programmed into Euphoria. I didn't have the immunity of falsehoods.

*This is real, Ellie!*

*Get it together.*

*Before it's too late!*

I bit my lip as my clit throbbed, angry that I continued to ignore its demand for more.

My heart seemed to stop with a horrifying pause before kicking back into its irregular swerving sprint.

If I gave in, I'd unleash a nightmare.

If I slid to the floor and fingered myself, they'd probably shoot Sully, then rape me.

Three men.

One of me.

I swallowed my groan as diabolical need poured indecent

gasoline on my delirious heart. Three men to pleasure me. Three men to make me come.

*No!*

*Stop it.*

*Enough!*

I grabbed my hair, bashing my forehead into Sully's shoulder blades, crying quietly.

He grunted at my torment, his violence lashing around us, on its leash for now but straining to get free. "You're right. She does want something." Sully's growl sent goosebumps over me, making it almost impossible to behave. "Just like, I'm sure…*you* want something too."

The tension in the room reached a new danger, thick with war and tight with suspicion.

My heart skipped a few fluttery beats, coughing with confusion on how to thrum.

"Gonna let us fuck her?" The taller dark-haired one raised an eyebrow.

"She's not on offer." Sully stiffened, struggling to hold me while my arms did their best to fondle my breasts.

"Too bad 'cause we're just gonna take her…with or without your permission."

"I have something better." Sully's voice was arctic, coating my skin with snowflakes, helping ward off the salacious heat I couldn't ignore.

"Better than fucking a girl who's dripping for it?" The copper-haired one lowered his gun. "Go on, I fancy a laugh. Tell us what we want more than that whore hiding behind your back."

"Money," he snapped. "Lots and lots of fucking money."

# Sullivan

# Chapter Twenty-Nine

I HAD NOTHING ELSE to play.

No way to stop what could be potentially become a mass fucking orgy.

The one saving grace was if I failed to protect Eleanor, at least elixir would keep her cushioned from her sins. She'd enjoy it. Her lust would provide a buffer between reality and myth.

She would survive being taken by them.

But me?

*Fuck.*

I would die.

I would die a million crucifixions if I had to watch one man lay a hand upon her.

Just the thought drove me mad.

Watching it?

*Yeah, I can't.*

I would sign over every penny and deliver any demand before I let that happen.

She writhed against my back, doing what I asked and fighting. I was so fucking proud of her for that—so grateful for her attempts—but I was also realistic. She couldn't keep battling. Her tenacity would fail soon, and the torment would begin anew.

For now, I kept her imprisoned behind me and worked against a rapidly ticking clock. I spread my legs for balance while my depleted system begged to sit and rest, and acted as if I wore my suit and Hawk diamonds, ready to interrogate three new guests onto my shores.

I stared past their hazel, brown, and blue eyes.

I rifled through their secrets and picked apart their transgressions.

Each one was lacking.

Each one wasn't worthy being afraid of.

They were just men. Men hired by my brother. Men who'd proven they could be bought, and luckily for me, I had untapped wealth just begging to be spent. Jinx had become the most important person in the world to me. Therefore, there was no amount I wouldn't offer.

"Name your price." I narrowed my hazy, hurting eyes. "Tell me what you want to walk away."

The tall dark one snickered. "Her. Give us her."

"She's mine, and I don't share."

Eleanor flinched behind me, a soft puff of need hitting between my shoulder blades. She still fought, but soon, she'd resort to begging. In a few minutes, she'd be on her knees again, scratching at my control, pleading with me to fill her.

These men couldn't fucking be here when that happened.

"How much?"

"Think we'll just take what we want." The copper-haired one waved his gun. "After all, you're not the one making the rules here. Your brother is, and he's paid us well. I'd rather have some pussy, thanks."

I bared my teeth, doing my best not to launch at him and leave Eleanor unchaperoned. "I'll pay you more than he ever could. I'll make you rich, then you can afford to buy plenty of pussy. This one is used. I've already fucked her. Don't you want your own?"

The filth falling from my mouth made them pause. I sensed a weakness and used it to my full advantage. "One million to walk out that door and leave. Get on a boat and never come back. You won't die. I won't come after you and extract retribution for what you've done. I give you my word that I'll forget about you. I'll even clean up your mess by killing my brother. Leave him in Euphoria, and I'll dispose of him."

"You'll *dispose* of him?" the shorter dark-haired guy snickered. "Yeah, right. Look at the mess you're in."

"I've been in worse where my brother's concerned and won."

"You're not exactly winning right now."

"I'm stubborn." I smiled savagely. "I have a knack for coming back from the dead."

The men shared a look, their guns wavering. "Why should we believe you? You could be a penniless little fucker—"

"I'm worth a thousand times more than my brother in assets. If I give you my word that I'll pay, I'll pay."

The copper-haired one wrinkled his nose. "Think we'll still help ourselves to that whore behind you. Her moans are making me hard."

I clutched Jinx tighter to my spine, my biceps bunching from holding her weight awkwardly behind me. "One million. That's generous."

"It's insulting," the taller one muttered. "A million split three ways? Fuck off and step aside. She's ours."

"How many of your men are left?" I backed up a little, keeping Eleanor's nakedness hidden behind mine, closing the gap between us and the wall.

The short dark-haired one seemed most open to my offer. His sneer had gone, calculations running through his eyes. He mulled over my question before answering, "We came as a team of ten. Why? Think you can kill all of us?"

"Already said goodbye to four." I grinned even though I wanted to trip to the floor and sleep for days. "What's another six?"

"Cocky bastard."

"Like I said, I won't kill you if you leave now."

Eleanor flinched, her body no longer just fighting against mine but seducing it. She rubbed against me. She pressed lusty kisses down my spine. She'd lost any sense of calmness, drowning beneath another wave of elixir.

"And by the way, I didn't mean a million total." I nodded like the unflappable hotelier that I was. "I meant a million. *Each.*"

A spark of interest finally arrived, followed by humour. "Expect us to believe you'll wire a million into our accounts in a week if we leave?" the tall one stepped forward, making Eleanor moan behind me.

Moan with need not fear.

*Fuck.*

"Sorry, mate, we're not idiots. We don't take IOUs. We take cash." He licked his lips as Eleanor writhed harder against me, forcing me to dig my fingernails into her arms, doing my best to keep her protected despite her undoing my control. "Hard, cold cash—"

"I have cash. In my office. Go see for yourself. The safe is hidden behind a painting of a caique parrot in the corridor. The combination is 44884."

The copper-haired one laughed coldly. "Just have a measly three million sitting around in a safe, huh? Yeah, right. We're not leaving. Not until we fuck that tasty thing behind you. We'll even be nice. We'll let you watch. And then we'll take you to Drake to finish what he started."

All three men stepped toward me.

Eleanor groaned, terror tangling with her thirst.

My muscles bunched with rage, preparing to take on three men regardless of my current condition. I might win another battle. I'd won the last one through sheer adrenaline. Tritec-87 had helped but keeping Eleanor away from my brother had been the reason for my invincibility.

This would be no different.

My heart pumped as they took another step.

Eleanor tried to get away from me, her skin flushed and sticky against mine. I wanted to snarl at her to quit it. To listen to me. To *help* me. Instead, I kept my entire attention on the pack of men slowly backing us into a corner.

"There's five million in there, not three," I hissed. "It's a bolt fund."

All three men froze. They shared a look.

"*Five?*" The copper-haired guy's eyebrows shot up. "You have five fucking million just sitting there."

"In cash and diamonds." I struggled to stay human and not crouch ready to attack. I hated that I bargained with these assholes. It felt weak, wrong. I wanted their blood on the floor and their hearts in my hands.

But...Eleanor.

*She's worth more than my idiotic pride.*

She moaned, wrenching their attention back to her.

*Goddammit, woman.*

Raising my voice over her debauchery, I growled, "You can have the lot. Every goddamn penny. Just leave."

"Sully...*please*..." Jinx's lips kissed along my shoulder, her teeth sinking into the sensitive flesh of my trapezius muscle.

My heart thundered; my own lust re-ignited. "Take the deal, gentlemen. It's the best you're going to get."

They eyed each other.

Stress poured through my veins, feeding fury and fatigue in

equal measure. I'd never been so on edge—never so hung up on a business negotiation. Never wanted anything this much. Never needed a *girl* this much.

Finally, the tall one nodded on behalf of the pack and holstered his gun. "If what you say is true, you have a deal." He pointed a finger at me. "*But* if I find out you're lying, I'm gonna fuck that goddess of yours until she's in pieces, and then, I'll personally save your cock and balls as souvenirs when your brother cuts them clean off your bullshitting corpse."

My lips thinned. My nostrils flared. I'd never permitted such disrespect, such fucking insubordination. A few months ago, if anyone had *ever* dared speak to me that way their tongue would've been shoved up their ass. Literally.

Turned out being in love had made me goddamn weak.

Swallowing back my rage, I snapped, "Go to my safe and then you'll owe me a fucking apology."

"We'll see." The guy snorted. "You two stay here. Watch them. I'll go see if he's telling the truth."

"Fine." The copper-haired one nodded. He crossed his arms, his gun dangling mockingly in his hand. "We'll just have a nice chat while we wait."

Eleanor almost slipped from my grip, her legs finally giving out. I clutched her close, my belly tense and leg pounding with pain.

*Shit, I need them all to go.*

She'd reached her limit. Her heat scoured my spine. Her lewdness and longing made my own spring fierce and greedy. I couldn't get her off this island, but I could help her escape it through an orgasm or two.

Would she cope waiting a bit longer? Would her heart remain intact?

Pika flew in through the open sliders, his glinting green feathers snapping with temper. He squawked, stealing the attention of the two men while the third rolled his eyes and headed to the door they'd broken down.

Eleanor quaked behind me, her gaze tracking Pika as he flew wildly around the room. She hissed between her teeth. I didn't know if it was in grief for Skittles or the unravelling of her self-control.

Her weight became heavier as she tried to slither to the floor.

Pika cawed and fluttered to the rafters, glaring at me with disapproving black eyes, almost as if he knew what I'd bribed and why.

If I had spare energy, I'd give him the finger—for his judgment and the fact that he hadn't stayed away like I'd hoped.

Eleanor groaned, jerking in my hold and falling backward. I spun to catch her, ignoring the two men and their guns watching our every move.

My heart fisted as her face scrunched up in agony. Her hands balled and wedged into her chest as if the elixir had formed a nucleus directly behind her ribs. Her skin gleamed with seawater and sweat, her hair tangled and ropy over her arms and shoulders.

She looked as if I'd caught her in a fishing net and dragged her from the deep. Dragged her into a world where she couldn't breathe, couldn't function, couldn't survive.

*Fuck, I'm so sorry, Jinx.*

Letting her fold to the floor, I glowered over my shoulder at the two remaining mercenaries, my eyesight flickered and faltered. "Do you give me your word that you won't interfere while you wait for your bribe?"

They snickered as Eleanor lost another element of her control, her hands splaying from fists to squeezing her breasts. "Dunno, depends how much of a show we're about to get."

"Vow you won't touch her, and I promise I won't kill you."

The copper-haired one raised his gun. "Yeah, good luck trying to kill us, mate."

"I killed four of you with my hands tied. I wouldn't fucking push me where this woman is concerned."

Looking back at Eleanor, her skin pale and washed out, her lips bright red from being bitten, her nipples peaked, and lust gleaming on her inner thigh, I pushed damp hair behind her ears and cupped her cheeks. "I'm going to keep you safe; I swear it."

Her eyes flashed open with grey lightning bolts. If her body didn't portray her need, her gaze was excruciating hunger. "*Sully...*"

Her hands landed on my wrists as I held her cheeks. Her touch was fire, her skin was fire, her very fucking soul was fire, and I threw myself into it. If she could survive what I'd done to her, then I could survive taking care of her.

With a heart-breaking groan, her hands slipped from my wrists and slid down her front. She hung her head in utmost shame, burying her face into my palms as she lost the final battle and reached to administer self-pleasure.

I caught her hand.

Not to prevent her from a release she so badly needed, but to protect her from the motherfucking bastards behind me.

"Come on." Hauling my rapidly failing frame upward, I bent and somehow found the energy to pick her up. Hoisting her higher into my arms, I glared at the two men. "Stay there." Not waiting for their reply, I strode into the master bedroom.

I tripped as my leg reminded me that stitches, glue, and nanobots couldn't repair a harpoon hole in just a few hours. That I was pushing myself to a limit I might not return from.

The bed beckoned.

The moment Eleanor noticed it, she bucked in my embrace. "Yes, oh, God. Please. I need it. I'm not feeling..." Her eyes snapped closed before flaring wide again. "It *hurts*, Sully."

Fear filled me. "Hurts? What hurts?" I almost dropped her as she spasmed again.

"*Everything.*" She stiffened as her fingers pinched her nipples and her legs scissored in my hold. "My blood, my breath, my *heart.*"

"Your heart?" I laid her gently on the bed, my voice snappish with worry. "What's wrong with your heart?"

*Please don't be like the others.*

*Please!*

Her ability at conversation broke. She writhed on the white sheets, her thighs parting wide, exposing every delectable inch of her.

My cock thickened, despite all the shit going on. She grabbed my hand, guiding it to her glistening pussy. I denied her, tugging back all while she dragged me forward.

I couldn't touch her. Not while her life still hung in the balance.

*Wait a little longer, Jinx.*

A cough sounded behind me.

Yanking my touch from Eleanor's greedy grasp, I spun around.

The two assholes hadn't obeyed me. They'd followed and stood on the threshold of the bedroom, gawking at Eleanor, seeing every indecent part of her.

She didn't care her most intimate places were on erotic display.

But I fucking did.

"Come another step closer...I dare you." My fists clenched into stones, planting myself in front of her exposure.

They crossed their arms, slouching against opposite ends of the double door entrance. The short one licked his lips. "Looking is free, and fuck, she's worth looking at."

I bared my teeth, wishing all over again that I had elongated canines that could rip out his jugular. "Come another step, and it will cost you your life."

The copper-haired one smirked. "The promise of over a million bucks will keep us right here. We won't come in, but we're not leaving either." He waved his gun, my faulty stare making it flicker. "So…give her what she wants." His head cocked, trying to see around my roadblock. "She's gagging for it. Might as well fuck her."

The short one shifted, his hand rearranging the front of his pants, clutching his disgusting hard-on.

It took every restraint not to murder them where they stood. I took a step toward them, my blood boiling, feeding yet more false power to my sadly depleted muscles.

But Eleanor cried out, a frustrated snarl tangled with a miserable whimper.

Her voice was a collar, yanking me back to her.

Dismissing the bastards without another thought, I turned to her, and my heart splattered cold and terrified on the floor.

She looked so, so white. Her usual island-glow horribly lost amongst the deathly pallor creeping over her. Even her lips were turning a nasty shade of purple, red gallantly clinging even as blue did its best to paint.

"Jinx." I snatched the spare cream-coloured blanket from the bottom of the bed. Covering her, I rubbed her arms, encouraging blood flow to heat her up. "You'll be okay—"

"I won't fucking be okay!" She tried to kick it off. "I *need*, Sully. I need. God, I *need*."

*Fucking hell!*

No more elixir.

No more fucking drugs.

I was burning every goddamn orchid and smashing every corrupting vial.

If she died because of this—if she took her last breath because of me…I'd never fucking forgive myself.

Violent guilt punched me as Eleanor shoved off the blanket and arched her spine. Her stretch accented every curve and shadow, intoxicating and inviting men to devour.

Her hand flopped to the side, imploring me to join her on the bed. "Sully. I need you inside me."

The men chuckled. "Gonna fuck her, mate? She's still begging. What sort of twat denies a woman when she begs?"

I swallowed dagger shards as I weighed up what the hell I could do.

Relieve her and run the risk of company? Don't relieve her and run the risk of her dying?

*Shit!*

"If you don't fuck her, I volunteer." The short one increased his voice. "Need a cock, pretty girl? I have one for ya." He grabbed his crotch with a sickening grin.

Eleanor's grey eyes flashed to him.

I froze, hoping to hell I wouldn't see an invitation there. That she wasn't so far gone to offer herself to him right in front of my miserable face. That she'd screw a goddamn stranger because of her elevated lust.

If she did…that was a punishment I deserved.

If she welcomed him to take her…that was my penance.

I'd made her become this wild.

She was this creature because of me.

And the reality of the situation smashed through the rest of my fucked-up morals, forcing me to admit that I couldn't *do* this anymore.

I couldn't be this asshole who played with other's lives.

*All* lives mattered.

Not just animals.

Human too.

And I'd been exploiting them.

I'd abused them for my own gains.

I'd killed without a second thought.

I'd farmed out their bodies because I didn't give a shit.

But watching Eleanor slowly fade before my eyes—to witness her vitality snuffed out by a drug that I'd created…*fuck, I can't.*

How could I ever feed a woman elixir again?

How could I accept money from men who were exactly like me with their empty hollow hearts?

Jinx had made me human.

Eleanor had made me care.

And just like that…my entire fucking empire was over.

If I managed to kill Drake tonight, I couldn't continue preying on any soul—four-legged or two.

Eleanor groaned as a full-body clench made her stiffen on the bed. The short mercenary left the threshold, daring to step toward her, transfixed by her parted lips and sinuous, sensual thirst.

I prepared to kill again. To steal his life for daring to steal the only thing that made sense to me.

Eleanor locked eyes with him. Her need flared, her eyelashes fluttered, and her gorgeous face softened in hello.

*No.*

My knees buckled.

Bile washed up my gullet.

The man grinned, and took another fucking step.

I didn't know if I wanted to goddamn cry or kill every last male on the planet.

But then…Eleanor mewled and tossed her head on the sheets, spreading knotted hair, her tongue licking her bottom lip, her gaze struggling to find mine. "Sully." Tears glossed the grey, spilling quicksilver down her cheeks. "Please, Sully. It has to be you. No one else. *You.*"

*Jesus Christ.*

She'd just given me redemption I didn't deserve. Her fidelity, even in the height of her heat, dismissed every other vow we'd uttered this far. She'd not only taught me how to trust, but in one sentence had evolved our connection from fledgling to forever.

Even out of her ever-loving mind, she refused another male.

She remained loyal and true to *me.*

*Me.*

My own greed spilled out of control. I was weak and sick, but seeing her so pure and potent undid me.

Snatching her wrist, I hauled her to the edge of the bed and kissed her.

I kissed her in thanks and worship, in punishment and promise.

She moaned so loudly, the men watching us groaned too. Sex exploded in the room, drowning us, making everyone fucking drunk. It would be so easy to pull her onto my lap and stick my cock inside her. So easy to take what she so desperately wanted me to have.

But our audience wouldn't stay voyeurs. I either had to kill them or get rid of them.

Tearing my mouth from Eleanor's, I bared my teeth at the men. "I suggest you chase your colleague. He's taking his sweet time…almost long enough to claim the five million for himself—"

"I didn't leave, you jackass."

All of us looked into the lounge where the tall mercenary stood, holding a duffel. It ought to be too heavy to carry with that amount of transportable value, but I hadn't just stuffed cash in there. There were envelopes of priceless diamonds, bought and stored from Jethro Hawk…waiting for a time when I needed to vanish. Fast.

There'd been a few instances when I'd reached for my emergency stash. A few court cases when I honestly didn't know if I'd get away with the convictions. But each time, I'd slipped conveniently through the criminal justice system thanks to philanthropy, hefty donations, and well-placed bribes on those I had dirt on.

Thanks to my Goddess Isles, I'd gathered more and more ammunition as I'd welcomed high-powered men to my shores.

Eleanor cried out with furious frustration, kicking off the rest of the blanket, leaving her ripe body on full display. Her eyes glazed with lunacy and her body swelled with a lust that'd transcended all control or care. She'd lost herself, not caring she was the only female in a villa of men.

My chest heaved as I growled at the three bastards, "I've kept my side of the bargain. Now, keep yours." I pointed at the door. "Time to go."

The tall one opened the duffel, letting his colleagues peer inside. Crisp bundles of hundred-dollar bills and velvet pouches of diamonds. A treasure trove of expensive loot.

They nodded and backed away, wincing from their engorged cocks.

I had no doubt they'd be masturbating on my beach before they left my island. But at least the sand would be smeared with their cum and not my goddamn woman.

I held my breath, waiting for them to leave.

Eleanor chose that unfortunate moment to lose herself further. To beg. Her hips soared into the sky, her fingers found her pussy, and her cry sent needles prickling all over my skin.

"Please." Her hips worked, thrusting into her hand, tears rolling down her cheeks. "*Please!*"

*Shit.*

The men froze.

All three switched from mercenary to monster. The duffel slapped against the floor as the taller one moved between his colleagues, gawking at Eleanor's stunning svelte body as she writhed.

I groaned as two fingers sank inside her while her other hand strayed to her lips. She fingered herself and bit on her hand as if she needed both holes to be filled, immediately, *now*.

She flinched, a gasp tumbling from her mouth. Her breath caught as if she couldn't suck in a proper breath. She choked.

Despite my desire to get rid of our audience, I rushed to her, catching her before she rolled to the side. Her body cooked in my arms, her pulse crazily out of control.

"Breathe, Jinx. Just…calm down."

*Don't let it kill you.*

*I fucking forbid it!*

Eleanor shuddered, her eyes fluttering and lips wide for breath. Before she'd even satisfied the urge for air, her hands once again crawled down her belly. "I need…I need…" Her beg had a different quality to it. Past desperate and into fearful. Her lust now blended with terror.

She'd been fed a liquid that dilated blood vessels and amplified adrenaline and dopamine.

She needed to come.

Yet I'd forbidden her from seeking relief, pushing her deeper into pain.

*No more.*

I couldn't cause her another ounce of agony.

I would wring that damn elixir from her system before it killed her.

I would give her whatever she damn well craved.

Scooping her into my arms, I snarled at the men. "You've got your payment. *Leave*."

Eleanor slinked in my embrace, twisting with inertia, tripping me until I sat heavily on the bed. The second I sat, she hooked her thigh over my lap and rubbed her drenched pussy against my boxer-clad cock. "Sully…"

Digging my fingers into her biceps, I held her hovering over me. My own heart turned sick with tremors. I caught the gaze of the tall mercenary, my possessiveness inching closer to wretched begging. "Take the cash and *go!*"

He shook his head. "I've changed my mind."

"My gift is non-negotiable."

He licked his lips. "We won't touch or interfere. We won't hurt you or her. But we aren't leaving." He looked at the two men on either side of him, his shoulders bracing with mutual conviction. "We've accepted your deal. She's safe from us, and we will get off your island without further bloodshed. However, we're not leaving until after the show."

My pulse boiled. "There *is* no fucking show."

"There's about to be." He crossed his arms, arching his chin at the velvet chairs by the small dining table. "We'll sit down. We'll stay out of your way and leave the moment you're done. But we're gonna stay and watch you fuck her as well as take your money."

The copper-haired cunt marched to the chairs, dragging two across the floor. The shorter one followed suit, parking his seat over the threshold of the bedroom just as Eleanor slipped her hand into my boxers.

I grunted, my belly clenching.

It fucked me off that I was hard.

This island had turned into a torture chamber and a mortuary, so sex should be at the very bottom of my priorities.

But not for Eleanor.

And not for me because I loved her, craved her, *owned* her. *Owe her.*

The men eyed up her beauty as they sat down. I clutched her harder, furious that they looked at what was mine. But...in some recess of my mind, some hidden feral part of me, the thought of fucking her in front of them turned me on.

To be the only one with permission.

To be the chosen one allowed to touch a queen.

Fuck yes, it turned me on, and it shouldn't.

I was sick.

But I was hers, and this was what she needed.

My own injuries and illnesses didn't fucking matter. Tritec-87 would have to deliver more strength, so I could save the only person who made sense to my murky, miserable world.

Whatever she asked of me, I would deliver.

I gritted my teeth as she fisted me, her breathing hitched and hurried, her heart pounding with irregular rhythm. I loathed the flutter and strange kick in her chest. I hated knowing I was the reason her system suffered.

I'd delayed for too long. I'd driven her closer and closer to an irreversible end.

Eleanor's lips landed on my throat as I released my hold on her biceps. The second I let her go, her hands scratched at my boxers, shoving them down.

Pointing a finger at the mercenaries, I snarled, "You come anywhere near us, and you motherfucking die."

"Deal." The tall one grinned, keeping my stare as he unbuckled his trousers and unzipped. The other two men followed suit, reclining enough to dig into their pants and fist their disgusting hard-ons.

Eleanor rubbed her face against my neck, her ass in the air and her whimpers in my ear.

Three men pulled out their cocks.

She fisted my erection.

She positioned herself above me.

I groaned.

She cried.

Men masturbated in unison.

And Eleanor impaled herself upon me.

# Chapter Thirty

HE STRETCHED ME IN all the right places.

His cock was made to fill me. His body tailored perfectly for mine.

The moment I claimed his every inch, he wrapped both hands around my nape, dove his fingers into my hair and slammed his mouth over mine.

He gave himself to me.

He shoved aside the worries, the weaknesses, the wrongness, and gave me everything I asked for.

Three pairs of eyes locked onto us.

Exposure and fear scratched my flesh.

Tears cascaded down my cheeks as I rocked in his lap. He flinched as I put too much weight on his sore leg but he didn't push me away, didn't stop me, didn't deny me.

The orgasm that'd tormented me with canes and floggers, the release that'd become so tangled with my heartbeats that I honestly didn't know if I'd die or come, no longer knew how to spindle.

I felt *strange*.

Sick.

Quivery and breathless and horribly aware that something had broken inside me. Elixir played havoc with the electrical pulses of my heart, revealing how fragile such a system was. It played piano with my veins and hammered drums on my muscles, making me weak and wobbly but also singularly obsessed with *lust*.

My denied orgasms mutated into something that transcended my out-of-control libido and systematically murdered the rest of my neurons.

My spine rolled as a full-body clench made me cry.

Sully kissed me harder, his tongue slashing into my mouth, his grip possessive and protective.

The rest of the world fell away.

There was just him.

Him and me.

And pain.

*God, make it stop.*

*Please, please make it stop!*

He thrust up, hitting the entry of my womb, bruising me in delicious, damning ways. My hips rocked, and we clung to each other. He permitted me to stay on his lap, taking from him all while an audience kept my shame levels astronomically high.

I burned with blushes.

I shivered with scandal.

I didn't want others to witness my unravelling. I only wanted Sully and my freedom from this sucking, siphoning death.

*I need relief.*

Bone-aching, scream-inducing deliverance, but the more I rocked, and the deeper Sully penetrated, the more profound my pain.

A peculiar, piercing pain that whizzed in my arteries and played havoc with my ability to stay alive.

*Stop.*

*Please, stop.*

I let more tears rain…my only avenue for release seeing as my body no longer knew how to spill with desire. I cried harder, my hips seeking an explosion. My breasts stung for touch; my core clenched with a never-ending contortion to come.

I gasped, once again forgetting how to breathe.

I was falling…gagging…dying.

My heart flailed in desperation and dementia.

But then, arms lifted me.

We were no longer joined but separated.

A kiss kept me distracted.

The bed cushioned my back as the only male I wanted climbed on top of me. Lips covered mine, weight warmed mine, and the thick consummation of Sully's affection for me slid hungrily between my legs.

He gave me every inch, driving into me, fierce and controlling all the while he kissed me, feeding the salt of my sadness back onto my tongue.

I gave in.

I stopped fighting to stay alive.

This man would help me.

He'd teach my body how to explode again.

He'd save me from the annihilation of my pulse and the ever-quickening blackness of nothing.

He thrust up hard.

I bit the tongue in my mouth.

I tasted the monster I'd always need and love.

His groan echoed through my ears, soaking into my belly as he kissed me harder, harder.

My nails scored his back as he rutted into me.

Every cell rejoiced.

Every atom did cartwheels and then turned crimson with dripping need.

I wrapped my arms around the head of the man kissing me.

Not just a man.

My *forever.*

We kissed and tongued; we smashed teeth and clawed.

His hands dug into the mattress by my head as his hips spread my legs wider. His thick cock did its best to teach my pussy how to orgasm again.

He let out a tattered groan as I bit his bottom lip, stiffening in his arms as my heart refused to permit a release. My pulse was sky high; my ability to see clearly and comprehend had fallen into impossible.

Everything was bad and broken…but not Sully.

I'd never felt anything so good, so perfect, so right.

I surrendered to him. I tore my lips from his and cloaked his wounded face with a million kisses. I was so grateful. So fucking grateful that he tried to help.

*It's too late.*

*Too late.*

My hips picked up a punishing tempo as I rocked with him, demanding a vicious, vile kind of coupling.

He groaned again, pouring fire on the inferno inside me. Trapped and tangled, the flames had nowhere to go. They incinerated my veins and charred my heart.

"Eleanor, please…breathe." His voice fed into my mouth.

His large hand cupped my breast, his fingertips pressing into my helter-skelter heart. "Please, Jinx. Come. Let go. Let me help you."

He drove his hips deeper into mine.

A flutter of a release feathered around my core, afraid to manifest after being told no for so long. It scurried back up my belly to my heart, hiding behind the rapidly failing organ.

"Sully—" I rocked and opened my mouth as a lash of agonising lust whipped up my spine. It tasted like liquorice and grave dust.

"That's it. *Come.*"

My pussy clenched around his girth. My clit throbbed and the tingling warning of an orgasm began. It tiptoed up my calves and trickled up my thighs. Buried beneath the excruciating pressure and tightness in every pore, it wasn't a relief, just more agonising temptation.

I no longer knew how to come.

I didn't know how to trigger the snarling, snapping savagery in my blood.

Sully sensed my struggles, rutting into me at a pace almost guaranteed to make me break apart. Short quick stabs, bitter and cruel.

My breasts bounced.

A climax once again whispered into being.

*Yes.*

*Please.*

*Yes!*

I gasped for air.

I suffocated on silence.

My fingers curled and toes spasmed.

But it didn't erupt.

It just sat there, growing fiercer and stronger, agony on top of razor-sharp agony, increasing my heart rate, sending me hurtling toward a wall I wouldn't survive. "Please! Fuck, *please!*" I scratched his back and bit his throat. I writhed beneath him and fought for reprieve. Some reprieve. *Any reprieve!*

Sully grunted as I started to sob.

I was so twisted and turned.

So knotted and knitted in one chaotic ball of skipping beats, pounding pulse, and an orgasm that'd been custom-designed to stop my heart entirely.

"I'm...I don't feel...I can't breathe..." I opened my mouth wide, desperate for air, my lungs only inflating with teasing taints of oxygen.

It wasn't my lungs failing, it was my heart.

It forgot how to beat.

It suffocated beneath the will to come that consumed my every existence yet refused to detonate.

Elixir had become my worst enemy.

A complex cocktail that'd poisoned me better than any virus or violence.

I contorted in Sully's embrace.

I bucked and swarmed with nightmares.

"Shit, Eleanor." Sully withdrew. Sitting on his knees, he scooped me from the mattress.

I dangled like an asphyxiated doll in his arms.

"Tell me what you need." He shook me.

My heart hiccupped. My eyes blurred with tears. "I don't know." I cried harder. "I can't—" My spine snapped backward as my body no longer belonged to me.

"Fuck, mate, you better do something," a stranger muttered. "Is this what happens to all the girls with elixir?"

Sully didn't answer him. "Come here." Snatching me from the bed, he spread my legs over his lap again. Brushing aside my sweat-sticky hair, he grabbed his cock and angled me until he fed his length inside me.

The moment he filled me, his hand went to my clit, rubbing me fast and quick, his rush to grant me a cure only making me worse.

I screamed as the pain became unimaginable.

I tried to get away, but I had no strength in my arms.

My head throbbed. My ears rang. He kept pushing me up and up an unclimbable cliff, too high, no air, too far, no breath.

"Don't do this to me, Jinx. Please don't die on me." He drove deeper into me. "Just come. Let go. I'm sorry I made you wait. I'm sorry. I didn't know what would happen if you didn't have the freedom to climax." He drove again and again, growling and thrusting, as deranged as I was.

My legs spasmed with muscle contractions. My toes curled until shooting pains ran down my soles. My fingers hooked into claws again, disobeying my instructions to uncurl, every part of me twining with unforgivable tension.

"*Please*, Eleanor." He fell forward, sandwiching me against the bed again, pumping viciously hard into me.

I was coiled in rope and bound by bars.

My convoluted orgasm snarled and turned rogue, no longer just teasing my womb but destroying it, shredding me from the inside out but *still* refusing to break.

Sweat coated every inch of me. The mattress was wet beneath me.

"Come for me. *Come.* I demand you to come. I want to feel your every clench, Jinx. You have my cock, so fucking use it." His voice slipped down my ears, clearing a path for his commands.

I seized with need. I clung to his rich baritone. My ears rang with gratefulness. They were the only part of me not wound tight with unbearable tension. The one sense still unhindered by my reckless, rampant heart.

The demons with their rabid claws snarled, switching from torturing to a fine shimmer of pleasure.

*Finally.*

*Finally!*

I groaned, arching my head, seeking, seeking.

*More.*

*Give me more!*

Sully understood.

His nose nuzzled my tensed throat, his teeth bit down on muscles far too constricted. "Is that what you need? Dirty words."

My pussy fluttered around his invasion.

My tears stopped, just for a second, my misery interrupted by the faint promise of a release.

"Okay, Jinx." Digging both hands into the mattress, he soared up, digging his hips into mine, making us join deeper and harder than we ever had before. "Do you know how much I love you? No other girl compares—"

My orgasm revolted, turning its back on him. That was too sweet, too full of love.

I needed anger to match my anger.

Filth to cancel my filth.

I cried harder as the faint promise turned once again into agonising misery.

"Jesus Christ." His lips found my ear again, our chemistry feeding him the exact knowledge how to fix me. He knew what I needed, but he hesitated.

His gaze went to the side, dragging my attention with it.

I flinched as I locked gazes with three men. Their hands locked around turgid erections, their breath quick, and faces etched with their own release.

I was jealous.

Fucking jealous that they could come and I could not.

The taller one licked his lips, his voice travelling over the floor to me. "You need to come. Let him fuck you."

Sully snarled. "Don't talk to her."

My back bowed.

The demons inside me reacted. They preened and simpered. Those men wanted me. They *all* wanted me. They wanted what I could offer. What my body was about to die for unless Sully could help.

With my eyes on the men and Sully thrusting deep inside me, I shivered as his lips found my ear again. He let down his shields and revealed his dangerous envy. He hissed with hate and hurt, "They want to fuck you. They wish they were me, balls fucking deep inside your delicious fucking cunt. They see me driving into you and contemplate killing me just to get a taste. One taste, Jinx. That's all they want. One opportunity to stick their cocks inside you. Do you want that? Do you want me to give you to them?" His teeth bit my ear, his cock diving deeper inside me. "Too fucking bad. I will *never* give you up. Never let another man touch you because you belong to *me*. Your pussy belongs to me, and I'll fuck you however I goddamn want."

A shooting star bolted around my core.

*Oh, my God.*

*Yes!*

"They all want you, Jinx. Every man who came to my shores wanted you. It took every shred of self-control not to fuck you myself when you first arrived." His cock hit the top of me, bruising and punishing. "I hated you for that. I hated that you made me so fucking weak."

My core twisted in all the right ways, not wrong.

"You're everything I ever dreamed of, and if you think I'm going to let you die on me…yeah, you're shit out of luck. I'm keeping you, Eleanor, so you better fucking come. There is no other alternative for you. *Come.*"

The tension in my muscles climbed another plateau, vibrating with anticipation.

"Sully…" I scratched his back. The pain in my womb finally switched. It stretched like a tigress, spun like a dancer, gathered to explode in a firework.

His teeth found my ear again, biting me as he growled, "It doesn't matter that every male wants to stick his cock inside you.

No one will ever have that privilege. They can watch you being fucked. They can fantasise about you, they can dream about you, but they will never touch you because you. Are. Mine." His thrusts turned quick and sharp, driving me to that final blistering edge. The edge I'd been cruelly shoved back from again and again until my system turned its warfare directly at me.

"Come, Eleanor. Give me everything. I won't deny you again. You want me to fuck you in a crowded room, I will. You want me to fuck you tied up in front of majesties and politicians, I will. I will fuck you wherever you goddamn want because you are *mine*."

Blades of fire.

Knives of pain.

Crashing, clenching waves that crashed through the barrier and poured free.

I screamed as my entire body seized.

Again and again.

I jerked.

I rippled.

I came.

I gasped for air as it went on and on and *on*.

I died and revived.

I rode through the crest and tumbled off the strongest, most spiteful climax of my life.

And when it'd drained me dry, I opened my eyes and looked directly at the masturbating men.

The tall one's hand thrust up and down, his thumb rubbed his tip, lips spread into a sinful smile. "He's right, you know. We all want to fuck you. Especially after seeing you break apart like that."

"Stop fucking talking to her," Sully hissed.

Tearing my eyes from inconsequential men, I locked gazes with the only one who mattered. Tears fell fresh, but they were cleansing.

I was reborn. Reincarnated.

Elixir returned to what it'd been designed for.

It stopped tormenting me with tombstones and only dealt in pleasure. I shivered as lust spread through me, hot and hungry, free to release rather than remain trapped within.

"Thank you." I kissed him. "Thank you."

He studied my face, searching for a sign of my tattered heart.

It still hurt.

It still flurried in odd ways.

But it was no longer the centre of my world.

*He* was.

*And I want him.*

Desire wriggled through me as I drank in the wounds he carried and the stubbornness he wielded. He needed to rest and heal, yet he'd put my needs before his own.

I wished I could turn off the rapidly building lust again.

I wished I could be the girl I was beneath the deranged desire.

But I hadn't reached that stage yet.

I couldn't allow denial to play games with my bruised heart.

I would listen to my body, and my body wanted another orgasm.

Three men continued to work themselves while Sully stared into my eyes. A personal, private moment. A moment when we fell deeper into love all while lust swirled around us.

He nodded once, accepting my climb back up a mountain, knowing I'd need his help being pushed off. "I'm sorry, Sully."

He shook his head, his lips twitching into a half-smile. "Not as sorry as I am that I created this madness." His head bowed, and his lips found mine.

We kissed sweetly, then greedily. His cock throbbed inside me, hinting he hadn't come, his focus on me rather than himself.

Placing my hands on his chest, I pushed him gently.

He moved instantly, keenly aware of my brittle state. He watched me like a hunter the entire time I shifted onto my knees and held out my hand to him.

He took it, linking his fingers with mine as I turned around and positioned myself on all fours.

He groaned as I arched my hips.

Elixir scrambled my thoughts again, turning me into a wanton goddess with impish wicked perversions.

Three men watched as Sully rose behind me.

My body was on display.

Our sex tainted the air.

In some segmented part of my mind, I knew this wasn't an illusion. This wasn't some fantasy coded in Euphoria. These men were real. The noises coming from their rising lust and the greed fogging the room weren't a computer program.

No sense deceptors would protect me.

No secrets would shield me.

This was real.

Real men watched me being fucked.

And I didn't care. I threw myself into elixir, preparing to give in until I could be free. I embraced the sensation of voyeurism because I had no choice. I needed this. I let forth the hidden sins that whispered they enjoyed being watched—enjoyed being hungered after, all while the only man I ever wanted grabbed my hips and jerked me back into his power.

I spread my legs.

I bit my lip.

I moaned as Sully mounted me.

Men groaned.

Sully snarled.

The mercenaries feasted their gazes on every sordid, swollen part of me.

Sully speared deeper, claiming me for his own.

An orgasm appeared with brisk haste.

Digging my nails into the bed, I gave in to it.

I let it consume me, splaying my legs, arching my back.

Sully's pace increased, mean and maddening.

And I gave in to him too.

I turned submissive and pliant.

I was no longer Eleanor.

I was theirs.

I was mine.

I was elixir's.

# Sullivan

# Chapter Thirty-One

DAWN HAD BECOME DAYBREAK, and daybreak had become early morning.

Eleanor had almost died in my arms.

I'd heard the sickness in her breath, listened to the jangle of her heart.

But now…finally, she slept peacefully. Flopped on her side, her skin full of fingerprint bruises, her hair knotted and tangled.

I sighed and pinched the bridge of my nose, doing my best to stay awake and not give in to my overwhelming need to rest.

The three men had watched their fill and left when Eleanor collapsed in my arms from her tenth or twelfth orgasm. They'd wiped away their spent pleasure, zipped up their pants, grabbed the duffel, and walked out the door as if our arrangement had been perfectly acceptable—a common transaction between a scientist who'd found a way to revert women into deranged goddesses and the infidels there to steal his creation.

The ironic thing was, I'd been prepared to kill Drake yesterday to protect what I'd designed, to keep my business, my girls, and my elixir for myself.

Today, I wanted to kill Drake so he'd never make the same mistakes I had. So no other girl would have to suffer the same way Eleanor had suffered last night.

That was the final straw.

I would *never* allow her to be so close to death again.

I wouldn't survive the powerlessness of not being unable to

help her, the fear of losing her, the guilt of being the cause of it all.

With a tortured groan, I slipped out of bed and stumbled to the walk-in wardrobe. As all our guests' villas, it was fully stocked with complimentary island attire in case the client arrived with inappropriate clothing.

Pika darted in from the bedroom, his small body descending onto my bare shoulder. "Sully!"

I sighed, snagging a pair of black slacks and black polo. "You watched too, huh?"

He squeaked, his tone full of disapproval.

"I know. It wasn't what I wanted either." Carrying the clothes back to the bathroom, I opened the vanity cupboard as Pika flew from my shoulder and scratched around in the cotton buds.

Grabbing the medical kit, I unzipped the case and inspected the bandages, antiseptic gear, and painkillers.

I had enough pharmaceuticals to treat myself, but I didn't have the time.

Tossing the painkillers on the counter, I braced myself and looked up.

I dared look into the mirror and study my broken appearance.

Thanks to Eleanor, I was drained to the point of death myself. My eyes were lined, and mouth bracketed with failure. The blue of my gaze muted, and the whites of my eyes still red and raw from Drake's lenses.

My vision operated below par, outlines still fuzzy and distance still muddy.

The first few layers of skin on my chest had been sloughed off thanks to the acid in the oil, but new flesh had covered the injury, shiny and vulnerable from the serum Campbell smeared on me. My wrists and ankles had suffered after Eleanor's refusal to swim to *Lebah*, and my stitched-together leg had once again stained my bandage with rust.

And the shitty thing was? I felt so much worse than I looked.

I still had so much to do, so many fights to win, and all my body was fit for was a crematorium and century-long siesta.

I sighed.

*Fuck.*

For all my improvements in the lab, I hadn't figured out how to make a reset button. A way to remove all trauma and leave the body fit and able.

Only time could do that.

Rest and nutrition.

All things I did not have.

Drake would've finished in Euphoria by now.

Jealousy would be free from the hallucination.

I hadn't forgotten what I owed her, nor could I stop the worry that she might not have survived another dose of elixir. After witnessing first-hand what'd happened to Eleanor, the guilt to help Jessica was a ruthless ruler.

If Drake was on his own, I would happily send him to death with a knife to his throat. But if he had guards…*well, I'll deal with that later.*

Gritting my teeth, I focused on the first-aid kit. Nothing I did would fix my rapidly fading system. Tritec still existed in my blood. It'd given me enough endurance to satisfy my elixir-drunk woman.

But now…now I felt the payment it demanded.

My body was sluggish. My mind not as crisp. My pain sharper than before.

I needed this to be over so I could attempt to avoid the rapidly encroaching end on my future. Heart attack, stroke, or coma.

Was I prepared to pay those terms? Had I earned enough time and strength to keep Eleanor safe?

The answer?

No, not yet.

I still had work to do, and I had to do it *now.*

Taking a handful of painkillers, I shot them back with a glass of freshwater from the tap, then took another fistful back to the bedroom. Pika flew after me, landing on the scrunched pillow next to Eleanor. She remained on her side where she'd passed out.

Her lips were parted and red from my kisses. Her cheeks pink with sex, but the rest of her remained white from exhaustion and suffocation.

She needed to sleep.

She needed to be safe.

Once again, neither of those things were available.

Pika nibbled on her hair, twittering and chirping as if he could sing her a lullaby and choreograph her dreams. My heart hurt just as much as my leg as I ducked to my haunches.

Swallowing my grunt of pain, I put the glass on the bedside table and cupped her icy cheek. Waking her up would almost be impossible, but I had to try.

I needed her help, just for a little longer. "Eleanor…take this." Pushing the pills into her mouth, I moved until I could sit her up a little. She mumbled something and tried to slip back onto the sheets, but I poured a mouthful of water into her, holding her chin until she swallowed.

Her throat worked, slipping the tablets into her stomach.

"Good girl." I kissed her head and let her collapse to her side again.

At least her system would have fortification while she slept. Hopefully, she'd wake with her pain dulled.

She really needed nutrition too. We both did.

We needed food and water and an island where we could be utterly alone.

But just like everything else…that would have to wait.

I swayed on my feet as I drank the rest of the water and abandoned the glass. I'd never been this tired or so useless. It would be so fucking easy to lie next to her…just for ten minutes.

To close my eyes and—

*Stop it.*

I shook my head, chasing away the insidious pull of sleep. Drake.

*Deal with him, then you can sleep wherever you drop.*

Quickly pulling on the clothes and draping Eleanor in an oversized canary yellow shirt, I sucked in a breath.

Last night had been my awakening. Today was my atonement.

*Just a little longer…*

A new fever made everything ache as I bent over the bed and scooped Eleanor into my arms.

Pika squawked and, just for a second, I didn't know if I'd have the strength to pull her up.

*Fucking hell, come on!*

My back tensed. My biceps clenched.

Anger at my weakness granted enough power to haul her from the sheets and into my embrace.

I wobbled.

I tripped backward.

I grunted as fresh pain from my leg ricocheted through my system.

*Ignore it.*

Hoisting Eleanor higher, I turned and stumbled toward the exit.

Pika chirped and chased after me with a worried huff.

He flew beside me as I carried Eleanor down the sandy pathways of an island that I no longer loved. His feathers whispered encouragement; his tiny parrot friendship keeping me awake, keeping me going, keeping me alive…for now.

* * * * *

I entered Euphoria's playroom and slammed to a stop.

I hadn't encountered anyone on my journey here.

Eleanor had slept soundly in my arms, Pika had fluttered beside me, and I'd focused on putting one foot in front of the other, steadily closing the distance on the final Sinclair battle.

I didn't bother being sneaky or trying to remain hidden on my journey. Drake had made it known that I knew things he wanted and I was not to be killed.

Hurt? Yes.

Killed? No.

And in reality, I was hurt enough.

I wouldn't prove to be too much of a risk unless someone threatened Eleanor.

Groaning with exhaustion, I jostled Eleanor higher into my arms and surveyed the aftermath carnage of Drake and Jealousy's BDSM fantasy.

They lay in the middle of Euphoria's bare and barren playroom. Drake lay on his back, one leg cocked and the other straight. His stomach was concave, the bullet graze and knife stab visible thanks to his bandages falling off, his cock flaccid and well-used.

Jealousy lay away from him, curled in a tiny ball as if she could become invisible. Her nakedness was white and as terrifying as Eleanor's, decorated with bruises and handprints.

Both she and Drake were out cold.

It would be too fucking easy to stroll over, grab a sword from the prop cupboards full of cavemen furs and highland weapons, and run it straight through his heart.

What would I fucking give to have a gun stowed in this room? To have armed myself to the fucking teeth for this eventuality. Instead, I'd left the weapon concealment to my hired guards—all who'd been murdered.

A noise dragged my gaze to the left.

*Shit.*

Killing Drake wouldn't be as simple with company.

My heart chugged as three men stood from their temporary resting area nestled against the wall by the bathrooms. They'd dragged the velour chairs from the guests' waiting area and made themselves at home. The reek of cigarette smoke and evidence of

255

midnight snacks littered my pristine villa.

They moved in unison, two raising guns while one snickered and looked me up and down. "Look what the parrot dragged in." Their eyes followed Pika as he zipped around Euphoria, swooping to Drake to bite his nose.

I tensed, but Drake didn't wake up.

Pika squeaked with pride and soared into the rafters, picking a perch to watch yet more drama unfold.

Eleanor grew heavy in my arms as the three men came forward. A blond with a bulbous nose snapped, "Where the fuck have you been?"

I shrugged, marching as firmly as I could toward them. "Dealing with business."

I'd been able to buy off three of these bastards. If I had more liquid cash, I could attempt to do the same. Unfortunately, five million was all I carried, and I was shit out of luck for such an easy overthrow.

Regardless, I tried anyway. "I'll give you a million each if you leave. I'll wire you the money the moment I kill that cocksucker over there."

The bald one muttered, "I'll give you a bullet if you try to low-ball us again."

"Fine." My arms ached under Eleanor's weight. "What's your number?"

"We want what he's promised." The blond smirked. "This place."

"It's no longer operational."

"Says who?"

"Says me."

The short one of the bunch chuckled. "We'll see about that when he wakes up."

I looked over at Drake, loathing him all over again for ever touching Jealousy. I had no ownership over her apart from her paid servitude, but I liked her as a friend, and I'd seen things between her and Cal these past few weeks that hadn't been there before.

She didn't deserve to be Drake's goddess last night.

She didn't deserve anything that I'd done to her.

Guilt swamped me, and my temper rattled.

*Fuck it.*

I was done bartering.

I'd just do what I'd come here to do and be done with it.

Ignoring the mercenaries, I marched toward Drake and Jealousy.

"Oi, where the fuck do you think you're going?" The blond followed me with his gun trained on my head.

"Providing aftercare." I bared my teeth. "Not that you'd understand what that is."

"Like hell you are. You're going back in your cage. Her too." He pointed the gun at Eleanor, coming close enough to nudge her cheek with the muzzle.

I lost it.

Finding strength hidden in broken muscles, I held her tight against me with one arm and lashed out to fist around his throat with the other. I squeezed, fighting through failure until his eyes flared with worry, and he held up the gun to my temple. "Let…me…*go*." He coughed, trying to get free. "I'll shoot."

"No, you won't 'cause you need me alive." I squeezed harder as his two friends rushed to save him. "This is what's going to happen so listen closely." I pressed against his larynx with fingers unforgiving in their message even with a gun in my face. "I am going to take care of my girls. I'm taking them to Campbell—the doctor who is the only reason you're here. He's going to treat them. Alone. While I'm doing that, you can decide if you want to accept my offer of cash and leave with your life or if you're staying and serving Drake until the end. Either way, I'm done with this shit."

I pushed him away, shaking out the pressure in my hand. "Drake has been a pain in my ass for three decades. I won't lie and say I wouldn't happily kill him right now if you accepted my deal, but if you don't, I don't fucking care. I've waited a long time for our feud to be over…I can wait a little longer."

The guy scowled. "Why do you think we're gonna let you wander around as if you own the joint?"

"I *do* own the fucking joint!" I snarled. "And you mean nothing to me. You can't kill me because Drake needs what I know, and you can't kill my goddesses because if you do, I will tear you motherfucking apart. Your only choice is to stand there like good little puppets and wait until your master wakes up. Or…allow me to kill him, and you can walk away with a payday. Either way, I'm providing aftercare."

Glowering at the three of them, I continued my path until I stood over Jealousy.

She looked even worse up close.

*Shit.*

How the fuck was I supposed to take two girls to the infirmary when I could barely walk under my own weight?

Eleanor squirmed as I bent over and gently placed her next to Jealousy. With my hands free, I checked Jealousy's pulse.

It was weak and erratic, her lips tinged blue and her skin clammy.

Ripping off my shirt, I slipped it around her frail form. "It's okay, Jess. I've got you."

Her lips twitched as I stroked her cheek.

The men surrounded me, their guns by their sides and eyes wide with disbelief that they permitted me to do my own thing instead of shooing me back into a cage.

That was the thing with authority. Display it correctly, own it completely, and weaker men slipped into line.

Electricity shot over my body as Eleanor opened her eyes, activating our bond as she blinked away her fatigue. She winced and tried to sit up, shaking her head. "Sully…"

No matter where we were or what we were doing, our chemistry and connection would never fail to reach into my chest and electrocute my heart.

Her lips formed the sweetest, caring smile, then vanished as her gaze locked on Jealousy. "Oh, no." Swallowing hard, flinching in pain from her own run-in with elixir, she crawled to Jess and ran her hand over her head. She ripped her touch away, her gaze connecting with mine in panic. "She's ice cold."

I nodded. "I need to get her to Campbell."

"Let's go." With gritted teeth, Eleanor forced her body to obey. Digging fingers into the tile, she clambered to her feet, only to fall back down again.

"Don't." I reached for her.

"We need to…go." Her eyes snapped closed, her head hanging with a tiredness she couldn't shed.

*Fuck.*

Tucking her close, I held her while she tumbled into exhaustion and clawed her way back in the same heartbeat. She pushed feebly against my arms. "Let me go…we need—" She yawned, making my heart fist.

Forcing her eyes open, her attention skipped over the men guarding us and fell to Drake still snoring on the floor. Pika swooped from the ceiling and landed on her shoulder, his feathers bristling.

"I'm okay, Sully. I can…I can do this." She sucked in a huge breath and raked both hands over her face, scrubbing away sleep, clinging to comprehension. "I *have* to do this."

Once again, she stunned me fucking stupid.

How strong was she to be able to stay awake after the dance with death she'd had? How fucking brave was she to immediately shove aside her own maladies and put Jess first?

Her grey gaze met mine. "Help me stand?"

I cursed the men watching us. I'd had my fill of goddamn audiences. But I also couldn't stop worshipping this woman, in awe of this girl, in love with every inch of her. "I'll carry you to Campbell and come back for Jess."

"No, you're fading too."

"I can manage."

"You can't carry both of us."

"That's why I said I'll take you first—"

"No." Her eyes flashed silver spirit. "She needs to see him, immediately."

My temper met hers. "I agree, but I'm not leaving you here alone. Not with him." My glare fell on Drake. Fuck, I wanted to kill him.

"And I'm not letting you push yourself so hard that you die on me." Her tone fell to a harsh whisper. "What did you tell me last night? You wouldn't let me die? Well…same goes for you."

"I'm not going to die, Eleanor."

She flinched. "We don't know that. Those side-effects you mentioned—"

"Won't happen to me." I pinched my nose, squeezing back nightmares, headaches, and agony. "Look, just let me—"

"Stop arguing. You carry Jess and I'll…" She pushed against me again, one hand rubbing at the spot above her heart as if palpitations still plagued her. "I'll…walk."

My eyebrows flew up. "*Walk*? You can't walk. Not after last night."

She gritted her teeth. "I'll walk." Pushing me away, she scanned my naked chest, seeing the stress and strain I did my best to ignore. "I'll help you carry her."

"No way." I snorted. "There is no way I'd let you do that. You're weak—"

"And you're hurt." She struggled to her feet again, the canary yellow shirt fluttering around her Bambi legs. Her attention split between me and the mercenaries. Her knees wobbled, her balance screwed from a night of mania. "We're all hurt, so we'll all help each other." Padding unsteadily, tripping to one knee and somehow standing again, she ducked by Jealousy and shook her shoulder. "Jess...wake up. Just wake up for a little bit and then you can sleep, okay?"

Jealousy groaned, her eyelids flickering but unable to open. Violent shivers wracked her as I moved to the two girls and tried to trust in Eleanor's strength.

*Could* she walk?

Could I seriously ask such a strenuous task of her?

My stomach clenched with possession. I wanted to take care of her the way she deserved, not demand she drain herself more, but...I wouldn't belittle her by commanding an alternative to the one she offered.

I'd let her walk until she passed out.

Then I'd decide which one to carry first to Campbell.

At least both of them would be free of Euphoria.

Her eyes caught mine, cloudy and tired but coherent and brave. "Are you okay? Do you have the strength?"

My nostrils flared, annoyance trickling down my spine. "Don't unman me, Jinx. I have enough."

She bit her bottom lip, fears for my own well-being ghosting over her face.

I cupped her cheek, and murmured, "I'm fine. Don't worry about me."

She turned and kissed my palm, shaking her head. "You're not fine, and I'm still worried, but...we don't have a choice."

Not replying, I scooped Jealousy from the cold sandstone and tripped backward as I hoisted her weight into my arms.

Holy shit, *did* I have enough strength? I honestly didn't know.

Getting a better grip, I struggled to suck up power and continue.

Jealousy's skin didn't make mine tingle like Eleanor's did. Her presence wasn't a curse or a blessing. She was just a girl who I would no longer rent out or misuse. A friend.

Eleanor stumbled and swayed, remaining on two feet but struggling.

I didn't know how long she'd last, so I strode ahead, rushing into another rescue mission that I hoped wouldn't be doomed to fail like the last one.

Drake mumbled something in his sleep as I passed him.

I kicked him hard for good measure.

"Hey!" the blond mercenary muttered. "He'll get you back for that."

"Or he won't remember because he'll be dead." I marched past them, one goddess by my side and one in my arms. "Think about my offer. I'll be back soon."

Eleanor eyed them up, jumpy and weak as if she couldn't believe they just let us walk away.

Cutting over the threshold and down the deck steps, I groaned as soft sand cushioned my bare feet. Warm sunshine broke through the gloomy morning, doing its best to paint my island in hope instead of despair.

Jealousy didn't move as I carried her farther down the pathway. I kept a strict eye on Eleanor as she parried and swerved, stopping occasionally to rest against a palm tree.

My baser instincts to protect her cursed my lack of power. I wanted to carry her too. I wanted her to give into the sleep clawing at her mind. But I gritted my teeth and kept an unforgiving pace, allowing her to trail behind, even though it killed me.

Pika kept flight with us, swooping ahead to perch on flowers before circling with chirps and urging us to keep going.

Every step whispered with warning that I was creeping closer and closer to the burnout I'd feared was coming for me. The mental and physical brick wall that didn't take kindly to me running face-first into it.

I felt it.

Its presence was unlike typical exhaustion.

It reached into my bones and bled my marrow dry.

*Just a little longer…*

*One step.*

*Now the other.*

My eyelids drooped, and my biceps threatened to drop Jess. I stopped for Eleanor to catch up.

Pika squeaked as she pulled up beside me, her face sweaty and hair a riot of knots. I'd loved her when she'd worn a gown of gemstones. I'd loved her when she'd been in a cave cuffed to the wall. I'd loved her even when I shouldn't. And I loved her the most as she staggered in stubborn, stunning perfection.

Her skin held so many of my crimes. Her figure hinting of our many couplings and carnality. She'd been sold to me poised and pissed off, the only girl with the ability to tumble me from my throne into dirt.

She'd been the catalyst for my undoing

Why I'd reached rock bottom.

Why I had no choice but to change.

She was so young.

So fierce.

So *wanted.*

If I survived this war, I would marry her and give her everything I had.

I would trade a life of empty loneliness for one filled with laughter and love.

*If I survive, Jinx…*

*I'm yours.*

*And you…I'm keeping forever.*

# Chapter Thirty-Two

"CAMPBELL, WHERE THE FUCK are you?"

Sully's voice ripped through the medical rooms where I'd woken on my second day here after fainting at Sully's feet. I'd rested on the bed by the wall. I'd glowered at Sully as he leaned nonchalantly against the drug cabinet, hating him with a thousand suns, and sucked up a smoothie full of delicious berries and banana and—

My stomach growled with starvation just as Dr Campbell appeared through the door separating this room with whatever surgeries and recovery rooms existed behind.

"Sinclair?" His white eyebrows shot up as his glasses slid down his nose. "What the hell are you doing here?" His gaze flew over me, swaying and clinging to the wall, Sully weaving and clinging to Jess, and Jealousy passed out and unresponsive in his arms.

We made a sad trio.

We dragged the stench of destruction and deceased hope behind us.

The doctor's shock spoke loudly: *Wow, you don't look so good. Holy shit, how are you still breathing?* But he wisely kept his lips clamped together and leaped into a medical professional who hopefully knew how to reverse the process of death.

Rushing toward Sully, he gathered Jealousy into his arms. The two men glared at each other. The awkward manoeuvre of transferring a girl from one embrace to the other made Sully clench his jaw and murder glow in his eyes.

The doctor swallowed hard and looked away, his body tensing as he took Jealousy's weight. The second Campbell held her securely, he rushed toward the door and pushed through it. Looking over his shoulder, he commanded, "Follow me."

Sully turned his head, catching my gaze. He shrugged wearily and held out his hand. "Can you walk a little farther?" The pride echoing in his tone made my heart kick with a healthy kind of joy.

Tripping to him, I slid my fingers through his. We used each other as crutches, our bodies kissing and skin singeing where we touched. "I can manage."

He shook his head as we slowly made our way to the door and pushed through it. "You've surprised me once again."

I shook away the cobwebs in my mind. "How so?"

He pulled me into a room reeking of potent antiseptic just as Dr Campbell placed Jealousy on a bed by a cabinet full of vials and concoctions. "You're still awake. After everything you went through. After your heart almost gave out—"

"Don't look at me as if I'm a miracle for staying awake. Not when you've endured days of torture and God knows what else. You're the one who's the miracle, Sully. Not me."

He scowled, guiding me to a second bed pushed on the opposite wall. "Tritec helped. You didn't have anything to boost you."

"Tritec better not hurt you any more than you already are," I muttered, sitting down gratefully, dangling my heavy legs off the edge of the bed.

Sully grunted and stayed standing, leaning against the bed, staying in touching distance while our attention fell on the doctor and his rapid work on Jealousy. "It should still be helping me. The drug is supposed to have a stacking effect. Energy is supposed to compound until the injected adrenaline overpowers the natural biochemistry." He shrugged. "It feels as if it's faded. Perhaps the dose Campbell gave me wasn't strong enough."

Campbell whipped his head to us as he cocooned Jealousy in blankets. "I gave you a full syringe, Sinclair. Any more and it would've been an overdose almost certain to kill you."

Sully crossed his arms. "If I'm to clean up the mess you made, I need another hit."

"You'll get nothing of the sort from me." The doctor pierced

Jess's hand with an IV, grabbed a bottle of who knew what from the cupboard, and injected her with a few needles and their contents. "Where's your brother?" He gently removed Jess's earbuds and eye lenses.

Sully yawned, clamping a hand over his mouth before answering sluggishly. "Out cold in Euphoria. He has three guards watching over him."

"Only three?"

Sully grinned cruelly. "Four are dead and three have been sent away."

"Are there any more?" Campbell continued to fuss as he treated Jealousy.

"Not that I should give you any information, you traitor, but according to one of their team, there was ten of them. Whether or not that can be trusted is another matter." Sully stroked my thigh, his touch bringing comfort and affection. "Whether or not I trust you is also a topic to be discussed."

"You need my help currently, so trust doesn't matter." The doctor peered into Jealousy's eyes, shining a torch over her pupils.

"When you cease to be useful, I will make a decision about your ability to breathe." Sully's tone was deadly as a shark. "Don't think this truce of ours will remain once I'm back in power."

Campbell flinched but nodded. "I'm aware I betrayed you but remember my aid when you make your final decision. *If* you come back into power."

"Drake is as good as dead." Sully's fingers latched around my knee with sudden violence. "His three guards are nothing."

"You are a force to be reckoned with, I will not deny that." The doctor continued working on Jealousy. "But even the strongest of us have failures."

Leaning forward a little, I caressed my fingers over the back of Sully's hand, reminding him that it was okay to rest…just for a little while. That here, in this surgery, we could try to regroup and heal.

Campbell wasn't our enemy…for now.

Drake would remain passed out for hours and, seeing as Jess had given him elixir too, his system would not only be exhausted but severely depleted.

Sully could easily overthrow him…if he regained a little strength.

"Sully…" I smiled tiredly, wishing I could snuggle into him and sleep. "Come here."

He came nearer, cupping my cheek with tender fingers. "Sleep, Jinx. Go to sleep. I'll stand guard."

My eyelids closed.

I wrenched them awake.

How dare he have the magic to send me under when I needed to stay coherent for him. "Sit with me."

He ran his thumb over my bottom lip, making me tingle. "I will. Soon."

My eyelids closed again.

I gritted my teeth and hoisted them up.

If I had to glue them open, I would. I refused to sleep until I knew Jealousy was okay and Sully wasn't about to die on me.

"For what it's worth, I'm sorry again, Sinclair," Campbell muttered, adding a different solution to Jess's IV.

Sully grumbled, "Help Jealousy and Eleanor, and maybe I'll think about accepting your apology."

Campbell wiped his forehead with the back of his hand, the muggy island refusing to abate even with the air conditioner cooling the space. "At least that was the last of elixir." Measuring out yet another injection, he tapped the syringe for air bubbles. "Drake came asking if I had any spare. I'm glad you only had a few left."

Sully stretched out his back, sighing heavily. "I have four hundred vials ready to go."

The doctor spun to face him, fury pinking his wrinkled face. "*What?* Where? Get rid of it." He waved his hand at me and Jealousy. "I'm guessing you saw the effects first-hand after last night. I heard the guards saying that Jealousy had a seizure while serving in the hallucination, yet Drake just kept right on fucking her."

"Shit." Sully hung his head, raking a hand through his tangled hair. "Will she be okay?"

"She'll die if she has another dose."

My heart flurried. "Is the damage reversible?"

The doctor made eye contact with me, his anger subsiding a little. "I don't know yet. Only time will tell. Time and detox from that heinous drug." His gaze narrowed, locking back on Sully. "What do you plan on doing with the four hundred vials you have? Tell me you're going to use them on those poor goddesses, and I'll march out of here and get a gun to shoot you myself."

Sully stiffened, sucking up the shadows of the room, wearing a cape of authority and dominion. "Not that it's any of your fucking business, but I'm destroying them."

Campbell glared, suspicion glinting off his glasses. "Why should I believe you?"

Sully tore his attention from him to me, saying, "Because my lab creation almost killed the purpose of *my* creation. I watched it try to steal my future, and I'm done. No more elixir. *Ever.*"

Goosebumps spread over me.

I wanted to kiss him.

Hug him.

Tell him just how much I loved him.

Dr Campbell sighed with relief. "I'm glad you're finally seeing sense. That you learned to love people and not just beasts."

Sully shook his head, lowering his voice to a murmur, "Not people, Campbell. Just one." He gripped my hand with possession, fire sparking and love tying us together with almost visible strings.

The doctor grunted and continued to treat Jealousy.

Sully swayed, bumping against the bed as his face contorted, and he rubbed his chest where his heart resided.

Fear sprang.

I was relieved Jealousy received help, but the longer the doctor fussed over her, the more my impatience grew for him to tend to Sully.

His knees suddenly buckled beside me, his own fatigue making it impossible for him to stay awake.

"Sully...are you okay?" I grabbed at him, trying to hold him up.

He groaned, pushing me away gently. "I'm fine, woman. I need to return and deal with Drake."

"Sit down, Sinclair, before you fall," Campbell muttered. "I'll tend to you shortly."

"But—"

"Sit just for a moment, Sully. Please." I tugged him with annoyance. If he went to deal with Drake now, the guards would kill him easily.

"Fine. Ten minutes, and then I'm leaving. I'm not dragging this out any more than it already has." Sully permitted me to pull him onto the bed. The frame creaked under his weight, and another heavy sigh spilled from his lips.

After everything he'd been through and everything I'd been the cause of...he couldn't escape sleep any more than I could.

*Please let it just be tiredness and nothing more.*

Needing him close, I tugged him until he scooted closer. We

leaned against the wall, every inch of our bodies—from our shoulders, hips, and knees touched—as if we couldn't bear to be separate.

My head fell into the comforting crook of his neck and shoulder.

His rested on the top of my hair.

Our hands linked.

Our breathing slowed.

And the world went dark as we lost the battle to stay awake.

* * * * *

"Here, drink this."

I hoisted up the heaviest eyes in existence, blinking back fuzz and cotton wool.

Pika was the only splash of colour in the otherwise white sterile room, his emerald feathers perched in the corner on a packet of gauze.

Dr Campbell leaned over me, his wizened face imploring. In his hand, he held the most delicious-looking smoothie I'd ever seen.

My mouth watered, my stomach snarled, and I sat up with a groan, allowing him to help me. Once I slumped in a sitting position, he passed me the smoothie.

A muddy colour, unlike the vibrant rainbow colours of Sully's other concoctions.

"Sorry if it doesn't taste all that appetising. I raided the kitchens and put in every vitamin and mineral I could find. Lots of tropical fruit along with kale and spinach and a bunch of other vegetables from the fridge."

I sucked on the paper straw, wincing as the icy, earthy liquid hit my tongue. I wouldn't have cared if it tasted like the bottom of a dumpster. I would drink every drop.

Slurping as fast as I could, tensing against the chill spreading through my stomach, I took in the rest of my surroundings. Sully lay beside me. We no longer sat like discarded toys against the wall but had been spread out on the bed, sleeping side by side, cramped and cosy, entwined in each other.

He remained asleep while Dr Campbell checked his vitals and added another bag of fresh liquid to the IV in the back of his hand.

A sharp bite in the back of mine made me look down, eyeing up the needle puncturing my vein.

The doctor saw me looking. "While you two were out, I took

the liberty of taking care of you." He glanced at Sully. "I sewed a few of his stitches that'd pulled apart again, rebandaged, injected more antibiotics, applied new eye drops, and tended to his other maladies the best I could. He's running on empty, but I hope I've given him enough strength to keep fighting." He smiled sadly. "I know this is all my fault, but…I couldn't keep letting him hurt those girls. I hope you understand."

I swallowed hard at the utmost sincerity and apology in his gaze. "You don't have to explain to me."

"I do. If only I'd waited a little longer. You would've stopped his use of elixir and Euphoria." He shook his head. "I'm not the reason he'll destroy four hundred vials of his drug. *You* are. He fell in love and earned a conscience along the way."

"I'm also the reason he strangled Calico, Neptune, and Jupiter."

He nodded. "You are but only because you finally woke him up that everyone deserves protecting. His violence came from affection for his own kind…something he never had before. So…thank you. And I truly am sorry for not waiting longer for you to succeed."

I blushed. "It wasn't my intention to make him change, Dr Campbell."

"And that's precisely why he has." He patted my shoulder. "You loved him as he *is*, not for what he could be. There's a difference in unconditional acceptance and being unable to see past the barriers we all erect. You forced him to look into a mirror and see what he'd become. *He* was the one who wanted change because he wanted to deserve you."

Goosebumps slid down my arms. I didn't expect nor want gratitude or worship. I didn't want this man to think Sully's evolvement had anything to do with me. I was just a simple girl who happened to lock horns with a god. I hadn't done anything special. I'd just *been* special. Just as he was special to me. "We were meant to find each other…that's all."

"You were. And I'm glad, because now that you've given him his freedom, perhaps he'll grant all those in his imprisonment the same luxury."

Smiling gently at me, he rocked Sully's shoulder and raised his voice. "Sinclair, time to wake up."

Sully groaned.

"Sinclair!" Dr Campbell shook harder.

Sully's eyes flicked wide, blank to start with, then filling with comprehension. He sat up stiffly, another groan rumbling in his chest. "Shit! I need to go."

"Drink this." The doctor shoved an identical glass into Sully's hand, eyeing us up. His tone switched from the soft conversation we'd shared to pragmatic surgeon. "You've both received anti-inflammatories and intravenous glucose and saline. Your systems are heavily depleted, but with some proper food and the six-hour sleep you just had, you'll rally round quick enough."

"Fucking hell. *Six hours?* Jesus Christ!" He tried to climb off the bed but Dr Campbell pushed him back.

"Don't worry. Drake is still comatose. His mercenaries left him on the tile in Euphoria so his wake-up call won't be nearly as beneficial as yours. You have time."

"Time is relative," Sully snapped. "I need every second I have to kill him."

"No, you need to be wise and heal. Drink your smoothie." Campbell padded across the room to check on Jealousy. He tapped her cheek lightly, his voice much kinder than he'd been with Sully. "Jess…time to wake up, sweetheart."

Nothing.

No twitch.

No try.

Just a girl with blonde hair spread over her pillow and her skin mimicking the snowy white sheets covering her.

My heart hurt. "Is she okay?"

Dr Campbell shrugged, leaving her be. "I honestly don't know. The scans show normal brain activity, so her seizure didn't disrupt her mental capacity. Her heart is still suffering arrhythmias, regardless of the beta blockers I administered." He sighed. "Only time will tell."

Sully finished his smoothie, wincing as he placed the empty glass on the cabinet close by. His actions jerked with nervous energy, ready to finish the war. "Is Eleanor okay? Her heart…it wasn't coping while in the midst of elixir last night."

I rubbed my chest, listening internally for any signs that I'd suffered long-term issues. The rhythm seemed regular. I felt a little bruised and delicate, but nothing a day of rest wouldn't fix.

Dr Campbell threw me a smile. "She's fine. Her pulse is a little faster than normal, and her iron levels are low, but her system will bounce back." He pointed a finger in Sully's direction. "As long as that was the last time she'll ever have elixir, you don't have anything to worry about. But if you dare—"

"Never again, Campbell." Sully cut in. "I give you my word. Not because of your ultimatums and betrayal, but because I fucking refuse to kill the only thing that matters."

I blushed as Sully cupped my cheek and kissed me. His lips pressed softly, his dark five o'clock shadow that'd grown into a cropped beard whispering against my skin. That damn electricity that never ceased to spark hummed between us, heating me from the inside out, proving to me that our connection was utterly irreversible. My cells had adopted his. His body had claimed ownership over mine.

We belonged to each other now, come what may.

When he pulled away, his gorgeous blue eyes dove into mine, firing its message of togetherness and true love. My healing heart hopscotched, switching regular into erratic just from a look. From a kiss. From the vow lashing us together.

*Till the end, Jinx. I'm keeping you 'til death do us part.*

My ears rang as if he'd actually said such things.

I gasped as he kissed me again, accepting Dr Campbell's insistence that we had a little more time before reality came crashing back.

Tearing his gaze away, Sully asked the doctor, "Is there anything you need for Jess? Trial drugs that you think will work? Any of our discarded mixtures?"

Campbell shook his head. "I've administered one trial that was said to stop the misfiring senses in Parkinson sufferers. However, it doesn't seem to have worked."

"Call Peter Beck. He might have something new brewing that could help."

Dr Campbell nodded. "Fine, I'll call him the moment I've checked on my other patients. It's a full house lately. You're lucky I'm not demanding another doctor to assist me."

Pika suddenly swooped to Sully's shoulder, squawking with an ear-piercing caw. Sully winced, rubbing his face with his hands. "Your other patients being Cal and Skittles, right?" He dropped his hands, peering at the doctor.

Pika continued to flutter and prance, his squeaks and chatters making my heart skip. Somehow, this tiny fluffy parrot knew exactly who the humans discussed and unnervingly knew he'd get to see his sister.

*How?*

*How does he know?*

What sort of instinct had animals tapped into that alerted

them to happenings before they occurred?

"Hush, Pika." Sully cupped the noisy bird in his hand, running his thumb over Pika's head. "She's fine. You'll see her soon."

"He can see her now. It's time I checked her splint anyway." Dr Campbell looked at his wristwatch. "I'm guessing you have another hour or so before Drake wakes. If you eat the mushroom wraps I made and allow your body to digest that smoothie and shed your exhaustion, you should be able to kick him from your island easily enough."

"Kill him, not kick him," Sully growled.

Pika nibbled Sully's fingers until he released him, then took off in a flurry of green to wing around Dr Campbell's head, squeaking, "Pika. Pika!"

Sully groaned, swinging his legs out of bed. "Fine, let's have a feathered family reunion because after, I have my own family reunion to finish." His voice turned black. "And a family burial to arrange."

# Sullivan

# Chapter Thirty-Three

"I THOUGHT I HEARD your annoying ass."

My head wrenched up as I crossed the threshold into the second recovery room. I had shit to do. No time to waste. Yet my exhaustion painted everything in a fugue. My urgency kept firing and then slipping.

I couldn't afford to waste a second, yet I couldn't seem to wake up fully.

Cal smirked as my gaze landed on him. His voice croaked and held a weak quality that hinted all his focus was on pain rather than the sarcasm he'd thrown my way.

A smile tugged my lips. "You're alive then. Figured you were shark meat." I tutted as I crossed the distance to his bedside. "Pity. They have the taste for humans now. They would've enjoyed your tasty hide."

Standing had been hard work, the first few steps after lying cramped on a small hospital bed had been agonising, and the hole in my leg refused to be ignored anymore, ensuring I had a goddamn limp. No matter how much speed or power I added, I couldn't get around the fact that most of my thigh muscle was out of service until it healed.

Cal noticed.

He'd always been razor-sharp at spotting vulnerability in the guests who came to my shore, using them to his advantage to keep men in line. It fucked me off that he assessed me with the same stare.

"Can't kill me off that easily." He grinned, his pallor pasty and body not its usual vital self.

"Ah, don't worry." I smirked. "I'll come up with other ways."

Dr Campbell rolled his eyes as Cal snickered and held up his arm. "Glad you're still breathing, Sinclair."

I clasped hands with him, squeezing with relief that my friend and second-in-command was still alive and his usual acerbic self. "Likewise, Moor." I glanced down his body at the tubes disappearing under the sheet covering him, the wheeze as he breathed, the etching of agony around his eyes that hinted his quips wouldn't last long until he either demanded stronger painkillers or succumbed to sleep to numb it.

"They might get to nibble on you after all, Cal." I forced a chuckle. "Who knows if you'll pull through. You look like shit."

"He'll pull through," Campbell muttered. "He's getting stronger every day. Only woke ten hours ago and has already improved rapidly…thanks to a few of your unapproved drugs, Sinclair."

I threw him a nod. "Use whatever you need."

Cal assessed me in the same way. "Know what? Those sharks of yours can have a chew on you. You're not looking so good yourself."

I scoffed and broke our grip. "Me? Nothing wrong with me."

"Of course there isn't." He grinned. His attention flicked to Eleanor as she slipped to my side. "So…you found your way back, huh?"

This joviality was wrong.

This was delaying a justified murder of my brother.

"I did." Eleanor nodded; her gaze direct but guarded. It hadn't escaped my knowledge that there was no love lost between these two. A competition lurked beneath their interactions. I supposed I should be honoured that the two people closest to me felt some sort of possession over me, but I wouldn't tolerate it.

*Not now Eleanor is a permanent fixture in my life.*

*However long that might be.*

"You told me to keep her if she ever came back." I crossed my arms. "Might just take your advice."

Cal's green gaze shot to mine. "Got yourself a new pet, sir?" He laughed under his breath, wincing as he held the two bullet holes in his torso that Campbell had hopefully fixed.

"Worse." I smiled. "If we get out of this mess intact, it seems I now have a wife."

Eleanor sucked in a breath beside me, her cheeks pinking as Cal's gaze popped wide. "Holy shit."

Cal stared at Eleanor, his blasé welcome switching to sincerity. "For what it's worth, I'm sorry for being a little, eh, cold to you. I was wrong. You're not like the others, and it seems you can be trusted. I told Sinclair not to send you away, by the way. I knew the asshole was in love with you before he did."

Eleanor rubbed the back of her hand where the IV line had been removed. "I don't really know what to say to that—"

"Say we can be friends and let it be the end of—"

Pika's screech shut Cal up as the chaotic caique ricocheted around the room. His feathers gleamed and his infectious joy dusted all of us as Campbell came through the door holding a silver tray, soft gauze, and a tiny patient in the middle.

"Skittles!" Eleanor headed straight toward the female parrot, the canary yellow shirt so big on her stunning frame. Skittles puffed up and screeched loud enough to hurt my ears.

Eleanor's legs still wobbled a little, her body would be undoubtedly sore from how rough I'd fucked her, doing my damnedest to get her to come before she died in my arms.

I sighed as my chest ached.

She'd been so fucking close to dying.

I could still feel the tremor of her pulse. The unbearable contortion of her body as she drowned beneath pleasure that'd become insurmountable pain.

She'd scared me.

Scared me straight in so many ways.

It was a minutely battle not to hover over her, to listen to her breath and press my hand over her heart to ensure it pumped reliably. It terrified me that we were such a fragile species. Ruin one organ and death followed.

*Have I shaved decades off her life because of what I've done?*

"Fuck, you've got it bad." Cal snickered under his breath.

I was tempted to punch him, but he hissed as the damage to his body dragged him under again. He had enough pain without me adding to it. Instead, I threw him a one finger salute and half-padded, half-limped across the surgery to where Campbell had placed Skittles on a bench beside the sink and antiseptic supplies.

Pika was beside himself, hopping, stomping, purring. He head-butted Skittles until she snapped at him, he pranced around with his wings spread like the savage dictator he was. "Hello. Hi. Lazy." He rolled over onto his back, his scaly legs kicking air, his happiness unable to be contained.

Eleanor laughed.

Such an innocent sound that had no place in the world we'd found ourselves in. This small oasis of peace wasn't real. We still had a fight to win, yet her laugh made me believe we had won.

That we could be happy...together.

That I could keep her and know she was safe.

*Fuck*, I wanted that.

I wanted her safe but I couldn't shed the creeping, cloying coldness beneath the spare white shirt Campbell had given me. Premonition or preparation...either one warned not to get too entangled just in case this pause in happily ever after was all I'd get.

Campbell stayed at a respectable distance, allowing our hellos. "Her wing will mend. I expect she'll be able to fly again in six weeks or so. Probably sooner but I'd like to err on the side of caution."

"That's good news." Eleanor smiled, continuing to cuddle the parrot.

Impatience slithered through my veins as I wrapped my arm around Eleanor's slight waist. It wasn't that I didn't appreciate this interlude...I just wasn't one to trust in seemingly perfect moments because there *was* no perfect moment.

*I need to go kill him.*

*Now!*

Eleanor kissed my cheek as I leaned over her and tickled Skittles under her chin, careful not to knock the small splint keeping her wing splayed and straight.

My heart squeezed at her swift, sweet affection.

Gratefulness filled me that Campbell had rescued the parrot who was such a fundamental part of Eleanor's enjoyment on my shores. I wasn't an idiot. She'd fallen in love with me, yes. But she'd also fallen in love with the world I'd conjured, the birds I shared my life with, the palm trees and beaches that were my playground.

Would she still love me if I didn't own an archipelago?

I couldn't punch Cal, but I could punch myself.

*Did she teach you nothing?*

*She would love you even if you were destitute and living in a cardboard castle.*

"Sully, what's wrong?" Eleanor whispered, her gaze tracking over my face. "You're gripping me so tight."

I relaxed my hold. "I'm fine." I hadn't meant to show my straying thoughts. That all this positivity and peace set my teeth on edge because I didn't trust it. We hadn't earned it. It was the calm before yet another storm.

*I need to go.*

*No more delays.*

Letting her go, I stepped back, removing myself from such a domestic scene. Jess had been tended to and was in the best possible hands. Cal was awake and inching farther from the Grim Reaper's sickle with each passing hour. Skittles and Pika were reunited. Eleanor was healthy despite the hurts I'd given her.

I'd fulfilled my responsibilities to those who deserved the best of me.

I was free to become the worst of me.

Released from my obligations so I could finally give in to the fury that constantly blazed in my belly. A fury I wouldn't be able to extinguish until my brother was dead and I'd delivered his demise personally.

Only then would I allow this sweetness to infect me.

Backing away, Cal caught my gaze.

He gritted his teeth but nodded, knowing exactly where I was going.

Campbell shook his head, and Eleanor spun with Pika on her finger, her face glowing with relief which quickly solidified into dread. "Sully...no." She stepped toward me. "Don't go back there. Not yet. You're not strong enough."

I held up my hand. "Stay here."

"No. I won't let you—"

"Stay *here*, Jinx." I pointed at the floor. "You will give me that respect. You will stay out of harm's way so you don't distract me from what I need to do."

"But what if—?"

"Stop." I held up my hand, putting more distance between us. "I'm going. I'll be back soon." Spinning around, I clenched my jaw against the need to limp and shoved aside my pain—both physical and emotional.

I grabbed the door handle and stepped over the threshold back into Jealousy's space where she lay unmoving by the wall.

A noise sounded behind me as Eleanor gave chase.

I slammed the door closed.

I braced myself, wanting to lock it so she had no choice but to obey me, but the soft snick of a gun set my senses into high alert.

*Mother. Fucker.*

Turning slowly, I glowered as the three guards from Euphoria aimed guns at my chest.

I didn't care about their threats.

I had a bulletproof vest thanks to Drake's decree that he needed me alive.

They didn't say a word as we squared off. The sound of heavy footfalls came just before Drake dragged his weary ass into the surgery and grinned.

Or at least, tried to grin.

His Botoxed face prevented any form of animation, but his exhaustion made him look like a discarded napkin. His cheeks slouched, his pupils dull, his shoulders rolled, and entire body looked like a sack half full.

He'd yanked on black combat gear a size too big for him. He trembled from the exertion of Euphoria and elixir. He looked weak enough to kill with a fucking feather.

I grinned, bending my knees, ready to pounce. Voices echoed behind the closed door where I'd left Eleanor with Cal and Campbell. Eleanor argued. The men kept her obedient. I tuned them out as I said, "I was just coming to find you, brother. How convenient that you came to me instead."

It wasn't convenient.

I wanted him far, far away from Eleanor.

But...beggars couldn't be choosers, just like my brother couldn't cry when I killed him for daring to come to me in pieces and think he could win.

Clearing his throat, Drake croaked, "Get away from the door. That bitch of yours isn't escaping so easily."

I balled my hands, stepping threateningly toward him. "You can choose to die in here or outside in the twilight. Your choice."

The mercenaries shared a smug smile, their guns still trained on me. "You're high on delusions, mate."

Drake sighed. "Shoot the goddess."

It happened too fast for me to choose.

A gun swung toward Jealousy, incapacitated and entirely vulnerable in bed.

Instinct kicked in.

I charged to stop it.

I left the closed door to Eleanor unprotected and failed to defend Jess as the crack of a bullet split the air, sulphur stunk the space, and a spill of blood stained the white sheet instantly.

She didn't even wake as he shot her.

"*Fuck!*" My leg bellowed as I tried to change direction.

Too late.

Two mercenaries bowled through the door, whipping guns up to aim at Cal and Eleanor.

Eleanor froze. Cal jack-knifed up in bed even with tubes and agony. His gaze fell on Jess bleeding in the other room and his face contorted with horror. "Ah, fuck!"

"*No!*" Eleanor screamed, trying to get past the guns and run to Jealously. "Oh, God."

For fucking shit, when would this fucking nightmare *end*?

Drake snickered. "Handcuffed ya, baby brother." He came toward me, reaching out to pat my shoulder.

I punched him square in the motherfucking jaw.

He collapsed.

The man wedging his gun into Eleanor's tangled coffee hair yelled, "Hurt him again and I'll shoot this bitch."

My fingernails dug into my palms as I fought every savage desire to kill three men. Three men holding my chosen family hostage.

Two humans, two parrots.

At least Campbell stood in front of the caiques, shielding them from my brother's view.

Drake clambered to his feet, rubbing his jaw and shaking his head. "I'll grant you that one, Sully. One punch. Do it again and I'll kill Eleanor Grace without any hesitation." His eyes flashed. "I'm not playing games anymore, baby brother. I'm as sick of this battle as you are. I'm tired and hungry and want to fucking rest. Be assured my temper is thin, and I *will* kill her, so be a good boy and listen up."

I cursed the coldness in his tone. The simplicity of finality.

He'd reached the end of his rope too.

Previously, our interactions had been a taunt, a test. The usual rivalry between siblings that'd mutated into murderous. But now, there was no quips or quarrels just the cold-hearted assurance that he was trigger-happy and impatient.

Still fighting my need to kill him, I snarled, "I will dance on your grave when you're dead."

"That's not very nice." Wiping blood off his lip, he cleared his throat and muttered, "I came here with an olive branch, would you believe? I actually came to congratulate you, Sullivan, before your anger made me do something I regret." His attention flickered to Jealousy. "She was such a good lay. Let me tie her in any position, stick any toy inside her. I didn't want to hurt her. I'd grown rather fond of her." He whistled under his breath. "But what you've created with Euphoria and elixir? Fuck. *Me*."

Blood seeped in an ever-widening stain over Jealousy's stomach. What the fuck had he hit? Her guts? Her womb? Was she dying and wouldn't even wake before her last breath?

*She needs Campbell, immediately.*

"You're a genius, baby brother, and I mean that sincerely. A goddamn prodigy."

Seething, I searched for a way to stop Jess bleeding out and the much-needed miracle of ensuring Eleanor, Pika, Skittles, and Cal weren't shot too.

"I don't want your compliments, Drake. They make my every achievement vile."

He ran a hand over his face. He looked like death had nibbled him, then spat him out—just as unwanted by the underworld as he was to the living. His fatigue almost promised an armistice but I knew better than to trust such a lie.

A thought wormed into my brain. A thought I wanted to kill straight away as it would delay this feud yet again. But at least it would buy me space for Eleanor and time for Jess. I'd already cancelled my business and removed myself from future dealings anyway. I no longer fought to protect my assets because they had become firm liabilities.

The only thing I wanted to protect was a *human*...

A complete switch from my previous apathy toward my own kind.

Keeping my voice as civil as I could, I snapped, "What do you want, Drake? You want this to end between us? Fine. Talk frankly and let's finish this."

*Hurry.*

Drake looked behind me, narrowing his gaze at the mercenaries keeping their guns trained on a sobbing Eleanor and a seething Cal.

I refused to look.

I didn't trust my restraint if I looked. I'd lose it, and do something that might get all of us killed.

Drake puffed up his chest, standing a little taller. "Talk

frankly? That will be novel for us."

"It might usher this bullshit along." I flicked a glance at Jealousy, her skin growing whiter by the second even though she already resembled a ghost.

"Fine." He cleared his throat again. "You want to negotiate? Let's negotiate. Elixir. If you don't have any more vials on this island, I'm guessing you have more."

"I do."

"Where?"

My voice revolted, unwilling to give up my secrets but I forced them out. "*Monyet.*"

"And what exactly is *Monyet*?"

"Another island. I have a lab there."

A lab unbound by FDA rules and bureaucratic tape. If I had a breakthrough in the Java Sea, I didn't need to worry that it would be stolen by greedy politicians or shut down by corrupt governments.

The lab out there was a country all on its own. Overseen by Peter Beck with regular live streaming and condemned to far less paperwork, breakthroughs on *Monyet* had far surpassed those of my lab in America.

"And how many vials are ready to go?"

"Sully, don't!" Eleanor's yell made me stiffen, but I ignored her.

"Four hundred."

Drake whistled again. "Does anyone else have the recipe?"

I tapped my temple with a smirk. "Just me. I give it to my scientists piece meal. No one knows the full ingredients."

He pursed his lips, thoughts racing in his gaze. He took a moment, deliberating for far too long. I grew angsty to help Jess. I grew furious to protect Eleanor. I honestly didn't know how long I could restrain myself from wrapping my fingers around his throat and strangling the bastard.

Finally, Drake sniffed and held out his hand. "A truce then. Give me the four hundred vials, write down the recipe, give me access to the codes for Euphoria, and sign the deeds for Goddess Isles into my name, and—"

"That isn't a truce. It's the exact same request that I denied at the start of this fucking war."

"Ah, ah, let me finish." He clucked his tongue like an asshole. "Give me those things. Let's face it…you don't need the wealth, Sullivan. Be generous and spread it around. Give me what I ask and…I give you my word I will not kill Eleanor…or you."

A laugh fell from my mouth. A bark of disbelief. "Yeah, right. You'd been better off telling me baboons can fly than promising not to hurt—"

"Calling me a liar?" His face darkened. "I give you my word, Sullivan." He waved his hand that still speared between us. "Shake on it, and my men will lower their weapons. You, me, and Eleanor will take a little helicopter ride to wherever this lab island is. If you're telling the truth about the four hundred vials and you sign over the titles to this sex-fest, I will personally drop you off in Jakarta where you two can go live happily ever after in some mansion elsewhere."

"Sully…he's lying." Eleanor's suspicion blended with my own.

Actually, it wasn't suspicion. It was damn right knowledge.

Drake had never conceded or compromised in his entire life.

If we flew with him to *Monyet*—if I signed those documents—he would kill me.

One hundred motherfucking percent he would murder me before the ink was dry.

He would put a bullet in my skull and then either abuse Eleanor until she begged for death or kill her and leave her to rot beside me.

I narrowed my eyes, studying him.

He licked his lips, his blue gaze doing their best to hide behind sincerity but far too smug.

He thought he could hoodwink me.

He thought he could keep me a pliant prisoner, willingly walking to his guillotine.

And the shitty situation about this was…I didn't have a fucking choice.

If I said no, he'd shoot Eleanor.

If I refused again, he'd shoot Cal.

If I continued to deny him, he'd rip off Pika's wings and break apart Skittle's body. He would revert to the psychotic child who got his kicks from mutilating animals who couldn't fight back.

*Jess is dying.*

*Hurry the fuck up.*

If I accepted his terms, at least I had an opportunity to protect Jess and everyone else behind me.

*Monyet* was a fifteen-minute helicopter ride.

That would give me time to plot.

Stepping into him, I gritted my teeth from the rancid sensation of touching him and slipped my hand into his.

"Sully, don't!"

"Be *quiet*, Jinx."

Drake grinned like a heartless mongoose as his fingers latched tight, and we shook. "Good choice, Sullivan. Good choice."

"I didn't have a choice." I yanked my hand away. "And we both know the outcome of what I've agreed to."

He smirked, his shields dropping, showing me the fate he had planned. "You always were too smart, baby brother. But smarts will get you killed. I've always told you that."

Snapping his fingers, he rounded up his mercenaries. "Gentlemen, I believe we have a flight to catch. Let's go."

# Chapter Thirty-Four

AS A GUN BIT into my lower back, ushering me down the bamboo jetty to a red helicopter manned by Drake's pilots and not Sully's, my instincts hissed a sinister warning.

The warning became louder with every step, evolving from a hive of bees to a swarm of plague-driven locusts.

As Sully winced and did his best not to limp on a harpoon massacred leg, he climbed regally into the cabin and a sixth sense bombarded me with pictures I hoped would never come to pass.

Sully shot.

Me dead.

Drake victorious with elixir.

My heart threw itself against my ribs, so convinced, so *sure* that if we flew with Drake, we would die with Drake.

I tasted the inevitability. I heard the bullet before it'd even been fired.

I didn't need puddles or masks removed in Euphoria for another kind of premonition. The kind that iced my blood and froze my bones. The kind that set my heart pumping in entirely new ways, seizing my muscles so I would not meet my end.

The mercenary behind me grunted when I refused to climb the steps into the aircraft.

Sully winced as the man wrapped his hands around my waist and tossed me into the cabin.

I fell on my knees, the bare floor cutting with its metal grippy covering.

Sully bent and gathered me tenderly, pulling me upright and placing me beside him. He didn't speak. He just stared. His sea-glass, waterfall gaze held mine, and I knew I wasn't wrong in my fears.

Violent sickness rushed up my throat.

The leather seats squeaked with promise as Drake and his men sat down.

The squeal of the engines and the growl of the rotors all added to the shivery sensation of dismay.

*Drake will kill us.*

The moment Sully gave him what he wanted…he would kill us, destroy our story, and end our love before we'd even had a chance to fully unfurl it.

*No.*

I shook my head as Sully cupped my cheek and ran his thumb over my lips.

Still he didn't speak even as the helicopter swooped into the dusky sky, sliced through ribbons of peach and gilded sunset and added power to the rotors to cut across the ocean in search of yet another island.

I understood Sully's unwillingness to talk with his brother sandwiching me between the two Sinclairs. I appreciated his desire to keep our bond as hidden as possible.

But he couldn't stop the crackle of connection between us.

He couldn't stop the tingle or tangle between our souls.

And he couldn't lie to me.

He could only nod and narrow his eyes, trying to convince me he had a plan to avoid death. I tried to trust him. To believe he had some mystical way to win.

But I wasn't convinced.

We were running on fatigue and the dregs of bad health. Sully had the added disadvantage of dealing with constant pain. Whatever he attempted probably wouldn't be rationally thought out. It would be instigated by sheer stubbornness and worry over my own survival rather than his.

I wanted to tell him not to put himself in harm's way.

To make him listen and agree not to be stupid.

But he let me go and stared out the window, looking far below where his islands were tiny gemstones and the jewellery thief was here to steal them.

The mercenary who'd clambered into the cabin last hadn't

closed the door. Wind whipped into the space, cooler up here than down below. My aches from elixir and my bruises from palpitations all ratcheted up my rapidly climbing worries.

*Something is coming.*

I could feel it.

Could feel the cloak of fate. Hear the inching disaster.

I just couldn't tell who would be the survivors—us or Drake.

My jumping thoughts collided around my head.

I leapt a mile as Drake planted his hand on my knee, squeezing cruelly from his seat across the cabin.

Sully instantly snatched his touch away, leaving Drake's fingernails burning tracks in my skin. "Don't fucking touch her." Sully's nostrils flared, and his entire presence bellowed in the cabin, seething with challenge. "Our truce will be over if you do."

There was nothing weak about him. Nothing more terrifying than a beast backed into a corner.

I'd never been more afraid of him or more proud.

His attention hadn't been on the vista outside, after all. His mind turned inward, problem-solving our predicament.

Drake sneered over the din of rotor blades.

The aura of anticipation and the sick taste of prophecy continued filling the small space. A trickle, a torrent, a gush of tense calamity. The lashing wind only made the waiting worse. It howled and clawed, my hair turned into live vines, slipping around my shoulders and dancing in the space above me. My skin erupted with goosebumps. My yellow shirt flapped around my body.

After playing the role of a goddess, I actually felt like one.

I stupidly bought into the illusion that I was more than human.

That I could feel fate stretching its powers and reaching for us over the sea.

My fingertips tingled with sick magic as I pressed them together. My stomach fluttered as if I'd swallowed a thousand hummingbirds. My rage at Drake's entrapment and my temper at not seeing a way free caused the strangest kind of power to arch and spark in my blood.

Maybe it was all a fantasy.

Perhaps elixir still played havoc with my nervous system.

Maybe all people facing imminent death felt otherworldly, ready to transform mortal shells and spread their wings to a new existence.

Perhaps it was all in my head and the hissing, heating

awareness, the tightening, tingling anticipation meant nothing was going to happen.

So how could I explain the three things that happened almost as if I'd foreseen them?

How could I predict that something was going to happen?

How could I have *known* that in the sky above Sully's paradise, one of us was going to die?

My heart galloped.

The world seemed to slow.

And the three things happened in quick succession.

One, the flight path flew us over *Serigala*.

Sully sucked in a murderous growl, his fury overflowing at the desecrated, blackened wasteland below. The soil stained with blood and rubble, workers and locals still picking over the refuse, doing what they could to salvage such a nightmare.

Two, the police finally arrived.

Far too late and far too below us. I caught sight of flashing lights and decaled boats racing with white water to our aid.

And three, Sully reached his threshold.

*Serigala*'s destruction and the police's useless arrival poured gasoline on a wildfire he couldn't control. I braced myself as he launched from the seat and threw himself at the guard sitting opposite with his gun resting warningly on his knee.

One second to punch him. Another second to steal his gun. A final second to pull the trigger and switch man to corpse, his cadaver thumping heavily at our feet.

For a moment, the world paused.

The rotor blades seemed to quieten. The sensation of doom stopped running its evil fingers down my skin.

But then, everything I'd been afraid of happened.

Drake yelled.

Sully attacked another mercenary.

The pilots swooped left, snatching the floor from beneath Sully's feet, sending him sprawling into the fuselage by the open door.

*"Look out!"* My voice tore over my tongue.

"Stop!" Drake bellowed as the mercenary grappled with Sully.

A gun went off.

A bullet flew from weapon to flesh.

Sully's eyes widened.

The mercenary's gaze narrowed.

I would never know who was shot because fate once again

became my enemy.

The helicopter swerved.

And my whole world tripped out the open, wind-lashing door.

**"NO!"**

I bolted to my feet.

I slammed to my knees as Sully fell.

And fell.

And fell.

*"No!!!"*

The mercenary plummeted to the sea.

Sully crashed toward his ocean.

Our eyes snagged and locked.

One second.

Two second.

Three.

And then…he was gone.

His body swallowed by a splash.

The blue wetness of his empire swallowing him whole.

Drake slammed on the cockpit partition. "Man overboard!"

I couldn't move. Couldn't breathe. Couldn't look away.

I stared at that ocean with every atom of myself.

I *willed* Sully to appear.

I dreamed and prayed and wished and *begged*.

But nothing.

No arms reaching for the surface.

No man swimming from the depths.

Just an empty ocean licking its lips after enjoying a snack from above.

The police boats added speed, chasing to Sully's and the mercenary's entry.

Loud hailers did their best to scream above the roar of mechanical blades. Threats and warnings, typical police menace to yank the helicopter to heel.

Drake snarled and punched the fuselage. *"Fuck!"*

A gun whistled from below.

"They're firing at us!" The pilots added speed to the rotors, shooting us out of reach. "The police fuckers are firing at us!"

Twice I'd been shot at in a helicopter.

Only once did I hope they'd succeed.

I wanted to be down there.

*I need to know.*

Crawling closer to the open door, I held my breath to jump.

I closed my eyes.

I pushed off.

But savage hands wrenched me back. "You're not fucking going anywhere." Drake held me tight, shoving me into the remaining mercenary's control. He raked both hands through his hair, anger and greed covering him. "Fuck!"

He wasn't afraid of his brother's demise. He was afraid that it'd happened before he'd taken what he wanted. "Fuck, fuck, *fuck*!"

"We can still get the four hundred vials already cooked," the mercenary yelled. "We can't go back. The police—"

Another bullet lodged in the fuselage.

"Fuuuuccccckkkk!" Drake stomped his foot like a spoiled brat.

"We have a goddess." The man held me tight as I fought. "She'll know how to load Euphoria. The last one did. You've got what you need, Sinclair. Let's go."

Drake glared at me. He pondered. He agreed. "Fine. Get us out of here."

The pilots added power.

Gravity made my stomach swoop.

Sully…

Thick tears tracked down my cheeks.

Sully…

My silence returned, thick and strong.

*Sully!*

My blood iced over.

My heart beat one last time.

And Drake dragged me onto his lap as he sat down.

The sky claimed me as the sea swallowed Sully.

Reversing our love story.

Deleting our beginning, erasing our journey, and flying me away from my forever.

# Pre-Order FIFTH A FURY

The fifth and final book of Sully and Eleanor's love story.
***Releasing 16th June 2020***
PRE-ORDER at www.pepperwinters.com

*From New York Times Bestseller, Pepper Winters, comes the fifth and final book in the USA Today Bestselling Series, Goddess Isles*

*"There was a beginning once. A beginning that started with being sold to a monster I fell for. There was an ending once. An ending that came cloaked in bloodshed and fury."*

Eleanor Grace is a simple mortal who has the power to topple a god. She captured his heart, fed him a different future, and fought for a fantasy that wasn't make-believe but destiny.

Sully Sinclair is a man masquerading as a monster. He let down his shields and allowed a goddess to show him a simpler path. However, neither of them could predict the war that was coming, nor the toll it would take.

A fated romance.
A fight that will finish in tears.
The age-old battle of good versus evil.

**Release Date: 16th June 2020**

# OTHER BOOKS AVAILABLE FROM PEPPER WINTERS

## FREE BOOKS
*Debt Inheritance (Indebted Series #1)*
*Tears of Tess (Monsters in the Dark #1)*
*Pennies (Dollar Series #1)*

## BOOKS IN KINDLE UNLIMITED
*Destroyed (Standalone)*

### Dollar Series
*Pennies*
*Dollars*
*Hundreds*
*Thousands*
*Millions*

### Truth & Lies Duet
*Crown of Lies*
*Throne of Truth*

### Pure Corruption Duet
*Ruin & Rule*
*Sin & Suffer*

### Indebted Series
*Debt Inheritance*
*First Debt*
*Second Debt*
*Third Debt*
*Fourth Debt*
*Final Debt*
*Indebted Epilogue*

### Monsters in the Dark Trilogy
*Tears of Tess*
*Quintessentially Q*
*Twisted Together*
*Je Suis a Toi*

### Standalones

*Destroyed*
*Unseen Messages*
*Can't Touch This*

# PLAYLIST

Bruises - Lewis Capaldi
Goo Goo Dolls – Iris
Use Somebody - Kings of Leon
Bittersweet Symphony - The Verve
You're the One – Rev Theory
And the Fire – Rev Theory
Pieces - Rob Thomas
You are the reason - Calum Scott & Leona Lewis
I won't give up – Jason Mraz
Dynasty – MIIA
Helium – SIA

# ACKNOWLEDGEMENTS

Fourth a Lie refused to be easy. I wrote this book (75,000 words) and scrapped almost every single sentence to begin anew, coming in at 88,000. I'm hoping the final product was worth the pain of deleting so many hours of work. A huge thank you to my beta readers who took the time to read multiple editions of this book and provide honest feedback that I needed to make the necessary amendments.

Thank you to hubby for putting up with my hermit ways and understanding when I lock myself in the rabbit's bedroom to write with my fluffy pom-pom muse.

Thank you to everyone who has joined me on this crazy, sexy ride!

Thank you to every blogger, reviewer, reader, and bookworm for all your help promoting.

Thank you to Danielle and Ashlee for the amazing graphics from the start of this series. I'm very lucky to have your skills!

Thank you to Next Step PR for all your help and support with releases and cover reveals!

And thank you to Sarah Puckett and Scott Rider for bringing the audio to life and for adding the extra lines and edits at such short notice!

I'm so grateful to everyone.

Stay safe!

Pepper x

CPSIA information can be obtained
at www.ICGtesting.com
Printed in the USA
LVHW011808070820
662641LV00004B/542

9 781653 895526